LET THE DEVIL OUT

LET THE DEVIL OUT

BILL LOEHFELM

SARAH CRICHTON BOOKS   FARRAR, STRAUS AND GIROUX   NEW YORK

Sarah Crichton Books
Farrar, Straus and Giroux
18 West 18th Street, New York 10011

Library of Congress Cataloging-in-Publication Data
Names: Loehfelm, Bill.
Title: Let the devil out : a Maureen Coughlin novel / Bill Loehfelm.
Description: First edition. | New York : Sarah Crichton Books/Farrar, Straus and Giroux,
    2016. | Series: Maureen Coughlin series ; 4
Identifiers: LCCN 2015036051 | ISBN 9780374298579 (hardcover) | ISBN 9780374711726
    (ebook)
Subjects: LCSH: Policewomen—Louisiana—New Orleans—Fiction. | BISAC: FICTION /
    Crime. | FICTION / Thrillers. | GSAFD: Suspense fiction. | Mystery fiction.
Classification: LCC PS3612.O36 L48 2016 | DDC 813/.6—dc23
LC record available at http://lccn.loc.gov/2015036051

Designed by Abby Kagan

Our books may be purchased in bulk for promotional, educational, or business use. Please
contact your local bookseller or the Macmillan Corporate and Premium Sales Department at
1-800-221-7945, extension 5442, or by e-mail at MacmillanSpecialMarkets@macmillan.com.

www.fsgbooks.com
www.twitter.com/fsgbooks • www.facebook.com/fsgbooks

10 9 8 7 6 5 4 3 2 1

Once again, for AC

The hardest thing in the world isn't to refrain from committing an evil, it's to stand up and stop one.

—DON WINSLOW, *The Power of the Dog*

LET THE DEVIL OUT

1

Late November. The time of the silver-haired man.

These past weeks, every gray cloud charcoaled across the pale sky brought him back to her. Every cold breeze coming down the Mississippi felt like his hands under her coat. His shadow walked before her everywhere she went, painting the buildings and the sidewalks of New Orleans like the shadow of a great carrion bird. When she awoke in the mornings, she felt he'd only just stepped away from the foot of her bed. The bed with bullet holes in it. Late at night, he whispered the names of the dead, his victims and others, in her ear during her last conscious moments, when she felt helplessly paralyzed by the coming sleep.

Which meant that most nights, Maureen did her best to stay awake until morning.

Maureen sat alone at a corner cocktail table at d.b.a., a Frenchmen Street bar, thinking about the silver-haired man speaking names into her ear. So, she figured, sipping her drink, she was now officially hearing voices. So be it, then.

Maybe that was for the best. Maybe they would help. Hearing voices gave her something in common with one of the women she was out here looking for: Madison Leary, the woman who killed men with a straight razor and who sang old folk songs about death and the devil into Maureen's voice mail. Maybe the connection, this new empathy, would inspire an idea. Maybe it would change her luck. Lord knows, she needed *something* to shake things up. She needed something to break. A break in the case, as they say. At this point, she'd take going half-crazy, even if it was the second half, even if it meant she was going the rest of the way crazy. As long as Madison Leary was there at the finish line.

She lowered her eyes to the table, avoiding the faces in the barroom, and sipped her drink again, embarrassed even though no one was looking at her.

The time of the silver-haired man, she thought. Oh, please, girl-friend.

What bullshit. Melodramatic bullshit, Maureen. You know better. Get over it.

He was just a man, she told herself, over and over again. *Just a man.* Repeating that sentence as if it were a stone she threw again and again at the great black bird overhead. Of course, she could never throw it high enough. And the bird never got frightened and never flew away. But that didn't stop her from trying.

She thought of the Greek god condemned to roll his stone up a hill, condemned to repeat the same meaningless task for eternity. She couldn't recall what his sin had been. Or his name. Didn't much matter. It wasn't much of a story, and Maureen knew what her own sins had been. The silver-haired man was just that, a man. Not a devil. Not a god. Not a ghost. He'd had an ordinary name. Frank Sebastian. And he was dead. Maureen knew this for sure. She'd been ten feet away from him when he'd died.

The time of the silver-haired man? His time was over. She had seen to that.

Sitting at her table, Maureen tried imagining herself as someone else. A different person. With a different voice. This was a new thing she'd been trying in her head. A way to hear herself tell the story of what had happened to her before she had come to New Orleans. She studied her pack of cigarettes. American Spirit. A chief in a headdress was on the front of the box. He smoked a peace pipe. Maureen lit up.

She closed her eyes and envisioned herself not as the thin, short, pale-faced redhead she was, but maybe as a stout, dark-haired, and tattooed medicine woman, crouched on her haunches as she told her story, surrounded by openmouthed, wide-eyed squaws circling the longhouse fire. She tried to hear herself, tried to listen to herself tell them the story of the Silver-Haired Man, the November Man, the one who haunted her in these late weeks of autumn. The one she saw reflected in store windows along Magazine Street and turning corners ahead of her along St. Charles Avenue. The one who lived in the blind spot over her shoulder, who hovered in her peripheral vision. The man she had seen in the soulless eyes of a sociopathic rich boy outside a party at his father's Audubon Park mansion, who she saw everywhere around her in the bars and clubs of New Orleans at night, in the glittering ravenous eyes of brown and black and blond young men.

But when she tried *listening* to her other self tell the story, as soon as she started paying attention and seeing everything again, seeing Sebastian, the cattails at the water's edge, the headlights of the oncoming train, Maureen's invented self fell silent. The story ended and the vision disappeared into a tiny point of light, as if someone had pulled the plug on an old television. At the table in the bar, the medicine woman vanished and Maureen was left alone again with her ache and her fear and her ghost, and she had nothing to say and no one to listen to her not say it. I need to find a way, she thought. I need to find a way to tell the story to someone.

She had hoped that this first anniversary wouldn't haunt her. The first six months after Sebastian had tried to throw her in front of a train, she still lived on Staten Island with her mother in the house she'd grown up in, on the same streets where everything bad had happened, and so it kind of made sense that those events had lingered. But *this* November, she had a new life, in a new city. She was a cop now, for chrissakes. A cop on indefinite paid administrative leave, she thought, which made her a cop without a gun and a badge at the moment, which wasn't much of a cop, but a cop according to her paycheck. And she'd get her badge and her gun back. Soon.

The point was she had put a lot of work into becoming a different woman, into building herself into a new person. A *real* new person. And leaving behind that bastard and the places he'd taken her was a big reason she had done that work.

But then the weather had turned at the end of the month, and Maureen learned that November in New Orleans could be, if it wanted to, as cold and gray and wet and bleak as November in New York. And at the turn in the weather had come her dark turn of mind. This year should have been much different from the last. She had expected it to be different. She *deserved* it to be different. And when it wasn't, she got pissed. More than pissed. Angry. Incensed. *Furious.*

The woman Maureen had been watching for more than an hour got up from her barstool, bringing Maureen back to the present. This woman was not Madison Leary. This woman was not part of a murder case. This wasn't police work. This was something else. Something private.

Just for tonight. Which was what you said the last time, Maureen thought.

The woman pulled on her coat, flipped her long black hair out from underneath her collar, gathered her phone and her purse, and headed for the door. The bouncer opened it for her, letting the cold outside air rush into the barroom as he said good night. Maureen pulled the hood of her baggy black sweatshirt tight against the back of her neck. She longed for her father's old blue pea coat, the one she had lost last November. The one she had left in a bloody heap on the floor of a Staten Island emergency room, soaked in Frank Sebastian's blood.

She drew her hands into her sleeves. She carried a weapon in the front pocket of her sweatshirt. She savored its weight on her lap.

A man Maureen had also been watching emerged from the dim and narrow hall that led to the restrooms. He froze, his face scrunching in anger, when he saw the empty barstool. He looked around the bar. Maureen could tell it was all he could do to keep from screaming the woman's name. They'd arrived at the bar at different times, the woman first and the man about twenty minutes later. Right away they had fallen into a bad argument, quickly enough that Maureen knew it was the continuation of a previous fight, badly enough that the bouncer had come over from the door to check on them. Maureen hadn't been able to hear much of what they were saying, but she'd heard enough to know that the man had followed the woman here from another Frenchmen Street bar she'd left to get away from him.

After the bouncer's intervention, the man had moved away down the bar, pretending, Maureen could tell, to watch the funk band that had taken the stage during the argument. But throughout the set he had kept a close eye on the object of his ire, glaring at her over his shoulder, his silver-labeled bottle of Coors Light raised to his lips.

From where she sat in the corner across the room, Maureen could see the wheels turning in his head. She could read his thoughts. She didn't like what they told her. Her fears were confirmed by the fact that the woman had waited until the man was out of sight to make her move for the door. She wasn't leaving. She was escaping. She was fleeing.

The man gave up searching the bar. He made for the door, shouldering people out of his way. He hurried out in pursuit, Maureen knew, of the woman who had slipped away.

She grabbed her cigarettes and slid off her barstool, pulling on her gloves and moving for the door as quiet as a shadow. She raised her hood over her head, slipped her hands into the pouch of the sweatshirt, gripping the weapon hidden there, a telescoping baton with a weighted tip called an ASP. She kept her head down as she passed by the bouncer and out the door. A few paces ahead of her on the crowded sidewalk, she spied the angry man searching for the frightened woman.

Like she had with the others, she'd take him from behind, start with a quick strike to his knee. A man who can't stand can't fight back. Then, before he even hit the ground, she'd go for his throat. For control of his voice, his breath, and the blood rushing to his brain. Destroying the knee hurt him, and it gave her strategic advantage. But compressing his throat in the bend of her elbow, *strangling* him? That was what induced the panic; that pressure conjured the terror. The terror was what she wanted. Terror left a lasting impression. She knew that from experience.

Maureen would make sure he never found the woman he pursued. Not tonight. Not ever. And that he'd never know what hit him.

2

Hours later, on a quiet residential street, a couple of blocks away from the late-night bustle of Frenchmen Street, Maureen climbed into her beat-up old Honda, the door creaking as she opened it. She sat in the driver's seat, the door open, one foot out on the sidewalk. She found her cigarettes and lit up. She was not quite ready to drive home. Too much to drink. She needed more time than one cigarette would give her, but that eight to ten minutes would have to suffice. What she should do, she thought, was call a cab. Maybe she would.

She put her head back on the headrest. Yeah, maybe a cab was best. In a minute, though. After this cigarette.

With her right hand she felt around on the Honda's passenger seat. Where was her gum? She always had gum in the car. Right? Where the fuck—no, wait—that was the patrol car, that was when she always had gum. Nothing but empty cigarette packs on the Honda's passenger seat. Well, whatever. Fuck it. If she wasn't going to be driving or kissing anyone, she didn't need the gum. Her eyes closed, she smiled. No, no kissing anyone tonight.

Only one man that night had attracted her attention.

And she'd left him, the man she'd followed out of d.b.a., crumpled on a curb on Burgundy Street, on the other side of the neighborhood from where she was now, but not far from the front stoop of the woman he'd followed. She'd left him weeping hot tears onto his bloody cheeks, bleeding from the mouth, and clutching his broken wrist to his chest.

But she'd left him hours ago. She should've gone right home after that. The interlude had left her spent. Now here she was, too drunk to drive and too tired to deal with a cab.

Instead of going home like she should have, she had restarted that night's intended mission. Hustling away from Burgundy Street, Maureen had worked her way deeper into the Marigny neighborhood, toward the Bywater, asking again at the neighborhood bars and corner stores if anyone had seen Madison Leary. Of course, same as always, no one had. This search had been going on for a month.

Maureen was asking the same questions of the same people in the same places every week. It was bad police work, and she knew it. Because now these people she pestered for information that they had already told her they didn't have were starting to ask *her* questions. When they did, she dodged. She copped an attitude. Or she tried to charm. No matter what tack she took, she tried to hide her face as best she could. She kept her hood up. She looked at the ground. Anything not to be memorable.

She couldn't tell the people she talked to that she was a cop. She definitely couldn't have them figuring it out for themselves. If anyone IDed her and called the NOPD to complain, she'd be sunk. She'd never get her badge back then. She was supposed to be staying at home this month. Behaving. Waiting. Being a good girl.

Conducting her investigation while half-drunk and totally disheveled made for good-enough cover, Maureen hoped. Her wardrobe helped her blend in with the neighborhood. She hoped to come across more like a desperate ex than law enforcement. She figured she hadn't been a cop long enough to emanate the vibe of a narc. While she hadn't scored the information she wanted, she hadn't gotten caught looking for it. And she hadn't gotten caught doing anything *else* she shouldn't be doing, either. But that night, she'd done something she'd never done before. Because she had gone out asking questions after dealing with the man, she had left witnesses to the fact that she was in the same neighborhood at the same time as one of her men.

And somebody had called for help for the rotten bastard. Maureen had seen the emergency lights of the cops and the ambulance flashing down Burgundy Street. Which meant there was a police record now of his beat-down.

Avoiding someone calling an ambulance, though, would've required hurting him less. But less pain and less injury left less of a lasting impression. She had the silver-haired man to thank for teaching her that.

So, so wise of you, Maureen. Every step of the way. You're letting him burn you down, she thought, from beyond the grave. After everything you did to get away from him.

How stupid can you be?

"Excuse me, Officer."

Maureen opened her eyes. Had she really heard that? Had she fallen asleep and dreamed it? That voice, she thought, feeling herself grinning, is in your head.

"Officer?"

It took Maureen a moment to recall that she wasn't in uniform. So was someone she knew approaching? She took a deep breath, willing herself attentive. Shit. Maybe someone she'd hassled in the neighborhood *had* figured her out. She checked her sweatshirt pocket for the ASP.

She put up her hood and climbed out of the car. Her legs were leaden. Her butt had fallen asleep. She slipped her hand into her sweatshirt pocket and gripped the ASP.

Blinking, she watched a short, slight figure approach out of the darkness, walking, no, not walking, more like sauntering, right down the middle of the street. Puffs of breath rose into the air around the figure's head. The night was so quiet Maureen could hear a metallic tinkling with every step the figure took, like the sound of spurs.

"I hear you're looking for me," the figure said.

Not spurs, Maureen thought. Metal buckles. Undone metal buckles running up the front of a pair of tattered, knee-high leather boots.

"Dice," Maureen said. "Not you, exactly. I've been looking for Leary."

Dice was a street kid, a skinny girl around twenty years old. Silver piercings adorned her nose and lips. An elaborate tattoo of Smaug the dragon wrapped around her shaved head. She and the other young homeless in New Orleans called themselves "travelers." Cops, shop owners, bar owners, and anyone else who didn't like them called them "gutter punks." Dice was a panhandler, a pickpocket, and a petty thief, depending on her needs. And she was also a heroin addict who, the last time Maureen had seen her, had managed to string together a decent amount of clean time through force of will alone. She often toted around a beat-up banjo that she plucked at for tips on street corners while sitting on an overturned pickle bucket. At least that was the theory. Maureen had never seen her do more than attempt to tune the thing.

Tonight, as Dice got closer, Maureen couldn't see the dragon. Against the cold, Dice wore a black knit watch cap, low over her eyes. The rest of her was wrapped up in a bulky wool herringbone coat many sizes too large. The coat fell below her knees. She looked to Maureen like a child in her father's overcoat. She didn't have her banjo, either.

"You've been following me," Maureen said.

"Only since you left the Spotted Cat," Dice said, grinning.

The last place I was in before coming to the car, Maureen thought. After the man on Burgundy Street. "Where have you been?"

"Here. There. Around."

"You've been hiding from me," Maureen said.

"How can I be hiding from you," Dice said, "when you aren't even looking for me? You said a second ago that you've been looking for Madison."

Maureen closed the car door. She stepped into the street to meet Dice. "Have you seen her? Do you know where she is?"

Dice pouted, toeing the asphalt. Maureen noticed the toe cap of her boot was wrapped in duct tape. "Nothing more for me? No 'How are ya' or 'How ya been' for me?"

Maureen rubbed her eyes. "You're right. I'm sorry. It's late and I'm tired. Of course I was hoping to find you, too, along the way."

"I'll forgive you for a cigarette," Dice said.

Maureen obliged. Other than Dice, Maureen wasn't sure there was another person in New Orleans who had spent any time with Madison Leary and lived to tell about it. As Dice had told the story, they had lived together at a hostel for a few weeks, when Leary had first arrived in New Orleans and before she had run out of the powerful medication that kept her demons at bay. Paranoia, schizophrenia, and who knew what else. Maureen had tried recruiting Dice to help find Madison when she'd first become a person of interest in a murder case.

Soon after that, though, Madison had gone from person of interest to number one suspect. Then things had gone to shit for Maureen on the NOPD, and Dice and Madison had both disappeared into the New Orleans underground. For the past six weeks, Maureen's conscience had been gnawed raw by the idea that she had gotten Dice killed for asking her to betray Leary.

Maybe she does know where Leary is, Maureen thought. Maybe she needs a way to tell me. "I thought maybe you'd moved on. The weather is turning, it's cold living on the streets. I thought maybe you'd headed for Florida or California."

Dice shrugged. She held her cigarette close to her mouth. On her hand was a fingerless black-and-white-striped glove. Tough picking pockets with gloves on, Maureen guessed. The things you learned staying out late in New Orleans, she thought.

"I considered it," Dice said. "Remember Taylor? The boy who wore the blue eye shadow over one eye, the one who wanted to fuck me so bad it oozed out of his pores? He begged me to come back with him to Orlando."

Maureen shrugged. "He seemed nice. Florida's okay. Warm. My mom and her boyfriend are thinking of retiring there."

"The Empire of the Rat? Seriously?" Dice said.

"Not Orlando," Maureen said. "But Florida."

Dice waved away the idea, a disgusted look on her face. "No offense to your moms, but fuck that." She tossed her cigarette in the street. "I like it here. New Orleans grows on you. I hear the winter doesn't last, anyway."

"I wouldn't know," Maureen said. "This is my first one, too."

"And really, it's only a couple of months, which is really only a few weeks, when you think about it, until Mardi Gras gets here. *That* I want to see."

I'm sure you do, Maureen thought. Tourist pockets to pick as far as the eye can see.

"Actually, it starts right after Christmas," Dice said. "So it's practically fucking here already."

Maureen could hear the hope in Dice's voice. She knew it wasn't for the holidays, or for Carnival. It was for the end of the cold, and for the chance to steal enough money to eat hot food, take a hot shower, and maybe to live indoors at a hostel or a flophouse until the Mardi Gras money ran out and she was back on the streets again. Many of the kids who Dice ran with had homes and parents to return to; it was an ill-kept secret on the streets. Maureen knew that Dice had neither of those things.

"She's a murder suspect, you know," Maureen said. "You withhold information and you're committing a felony. And she's dangerous. You know that as well as anybody."

Dice cocked her head, studied Maureen out of one eye. "Are you even a cop anymore?"

"Of course I am," Maureen said. "I've just been on kind of a hiatus for a while."

Dice nodded, sagely. "Because of that cop you knew who died in the river."

"Madison doesn't have to talk to me," Maureen said. "She can reach out to Detective Atkinson. She's the one working those murder cases now. I know Atkinson. She's the best there is. She's good people." She stretched out her empty hands. "You could talk to Atkinson."

"You've told her everything I told you?" Dice said.

"Weeks ago."

"Then what's the point?" Dice said. She turned in a circle on her boot heel. "This Atkinson's already heard what I have to say. Why does she need to hear it from me in person?"

"We could help you," Maureen said. "Quid pro quo. You help us; we help you. Atkinson has a lot more juice than I do."

Dice laughed out loud. "The police? The city? Help me? Help me do what?"

"Sure," Maureen said. "There are diversion programs, shelters, halfway houses, all kinds of resources."

"Diversion programs," Dice mocked, making air quotes with her fingers. "Because I need my face jammed into some bull dyke's muff in the middle of the night. Or some creepy old perv slipping his cold fingers down the back of my pants. No fucking thanks." She laughed again. "You're terrible at this, Officer. You're a terrible storyteller. You don't believe a single word coming out of your own mouth."

"Fine, you're right," Maureen said. "But you know as well as I do that Madison killed two men."

"Allegedly."

"You're her attorney now?" Maureen said.

"Those two men followed her to New Orleans," Dice said, her voice heating up, "and hunted her when they got here. All Madison wanted was to get away from them and the rest of their stupid group of fake soldiers. What did they call themselves?" She made air quotes again. "The Watchmen Brigade." She made a show of rolling her eyes. "Whatever. Those two men who died, you and I both know they had it coming. The world is better off without them. Don't even tell me you don't believe that."

"We don't get to make those decisions."

"There you go again," Dice said, "spouting shit that you don't believe." She moved a step closer. "Think of it this way, then. If Madison *is* the killer you seem to think she is, look at what she did to those Watchmen. She cut both of their throats. You think it's best being out here alone after dark chasing after her when she's this crazy murderer?"

Maureen scratched at her scalp. Why had she not gone home hours ago? She'd forgotten what a pain in the ass Dice could be, like a gremlin you couldn't quite grab. And how *smart* she was. "Can you even tell me if she's stayed in town?"

"I could," Dice said, smiling, "but I won't." She paused. "Maybe."

"Look who's playing games now," Maureen said. "What does that even mean?" She reached for her wallet. "You know what." She pulled out a ten, handed it to Dice. "This is why you followed me. Because you need fucking money. The rest of this is playing games to make yourself feel better about *begging* from me."

Dice shook her head. She didn't take the money. Her face had darkened. The games were over. "You should stop looking for her."

"And why is that?"

"People are starting to talk about you."

"Like I give a fuck about that," Maureen said.

Dice picked at a thread on her glove, considering, Maureen could tell, what to say next, how much of a chance to take. Dice said, "You're not the only one looking for her, either. Someone else has been coming around asking questions."

"Who?"

"It's not important," Dice said, "and I don't know who he is or who he's with, I haven't talked to anyone in person about her myself, I'm only telling you what I'm hearing. Now, the other street kids, they're starting to talk. They want to know who this Madison Leary person is that the cops are looking for, that other people are looking for. None of this attention is doing anybody any good. There's a mess about to be made."

"Tell me who this guy is," Maureen said. "Tell me what he looks like. I can help back him off. Trust me on that. Is he with the militia, too?"

She waited. Dice said nothing.

"Can you tell me if he's law enforcement, then?" Maureen asked. "Can you tell me that much?"

"No," Dice said. "I can't."

"Can't or won't?"

Dice sighed. "This conversation is having the opposite effect I wanted it to."

"Is it the Watchmen again?" Maureen asked. "Is that who's looking for her? She stole from them. She knows things about them law enforcement can use against them. They're going to keep coming after her. These guys, Dice, you laugh at them, but they're fanatics and they're armed to the teeth. Completely psycho. They shot my house to shit in broad daylight. I have bullet holes in my headboard."

"You're bragging," Dice said, giving Maureen a wry smile.

"These guys think of themselves as an invading army," Maureen said. "They're moving *crates* of guns into the city."

"Tell me more about your headboard."

"Spare me the flirty bullshit," Maureen said. "They'll kill you without a second thought."

"You should leave her be," Dice said. "Leave Madison alone."

"So she's in town," Maureen said. "If she wasn't here you wouldn't tell me to leave her alone."

"She only did what any woman would've done," Dice said. "What you would've done, what I would've done. She was just defending herself. As is her right as an American. She was standing her ground."

"If you've got nothing useful to tell me," Maureen said, "why'd you even come find me tonight?"

"Word's around that you're looking," Dice said. "It's in the streets. I heard people talking and I knew it was you. I don't think they've figured you out for a cop, but that's coming. And if they don't figure you for a cop, they might figure there's something valuable in protecting her in a more emphatic way than just saying they don't know her, since she's so interesting. So what I came to tell you is that you should stop looking."

"Is that a threat?" Maureen asked, laughter in her voice. "Who are you delivering messages for? Who's got you making threats for them? How well do the Watchmen pay?"

Dice sighed. Good, Maureen thought. Her turn to have her patience tested. "You're *such* a fucking cop. Everybody always with an ulterior motive, even me."

"*Especially* you," Maureen said. "Are you kidding me?"

"You tried to do good by me before. I'm only trying to do you a favor, one woman to another."

"How do you know," Maureen said, "that you're not next on Madison's list?"

"I just do," Dice said. She snatched the ten-dollar bill from Maureen's hand, stuffed it into the deep pocket of her big coat. "Besides, I know how Madison operates." She started backing away down the street. "Leave her be, Officer. Like there's no other crime in this town? From what you tell me, you cops are about to have your hands full, more than ever. Get on with your life, Officer Coughlin. Do that, and you and me, we can stay friends."

3

Late afternoon the next day, Maureen left her house in the Irish Channel for a run. She jogged up Sixth Street, crossed Magazine Street, crossed Prytania Street, and then made a left turn onto St. Charles Avenue.

She wanted to reach Audubon Park, circle the park twice, and start heading home before dark. She had plans for that night. Big plans. If she didn't run and lingered around the house, she wouldn't be sharp later. She'd feel slow and tired, especially after seeing so little daylight. She'd start drinking early. Earlier. She might even change her mind about going through with her plan and stay home, hiding in her living room. Not an option.

At a half mile or so into her run, when she hit the intersection of Louisiana and St. Charles, her legs started to lighten and loosen. Her blood pumped hard through her arms and legs. She flexed her fingers as she ran. Her chest burned from the previous night's abundance of cigarettes, but her wind was good overall. She felt her body coming back to life for her once again, her run beating back the ravages of another daylong hangover. She knew she demanded a lot of her body. Between what she did with it and what she put into it, she also sent it a lot of mixed signals. It always responded and gave her what she demanded of it. Pretty quickly, too.

How long her body would remain so responsive, she didn't know. She was thirty. She lived hard, had done so since eighteen. These past few weeks, the ones away from work, she'd begun bumping up against her physical limits. By the time she'd gotten home from Frenchmen Street, cleaned up, and climbed into bed, her conversation with Dice turning over in her head, the sunrise, and her hangover, had arrived.

No Frenchmen Street tonight, she thought. That had been dumb luck, a surprise opportunity, running into that feuding couple in d.b.a. Tonight, she was getting back on target, back to her plan, and the hunting ground was closer to home. Right in the neighborhood. Which, of course, made things much riskier. This project was as important, she reminded herself, as anything she'd be doing were she on the job. And not only important to her. She might quite possibly be saving someone's life.

Picking up her pace, she followed the streetcar tracks along the dusty neutral ground of St. Charles, passing under the branches of the live oaks, their leaves staying green into the heart of November. Three miles later, she'd reached her destination.

She skipped across St. Charles through stopped rush-hour traffic and into Audubon Park, chastising herself for being tempted not only by the water fountain, but also by the empty benches on the banks of the lagoon. Maybe tomorrow, she told herself. Maybe later in the week she'd get up to the park to hang out and relax for once, to read a book, to watch the ducks and squirrels from one of the benches. Everyone else could rush by *her* for a change. Such a beautiful park, she thought. She couldn't believe sometimes that she ran under the boughs of oak trees draped with wispy gray Spanish moss. Like something from a movie or a postcard. Right there, inches above her head. So many gorgeous, quiet hideaways in the park, and she was always running right by them. Panting. Pushing. Of course, park benches and ducks, peace and beauty, they were not the reasons she had added the loops around the park to her runs.

A couple of circuits helped Maureen accomplish two things. First, the extension added almost four miles, bringing her nearer an even ten miles.

Second, it gave her a reason to pass by the Heath house.

Solomon Heath's mansion sat on the edge of the park behind a screen of squat, sprawling live oaks, ancient dark-bodied trees whose knotted branches dragged in the grass like the impossibly long and bendy arms of great jungle apes. Running by the mansion in the late afternoons and evenings, Maureen had often glimpsed Solomon sitting in one of the throne-like white rocking chairs on the wraparound porch, his hand gripping a highball glass. He seemed to be watching the birds and squirrels flitting about in the branches of the oaks.

One evening she'd seen him standing, looking contemplative, at a tall second-floor window, the curtain held aside with one hand. That time he seemed to be looking at her instead of the park's modest wildlife, watching her as she ran past his property. She'd seen him on several evenings standing watch over a generously smoking grill.

Every time she saw him, he was alone. Every time one hand clutched a glass. Bourbon, she figured. Really excellent bourbon, she imagined, that he bought by the case.

Half a dozen times Maureen had taken the liberty, during the day, of following Solomon's black Jaguar in her Honda from his Central Business District offices to the job sites of Heath Design and Construction's larger current projects: the housing development on the edge of the Quarter, the new jail and new hospital in Mid-City. Even on weekends, she never saw anyone else at the house. Solomon was a man who had his work and nothing else. At least, she believed, that was what he wanted anyone who might be paying attention to think about him.

She'd been to the house once. Not long before her suspension she'd worked a security detail at a cocktail party fund-raiser hosted by the family. She'd met Solomon, shook his hand. And she'd had a run-in under the live oaks of the park with his troublesome sociopath slumlord of a son, Caleb. She hadn't actually made it inside the place, restricted that night to the mansion grounds like a guard dog.

She watched Solomon, but the Heath she wanted most was Caleb. He had fled the country following the death of his friend and Maureen's coworker, NOPD officer Matthew Quinn. The cop in the river whom Dice had mentioned. A schoolmate of Caleb's, Quinn had been in Solomon's pocket since he'd gotten his badge. Six weeks before, in an effort to protect Caleb from being outed as a member of the Watchmen by a drug dealer and murderer they'd worked with named Bobby Scales, Quinn had snatched Scales from Orleans Parish Prison and drowned him in the Mississippi.

Problem was, Quinn had gone in the river, too, sucked by the wake of a passing freighter under the same currents that swallowed Scales. Maureen had been there at the riverside, had watched them both go under the frothing water, helpless.

Nobody knew when, or if, Caleb was coming back to New Orleans. A few people knew—and Maureen was one of them, Solomon had to be another—that Caleb had played a role in Quinn's death. And had played a larger role in an attempt on Maureen's life. Caleb Heath was the reason she had bullet holes in her bed. Caleb had given her address, which he had gotten from Quinn, to a van full of heavily armed Watchmen. She wanted to talk to him about that. Preferably in an interrogation room, handcuffs cutting into his bleeding wrists. And with a black eye inflating one side of his face.

She watched Solomon because he was the only man with the power to call Caleb home. Not that NOPD had tried. Maureen got the impression they were relieved he was out of reach. As far as she could tell, Solomon had no interest in bringing the boy home. Judging by what she had learned about their relationship, Maureen figured Solomon was only too happy to be rid of his youngest son. And there was quite possibly another reason Caleb had been sent halfway across the globe. The two men Madison Leary had killed knew each other, did things together. Those men knew Caleb Heath and did things with him, too. Things for which Caleb put up the money. It seemed Madison Leary had a list, and Caleb Heath was probably on it. Maybe even next. And Caleb knew it. Maureen was the one who had told him so.

Information about the rest of the Heaths hadn't been hard to find around town. They were a prominent New Orleans family, and had been so since the days of Queen Sugar. For a generous tipper, and Maureen was surely that, stories passed readily across the top of any old-line bar in Uptown. One red-faced, white-haired barkeep at the Columns Hotel proved to be positively encyclopedic. Maureen knew she heard a lot of rumor and conjecture, and that much of what she was served came spiked with the moonshine of vitriol and resentment, or smoothed out with the sycophantic admiration granted the extremely wealthy, but she was good at distilling gaseous rumors into compounds of truth.

She'd learned a Mrs. Heath existed, and that the lady was a tall, stale whisper of a name around the city and a wife to Solomon in paperwork and bank account only. She'd been in Paris since Katrina. She, apparently, did not come home when called. Good for her, Maureen thought. She didn't care much; a lost wife was of no use to her.

An older brother named Torben was the one charged with sheltering Caleb in Dubai, where Torben oversaw the Heath company's international offices. Maureen had no idea if Torben knew why his black sheep brother had been dumped in his lap. The older brother had a twin sister, Holiday. She lived in the Emirates as well. What she did there, Maureen had no idea. Probably not much of anything. She lived in a Southern California–style expat compound on the sandy shores of the Persian Gulf. In the Heath family, the work gene, profitable as it was, had passed from Solomon to Torben and spread no further. Maureen had tangential interest in these other Heaths. She cared about Caleb. She only had eyes for him.

As she ran in circles past Solomon's house, Maureen weighed the consequences of approaching him, of stopping her run and walking right up to him on his porch. Sweaty. Smelly. Asking for a glass of water. To see if he remembered her from the party. Or from the trouble with his son. She wondered if he even knew who she was. If he didn't remember, would he ask her name? But Maureen never went anywhere near him. She'd never get her job back if she pulled a stunt like that. And she had no idea what she would really say to him were they ever face-to-face again.

Maybe to talk to him *wasn't* what she wanted, she thought, her feet pumping under her along the track like a heartbeat. Maybe what she really wanted was for Solomon to see her. Every. Single. Day. From his rocking chair. Through the glinting windows of his mansion. In the security cameras he kept trained on the park around his house. So he would know. So he would be forced to remember her. He would know she hadn't gone away for good. He would know that she wasn't afraid of him, of any of them.

Not the Heaths, and not the cops and criminals alike, whom they paid off with stiff new bills passed hand to hand in unmarked envelopes. Like the envelope he had given her the night she'd worked the party. Trying to buy her, and assuming she came cheap.

4

That evening, as she rounded the turn past Bird Island out in the lagoon, Maureen could see high in the island's trees, settling into their nests for the night, great white egrets holding their long beaks open and squawking and beating their wings, the feathers of their wingtips thin and spread wide like human fingers, silhouetted against the sky. In the lagoon, brown-and-green ducks paddled with purpose along the water's smooth surface, their eyes fixed straight ahead, the upright triangles of their tails wagging, their V-shaped wakes splitting then fading behind them.

Maureen continued running along the track, closing in on the Heath house. She dipped and dodged as people of varied shapes and colors, wearing everything from shiny skintight biking gear to fluffy pink tracksuits, cycled, jogged, power walked, and Rollerbladed around her, talking and talking, those moving mouths always talking, to each other, to their babies, to their dogs, into their phones, or maybe all at the same time, as far as Maureen could tell.

In her own ears, music pounded. Trombone Shorty & Orleans Avenue.

An instrumental track, one of her favorites: "Hurricane Season." She could hear nothing else around her. She ran lost in a wash of horns so loud she couldn't think, her preferred state. The sinuous, repeating sequence of notes blasting in her ear worked like the expert combination punches of a boxer. The bass and drums and guitar rolled and thundered underneath the lightning of the horns like a runaway locomotive threatening to jump the track. But the horns were what got her, what held her. She'd never heard anything like those horns until she got to New Orleans.

The infectiousness. The irresistible raw and ecstatic power.

Where was this music when she was growing up?

As if she hadn't gotten in enough trouble as a teenager, she thought. She could only imagine what would have become of her had she hurtled through adolescence with brass band music percolating her blood and her brain tissue along with everything else drenching her system in those days, both what came naturally and the other chemicals she had added herself.

Maureen ran past the island, putting the noisy birds behind her, and the great house appeared on her right. And there he was standing in the yard, highball glass in one hand, the man himself. Solomon Heath. He was getting nearly as regular as she. Was it he, she wondered, who had dispatched someone to search for Madison Leary? Was Solomon's agent the man Dice had been talking about? New Orleans would be safer for his son if Leary was behind bars, or in the river. She put neither option past the man.

She kept an eye on Heath while navigating the obstacles around her.

He was looking right at her, watching her as she ran. Even from a distance, she could tell that something about him that evening was off. No smoke rose from the grill. He just stood there, not moving, halfway between his house and where the edge of his property melted into the park. Like he'd been waiting for her. In his right hand was the highball glass, tilted at an angle where it might spill its contents. In his left hand he held a short golf club against his pant leg, the club's metal shaft glinting in the fading sunlight.

As if whatever signal he'd been waiting for had arrived, he started walking toward the park, toward her, raising his glass to his lips and drinking, never taking his eyes off Maureen. His steps were unsteady. She wouldn't have to speed up much, she thought, to run right by him. He was in no shape to chase her, not at his age, not with the way she could run.

But she didn't accelerate; she held that option in reserve. Instead, she slowed down, letting him know, she hoped, that she had clocked his approach.

The golf club, she decided, was a prop. Something he could lean on while he'd waited for her to run past that wasn't a sign of weakness, like a cane. Not that she'd ever seen him use a cane. Not that he'd ever appeared to her a weak man. She noticed his steps in her direction had quickened. His gait had steadied. He was determined to intercept her.

Okay then, she thought. Let's do this.

At most the club was an implied threat, she decided, not an actual one. He'd have to do better than that, Maureen thought, considering what his son and his friends had already put her through. She drifted across the track in his direction. She might leave the running track, she decided, but she wouldn't stray far enough from it to cross from public property onto his. But if Solomon was going to approach her on park property, she wasn't going to stop him. She welcomed the interaction. She was glad she'd finally reached him, and without her once knocking on his door or invading his private space in any way.

Then, on one of the benches ahead of her, Maureen saw a familiar sandpaper-colored head. The head turned and Maureen saw the full-cheeked, green-eyed, red-pepper-flaked face of Sergeant Preacher Boyd, her former field training officer and her duty sergeant at the Sixth District. He turned on the bench and waved at her. Preacher wore civilian clothes: pressed dark jeans and a black Saints hoodie, and a dark knit hat. A group of white ducks crowded about his feet, complaining, Maureen figured, that they weren't getting fed. A single massive goose stood off to the side, observing the proceedings. Now this, Preacher being here,

Maureen thought, this could fuck things up with Heath. She slowed to a walk. She looked over at Solomon.

He had stopped, maybe ten yards away from her. Close enough that Maureen could hear the clink of the ice in his glass. He tapped the head of the golf club on the toe of his shoe, watching her. He sees Preacher, too, Maureen thought. But does he know who Preacher is? He must, she decided. The two of them were both so deeply woven into the tapestry of the city, they had to know each other.

Preacher rose from the bench, narrowing his eyes at Solomon, frowning when he realized who he was observing. They knew each other, all right. The three of them stood, looking at one another, the points of a triangle. It wasn't Solomon putting the frown on Preacher's face, Maureen realized. It was her.

She felt caught out, embarrassed, as if she'd been busted meeting a boy she'd promised her friends she'd left behind. In reality, she had been caught doing, or been caught *about* to do, something technically much worse than meeting a bad-for-her boyfriend. According to her superiors at the NOPD, Maureen was banned from having anything to do with Solomon Heath. The excuse that he'd approached her in a public place would never wash. Not with them and not with Preacher.

"Coughlin," Preacher said. Not loud, but authoritative enough that Maureen didn't want to hear him say it again. He would never order her to do something in public, not when she was out of uniform, but when he spoke to her like that, the command was implied.

Maureen glanced at Heath one more time. He stood his ground, staring at her, swinging the golf club through the dead leaves at his feet like a pendulum.

She sighed, turned her back on him, and jogged in Preacher's direction, her head hung low like a ballplayer on her way back to the dugout, upset with the umpire's decision. She could feel the heat of her blood as her neck and cheeks flushed. She was not happy, very not happy, about being brought to heel by Preacher in front of Heath. Part of the point in her running by his house so often, she thought, had been to demonstrate her freedom; to imply that she might be more dangerous on the loose than she had been on the job. Now, this moment she had been waiting for, that she had so carefully orchestrated, was backfiring on her. Not the first time that's happened, she thought.

Maureen and Preacher had been meeting in the park for the last month. They didn't communicate beforehand to set up the meetings. She ran through the park at about the same time every day. When Preacher needed to see her, he went to the park and waited on the bench. If Maureen saw him there, she stopped and they talked. Usually, he'd have some tidbit of department gossip for her. He kept her apprised of daily life in the Sixth District. Sometimes he had something he'd heard about the Leary case and things surrounding it. What he had most often was no news about that case at all.

Maureen knew, though they never discussed it, that the main reason for the meetings was Preacher's constant worry about her. He was checking up on her. Until today, she had appreciated the attention. She knew he was taking a risk. They both were.

Maureen and Preacher weren't supposed to see each other, to have any contact, until she'd been officially reinstated to the police department. Or fired from it. She didn't know who at the NOPD, if anyone, watched or kept track of such things. She certainly couldn't see Preacher reporting to or checking in with anyone. And if someone was watching the two of them, there was no way Preacher didn't know about it. He probably knew the person doing the spying, and that person probably owed Preacher any number of favors. Everyone in New Orleans, cop or not, owed Preacher a favor. In his way, Preacher could reach as deep into the convoluted viscera of New Orleans as the Heaths. They reached down from the top. Preacher reached up from the bottom. Both got results.

Maureen coasted to a stop, stepping off the asphalt track onto the grass to meet him. She plucked out her earbuds and silenced the music on her iPod with her thumb.

"I'm waiting," Preacher said.

"For what?"

"For you to say thank you," Preacher said. "Because I just saved you from making a huge mistake."

"I don't know what you're talking about," Maureen said, studying the tops of her running shoes.

"We really going to play this game?"

Maureen set her hands on her hips. She puffed out her chest and raised her chin. But she said nothing.

"What you're doing right now," Preacher said. "Not talking? You should do more of that."

Preacher scanned her with his eyes, evaluating her from her head to her feet, as she approached. She couldn't miss the scrutiny; he didn't even try to hide it. It was the first thing that happened each time they met. It wasn't a sexual appraisal. She'd never gotten the slightest kind of attention from him that way. This time, Maureen wasn't sure what he was thinking as he added up what he'd observed about her. Whatever it was he saw today, she could tell from his face that he didn't approve, beyond what she had tried with Heath.

"What now?" she asked.

"Do you ever eat?"

"The amount of exercise I get?" Maureen said. "I eat constantly."

"Not that nuts-and-berries shit," Preacher said. "Real food. Cooked food."

"We've only known each other a few months," Maureen said, grateful for the change in subject, "but we've spent a lot of time together. You've seen me eat. You really think I'm a nuts-and-berries kind of girl? C'mon."

She bent forward, her hands on her thighs, huffing for breath, sweat trickling from under her headband and down the sides of her neck. She gave Preacher a hard time, goofed at things he said, but she understood his point. It wasn't like she didn't know what was happening to her.

She was losing weight. A lot of it. No one needed eyes as keen as Preacher's to see that. She'd never had much extra weight to spare, she'd always had angles where other women had curves, but during her suspension she had started losing the muscle she'd added over the summer in the police academy and her first months on the streets. Muscle she had worked hard for, that she needed in her arms and shoulders and back and backside to meet the physical requirements of her job. To protect herself on the streets.

She'd noticed this wearing away. She saw it in her hands, which were looking almost like a waitress's hands again. She saw it in the way her newer clothes no longer fit her. The running shorts she wore had fit when she'd bought them online two weeks ago. Now they sagged on her hips. She studied herself in the mirror after showers. Her ribs showed like they had in her cocaine-fueled middle twenties. Her hip bones were visible, too. For a few weeks there she'd almost had an ass. She was even losing that.

More than what she saw in the mirror frightened her. The visuals may have been what hurt her the least. What made her more nervous was that she could hear it, too, what was happening to her, when she was alone in the quiet of her house.

She could hear the grinding, the sound and the feel of stone working on stone, a feeling like the grinding of gears in her belly. Each day she was having a harder time ignoring the fierce devouring machine running every hour of the day and night in the arch under her ribs. And so *she* ran to take the machine's energy away. To burn the fear and the rage that she knew fueled it. To exhaust it before it ate her alive.

Her suspension was the first time since she was eighteen years old that she'd gone more than a couple of days without a job or a class or both to go to. So she ran.

She ran too often, too long, to the point where her body had started breaking down in protest. She ran through shin splints. Through swollen knees. Achy hips. She ran through every caution sign her body threw up in front of her.

Because she needed it.

Running, being in motion, was the only time that the world these days wasn't blurred and tilted ever so slightly on its axis, like she was looking at her surroundings through a turning wineglass. She needed the percussion of her feet pounding the dirt of the neutral ground between the iron rails of the streetcar tracks. Every long daylight stride pushed the silver-haired man farther back into the shadows. Every mile put the frightened, on-the-run woman she used to be farther behind her. She needed the shelter of the streetlight's curled arms and the stretching boughs of the live oaks arcing over her head. She needed to feel protected, to feel embraced by her new city. Running was the only time she felt safe anymore.

Well, when she was running and when she was chasing. And when she was hurting someone else.

One thing that being a cop and these past few weeks of night work had taught her—chasing after something or someone could feel as good, maybe better, than running away. Maybe because there was a real, live person at the end of the chase. Someone you could catch. Tangible damage you could do. The things she was running from, they weren't outside her, they were in her, and so she carried them with her. She knew that. One thing Maureen knew for sure was that neither the chasing road nor the fleeing road was anywhere near as frightening as the thought of standing still.

As she stretched in the soft grass of the park, she focused her vision on an ant crawling through the blades between her feet. She blew out her breath and the ant fell over on its back.

She moved her hands to the small of her back, did a slow back bend. When she'd righted herself she said, "You couldn't have picked a spot by the water fountain, at least? I'm putting in work here."

"We can walk over to it if you like," Preacher said.

Maureen looked out over the lagoon, eyes narrowed. She had an idea why he was there. Disappointment crept over her. This evening was crashing down around her ears in a hurry. "We're fine right here," she said. "Go ahead and get it over with. What have you heard? Is the axe coming down?"

"Excuse me?"

"I told you last time we met," Maureen said, "that I have my meeting tomorrow morning with the district commander. You're here because you've heard how it's gonna go. And you wouldn't be if things were gonna go well."

"Come sit on the bench with me," Preacher said.

"Wow, that bad." Maureen set her hands on her hips. She looked over her shoulder at the spot where Solomon had stood with his cocktail and his golf club. He was gone.

Preacher ambled over to the bench and sat. Half a dozen ducks waddled to him, quacking, their expectations renewed by his return.

Maureen hadn't realized until that very moment that, despite everything she'd done wrong both to earn her suspension and while serving it, she had been completely confident the DC would reinstate her. For the past six weeks, as far as the NOPD knew, she'd done everything the department had asked of her. She had kept quiet and stayed away from other cops. She had told no one about her searching the streets for Madison Leary, not even Preacher. Had the NOPD found out anyway? Where had she blown it? Dice had said no one she had questioned while searching for Leary had made her for a cop. She couldn't see how any of the guys she'd dealt with in the streets could know she was police. Not one of them got a good look at her face. They'd hardly heard her voice. She wasn't sure any of them even knew it was a woman who had taken them down.

But why would Preacher cross town to stake her out in Audubon Park the night before her big meeting other than to cushion the blow of the bad news in person? He was brave. And professional. And he had always looked out for her. If she were walking into an ambush in her meeting tomorrow, Preacher would warn her.

"Do I need to buy a plane ticket and get out of town?" Maureen asked. She looked through the trees at Solomon's house. He knew by now his bribe hadn't worked. Maybe he'd tried different tactics and reached into the department. "Have the brass changed their minds and decided to bring charges?"

Preacher turned on the bench when he realized she hadn't followed him. "Good Lord, woman. Would you come over here and sit? Did I say I'm here about your meet with the DC? I'm not. It's something else entirely. You Irish, you always expect the worst. Most dour motherfuckers I ever met. How any of you ever had the nerve to get on a boat I have no idea."

"We were highly motivated," Maureen said. "Our survival instinct is epic."

"Some of my people," Preacher said, "they were highly motivated, too."

Maureen sat next to him on the bench. A couple of noisy, dissatisfied ducks tottered in her direction. They had an arrogance to them, Maureen decided. The way they demanded things from you but never looked right at you while they did it, giving you one reluctant eye, like aristocrats demanding tribute. She kicked at them. "Beat it." The goose hissed at her, lowering its head and spreading its broad wings. "Jesus."

"This is their turf," Preacher said, his thick arms extended over the top of the bench. "Most people feed them. You really gonna hate on them for expecting to get what they've always gotten? You don't look any different to them than the rest of us do." He smiled. "Just another sucker."

"They're fucking annoying."

"They're fucking birds in a park," Preacher said. "They're doing what they're supposed to, tryin' to eat. It's not personal. They'll go away in a minute." He raised his chin at something over Maureen's shoulder. "Look, there you go. Salvation."

A young girl, no more than two or three years old, waddled much like a duck to the edge of the lagoon. Her pink puffy jacket rode up on her ribs. Her shock of curly red hair blew in the breeze. In one hand she held a plastic Bunny bread bag. She reached into the bag with her other hand, throwing fistfuls of white bread into the grass. Crumbs stuck to her fingers. She screamed with delight as the ducks headed in her direction, quacking up a storm, wagging their tail feathers, putting on a show as they snatched the bread out of the grass. More ducks came paddling over from out on the lagoon, attracted by the fuss. Maureen worried the goose would make a power move for the bread bag. She wondered if the girl's parents stood close enough to protect her from the goose if the bird got aggressive, or to rescue their little girl if she got overexcited and tumbled into the lagoon.

Maureen decided *she* was close enough to the little girl to intercede if disaster struck.

Or maybe, just maybe, Maureen thought, a little girl could feed the ducks at the park on a fall afternoon for a few minutes without something terrible and violent happening. She rubbed her temples with her fingertips. She wished she'd brought her cigarettes on her run.

She turned to Preacher. "Tell me you've got *good* news."

"You're not going to take it that way."

"You're killing me, Sarge," Maureen said. "Just straight killing me."

"When you go see Commander Skinner for your badge, he's going to ask a favor of you."

Maureen took a deep breath and held it. Keeping quiet these past six weeks, she'd been led to believe *that* was the favor. Now there'd be more. She felt foolish for being surprised. She blew out her breath. "How big a favor?"

Like it mattered, she thought. Like she wouldn't do it, whatever it was, to get her badge back.

"The FBI wants to talk to you," Preacher said.

Maureen sagged on the bench, as if her bones had turned to putty. "You are fucking kidding me. That wasn't supposed to happen. That was the deal."

"I'm not kidding," Preacher said. "And it's not as bad as it sounds."

"Is my phone tapped?" Maureen asked, sitting up. "Is that why we've been meeting in the park like a couple of fucking spies? Am I being surveilled?"

"I wanted to talk to you," Preacher said, "before the FBI did, and before you went in to see the district commander. So you could have your tantrum with me, instead of the DC." He turned to her. "Is that even a real word, *surveilled*?"

"What do they want?" Maureen asked. "I made my statements already. Detailed statements."

"The Sovereign Citizens kid," Preacher said, "the one who that Leary woman murdered on Lyons Street, the one who went to that reform school with Caleb Heath, name was Gage. Clayton Gage. His father has been in town asking questions. He's been to HQ and Homicide a couple of times, making angry demands." He shrugged. "It *was* his son who got killed, peckerwood shitheel that he was."

Maureen winced. "Tell me we're not back to covering up that traffic stop again. I can't. We did our best with that. It wasn't worth the lies we told. Not about Gage, not about Leary. I'm exhausted even thinking about it." She waved her hand. "Atkinson is lead detective on the Gage homicide now anyway. I secured the scene the night it happened, took a quick look at the body. The FBI knows all this. That was it. The father can talk to Atkinson. She doesn't want to do it, that's not my problem."

"What I'm hearing," Preacher said, "is that the feds think the father might be a source of useful intel on the Citizens and the Watchmen Brigade militia and whatever else his son might have been into. The money, the guns."

"He's involved, the father? He's part of the Sovereign Citizens movement?"

"Unknown at this time. That's probably the main thing the FBI wants you to find out when you talk to him."

"Wait—what? You're *shitting* me. Preach, the Citizens, the Watchmen, they tried to kill me. And the feds picked me for this because . . . ?"

"I don't have specifics on that," Preacher said. "But as near as I can figure, while Atkinson is lead on the murder, *you've* had more direct contact with the players." Preacher ticked off Maureen's connections to the case on his fingers. "You pulled over the truck with Gage and Leary in it. You took her to jail. You worked the Gage murder scene. Before that, you discovered the Nazi guy's body, the first victim, what was his name, Cooley." He raised his hands as if to fend off blame for the FBI's choices. "Anyways, looks like as far as the FBI's concerned, you,

Coughlin, are the resident NOPD authority on these psycho patriot derelicts."

Maureen sat up straight on the bench. Livid, she didn't know which way to look. "Man, *fuck* the FBI. Those terrorist motherfuckers in the Watchmen are *already* pointed in my direction. With guns blazing. Where was the FBI when these guys were stashing guns all over Central City? Where were they when these guys used their guns to try and kill me? They gotta be kidding me. Papa Gage is *their* problem. I don't get paid enough for this shit. I'm doing federal work, I want federal pay, and federal benefits."

She stood, her legs feeling thick and heavy. She needed to get moving again. She shook her head, turning to Preacher. "The feds knew I'd react like this, didn't they? They knew I wouldn't like this idea. That's why you're here, isn't it?"

"You got it wrong," Preacher said. "You're way ahead of yourself, as usual." He threw a glance at the little girl's parents, who had started eavesdropping. "And lower your voice."

"They sent you out here to soften me up to the idea." Her tone was derisive. She should've known, Maureen thought. She should've known there'd be more dues to pay, even after her suspension ended, to get out from under what had happened with Quinn a month and a half ago. She *and* Preacher, they were the only ones left around and they'd never stop paying. But, wow, she thought, Preacher tasked with the FBI's foreplay? It stung that he would go along. That he would deceive her on their behalf.

"Look at you," she said, giving him the up-and-down now, "a fucking butter man for the *federales*. Who'd a thunk it?"

Preacher rubbed his palms on his wide thighs. Maureen knew as soon as the last words left her mouth that she'd overstepped, even for her. She thought for a moment he might get up and walk away without another word to her. She took a deep breath. She forced herself to forget they were talking in the park, wearing their civilian clothes. Preacher was her direct superior. She had to stop abusing his patience.

"That's not the case," he said. "I'm not applying grease on anybody's behalf. This comes on the QT from my sources in the department. *Our* department. Like maybe somebody in Homicide, a tall blond Detective Somebody who you already owe a world of favors, is tipping me some info. I'm not supposed to know this shit, and you *sure as hell* aren't supposed to know it. We're not even supposed to be talking, remember? But here I am anyway, like I've been the past six weeks. I'm here for you, Coughlin. For your sake. Not for anyone else's. You should do this favor for the FBI. It could be good for you. It could be good for the department, which you owe a few favors. Most important, lest you forget the point of what we do, helping the FBI might help us catch some bad guys. Serious bad guys out to hurt cops. Learn how to accept a favor."

Maureen felt a hot wave of shame. She raised her hands, puffed out her cheeks. "Shit, I'm sorry."

Preacher had protected her from the moment she had climbed into the police cruiser as his trainee. He had protected her from the bad guys, from bad cops, from herself. And not just her. He watched over everyone in the Sixth District. Here was the one guy in New Orleans she could trust, and she was shit-talking to his face. She'd stop, right then.

Tomorrow, she thought, she would be a real cop again. No more pretending, no more running the streets in an oversized sweatshirt, hiding her face. She should feel nothing but relief. Instead, though, she felt the oily stain of compromise.

Do us one more favor, the men in charge said. It's right here in my hand, what you want. All I have to do is slide it across the table. Shake that ass for tips one more time. Then we'll stop asking. Except they never did. Not today. Not tomorrow. She thought of her plans for later that night. She could let them go. She could stay home. Tomorrow, she would be a cop again. Right, she thought. Tomorrow. Which meant not tonight. Tonight she remained whatever it was she had become, what she had made herself into, over the past six weeks. She'd refused to put a name on it. If she named that other self, she thought, it might stay.

One more night, she thought. One more time. On my terms.

Because you've never told yourself those words before. Not ever. Not a million times.

"Tell me one thing," Maureen said. "Tell me they're not making me a rat. Promise me that they're not gonna sell me to the DOJ when they're done with me. Tell me that's not the price tag. That Justice wants someone of their own undercover in the department. Someone easy to use, who they can hurt. Did they come to me because they don't have the nerve to ask this of Atkinson? Because she's clean. Because they got nothing on her."

"I've heard nothing," Preacher said, "about the Department of Justice. Or about this being some kind of permanent snitching gig for the feds. It should be the one favor."

Maureen laughed. "C'mon, Preacher. There's never just one favor. Admit it. Skinner *finally* decided to bring me back because the FBI showed up and gave him a chance to do them a favor. I do this favor for the feds and I get my job back. I'm not stupid. Nobody's doing anything for my benefit. I'm the perfect puppet. Quid pro quo, little bird." She rubbed her eyes, sat on the bench. "Here I am accusing you of being the FBI's bitch, when in the end, it's me who's going to be their bitch."

"I don't know for a fact," Preacher said, emphatic, "that your reinstatement continges on you talking to this FBI guy, but, whether it does or it doesn't, doing the feds a solid can't hurt your chances. You're a good Catholic girl. Don't think of it as a price tag, think of it as penance."

"I gave up that Catholic shit," Maureen said.

"Then think of it as karma," Preacher said. "I don't judge. Think of it as a mutually beneficial opportunity of which you've been availed. I don't much give a shit how you sell it to yourself. Just, for once, make the Man happy. It won't kill you. I've dabbled in it in my three decades on the job and I survived. And I remind you, if the bosses wanted to be cruel to you and roll around in their own shit in the process, which wouldn't be a first for this department, criminal charges around this Quinn thing and the Gage murder *are* a real possibility. You gotta live with that. You gotta factor that in."

"And I remind you," Maureen said, "this bird can sing. Factor *that* in."

"Sing about who?" Preacher said. "Quinn? His partner Ruiz? Not much point to that, is there?"

Maureen knew there was a third name Preacher had left off the list. His. He knew he didn't need to say it, that she'd register the omission.

"Listen to me, Coughlin. The best thing that could've happened for you did happen. The people in power, they've decided they need you. That only you can do what they need done. Be smart. Take advantage of it. Pride has no place in this job we do. Results are what matter. Favors. Debts. Information. Get your badge back so the Man can forget about us and we can get back to doing the work we were put on God's green earth to do. Catching the bad guys. Believe."

Maureen got up from the bench. "Speaking of bad guys, I saw Dice yesterday. Downtown."

"I don't want to hear about it," Preacher said. "Not my case. Not even my district. Not your case, either. And you're not a cop again until to-morrow. So shit that happened yesterday needs to stay there."

"She had nothing to say about Leary anyway. Except that there's been people looking for her. I think maybe Solomon sent someone after her, to protect Caleb."

"What did I just say? What did I just say to you about yesterday?"

"What? She followed me to my car and started talking. I was at the Spotted Cat having a drink and she saw me. I think she needed money, really. I think that's what it was about."

"And you just decided, hey, while I've got you here, let me ask about that murder suspect you know."

"It wasn't anything," Maureen said.

"Then why tell me about it?" Preacher asked. "Why mention it?"

This motherfucker, Maureen thought. Honesty. Up to a point. "I thought you'd be happy to hear the girl's not dead. That's what I meant by bringing it up."

"I am glad," Preacher said. "I am. When you're official again, reach out to Atkinson, let her know Dice is breathing and in town. Then maybe stay this side of Canal Street for a while."

Maureen pulled her heels to the small of her back one at a time, stretching her thighs. "I'm with you. I am."

Preacher was giving her that disapproving look again, like every wrong thing she had done over the past few weeks was scrolling across her body like a movie on a screen.

Maureen bounced on her toes. She was ready, more than ready, to start running again. "What? Why are you looking at me like that? I said I heard you."

"Make sure you hear this, too," Preacher said. "Tomorrow you'll be back at work. So if there's any business you need to finish up, anything pressing or lingering that you need to get out of your system before you come back, go ahead and let the devil out tonight. One last blowout, one last hurrah, whatever. Because tomorrow you need to be ready to be a cop again. One hundred percent."

He waited for her response.

He knew, Maureen thought. Somehow, some way, Preacher's preternatural cop intuition told him she'd been up to no good. Like when you were out on patrol and you talked to a guy on the street about the Saints or the weather, and you just knew somehow he had something in his pockets that he shouldn't have. Like whatever impulse, she thought, that had told her to pull over that pickup truck with Clayton Gage at the wheel and Madison Leary in the passenger seat. Maybe Preacher didn't know the specifics of what she'd been getting up to at night, Maureen thought, but he knew something was going on. And he knew it was wrong. Maybe he didn't know how far she'd gone, but he knew she'd strayed from the one true path.

"And leave Solomon Heath alone," Preacher said.

"I haven't said two words to that man since I worked his party."

"The man, his house, where he does his business," Preacher said. "Stay away."

Maureen opened her mouth to speak, to spit out some bullshit denial, but Preacher raised his hand against it. "You gonna hurt my feelings, Coughlin, you keep this up."

"Sorry."

"So we understand each other?"

"We do," Maureen said.

"We're clear, Officer Coughlin?"

"We are, Sergeant Boyd," Maureen said. "Crystal clear."

Preacher nodded. Maureen watched as he got up from the bench and walked down to the water, his hands buried in the pocket of his sweatshirt, his broad back to her. One more time, he was telling her, he would look away from what she did next. Once more.

5

Late that night, Maureen sat alone in the corner booth of a boisterous Magazine Street bar, called the Irish Garden, a few blocks from where she lived. She was cocooned and anonymous in the hive-like buzzing and activity of the partyers around her. She excelled at this, finding the blind spot, the blank space in an otherwise crowded room, and hiding there, looking out at a room full of strangers, watching and listening, an owl in the crook of a branch, absorbing the nighttime wilderness around her, invisible and calculating. If she ever got to do undercover work, she thought, she'd be great at it. If she could keep her job long enough to get there.

She'd also found, as best as she could figure with limited reconnaissance, a blind spot in the Irish Garden's security cameras. That was if the cameras were on, something she doubted, considering the clumsy minor-league hand-to-hand drug deals she'd witnessed by the restrooms and around the pool tables. One of the bartenders was blatantly stealing. Still, she figured, one couldn't be too careful while being completely reckless and endangering everything one had worked so, so hard to get.

That round, silver-crescent-over-a-star badge—like her whole future in New Orleans—had been hidden from her for six weeks, disappeared into an amorphous legal limbo and the power and whims of others. She realized that when she had thought about her badge over the past weeks, she had assigned it a mystical identity, like a lost relic in an old adventure movie, a glowing and humming talisman lost in the depths of a yawning cave or a crumbling temple. An object of power and value like Excalibur or the Ark of the Covenant or the One Ring, it waited for her, only her, to rescue it from useless oblivion. The badge had become her Precious.

But a badge wasn't a hero's sword lodged in a stone that she could claim, it wasn't a mystical Old Testament talisman she could unearth, or a piece of magic regal jewelry that she could steal as she fumbled about in the dark. She couldn't *take* her badge back; it had to be awarded, given to her, like a secret. She needed someone to reach a hand into that drawer and liberate that badge for her. She needed *someone else* to decide she deserved it, like on the first day she wore it, her graduation day that past summer from the NOPD academy. And she just hated that *need* of someone else's power. Of their permission. Of their approval.

Her need made her feel small and fragile, blind and weak, her skin tingling in anticipation of being violated or betrayed, the usual outcomes, she'd learned, of need. This time of year, she found herself especially conscious of that lesson.

What you *need*, Officer Coughlin, she thought, picking up her drink, is to be home getting a good night's sleep for once, instead of sitting in this bar, waiting for trouble. Waiting for the chance to make things worse right when your life is about to get better.

She looked down into her drink, an underpoured, watered-down, double-in-name-only Jameson rocks in a plastic cup. She wasn't going to change her mind about tonight. She needed to quit worrying, quit thinking, and focus on the task at hand. Focus was key. Somebody in this bar who didn't even know she was there needed her.

She poked at the ice in her cup, the cubes melted through in the middle, with the hard plastic cocktail straw. She slipped the straw through a cube, fished it from the whiskey, raised it to her mouth, and let the ice slide onto her tongue. She savored the cool, the ice whiskey-slick, before crushing the cube into shards between her back teeth.

She picked up her burning cigarette from the cracked plastic ashtray, took a deep drag, pulling the smoke over the whiskey and the ice chips, blending the temperatures and flavors.

Rattling the ice in her cup, she again looked over the men in the room. Stop lying to yourself, she thought. She wasn't only there for the sake of someone else's needs. It wasn't like she didn't have needs of her own, didn't enjoy the anticipation of meeting them.

She crushed more ice in her mouth and watched the room through the smoke of her cigarette.

This wasn't her first time in the Garden; she'd lived in a tiny studio across the street from the place for her first six months in town, during her time in the academy, during her field training—in a big old mansion that had been carved up into apartments decades ago.

She'd dated a cook from the bar's kitchen. Briefly. Things with Patrick hadn't worked out. Or, Maureen thought, they had worked out perfectly, considering what each had been looking for going in. She wasn't sure why she used that term—not working out. Not marrying the guy didn't mean the relationship, if she would even give it that name, had failed.

Either way, whatever they'd started had ended amicably, and she and Patrick hooked up once in a while, creating a situation only slightly different from the original incarnation, she thought. What made things different now, and possibly better, was the mutually acknowledged fact that they were now in the aftermath of something and were no longer at the beginning. The fact that there was no future in it took a lot of the pressure off. The really important part was that he was good in bed, patient and mature enough that she could take her time and get what she wanted, but not some kind of sexual martyr who acted like waiting for the woman to come first was an act of enormous personal sacrifice.

They'd ended their regular thing when Patrick had landed a new gig at an upscale restaurant farther uptown. He'd made the kind of all-consuming career move that Maureen understood very well. Well, if she was gonna be honest about it, *they* hadn't ended it. He had called it quits, while the smell of sex lingered on them, as a matter of fact. But she hadn't fought him on it, which kind of, pretty much made it mutual. That was what she told herself.

Christ, she hated this fucking bar. She wouldn't have set foot in the place except for the task at hand, searching out one special man, the one in whom she saw herself reflected back to her, the one hiding in plain sight. She took a tiny sip of her drink, nursing. Don't get up for another whiskey, she thought. Limit your motion, your interaction with the staff and the other patrons. Don't do anything that might make you memorable.

Truth be told, she didn't much want to see her face in the mirror behind the bar.

She wasn't there to drink whiskey, anyway, good as it tasted.

Look at these men, she thought. So similar, like they rolled off an assembly line. Thick unbrushed hair. Khaki pants. Checkered shirts. Hours after the sun had gone down, their wraparound Oakleys hung around their necks on leather straps. Leather boat shoes in hideous colors. Hairy forearms. Thin and bony ankles and wrists. So breakable. And those perfect white teeth. So expensive and so fragile.

Her eyes flitted from face to face. The same, the same, the same.

So loud, their ever-running mouths. Loud voices, loud laughter. Everything they said was shouted. Every insult, every joke, every reaction to whatever game played on one of the twenty televisions or whatever played-out song came on the jukebox.

How would she ever find that one special man she was looking for? Her last mystery man. Because, she told herself, you've spent enough time as prey to know a predator when you see one. And a predator is hunting out of this bar. This was her third night in the past week camped out in the Garden, waiting for him to appear.

One night a couple of weeks ago, after a show at Tipitina's, Maureen had stopped in a bar called Ms. Mae's for a late-night drink or three. There she'd bumped into a couple of off-duty cops, Wilburn and Cordts, guys she knew from her district. Day-shift guys.

They should've avoided each other, everyone in her district knew about her suspension, but the hour was late and the drinks had been flowing. Who could possibly be watching them in a dive bar like Ms. Mae's? Maureen bought a round of whiskey shots. She bought another. She asked if any good stories floated around the station. The only interesting thing, Wilburn told her, was that in the past two weeks, three calls had come into the Sixth from women worried they'd been followed home from the Irish Garden.

Didn't she live right by there? Cordts asked.

What had been done about it? Maureen asked.

The guys told her that responding officers had put the calls down to scaredy-cat girls and clumsy young guys too full of hormones and drink. That bar was a pain in the ass, you know that, they said, the way it dumped drunk meatheads into the neighborhood every night.

But the Irish Garden's owner was ex-NOPD, Wilburn said with a shrug, a former detective who'd taken early retirement under a cloud five years ago.

Brutality! Cordts coughed into his hand.

Wilburn threw him an elbow. *Anyway,* he said. Circumstances made it hard to look at the bar as a trouble spot. The place was protected. There was certainly no going in there asking questions. The cops who took the calls had followed procedure and taken reports at the scene, Wilburn said, as was their duty.

Maureen had said nothing, had asked no more questions, instead lighting cigarettes for the three of them, and buying herself one more drink for the walk home before she left.

The story of those frightened women stayed with her after that night. Her coworkers' easy dismissal of those incidents, not only the officers who had responded to the calls but also the men who had told her the story, ate at her, scratching at her brain.

Against her better judgment, the next time she saw Preacher in the park, she had asked him about the calls. Were she to take matters into her own hands—and a plan was already forming—and if she got caught doing it, having tipped off Preacher that she knew of the incidents would put both of them in a tough spot. So don't get caught, she told herself.

Preacher told her each woman had made it safely back to her apartment, shaken but untouched by her pursuer. The first and second callers had both quit talking in the middle of their interviews, having convinced themselves in recounting the events while surrounded by impatient police officers and nosy neighbors that perhaps they had overreacted. But maybe not, Maureen had thought, because the third caller had complained of the man banging on her building's front door for several minutes after she had gone into her apartment and called the police.

She'd said he wore a ring. That she remembered the sound of it, would for a long time, the metal banging on the thick glass on the front door as he slapped his palm hard against it.

Maureen knew that if three calls had come in, then half a dozen other incidents had gone unreported. And that the stalkings had been happening for more than a couple of weeks. Other women hadn't called the police.

Women too frightened or tired or intoxicated. Women with a few pills or a bag of weed in their underwear drawer who didn't want cops in their house, or who didn't want to stay up another hour or two or three waiting for those disinterested, irritated cops to show up in the first place. Or worse, women who didn't call because they were conditioned to believe the threat existed only in their heads, or to believe that, because of the late hours they kept or the booze or the pills or the weed or because of what was, or wasn't, between their legs, they'd brought it on themselves. That they had it coming to them. Whatever *it* was that had happened to them. They believed that being made afraid didn't rise to the level of a crime. That they were *silly*.

They believed what boyfriends and, unfortunately, some of their girlfriends told them—that they'd scared themselves into seeing threats where none existed, that they were paranoid, like anyone really knew what that word meant. Or brainwashed. That they should doubt their deepest, primal natural instincts for self-preservation so as not to be embarrassed.

It was part of the problem, Maureen knew, the hard part of trying to convince people to see threats, to be wary, to be hard targets. If you over-sold the message, people saw danger so often that they stopped seeing it altogether. They stopped believing in it. Nobody wants to believe they should be afraid. And too many people, thought Maureen, thought that acting careful and living afraid were synonymous, that being wary of your surroundings constituted a character flaw.

Sitting in the booth, her eyes moving from guy to guy, Maureen recalled Preacher telling her that the description of the stalker was similar in all three incidents, but was so generic as to be useless: white, dark hair, medium height, medium build. Only the ring stood out. Only every other guy in this bar, Maureen thought, matched the physical description. None of the women could describe a face in detail. No one could offer a name. The women were convinced the stalker couldn't be someone they knew. Why would someone they knew treat them like that? He hadn't been someone they'd talked to that night. If someone they knew or had met was capable of acting like that, surely they would see it. They would feel it. Right? They would know better.

The night of her talk with Preacher, sitting at her kitchen table later, in a notebook Maureen had sketched out the details of the cases. She saw plenty to worry about.

She saw a predator practicing the hunt, learning his territory, honing his timing, and working up his nerve. Already a pattern was emerging. Somewhere in the near but indistinct future, somewhere in her neighborhood, a rape was going to happen. That it hadn't happened already was a small miracle. Maureen had no intention of relying on the miracle to endure. She would indeed take matters into her own hands. She thought of one of the nuns' favorite sayings from her Catholic school days. "The Lord helps those who help themselves."

Right at that moment, somewhere around her in the Irish Garden, mixed in with the boring, harmless men she was looking at, hiding in plain sight, was a soon-to-be rapist. She knew it. She could feel it. She had experience with predators and she had an eye for victims. She'd known them. She'd been one. Like recognizes like.

What she needed to do tonight was spot the matching pair. That she could recognize both predator and prey, she thought, that vision, that slice of wisdom, more than anything she'd learned at the academy, would make her a cop to be reckoned with, to be feared. Being able to see both sides, to see the world as both the owl and the mouse, was a dark gift that the silver-haired man had given her. A gift she'd use against every man like him that she met.

She sipped her whiskey.

How long had she been sitting in this bar tonight? Long enough that the smoke from other people's cigarettes burned her eyes.

She checked her phone. It was after one. She'd been in the bar since ten.

She'd find her target. She'd see him first and he would never see her. Not before, not after, she was sure of that. Plain and pale and thin, her unwashed, cornflake-colored hair pulled back in a ponytail, not made-up, in jeans and a T-shirt and an unzipped hoodie, she would never be noticed by the man she was looking for. Not by any man in that bar. Not until she wanted him to. At her time, on her terms, she would make her move. He would never see her face, but he would remember her for a long time. A *very* long time. She'd create a lasting, life-changing memory for one special man.

The ASP, sleek and black, rested beside her on the bench.

Killing a man with an ASP was tough, but not impossible. What it did best was wreak agonizing, emergency-room-level havoc on jaws and joints and teeth and the small bones of the extremities. The bigger bones broke, too, if you caught them right. The weapon was an academy graduation gift from her mother's ex-NYPD boyfriend. In Nat Waters's time, in Nat Waters's hands, that ASP had broken more than a few bones on the streets of New York City, Maureen thought. It had changed the course of several lives before lying dormant for a decade, waiting to come to her.

Now Maureen had it, and she had put it back to work on the streets of New Orleans.

6

Shortly before two a.m., Maureen spotted a match. The target and the stalker revealed themselves to her one right after the other, exactly as she had expected it to happen.

The target was young, early twenties, blond, pale, and thin and chirpy as a baby bird, one of a small flock of potential victims Maureen had been watching. She wore billowy cotton pants in a fake African pattern, a charcoal top about a size too large that almost matched the pants, and wedge-heeled shoes. She had the look of someone who'd borrowed her curvier roommate's clothes. Maureen had seen her come in around eleven, alone and already listing from drinking at home. She wore only a thin jacket against the cold night, which told Maureen she lived nearby. She'd spent most of the night squinting at her phone, texting. The girl was upset about something, Maureen figured, that had happened before she'd left home. Her outfit had a touch of "Fuck you, I'm going out." She'd *almost* had the energy to get dressed up, but hadn't quite made it. She'd done just enough preparation to convince herself she wasn't going out purely to get shit-faced, which gave her permission to do exactly that.

As for what had wounded her, Maureen thought at first that a job interview had gone wrong, or maybe a rejected grad school application, but Maureen soon noticed that the girl emanated a swoony neediness that repelled everyone around her, male and female, like a bad smell. That stench, Maureen knew, was heartbreak. The girl had been dumped. Some boy's job interview or grad school application had gone really well, and this girl was now collateral damage to his success. She watched as the girl stood on her toes on the bar rail, leaning over the bar, talking to, talking *at* the seething bartender, who Maureen could see had no interest in the sob story being shouted in her face.

At about half past midnight, the girl had started bumming cigarettes from anyone whose attention she could corral. She'd have one burning down in the ashtray while she was bumming another from whatever bland boy drifted by with a Marlboro in his hand. She was light-eyed and banally cute and alone, Maureen saw, but not one of those boys hung around to talk to her. Not one of them bought her a drink. None of this was surprising. The girl was not out to hook up. This wasn't an "I'll fuck him over by fucking someone else" outing. This was "I can't stand another minute of my own company alone in that fucking apartment."

Maureen could see the girl's emotional defenses whirling in the air around her like a cloud of stinging insects. Unfortunately, while the emotional defenses were working overtime, Maureen feared alcohol and the late hour had dulled the girl's other self-protective instincts. And she was not the only one who had picked up on that weakness.

A dark-haired, clean-shaven man, his thin shoulders hunched, sat alone at a small table under a huge television, a collection of plastic cups on the table in front of him. He wore a black hoodie, deep indigo jeans with the cuffs folded up, expensive and well-worn black work boots. He wasn't dressed breaking-and-entering dark, Maureen noted, that might be too conspicuous, but dark enough to hide in the nighttime shadows. He was pretty good at hiding, she had to admit.

She hadn't seen him enter the bar, hadn't seen him order a drink and sit. She'd been scanning the room like she'd done fifty times that night and had missed him, until that last time. Like a ghost, he wasn't there, and then he was—alone, disengaged, hiding in the shifting light of the big television screen over his head. He was collecting plastic cups in front of him instead of throwing them away as he got another drink. To Maureen, that was the tell. He was measuring something, Maureen thought. Something inside himself. Adding up, piling on. Keeping count. Trying to hit a target. Proving to himself how much liquid courage he'd poured into getting his nerves up. See what you can do, he'd tell himself. You're ready now. How many drinks lit the spark, Maureen wondered. How many to turn the power on? Six? Seven? Was there a magic number he needed to reach? Or did he wait until some internal switch he hadn't quite learned to throw on his own turned over?

Maureen watched as the girl signed for her tab, chattering away at the ever-bored bartender as she did so. She staggered to the door. The man ran his fingers through his curly hair. He zipped up his sweatshirt. Maureen saw the thick ring on his finger. She had her man. He used the glass of the bar's French doors to track the girl. Maureen downed the last of her watery whiskey, slid to the end of the bench in her booth to get a better look at the man. She slipped the ASP into her back pocket, pulled her sweatshirt low over her backside.

The girl paused in the open doorway, not five feet away from the man in the black hoodie, opening her clutch and removing her phone. Maureen hoped she'd had a moment of clarity or instinct and was calling a cab. No such luck, as the girl frowned into the blue glow of the small screen and her thumbs went to work.

Can't you leave it alone, Maureen thought, for ten minutes and get yourself home in one piece?

The girl stepped out of the bar and staggered down the sidewalk, focused on her phone. Maureen risked losing sight of her for a quick second as she slipped out the side exit instead of taking the more exposed path through the barroom to the front door. She pulled up the hood of her sweatshirt, hiding her face and hair, and stood beside the door, pretending to be checking her own phone. The girl drifted by, texting away.

Not ten seconds later, the stalker passed by right behind her, hands in his pockets, silent as smoke. Maureen fell in step behind him, as far from him as he was from the target.

Maureen knew well how vulnerable most people were from behind. Few had the 360-degree radar that was the province of being a small woman with a late-night job. She knew most people couldn't feel the devil himself coming right up on them until he was close enough to plant a hot kiss on the back of their neck. How many times had she already heard in her short career as a cop: "I never saw him, he came from nowhere and took my purse, took my phone, took my wallet, hit me in the head, pulled a knife on me, put a gun in my back. I'm usually so careful."

The girl continued walking, unsteady and slow on her wedge heels, distracted by her phone. The man kept his distance.

A cold wind blew down Magazine, biting through Maureen's clothes, sending a chill rippling over her skin. She thought of that night with the silver-haired man a year ago. She thought of distractions. Of a red traffic light you watched so hard it took you far too long to notice how fast the headlights in your rearview bore down on you. And before you knew it, because you'd let your guard down for maybe nineteen seconds, the guys who'd rear-ended you, killers you'd dodged for weeks, had you locked in the trunk of their car, your nose full of mold and your mouth leaking blood.

Stay here, she told herself. Stay here in New Orleans. Stay with that oblivious girl.

She reached into her hoodie pocket for her cigarettes; she craved smoke to cover the taste of the trunk of that car, but she stopped herself. She didn't want to illuminate her face for anyone else on the street, and she didn't want to risk the man she was following turning at the flick of the lighter or the smell of the smoke.

She concentrated her vision on the hunched shoulders of the man walking in front of her. Look to the future, she told herself, boring into the space between his shoulder blades with her eyes, to what's ahead of you. Don't give him any reason to turn around. She was counting on the man's own vulnerability, on that unattended and forgotten space a breath-width behind his back.

The blindness she lamented in the girl was Maureen's best advantage over the man a dozen paces ahead of her. Watching him, she thought again of hot smoke in her mouth, of that next cigarette. She'd save it for after her work was done, savor the anticipation of it.

When they had walked three blocks along Magazine, the girl made a wide, slow turn down Philip Street, taking her pursuer and his pursuer toward the river and into the Irish Channel, where the streets got quieter and darker. Fewer porch lights. More broken streetlights. Virtually no car or foot traffic. Maureen thought the girl might on instinct turn and look behind her up Magazine as she turned the corner. She didn't.

The girl did stop half a block down Philip, her back to Magazine Street.

Maureen watched as the man hesitated, slowing almost to a stop.

The girl never sensed him. Never turned. She stuffed her phone in her purse, continued digging around in it as she continued walking. Maybe she's smarter than this guy and I both assume, Maureen thought. Maybe she's reaching for a gun. The purse was big enough to hold a smallish weapon, a .38 or a .22. Maybe she had heard the stalker stories. Maybe she had been waiting to make the turn onto the darker, quieter street because she thought that gave *her* an advantage, or because it reduced the chance of witnesses.

Maureen had a disappointing realization.

If this girl pulls a gun, she thought, and if it looks like she might pull the trigger, I have to intervene on the stalker's behalf. A telltale metallic jingle made the issue moot.

No gun in that purse, only house keys.

The girl walked quicker. The stalker hastened as well, closing the gap between him and the girl. Maureen moved closer, too, convinced that neither player knew of her presence.

Whatever was going to happen was happening very soon. Like in-less-than-a-minute soon. Maureen had waited hours to hit this spot. Now she was down to the final seconds. The girl reached for a wrought-iron gate. Maureen heard the stalker catch his breath.

Here it comes, Maureen thought. Don't miss it.

The gate creaked as the girl swung it open onto a walk leading to a small cottage. No lights were on inside. Not even a fucking porch light burned.

What was wrong with this girl? Maureen thought. Did she know nothing about the city, about the world she lived in? There are people in this world, Maureen remembered, to whom awful things haven't happened yet. And I'm here in the dark, she thought, to keep that true for this dumb girl for one more day.

She pulled the ASP from her back pocket. She gave the man half a moment to acquit himself, to let the girl know he was there, to call out her name. Anything to tell Maureen he wasn't following this girl home with ill intent. Anything. To not be what Maureen knew in her bones he was. Do that, Maureen thought, show me you're not what I think you are and I will walk on by. I will let this go. The man said nothing. He did nothing but reach for the gate. He'd been smart enough to let it bang closed before he opened it, knowing some part of the girl's brain waited to register that sound.

The man slipped up the walk behind the girl, impressively silent, had her within arm's reach. Maureen darted through the gate behind the man. She didn't wait for him to reach for the girl.

She fell on him from behind, kicking out the back of one knee, locking his throat in the crook of her elbow. He lurched forward, gasping, knocking into the back of the girl, who went facedown without a sound onto the brick steps leading up the porch.

Maureen hammered the ASP down on the knee she'd kicked. The joint gave out. As they fell, she and the man she'd pursued, her foot slipped off the edge of the walkway, and she rolled her ankle. Electric pain shot through her ankle and up her calf. The pain made her gasp.

Not again, she thought. This fucking ankle will never heal. Forget it, she told herself. Use it. Let it hurt. Use the adrenaline, the anger.

They tumbled into a row of ginger plants, falling to the ground among the stalks. The man landed facedown, Maureen on top of him. He clawed at Maureen's forearm with both hands, trying to pry her arm away from his throat. He yanked at the sleeve of her sweatshirt. Her grip wouldn't give. When she felt him weaken under her, she released his throat, letting him breathe. She didn't want to strangle him. Grabbing him by the back of the head, she pushed his face into the dirt. He couldn't be allowed to get a look at her. He flopped under her like a fish. He was a fighter, but not much of one. He was a weak man.

Inside the house, a dog barked, a crazed yippy thing that would wear on the nerves quickly. Maybe panicked enough to get people looking out the window. She'd have to work quickly.

She straddled the small of the man's back. She cocked her arm and thumped him a hard shot to the rib cage with the ASP. The blow made a sound like she'd slapped a pumpkin. He cried out into the dirt, his breath exploding from him.

"Stop fucking moving," she said, "and lie there."

"I can't—I can't breathe."

"Lie still," Maureen said, "and take it like a man."

"My fucking ribs. Fuck." He squirmed and cried out. "I can't—you broke my fucking knee. Christ, it fucking hurts."

"Let it," Maureen said. "Let it hurt."

She tapped the weighted ball of the ASP against his cheek, traced the underside of his eye as if caressing it with her fingertip. Blood stained his teeth. Dirt dusted his hair. She watched his terrified wild blue eye roll around in its socket, searching for her, for her weapon, for an escape. She knew she sat back far enough that he couldn't see her face.

"Lie there and let it hurt," she said, "and no more talking."

"What the fuck?" Maureen heard the girl say. "Holy shit, my face is bleeding."

"Go in the house and clean up," Maureen said, not turning, not looking up or at the girl, hiding her face with the hood of her sweatshirt. "Go in the house and clean yourself up and don't come back outside. Do not call the police."

Maureen heard the sniffles as the girl started to cry.

"Everything is fine," Maureen said, with as much gentleness as she could muster. "Take care of your dog." She used the voice she'd been taught to use with witnesses at a crime scene, which was exactly what, she realized, this girl had become. Well, better to be the witness, Maureen thought, than the victim. "Go inside."

The girl did the smartest thing she had done that night. She went inside the house.

Maureen turned her attention back to the panting, bleeding man beneath her.

"Now it's you and me, handsome. Alone in the dark."

He had stopped struggling. His pain made it impossible for him to lie motionless. There was no comfortable position for him, wouldn't be for months, but he was listening. He was trying to obey her.

Maureen rose up on her knees, lashed down again with the ASP on the man's injured knee. Something shattered in it this time, and something broke in him. He sobbed.

She leaned her face down to his ear. She was hunched over his body as if he were felled prey, which, she supposed, he was. She could smell the cheap vodka on his breath, sweating out of his pores. Her ankle throbbed. She hated him, blamed him, for the pain she felt. She could smell her own whiskey breath on his skin. He cried underneath her, biting his bottom lip to stifle the sound. She could feel his chest pulsing with sobs between her thighs. She'd lose him soon to the pain and the damage she'd done. She was losing her chance to talk to him, to deliver the rest of the message she'd prepared.

"I know you," she said. "I know what you are. I know what you do. I know what you want, what you think. I *see* you. You ever try this shit again, and I will know. It will come to me like a dream and I will re-appear. Things won't go down like this next time. There won't be any pain next time. This time you saw stars. Next time the lights go out."

She rose to her feet. She glanced up and down the block, gave the cottage windows the once-over. She settled her sore foot on the small of the man's back. She leaned more of her weight on it to increase the pain she felt. She listened for sirens, heard none. No one was coming. Not for him. Not for her. "Stay here. Stay here and count to one hundred before you move a muscle."

If he'd heard, he didn't acknowledge her. Didn't much matter, Maureen thought. With what she'd done to his knee, he wouldn't be following her, or making an effort to get into that girl's house. Hell, he might be lying there in the crushed ginger in the morning. She didn't much care. She backed away up the walk, collapsing the ASP and slipping it into her back pocket. She'd clean it off when she got home.

She passed through the gate and out into the street. She pulled her hood close around her face. Her rolled ankle would hurt like a bitch in the morning, swell up to grapefruit size if she didn't get ice on it soon. She couldn't exactly load up on Percocets before her sit-down with the district commander. But right then and there, having left a would-be rapist sobbing in the shadows, her insides felt right. The engine that tremored in her belly twenty-four-seven had gone quiet, like it had those other times. She didn't care about anything that had happened before that very moment. She didn't care about the future. What she cared about was the quiet. The past was so very far away. The entirety of her future was her walk home.

The satisfaction was a dangerous feeling. She knew that.

I could do this every day, she thought.

Well, no, she corrected herself. Starting tomorrow, you can't do this ever again. You'll have to find another outlet, another answer, sweet as this one has been.

Her first time really going after someone had just kind of happened. She wasn't looking for it. An opportunity arose in front of her, an accident, even, in the form of some dumb boy. So she did it. To see what it would feel like. And she found she liked it.

She'd been in the Marigny most of that night, skipping dinner, catching a band at the Apple Barrel. She'd had a few during the set, which ran late. After the drinks and the music, she'd stayed out and hung around Frenchmen Street, chatting up the street musicians and the homeless kids, looking for Madison Leary. Maybe for Dice, too.

A few blocks away from Frenchmen, across the wide lanes of Elysian Fields, behind the warehouses, the Marigny neighborhood turned more residential. The narrow streets were dark with the shadows of crepe myrtles and banana trees.

In those shadows, Maureen spotted a drunken kid standing between two cars in the unmistakable wobbly posture of someone trying not to piss on his own shoes.

She'd shouted out to him, "Why don't you go home and piss on your own neighborhood?"

The boy hadn't looked over, hadn't altered his posture or pinched off his stream, but he'd responded, "This *is* my neighborhood, *bitch*."

That had stopped her in her tracks. "That makes it worse, not better, you asshole," she said. And then she crossed the street in his direction.

The original plan was to tell him she was a cop, and that she could have him locked up for what he was doing. That he could've used one of the dozen bathrooms available to him only blocks away back on Frenchmen Street. She wanted to intimidate him, maybe shame him for being confronted by a grown woman while he stood there with his limp dick in his hand. But then she thought, as she got closer, her boots crunching on the crackled asphalt, why tell him anything? Why waste her time and her breath? He'd had his chance to do the right thing when she'd yelled at him, and he'd chosen not to. He'd had his chance to be a decent human being, she thought, before he'd ever unzipped his pants, and he had passed.

Now came the consequences.

When she got close he looked up, unsteady. She anticipated another smart-ass remark. She expected to hear "bitch" again, once if not multiple times. She noticed he had his car keys in his hand. His blond head with its puffy pink face rotated in her direction.

"Wha'?"

She slapped him in the mouth. Hard enough that the crack of it echoed down Dauphine Street. And then she slapped him again. After the second slap, blood trickled down his chin like baby's drool. He sputtered, staggered, and dropped his keys in the puddle of piss in the street.

"Wha'?" he said again, and he leaned against the trunk of one of the cars. He belched.

Maureen did a quick check of the block for foot traffic. Her palm stung. Her knuckles throbbed. So far, so good; they were far enough away from Elysian Fields that they wouldn't attract attention. Maybe they looked like a couple arguing. Maybe they weren't worthy of anyone's attention. She grabbed a fistful of his hair at the back of his head, forced him down onto his hands and knees in the piss puddle.

"These people who live here," she said, "don't need to be smelling your piss with their morning coffee. Mind your fucking manners next time you go out. Or better yet, stay home."

Then she kicked his keys under a nearby car. She heard them jingle as they dropped down a storm drain. A happy accident, she thought. She pulled a ten-dollar bill from her pocket, tossed it in the puddle.

"Call a cab," she told the man at her feet.

Walking away, her heart racing, sweat beading along her hairline, she felt better, higher, smoother than she had since they'd taken her badge. Like cold, clear water had flushed out her veins. She took what felt like her first honest deep breath in months. Once, she'd told herself as she popped a piece of gum into her mouth. I do this *once*.

Kid had it coming, she thought. I didn't really hurt him. He'll hardly even remember it. Just this once.

Turning from Philip onto Constance, she finally lit that cigarette she'd been craving. The pink-faced boy with piss on his shoes had been her first time. And now she'd done it for the last time.

Tomorrow she'd be Officer Coughlin again. She'd find other ways to satisfy her less professional cravings. The job and the city she did it in were good to her that way. She and New Orleans, they were made for each other.

Maureen limped off into the dark, trailing smoke behind her into the night sky like a dragon.

7

The next morning, in her sunlit bedroom, her closet half-empty, her clothes strewn across her bed, Maureen changed her outfit five different times. She'd be so glad to be working in a uniform again.

She finally committed, more out of frustration than preference, to the outfit she'd started with: black cotton slacks and a matching jacket, under which she wore a button-up white top. Instead of her black boots she wore a pair of black patent-leather wedges. The combination made the closest thing she owned to a business suit. This was how you looked like you meant business *off* the streets, she thought. Clothes like this proved you were a grown-up. This was the uniform of offices, of court-rooms, of people talking over a desk or a conference table and not over the hood of a patrol car at three in the morning. People who weren't borderline crippled by what they'd done the night before. She bent forward, her hands on her knees, taking deep breaths.

Her hangover was brutal. Epic. A record-setter. Her ankle throbbed like a second panicked heart. A pulsing reminder of the violence she'd dished out. At least, she thought, someone out there was having a worse morning than her. She felt like she was moving through glue. She was almost ready to leave. Almost.

She took off her jacket and blouse, laid them carefully on the foot of the bed. In her bare feet, she walked into the bathroom. She tied her hair up, and in her slacks and white bra, made herself throw up one more time, her knuckles white as she gripped the cold rim of the bowl. Nothing but bile came up; she was empty inside.

She struggled to stand up straight, her stomach muscles sore and cramping from the morning's efforts. At the sink, she blew her nose, brushed her teeth again, and rinsed her mouth with cold water and mouthwash. She rinsed her eyes with Visine, blinking at the bathroom ceiling as the saline ran down her cheeks. She checked her nails one more time. Her fingers were raw from the scrubbing she'd given them, but no blood remained, no dirt. Relax, Lady Macbeth, she thought. That was the beauty of the ASP. Using the weapon saved her hands. Sticking to body shots minimized the blood. Externally, anyway, which was Maureen's main concern.

In front of the mirror, leaning over the sink for a closer look, she touched on modest makeup, mostly around the eyes. She let her hair down, brushed it.

Returning to the bedroom, she dressed again.

She searched the jewelry box on top of her dresser for her favorite earrings, a pair of sterling silver fleurs-de-lis. She should show loyalty to the cause. They were a gift she'd given herself on her thirtieth birthday. For twenty-nine she'd gotten a nose ring. Her nose had gotten infected and she'd hardly worn it. A dumb idea, anyway. She checked her nostril in the mirror, touched the side of it with her fingertip. The tiny hole was gone. As if it had never been there. As if she had never made that bad decision. She touched the space under her nose, the indentation in her top lip. She thought of Dice, who had a stud punched through her own top lip, right there in the middle.

She tossed the earrings back in the jewelry box. Whatever. Fuck it, she thought. She's not my problem. I'm not a goddamn social worker. She slammed the box closed.

She realized, taking one final look in the mirror, that she had picked out, with the exception of having switched out a blue top for white, the same outfit she'd worn to her hearings with the Public Integrity Bureau. That wasn't bad luck, right? No. It was good luck, she thought. She'd survived and was on her way to get her job back. Things had worked out for her.

She had a horrible thought.

Things had worked out provided the DC wasn't putting her on a desk in the motor pool or the evidence room. What if that's what waited for her after this favor for the feds?

She put her hand over her eyes, as if hiding from the sight of her foolish self in the mirror. Oh God, she hadn't considered that option until that very moment. Her stomach dropped through the floor. The brass and administrators knew how badly she wanted to stay in New Orleans. She hadn't exactly kept it a secret. They knew she wanted to buy the house she was renting. That she had bills in the present and plans for her future.

For the first time in her life, she had plans beyond surviving the next shift. She needed her paycheck. She needed her benefits. Why? Why had she let them see, let them know what she wanted, what she hoped for? They'd use it against her. Especially if she bungled this thing with the FBI. Then the brass would really screw her. Royally.

Calm down, she told herself. Preacher would know if the DC planned on backstabbing her. He would have warned her. He wouldn't let her get her hopes up if he knew she was getting shafted. Preacher wouldn't let her go blind and unaware to her own demise. She had faith in that, in him.

She checked her phone. Twenty minutes to get to the DC's office. These questions, she'd have answers to them soon enough.

8

Maureen arrived at DC Skinner's office with three minutes to spare. He came out into the lobby, met her with a smile and a handshake. Skinner told her he was sorry but she'd have to wait another fifteen minutes or so. She didn't care. She'd survived six weeks in exile. She could wait another fifteen minutes. Hell, she could wait twenty. He made her wait twenty-five. She did the last minutes of her penance with a smile on her face. She drank three cups of ice-cold water from the cooler. She practiced her deep breathing.

She was checking her hands one more time when Skinner opened the door. He smiled at her, beckoned her into his office. Maureen brushed her hair off her shoulders and followed him in. As she entered and eased closed the door, Skinner returned to his seat behind his desk.

Deep breaths, she told herself. A steady voice and eye contact. Show him, she thought. Prove to this man that he can trust you.

Skinner's office reminded Maureen of what she imagined a small-town politician's might look like. Big desk. Shelves heavy with books that had probably never been read. Framed awards and photos on the wall. A clean window with dusty blinds overlooking the police parking lot and Martin Luther King Jr. Boulevard. Local politician, she supposed, was part of the district commander's job. Skinner looked the part. He was a tall, amiable, white-haired white guy with red cheeks and a jowly neck spotted red with shaving nicks. Bright, bright blue eyes.

"Have a seat, Coughlin," he said, his voice scratchy, as if maybe he'd had a few too many drinks himself the night before. Maureen noticed the office, or more likely the man, carried a whiff of expensive cigars. Definitely better quality than the shit Preacher smoked. "Certainly no need to drag this out any longer than we have to."

Maureen sat in the office chair before his desk. She crossed her legs, folded her hands in her lap. She uncrossed her legs, settled her arms on the arms of the chair. She had to pee. She cursed herself for the agitated fidgeting. She hated herself for wearing her hair down, for playing at being a girl. Skinner moved papers around on his desk. She'd been so much calmer following a strange man down a dark street. A man, she thought, who didn't know she was there, who wasn't looking right at her. A man with no power over her.

"A month and a half off with pay," Skinner said, rocking back in his big leather chair, "and without a damn thing to do. Not a lot of people would consider that punishment."

What Maureen wanted to say was *You have no idea*. What she wanted to tell him was *Having not a damn thing to do made me fucking crazy*. Another two weeks, she thought, and y'all would've been coming to get me, blue lights blazing.

What she said was "I'd rather have been on the job, sir. Earning my pay. I'm not a fan of the sidelines." Her mouth was bone-dry. She licked her lips. "Though I certainly understand why things had to happen the way they did."

"What's happened over the past month and a half took a lot of thought, and a lot of planning. The final decision was not unanimous." He came forward in his chair, his feet on the floor. "I handpicked you for the Sixth District out of the academy. Made a big deal of it. Both the Eighth and the Second wanted you, too, but I got you, because I'm the senior man. You remember that?"

"I do, sir," Maureen said. "Preacher made sure I knew. And I'm grateful."

"I bragged about you. Academy valedictorian. First place in the hand-to-hand combat competition. Smart, tough, and female. Everything that makes me and my district look good. How you think it looks if my super-girl implodes after three months on the job?"

"You look like Mickey Loomis wasting a first-round draft pick, sir."

He grinned in spite of himself. He knew she was kissing his ass with the football bullshit, Maureen realized. She could tell he appreciated the effort.

"And that is a thing that Mr. Loomis does not like to do, is it, Coughlin?"

"I'd imagine not, sir."

"The reason I say these things, Coughlin, is this. What you do on the job, in our uniform, affects a lot more people than you—like the next woman who shines coming through the academy, for instance. Three DCs don't chase her for their districts like we did you if you blow it, Coughlin."

He slid open a desk drawer, removed something from it. Her badge and her ID. Maureen felt her eyes widen. She tried to stop her reaction, and failed.

The DC set the badge in the center of his desk. "I want you to have this. A lot of people around here want you to have it." He paused. "And there are some that don't. Quinn was a cop in this city a long time. He stayed for the storm. He stayed after."

Maureen leaned forward to speak. Before she could say anything, Skinner raised his hand to stop her.

"The fact that you're even here," Skinner said, "should tell you that you've been heard on the Quinn matter. I'm not telling you what's right. We're not here discussing principles. I'm telling you how some of the people you work with think. What they know Quinn did, what they saw, will always count more with them than the things you said he did."

Don't reach across the desk for that badge, she told herself, don't reach for it until he offers. Skinner noticed her staring. She couldn't hide it.

"I want you to keep it," Skinner said. "You'll outlast this bullshit. You're already most of the way there. I want you to sit in this chair some- day. Or the next chair up. Or as head of Homicide."

And you'll be there to take credit for it, Maureen thought, and to brag to your buddies. "Thank you, sir. I appreciate your confidence."

"You can be a hell of a cop, Coughlin, if you can just get your shit together." He picked up the badge and held it out to her. "And keep it together."

When Maureen leaned forward and reached for her badge and ID, he pulled it back.

She froze, her rear end half a foot off the chair. "Sir?"

"There's one thing you have to do for me," the commander said.

Shake that ass for me, Maureen thought. One more time. She settled back into her chair. Here it comes, she thought, the deal with the FBI. In her excitement, she'd forgotten about it. The reason she was here. "I'm all ears."

"You have to promise me," Skinner said, "that you will consider seeing someone, talking to someone about what you've been through."

For a fleeting moment of high panic, Maureen thought he meant the silver-haired man. How could he *possibly* know?

Or did Staten Island have nothing to do with it? Had her recent night work in New Orleans come to light? That was more likely.

Wouldn't make sense, though, she thought, to be giving her back her badge if he knew she'd been out at night playing vigilante.

"Between what you went through with Quinn," Skinner said, "and what happened at your house, those things are tough on anyone. To be honest, you look considerably frayed. Even after the time off. I expected better." He paused, waiting for Maureen to consent to his assessment.

"Maybe too much booze and not enough sleep," Skinner said. He paused again.

Maureen blinked at him. Wow. It was that bad. Her hand went to her mouth. As if her breath were the only thing that might give her away. She wanted to crawl out of the room.

"I've been around cops a long time," Skinner said. "I was here during Katrina, and for after. I have a pretty good eye for what a particularly stressed officer looks like."

Maureen straightened in her chair. "I'm in the best shape of my life. My doctor says I have the resting heart rate of a professional athlete."

"You don't have to see a department shrink." If Skinner was impressed with her physical conditioning, she thought, he hid it well. "Or any shrink. But collect yourself. Smarten up." He touched his finger to his chest. "I'm sending you out on the street with a gun. Me."

"I will take care of it," Maureen said.

"I have your word?"

She swallowed. She remembered that being a cop meant she would now spend a lot of time around people who read others as well as or better than she did. Skinner didn't get where he was by being easily fooled. "You do."

Skinner reached her badge across the desk. Maureen took it, the badge warm from being held in the DC's hand. Her hand shook. She didn't care if he saw. She slipped the badge into her jacket pocket. She felt a foot taller with the weight of it against her breast.

"Becoming a cop is one thing," the DC said. "Staying one, that's another thing entirely. And surviving New Orleans, that's its own thing again. Nothing wrong with getting help. Even Drew Brees has coaches. Going back to our talk of Mr. Loomis, you got drafted, and you made the cut at training camp." He waited for her to finish the story. She wasn't sure what was supposed to come next.

"Sir?"

"The easy part is over, rookie. The academy, the training. The coddling, the encouragement, that's done. Time to do real work starts now if you want to stay on the team. These are the times that separate the men from the, well"—he smiled—"you know what I mean."

"I do, I'm ready," Maureen said. "I'm good to go. Who dat."

"Good, that's what I like to hear." He studied her, thinking. "The department has looked out for you. It's time to start paying back the favors."

"Name it, sir," Maureen said. *This* was it, she thought. She was ready.

"The FBI has reached out to us in the Sixth District," Skinner said, "about the Clayton Gage homicide. The father of the victim has come to town asking questions. The FBI wants you to talk to him. You feel up to the task?"

"I don't know a whole lot about what happened," Maureen said.

"If what you want to tell the man," Skinner said, "is what you don't know, that's fine with me. I was asked to ask you to take the meeting."

"I'll meet him. Of course. What do I do? I don't know how these inter-agency things work."

Skinner shrugged. "They work however the feds want them to work. I was told someone from the FBI will reach out to you, sometime today. He'll have the details. He'll probably coach you up a bit, too."

"So this is part of a bigger investigation?" Maureen asked.

"Like I said, I was asked to ask you if you would take the phone call and the meeting. That's as far as I go in this."

"Yeah, tell the agent to call me. Absolutely, sir."

"I don't have to tell you," Skinner said, "that pleasing the feds—FBI, DOJ, feds of any stripe—is good for the department. Part of the reason I recruited you for the Sixth was to make me look good. Here's a big chance for you to contribute."

"Happy to have it, sir," Maureen said. "I won't let you down."

"You're on night shift tomorrow," Skinner said. He stood, extended his hand across the desk. "Welcome back, Officer Coughlin. What is it the kids on the street call you?"

Maureen shot up from her seat and reached for his hand. She shook it hard. She had her badge in her pocket. Tomorrow night she'd be back in uniform. Everything was right with the world. "OC, sir. They call me OC. Some of the other officers, too. You know, for Officer Coughlin."

"Now, please," Skinner said, checking his watch, "let's get back to what we call normal around here." He sat back down behind his big desk. "Don't let me see you in here again unless it's for a commendation or a promotion."

9

That afternoon, groggy from a long nap and pain pills, Maureen sat on her front porch wrapped in a Mexican blanket, her legs folded beneath her. She clutched a steaming cup of fresh coffee. In an ashtray on the table beside her a cigarette burned. The sky over the Irish Channel was the color of her ashes and the air was cold and damp. The warmth in her palms from the coffee mug helped push back the chill.

She'd slept away most of the afternoon in a deep, dreamless slumber, the best hours of sleep she'd had in weeks. She felt as if she'd awoken from hibernation.

When she imagined her next roll call, she couldn't help seeing Quinn and Ruiz waiting for her, cracking wise in the corner like schoolboys and smirking at their private jokes that no one else on the squad understood. But they weren't schoolboys, she thought, the warmth in her hands dying as she squeezed the mug tighter in search of more. And they weren't cops anymore. And it wasn't always jokes that they whispered back and forth and hid from the rest of the squad. Sometimes the secret commentary had been flat-out criminal. Her ankle ached.

As she shifted her weight in the rocking chair to relieve the pressure on it, the wood creaked beneath her and she remembered that this new chair was a replacement for the first one, a gift from her mother that had been shot to pieces by automatic-weapons fire. Quinn and Ruiz had been connected to the people who'd shot at her. Quinn and Ruiz had been criminals in cops' clothing, Maureen thought, and they had almost gotten her killed.

She picked up her cigarette, took a long drag, and picked up her phone. Time to call her mother in New York, she thought, blowing out a plume of smoke. Time to let Amber Coughlin know that her daughter had kept her job.

Amber's feelings would be mixed, Maureen knew, as they always were concerning her daughter's choices. Part of Amber would be glad for Maureen; she knew how much Maureen's new career and new city meant to her. And even if Amber didn't understand Maureen's love for what she did and where she did it, Amber believed that her daughter's love for both of those things was real. But Maureen knew that another part of her mother had rejoiced at the thought of her daughter flaming out in New Orleans, because failure in Louisiana kept alive the possibility of Maureen's return to New York.

Amber answered on the third ring. "What's wrong?"

"Really, Ma? I can't call to check in?"

"Sure you can," Amber said, "but you never do. Whenever you call in the afternoon, it's because you have bad news. When you want to check in, you call in the evening."

This is what happens, Maureen thought, when your mother falls in love with a detective. Weird, she thought, she never considered what had happened with Nat Waters and her mother "falling in love." Had she ever even used those words? Her mother and Waters certainly never had. But here they were coming up on a year together, and they were happy, what else could it be? What else could she name it but love? And Maureen liked thinking about the relationship that way. She had never known her mother happy. Part of her ached at being so far away while it happened. But in her own way, Maureen realized, she was in love, too.

"Your old mother's smarter than you think," Amber said. "So out with it."

Not that love and happiness had changed Amber much when it came to her daughter.

"Shows what you know," Maureen said. "I'm calling with good news. Great news, in fact. I got my badge back today. My next shift is tomorrow night."

Maureen heard the instant's hesitation before Amber's answer as she adjusted her response from what she really felt to what her daughter wanted to hear. "I'm happy for you. I know this is what you wanted. And I'm glad they didn't use what those crooked bastards did against you. I have to say, I wasn't optimistic."

"I was," Maureen said.

"I know, though I don't know why. You always see the world the way you think it should be. It's why you're always getting disappointed."

Maureen set her coffee down. She lit another cigarette with the embers of the first. Whoever invented e-mail, she thought, had conversations like this one with his mother. "Ma, did you miss the part where I said I got what I wanted? That things worked out for me."

"You need to quit smoking," Amber said. "How can they let you smoke at that job? Don't you have to chase people, be in shape?"

"Hey, Ma, my doctor says I have the resting heart rate—you know what, forget it. I wanted to let you know things worked out. I know you were waiting to hear. Tell Nat I said hello."

"Maureen, wait," Amber said, "while I have you, there's something we should talk about."

"Is it Nat?" Maureen asked. Please, she thought, don't let there be a breakup. Or worse, another heart attack. The first one had been bad, a real close call, and he struggled with his weight. "Is he okay?"

"He's fine." A long pause. "Well, do you remember Lori DiNunzio from across the street?"

Maureen sighed. She didn't know where this was going, but she was sure Lori DiNunzio wasn't what her mother wanted to talk about. "Yeah, of course, Ma, we walked to P.S. 42 together almost every day for years."

"I always thought it was a shame you two drifted apart. You two played at her place every day and then you never saw each other."

"We went to different schools after 42," Maureen said. "You know how little girls are, everything or nothing." Which was true, though it didn't help the friendship that Lori's skeevy older brother kept trying to put Maureen's hand down his pants when Lori was in the bathroom or went to get snacks. And that Lori pushed Maureen down on the sidewalk when Maureen told her what her brother had been doing. "It was no big deal. We stayed friendly when we grew up. I'd see her around the island. She'd come in now and then where I worked sometimes. Have a drink."

"You know, you never had another friend like that," Amber said. "A close one."

"I had no friends after the fifth grade," Maureen said, "that's right, Ma. That's so true. Thanks for reminding me. I guess it's why I'm so easily disappointed. And I did so have friends. Like the whole track team in high school. Just 'cause you didn't meet them." Maureen caught herself. She knew she sounded like she did when she was fifteen. Lying then, lying now. She took a deep breath. "Is Lori okay? Did she die?"

"Good Lord, no," Amber said. "The morbid way you think. She got married. Finally. I was worried. She got so heavy when she moved back in with her mother. And I don't think she works."

Aha. *There* was the point, Maureen thought. Thirty-year-old, living-with-her-mother fatty Lori DiNunzio had landed a man. And I have this backwater career. "Listen, Ma, if you want me to move home and get fat so I can land a man, just say so."

"It's lovely," Amber said. "To be reminded that there's someone for everyone."

Who was this person she was talking to, Maureen wondered. "Ma. Are you drinking in the afternoon again?"

"It gives you hope."

"Ma."

"Who's gonna love you when I'm gone?"

"*Ma*." Amber was hitting the box wine again, had to be. Though she didn't sound like it.

"Maureen, Nat and I have been talking. We've been discussing the future."

"I'm staying in New Orleans," Maureen said, exasperation creeping into her tone. "I'm staying a cop in New Orleans. I'm sorry if that doesn't make me as marriageable as old pride-of-Eltingville Lori DiNunzio."

"Young lady," Amber said, "we weren't talking about *your* future. You're a grown woman. You can do what you want. We're talking about *our* future, his and mine."

"Oh, wait, what are you trying to tell me? Did y'all decide about Florida?"

"Kind of."

Maureen stood up. The blanket she was wrapped in fell to the porch. Amber and Nat had been discussing the move south for a while. Maureen knew this; they'd kept her in the loop. Amber had hesitated to consent, though, claiming reluctance to part with the only house she had ever owned, the only thing of real financial value that was hers. Maureen partially believed her. She also thought Amber was old-fashioned and wouldn't move and cohabitate with a man she wasn't married to. The obstacle there was Maureen's father, twenty years in the wind.

"Ma, did Nat propose?"

Amber waited a long time to respond. "We're not kids. It's not like he's going to get down on one knee and do something silly like that. Lord knows, we don't need to be throwing away money on a ring."

Maureen felt such an ache in her heart for her mother to have those things that she could barely breathe.

"But, yes," Amber said, "Nat and I have discussed it. It would be much easier for us to move, to get a mortgage on a condo if we were married. And I could drop my insurance and get on his plan. With his retirement package from the city, it's a much better plan than mine from Macy's, and, well, I'm not getting any younger."

"Ma, that's amazing," Maureen said. That sly devil, he hadn't dropped a single hint. Even off the force and out of practice he could play it close to the vest with the best of them. Or maybe, Maureen thought, you're not much of a detective yet. "I'm so excited. Is Nat there? Can I talk to him?"

"See, there you go again," Amber said. "We're *talking* about it and you're ready to send out the invitations. And before any of it goes any further, there's something we need to discuss, you and me."

"What's that? The honeymoon?"

"Your father," Amber said. "We need to talk about him."

"I forgot about him," Maureen said after a moment.

"I didn't," Amber said.

"Of course not," Maureen said. "And I didn't mean I *forgot* forgot. I just, I don't think about him much."

"You know that I never divorced him after he disappeared," Amber said. "I never did anything about it. Legally, we're still married."

"I hate that thought," Maureen said.

"So I'm looking into something," Amber said. "As a possible solution."

"And what's that?"

"Having him declared dead."

"I can get behind that," Maureen said.

"So if Nat starts the process of having him declared dead, which may involve looking for him, you're okay with that."

"I have one request," Maureen said.

"What is it?"

"If you find him," Maureen said, "don't tell me. I don't want to know. Where he is, where he went when he left."

"Believe me," Amber said, "I don't want to know those things, either."

"Good," Maureen said. There was one thing concerning her father, she realized, that she wanted to know. "So this is kind of a weird question."

"Yes, we're having sex," Amber said. "We are consenting adults. We're old, we're not dead."

"Oh. My. God. That was not what I was going to ask. At all."

"Well, then," Amber said, "what was your question?"

Maureen struggled to recapture the original thought. "Oh, I got it. Daddy's ring, the wedding ring. You won't wear it anymore, will you? Nat will give you a new one."

"I stopped wearing it not too long after you left New York," Amber said. "I think maybe I took it off after we got home from your academy graduation. I forget."

That's a lie, Maureen thought. Amber had worn that gold band for eighteen years after the man who'd given it to her was gone. Amber would remember not only the day, but also the hour she took off that ring.

Maureen waited, listening to her mother's breathing through the phone, knowing Amber was carefully weighing what she would say next, and how much she would let it reveal.

Amber said, "It all, it seemed so much more over when you left. More final. Like that was really the end of me and you and . . . him."

Maureen swallowed hard. "I never knew that."

"Why would you?" Amber said. "Nothing would've changed if you did. And I didn't even know I'd feel like that until after you were gone."

"What did you do with the ring?"

"Why, do you want it?" Amber asked, forced brightness in her voice. She was wearying of the topic, Maureen could tell. "I know you don't have much of his, not since you lost that coat."

I didn't quite lose it, Maureen thought. The hospital burned it because they couldn't get Sebastian's blood out of the wool. But, she thought, her mother's point was the same. Her father's coat was gone and she had nothing left of him but his last name.

"I don't want that ring," Maureen said. Except maybe to toss in a volcano. "It's of no use to me."

"Oh, okay, then. I guess it's in a drawer somewhere. I can't throw it out, I'm sure it's worth something. Just not to me. Not anymore."

10

Shortly after nine the following morning, Maureen was down in the Central Business District, sitting at a small table outside the PJ's coffee shop on the corner of Camp and Girod Streets. Despite the day's early hour, she felt more calm and clearheaded than she had any number of the past days when she'd slept much later, rolling around sore-legged and headachy in the tangled sheets into the early afternoon.

She lifted the lid off her paper cup and blew on her coffee, the rising steam fogging her sunglasses. She wore boots and jeans, and over a white thermal undershirt she'd pulled on a gray V-neck T-shirt featuring a gas lamp emblazoned with the name Kelcy Mae, a local singer-songwriter. She'd caught the show a couple of weeks ago, a good one, at a small bar in the Riverbend neighborhood called Carrollton Station. She didn't remember buying the T-shirt after the show, which was fine; she liked the music and the band, and the shirt, but she didn't remember the drive home, either. She didn't remember much of anything after the fourth double Jameson, and that was a problem. At least she'd woken up alone that morning. Thank the Lord for small favors. She was looking forward to putting those days behind her.

She tilted her chair back against the building, her face turned up into the sunshine, her eyes closed behind her sunglasses, her back pressed against the warm wall of the coffee shop. The air was cool but the sun warmed her face, the cotton stretched over her chest, and the denim stretched over her thighs. She felt as if she hovered slightly above her own body, lifted skyward, lightened by the autumn sun. Not asleep, but not entirely present. This is what it's like, she thought, to wake up without a hangover. To wake up not wondering who saw what you did last night. Remember this? This is what it's like, she thought, to relax. Having that back, even for a few short moments, was serious progress. Maybe now that she was a cop again she'd fight her way back to sane.

At the next table along the wall, not five feet away, sat Preacher. She'd called him last night, told him about the meeting with Skinner. He'd agreed to sit in on her meeting with the FBI before she'd finished asking the question. He wore civvies like Maureen, dressed in an olive Guevara shirt and matching pants, sandals and thick black socks on his feet, a black felt porkpie hat on his head. He sat with his wide face held at the same angle as Maureen's, soaking up the sun. Taken together they gave the impression of two beach bums wasting away the day, as if the concrete sidewalk they sat on was instead white sand, and the parking garage across Girod Street was a green and rolling ocean that smelled of salt instead of car exhaust.

"You feeling okay?" Maureen heard Preacher ask.

"Never better."

"Long night?"

"Nope. Quiet. I talked to my mother. I read. Slept like a stone."

"Sounds nice," Preacher said. "You look pale, though. Even for you."

"I'm redheaded Irish, Preach. And a Yankee. Cadaverous is my natural look."

"I see you're limping again," Preacher said.

"It's that ankle thing. It comes, it goes."

"I don't know if you heard," Preacher said. "I'm guessing you didn't, but some guy in the Irish Channel had a rough time of it the other night."

"I'm sure there's more than one of them out there."

"Young man took a hell of a beating," Preacher said. "Got left bleeding in the bushes. Couldn't talk much since he had a couple of cracked ribs. Punctured lung, as it turned out. Could've gone way worse for him. He woulda died there in those bushes if he'd been left there much longer. Wouldn't have made it to dawn. We'd be calling your buddy Atkinson for him."

Maureen willed herself not to look at Preacher. Instincts, or was it her guilty conscience, warned her that he was fishing. He had instincts of his own, she recalled, and they were much better than hers.

"What saved him?" she asked.

"Girl who lives in the house where he took the beating, her dog wouldn't stop barking. She finally went out to check, found the poor bastard in the bushes. Girl called nine-one-one. Turns out she was a witness to the beat-down."

"Good for her for making the call," Maureen said. "She's a fine citizen. And why would I have heard about this?"

"It happened in your neck of the woods," Preacher said. "On Philip Street. Only a few blocks from your house. You must've heard us coming out, the sirens."

"I miss the job," Maureen said. "I'm eager to get back to work tonight, but I haven't been sitting home listening to the scanner. I hear sirens every night, up and down Magazine, Tchoupitoulas, all over Uptown."

"The girl with the dog," Preacher said. "She'd had a few at the Irish Garden. She said the guy was attacked right there in the front yard. He appeared out of the dark. Like he'd been there in the bushes waiting for her to get home."

"Or like he followed her home," Maureen said. Nailing the guy had taken strong detective work. Having to hide that part of what she'd done gnawed at her professional pride.

"So this guy appears and then, boom, out of the shadows leaps contestant number two, who then proceeds to kick this guy's ass six ways to Sunday." Preacher shrugged. "Girl did say she might've walked into a fight that had already started before she got there. She couldn't say for sure the order of what happened. One of them yelled at her to get inside. She was scared enough to listen. Never got a good look at either the victim or the assailant."

"If she'd had a couple of drinks," Maureen said, "her facts might be off. Even so, it's a shame we couldn't get any kind of description from her on the guy giving the beating."

Preacher raised his hands. "Yeah, a shame."

Maureen reached for her coffee, lifted the lid, and sipped, content to let the subject drop. Where in the hell, she thought, was this FBI stooge?

"It got me thinking," Preacher said.

Maureen's stomach dropped. She did *not* want Preacher thinking about crimes she had committed. "Were you at the scene? Did you work this?"

"I was at the St. Charles Tavern," Preacher said. "I caught the details on the radio. Figured I might as well swing by. It was you that put the idea in my head. Those calls you were asking me about last week at the park, with the girls getting followed home from the bar. It was that Irish Garden bar, wasn't it?"

"Is there a point to this?" Maureen asked.

"The address, it was another one not far from the bar." Preacher rolled out his plump bottom lip. "I wanted to see what I could see. I'm curious, I'm thinking, what if maybe that was our guy? Maybe somebody caught on to him, lit him up on their own."

"The girl," Maureen said, "she have a boyfriend? Someone that could've seen this guy following her, like from the apartment or the porch or something?"

"No boyfriend," Preacher said, shaking his head. "He'd dumped her that afternoon." He rolled his eyes. "I heard *plenty* of detail about that. Job transfer. He ditched her by text. Anyway, that was why she was out alone in the first place, she said. If anyone saw what happened, we don't know who they are."

"So is there anything to move on?" Maureen asked. "Or are we shelving it?"

"I want to see if those calls stop coming," Preacher said. "Far as I'm concerned, that'll tell us if Johnny Lungblood is our man."

"Or maybe the calls stop coming," Maureen said, "because we never did anything about the first few."

"Maybe."

"The guy," Maureen said, taking a deep breath, "he have any idea who put the hurt on him?"

"Beats me," Preacher said. "I haven't heard anything since he got taken to the hospital. They were working on him in the yard when I got there. I don't think anyone at the scene talked to him much. Wasn't much he could say. I'm sure the detective will talk to him. Eventually. Maybe when he gets out of the hospital."

"So no one at the scene questioned this guy?" Maureen asked. "No one asked him what he was doing in that yard? If he knew that girl?"

"Coughlin, somebody caved in the guy's ribs for him," Preacher said. "Somebody nearly *killed* him. Did you miss that part of the story? Because I'm pretty sure I told it. Ambulance guys suspected a weapon like a pipe. Maybe a bat. Guy has a knee that looked like a fucked-up hamburger cauliflower. EMTs had to cut his pants off him right there in the yard." He brushed his fingers over his pants, dismissing imaginary crumbs. "We'll see tonight if there's any updates when we go in. Anyways, it'll be easier for you to stay in the loop, now that you're back on the job."

"Believe it," Maureen said.

Preacher puffed out his cheeks, blew out the air in a long sigh. He raised his chin at something over her shoulder. "Hey, look, I bet this is your FBI guy."

11

Maureen turned her head, rolling her skull along the concrete wall of the coffee shop.

A short, slender, clean-shaven black man in a charcoal suit, his head down, phone at his ear, stood at the nearby corner. His name, as he'd told her on the phone last night, was Clarence Detillier, and he was an FBI agent, domestic terrorism unit. He was going to give her a chance, he had said, to go from being a liability to a commodity. His words. She could tell over the phone that he was proud of them. She'd told him she'd be happy to talk. She even let him name the time and the place. Then she had called Preacher. She knew when to roll with backup.

Preacher had worked his web of New Orleans contacts and called Maureen back to vouch for the guy. It was Preacher who'd found out he was in the domestic terrorism unit. So it didn't seem, as far as Preacher could tell, that Detillier was setting her up for a fall, or worse, looking to somehow use her against her fellow cops in the Gage murder case.

The FBI agent finished his phone call, tucked his phone in his jacket pocket, and headed for Maureen's table, where an empty chair awaited him. He dusted it off with a handful of paper napkins before he sat. He extended his hand across the table.

"Clarence Detillier, FBI, New Orleans office," he said. "Thanks for meeting me."

Maureen shook his hand. It was cold and dry. "Maureen Coughlin, NOPD." She turned toward Preacher, who sat silent and stone-faced, his hands spread on his thighs. "This is Sergeant Preacher Boyd."

"From the union?" Detillier asked, his eyebrows raised. Maureen could tell he hadn't expected her to have company. *Good*, she thought. She'd already thrown the FBI a curve.

"Sergeant Boyd is my current duty sergeant."

"So you're no longer suspended?" Detillier said. "Congratulations."

"Thanks." *As if you didn't already know*, she thought.

"I'm here in an advisory capacity," Preacher said, watching pigeons work a chunk of bagel in the gutter. Maureen heard protective muscle in his voice. He was advising her, and Detillier, too, that he had her back. "Moral support. Backup. Standard operating procedure."

"You've had bad experiences with the federal government, Officer Coughlin?"

Preacher laughed out loud. "We're sitting in New Orleans and you ask that?"

Detillier leaned over the table. "Hey, Sergeant Boyd, I'm as 'from here' as you are. Born and raised."

Maureen straightened in her chair. "Fellas, fellas." She turned to Detillier. "Let's be straight about one thing. I know you said you're bringing me an opportunity, and I'm not trying to sound ungrateful, but everyone here knows the NOPD is scared shitless of the feds these days. For reasons that have nothing to do with Katrina. Between y'all and the Department of Justice, we're every one of us waiting to hear the ring of the blade in the air."

Detillier folded his hands in his lap, leaned back in his seat. "Tell me your specific concerns."

"As soon as I get my badge back," Maureen said, "I'm talking to the FBI. The next day. How do you think that makes me look around the district, to other cops?"

"No one needed to know about this meeting except you and me," Detillier said. His eyes shifted to Preacher. "You're the one who brought a witness."

Maureen laughed. "This would've stayed a secret? Because that would look so much better, a *secret* meeting with the FBI after I get my badge back. Please. Yeah, I brought a witness. So that when I'm back on the job and the rumors about me start I have an impeccable source to vouch for me. So y'all are watching us, but we're watching y'all right back."

"You agreed to this meeting," Detillier said, "of your own free will."

"We're under a consent decree," Maureen said. "Big Brother is watching. I'm a rookie. The only reason I'm not out on my ass already is because I'm a woman and I have dirt on the department."

"Dirt on the NOPD," Detillier said, "is not why I'm here. I'm interested in the future, Officer Coughlin, not the past. That's not my department. And I think you already know that."

"So what is it exactly about the Gage murder that interests you?" Maureen asked.

"Where he came from, for one."

"LaPlace?"

"The Sovereign Citizens," Detillier said. "And the Watchmen Brigade, specifically. They are of interest to us. You are of interest to them. You see where I'm headed with this."

Preacher leaned forward in his chair, the plastic creaking under his shifting weight. "Interested in her? They tried to kill her."

"We know that," Detillier said. "It's the reason we're sitting here today."

"You know something," Maureen said. "What do you know?" Her heart rate doubled, tripping over itself in its effort to accelerate. "They're going to try again. When? How?"

Detillier threw the quickest glance at Preacher before he spoke, his hands raised in a calming gesture. "We don't really know anything. I have no knowledge of another planned attack. But we're worried about it, an attack on you, or on another officer or officers. Losing the gunrunners Gage and Cooley from their own ranks, losing their local connection, the drug dealer named Scales, we don't believe any of that has deterred the Watchmen from moving men and weapons into New Orleans. None of those three men were in charge. None of them made decisions. They were expendable."

The agent leaned forward, elbows on his thighs, looking at his hands as he spoke. "The Sovereign Citizens, the larger, umbrella cause that the Watchmen align themselves with and claim to support, or represent, or whatever—it's all very fluid—are a problem. They have been for some time. Until recently, they mostly confined their efforts to the courts— filing crazy lawsuits, clogging up the system with paperwork, suing townships and judges and anyone else, squatting in foreclosed houses and filing ownership claims—shit like that."

"More recently, my ass," Preacher said. "Timothy McVeigh was a Sovereign Citizen."

"There have always been outliers," Detillier said. "Individuals. Duos and trios. Cells, if you want to call them that. We're starting to; the language is changing. The terms we use in the U.S. are becoming more familiar in ways that nobody likes. The outliers, the extremists, they're impossible to predict, nearly impossible to find before they act. And yes, Sergeant Boyd, I admit, we spent recent years watching for international dangers and for threats coming into the country. As a result, we are now woefully behind on what's been growing here at home. We're human like you. There's only so much we can do.

"What worries us much more now is the growth, the *exponential* growth of these armed and dangerous militaristic offshoots like the Watchmen Brigade. These patriot groups not only don't fear law enforcement, be it local or federal; many of them antagonize law enforcement." He gestured toward Maureen. "They target law enforcement. And their influence is growing.

Detillier ticked off names and places on his fingers. Maureen grew ill as they added up. "That rancher in Utah and his gun buddies. The Oath Keepers, who are now national, the West Mountain Rangers in Montana, the Indiana Rangers, the Massachusetts Fighting Wolves, the Radical American Patriots, the Guardians of the Free Republic in Texas." He shook his head. "The list goes on, and it grows. Now we have the Watchmen Brigade in south Louisiana."

"The conspiracy in Vegas," Maureen said. "The cops killed in the ambush, in the restaurant. That was these people you're talking about. These are the people who are after me."

"They got our attention around here before that," Detillier said. "When those state police got killed in LaPlace. But, yes, the killers in Vegas called themselves Sovereign Citizens. The man they just caught in Pennsylvania who killed those state troopers at their barracks. Him, too."

"LaPlace was three years ago," Preacher said. "Vegas was last summer. Pennsylvania was last month. You're not making much progress. They're still there, and probably elsewhere in Louisiana, and now they're here in New Orleans, too." He nodded at Maureen. "She's got a front door full of bullet holes to prove it."

Maureen shook her head. "Not anymore. Rehab is done on the outside. Can't even tell it happened anymore. I don't even wanna think about what it cost the landlords to get it done that quick."

"What about the inside?" Preacher asked.

"That's got some work left," Maureen said. "There are bullet holes above the fireplace. In my bed frame."

"That's gotta frighten the boys away," Preacher said.

"Well, good luck with that," Detillier said, loud enough to get everyone back on point. "If the events of last month have checked the Watchmen's move into the city, it's not for long. We're planning aggressive countermoves. We would like your help with that."

Maureen stretched her legs under the table, crossing her ankles. "In what capacity?"

"This is not the part where I make you a federal agent," Detillier said. He reached into his suit-jacket pocket, produced a notepad and a pen. "This is the part where I ask you some questions. Hopefully, you give me useful answers, and we move on from there." He clicked the pen. "What can you tell me about Madison Leary?"

Maureen crossed her arms. Not the question or the name she'd expected to hear. Leary was a New Orleans case. Skinner had told her the feds had dead Gage's father on the hook, and that he was the person they wanted to talk about.

"She came here from LaPlace on the run from the Watchmen," Maureen said. "Allegedly carrying a sizable wad of cash that she'd stolen from them. As far as we were able to figure, both Cooley and Gage were in New Orleans looking for her and the money. But she's not who you want. A man named Caleb Heath, he's the one you want."

"Coughlin," Preacher said, caution in his voice.

"Leary knows the Watchmen," Detillier said. "She lived with them in LaPlace. She was one of them. The last place she lived before she came to New Orleans was with the Watchmen."

"She's a crazy drifter who fell in with the wrong guys at the trailer park," Maureen said. "That's not the same as joining a terrorist cell. She came to New Orleans to get away from them. To escape, and they hunted her here."

"According to your friend Detective Atkinson," Detillier said, "this poor, unfortunate victim you describe, she's the lead suspect in the murders of Gage and Cooley."

"Then ask Atkinson about her," Maureen said.

"We did," Detillier said. "And she sent us to you. She said you knew her first."

Maureen turned in her chair and looked at Preacher, expressionless behind his dark glasses. In the park, they had theorized about how Maureen had drawn the FBI's attention. Atkinson was the answer, then. Maureen wondered what else the detective had told the feds about her. Not too much, not everything she knew if Detillier wasn't coming after her with cuffs.

"If you want the Watchmen," Maureen said, turning back, "if you *really* want to hurt them, find Caleb Heath." She waited for Detillier to write the name down. "Caleb Heath, son of Solomon, the owner of Heath Construction and Design. They have a house on Audubon Park. You need me to spell it for you?"

"I see their signs around the city," Detillier said. "I know who they are."

"They've rebuilt half of it," Preacher said. "And they're tearing down the other half so they can rebuild that. City dollars, state dollars, federal dollars. Katrina made Solomon Heath even richer than he was before the storm. And that's saying something."

Detillier chuckled, shaking his head. "Caleb Heath is in Dubai. You both know that already."

"He can't stay there forever," Maureen said.

"I don't know about that. He's got a brother who lives there. Heath Construction has an office there. Among other places." Detillier leaned across the table. "Do you have any idea how big these people really are?"

"I get the feeling you do," Maureen said, leaning away from him. "And that you're making your decisions accordingly. The poor people like Leary put up so much less of a fight."

"It's the poor people, as you put it," Detillier said, "who shot up your house."

"Caleb Heath bought them the guns they used to do it," Maureen said. "Caleb Heath gave them my fucking address."

"You have proof of this," Detillier said. "Ironclad proof? Because that's what we need to send agents to Dubai to arrest this man's son. Otherwise, I don't have taxpayer dollars for a wrongful arrest suit. Not with my budget. Not with the lawyers the Heaths can afford. That's what I mean when I talk about how big they are."

"I do not have that kind of proof," Maureen said. "I did. I don't anymore."

"Officer Quinn?" Detillier asked. "I take it he's one of your sources." Maureen nodded.

"Well, he's dead," Detillier said. "Which means anything he ever said to you is meaningless."

"Caleb knows everything Quinn told me," Maureen said, "and more."

"Rebuilding New Orleans is only part of what they do," Detillier said, shaking his head. "And a small part at that. It's building sand castles to these people. They're worldwide. If they get sick of Caleb in Dubai, they can send him to Jakarta, to Buenos Aires. That's how big these people are, how deep their pockets go."

"Here in New Orleans," Maureen said, "the big boss lives on the edge of the park four miles away. I can show you which house. I can give you *their* address. Solomon seems like a decent guy. I only met him once, but I've seen him a bunch of times since then. I can give you a general impression. He has to know what his son is mixed up in. Have you even talked to him? Made him try to understand what his son was doing?"

Detillier sat silent and stone-faced.

Maureen turned to Preacher. "Do you believe this guy?"

"I do," Preacher said. "Sadly enough."

"Caleb Heath is a direct connection to the Watchmen," Maureen said, rising from her seat, pressing her finger into the tabletop. "Direct. He's done business with them. For them. He knows any number of them personally."

"This business is?" Detillier asked, sighing.

"Guns," Maureen said. "Lots of them. He finances them, bankrolls them. Or he did, through Clayton Gage, who was an old friend of his from school." She sat back down. "Now that Heath is out of the country, I don't know if the pipeline stayed open."

"Clayton Gage," Detillier said. "He's dead, too. He was the second murder." He drew a finger across his throat. "The necktie outside the bar."

"Indeed," Preacher said.

"So with the deaths of Quinn and Gage, and the disappearance of"— Detillier flipped through his notebook—"former officer Ruiz, this direct connection from Heath to the Watchmen has been totally cut off. So to speak."

"Ruiz hasn't disappeared," Maureen said. "He left New Orleans."

"And went where?" Detillier asked, his eyes moving back and forth between Preacher and Maureen. "He resigned in disgrace, not the best witness. He's a waste of resources."

"You're the federal investigator," Maureen said. "We're just beat cops, us."

"These connections were cut off by the murders," Detillier said, "in which Madison Leary is a suspect. She seems to know how to find these guys better than anyone else in New Orleans. I'd like to talk to her about that."

Maureen shrugged. "I'm telling you, she's not your best way in. She's not the trick to shutting them down. She's her own violent offshoot of their violent offshoot."

"I can be the judge of how important she is," Detillier said. "Or isn't."

"You know she's mayor of Psycho City, right?" Preacher said.

Detillier frowned at his notebook, flipping back and forth between pages. Maureen didn't know who else he had talked to about the case, but he'd made a lot of notes. She could tell from his furrowed brow that ideas were starting to lock together in his imagination.

Detiller said, "We'll come back to Ms. Leary."

Maureen wondered if Madison had ever been called *that* before. She had a crazy idea. She decided she'd say it out loud. To see what Detillier would do.

"She's one of yours, isn't she? Madison Leary. She was some dopey bastard's drug mule, or some gunrunner's scagged-out girlfriend, and you flipped her and put her to work for you, made her an informant. You brought her to Louisiana and pointed her to the Watchmen. And now you've lost her and she's running around New Orleans killing people. She was a mole for you, into the Sovereign Citizens down here. And she's gone rogue in the worst possible way. That's why you're so interested in her."

Detillier stared at her for a long time. "I can see you've put a lot of thought into her."

Maureen couldn't even hear Preacher breathing.

"Let's talk about the father," Detillier finally said. "He's of interest to us." He paused. "I'm talking about *Clayton's* father. I'm talking about Napoleon Gage. Goes by Leon."

"Yeah, I got that," Maureen said. "What about him?"

"We're wondering what he knows, if anything, about *his* son's activities," Detillier said. "He went to Homicide demanding information about his son's death. He dropped off a two-inch stack of bullshit paperwork there that he says compels the NOPD to talk to him. Apparently, he spent three days going from courthouse to courthouse trying to see judges and trying to file these legal forms he drew up himself. This is before going to Homicide. After his visit there, Detective Atkinson reached out to us, which she did because we asked the division to do so. We've been waiting to see if anyone would surface over these deaths. Now someone has."

"And you can't question this guy yourself?" Maureen said.

"He's demanding an audience with law-enforcement personnel who worked the scene. We hear he's filed a bunch of papers with the coroner's office, too."

Maureen turned to Preacher. "And we honor demands like these? Is that common NOPD practice?"

"Fuck, no," Preacher said.

Maureen turned back to Detillier. "But this guy is an exception because?"

"Because his son was a member of a violent patriot militia," Detillier said. "And because this business with the bogus paperwork filings is typical of Sovereign Citizens. It's our first real sign he may have been involved in his son's activities."

"How does Detective Atkinson feel about the FBI stepping into her investigation?" Maureen asked. "About you bringing me into it like this? She's okay with it? The two Watchmen deaths are her case now. Leary is her suspect. Why doesn't she get a chance to talk to the father? He may know a thing or two about Leary. Put him in a room with Atkinson, she'll have him squawking in three minutes. She's the best interrogator probably in the state."

"We asked her," Detillier said. "She told us to come to you."

"If you think this guy's a Citizen," Maureen asked, "why not have one of your guys handle him?"

"As far as Napoleon Gage knows," Detillier said, "his son is the victim of a random street crime. He expects to deal with the NOPD. The FBI suddenly appearing would change that. We don't want to scare him out of town. We don't want to make him more reluctant to talk. We want him very much to talk to someone, and we agree with Atkinson that the someone he's most likely to be comfortable with is you."

Preacher laughed out loud, trying and failing to cover by coughing into his fist. "Because of her sparkling personality."

"You have to admit, Preach," Maureen said, "that I'm a whole lot less scary than Atkinson."

"You're the one the Watchmen shot at," Detillier said. "Nobody's forgotten about that. We thought you'd like to get in on bringing them down." He shrugged. "But if you're happy writing speeding tickets . . ."

"I'm going to tell Atkinson everything that I learn doing this," Maureen said. "Anything I learn from Gage that might help her find Madison Leary and close her case, I'm going to tell her."

"Bringing Leary in could only be good for us," Detillier said. "If you can help Atkinson while keeping the father in play for us, I have no problem with that.

"Listen, let's not get distracted by interagency politics. I want to keep you alive, Maureen. The Watchmen present a direct physical threat to New Orleans law enforcement. They've targeted you specifically. Leon Gage may have useful information about them, and we feel that humoring him is the best way to get that information, should it exist. No matter how she feels about me and what I do, I'm sure Detective Atkinson is keen to eliminate the threat the Watchmen present. And I think she would agree that pulling apart the Watchmen is more important than her murder investigation into the deaths of two guys who, quite frankly, no one will miss."

Maureen reached for her cigarettes. She lit one.

She wanted to believe that Detillier was telling her the truth and that the feds were on her side. That they were generous and team-oriented. That all law enforcement was created equal. That a badge was a badge to them. She knew better. They didn't want her killed, but the feds acted only in their own interests. They came to her because it was the best move for them. She exhaled a long plume of smoke.

"So you get my help with the father and the Watchmen," Maureen said, "and Atkinson maybe gets help with finding Leary, which may also benefit you guys. What I want to know is, what's in it for me?"

"Preacher will tell you," Detillier said, unfazed by the question, rolling into an answer that sounded like he'd prepared it, "that plainclothes work is the quickest way to a promotion in any police department. That's *especially* true of the one that you work in. Here's your chance to build that résumé, with an endorsement from the FBI to put in your file. Your coworkers may twitch at the idea of you doing a favor for the feds. They'll get over it. The brass and the suits look real favorably on that kind of thing, on anything that makes them look good. The brass are the ones who give out the gold shields. And I know one DC I figure you owe some good turns."

Maureen turned to Preacher, who shrugged.

"Believe him," Preacher said. "It's not like you'll be in Narcotics in two weeks, but you have to start somewhere. Sounds like a cake gig to me. This is a legit opportunity." He glanced at Detillier then looked back at Maureen. "If they want to overpay for a small favor, fucking let them."

"Your department is bleeding cops at a near-terminal rate," Detillier said. "From top to bottom. You didn't hear it from me, but your SVU is about to lose five detectives. Five. Someone's getting sucked up into that empty space in the departments above you. Why not make it you? We want one hour of your time. Have coffee with the man. Tell us what he tells you. Couldn't be simpler. If it's nothing, well, we tried, and the effort looks good on you."

He checked the time on his phone, reached into his jacket pocket, produced a business card. He placed the card on the table between them. "Take a few minutes to discuss things with your duty sergeant here. But call me soon. Later today or tonight. We don't know how long Gage is staying in the city. If we wait too long, we may all of us lose our chance to get what we can from him." He raised his hand to Preacher. "Sergeant Boyd, a pleasure." He shook Maureen's hand. "Officer Coughlin, we'll speak soon."

Maureen left the card on the table until Detillier turned the corner. When he was out of sight she picked up the card, tucking it into the inside pocket of her leather jacket.

"What do you think, Preach? Straight up. Do I trust this prick?"

"You have to make that decision," Preacher said. "I'm not seeing a downside for you right now, but they set it up that way on purpose. I will tell you this. If you get them something good for Detillier, if you put the NOPD in the middle of the FBI making a major bust, you will have gone from the shithouse to the penthouse faster than any cop in department history. We could really use a gold star around here. Believe it."

12

That evening Maureen arrived an hour early for roll call. She'd always been prompt, but an entire hour set a personal record.

She sat alone in the room at one of the two-person desks, a cup of terrible station-house coffee steaming in front of her. She sniffed it. She added a fourth packet of sugar. Okay, maybe the horrible coffee was one thing about her job she hadn't missed. She rubbed stray sugar crystals between her fingers and thumb, waiting for the other night-shift cops, trying to enjoy the quiet. She savored silence on the job. How she hated the quiet, she thought, when it filled her own house. Because when her house was quiet, she thought, that was when her brain ran at its loudest.

The day shift was still on the streets when she'd parked out back and headed into the building. She'd taken her time getting dressed in the locker room, having the place to herself. No other women were on duty that night.

She'd remained on the bench in front of her locker for a long time, stripped to her underwear and a white T-shirt, her hair down and loose on her shoulders, the lacquered wood of the bench cool on the backs of her thighs though the heat was on. The locker-room air had that dry, close feel she remembered from New York City school buildings. She breathed in the institutional antiseptic smell of the room. She listened to the occasional squeak of boots on the hallway tile as other cops passed by. She heard their muffled voices as they talked on their phones, or to one another. Overhead, water surged through the old pipes. The elevator thumped to a stop in the front of the building. The fluorescent lights hummed.

She'd had a boyfriend once who'd been a swimmer. She hadn't quite believed him when he'd talked about the sedative effects the sounds and smells of the pool, any pool, had on him and how they eased his mind, the sharp tang of chlorine in the air, the thumping splash of a flip turn, the whistle of a swim coach. Sitting in the Sixth District locker room, she now knew exactly what that boy had meant.

She studied her blue uniform hanging on her locker door, cleaned and pressed, the plastic covering from the dry cleaner's now torn off and crumpled on the floor like a shed skin. Her gun belt rested at her side on the bench. She stood, rubbed her thumb over the yellow police department patch with the blue crescent sewn onto one sleeve of her uniform shirt. She touched the plastic name tag that read M. COUGHLIN pinned onto the pocket.

Her plan had been to return to work recharged and ready for anything. She'd wanted to rest while she didn't have to work. That was why she'd rented a cottage on the beach those first two weeks of her suspension. She wanted to come back to the job and the city strong and clearheaded. Calm. Instead, standing there, the day she'd longed for finally arrived, she felt raw and hollowed out inside. The free time had revealed a pit at her core that was bottomless and lightless, smooth and cold to the touch. It was more than sleepless nights and whiskey that ate at her. She felt like a parasite had burrowed through her. She feared that maybe it remained inside her, chewing. Was that the noise she heard when the house was quiet? The gnawing away of her insides? She couldn't figure out who or what she was afraid of anymore. The past? The future?

She folded her hands over her badge and closed her eyes. She promised herself again she was safe now. She was being ridiculous. Her life was different now than it had been a year ago. *She* was different now. The evidence was everywhere around her. Ironclad evidence. Be a good cop, a smart cop, she told herself. Trust the evidence. The silver-haired man was not coming to get her. There had been nothing supernatural about Frank Sebastian. Nothing.

Maureen knew that the power to haunt her was power she gave him. His specter was her creation. She was being silly, a child who missed her night-light. Frank Sebastian wasn't under her bed. He wasn't out there on the streets. He wasn't in a big house on the park. He was dead. He was staying dead, and she had run so far and changed so much that his ghost, should it ever manage to sneak out of hell, could never find her. Would never recognize her. She would stop going out at night looking for him. She wouldn't take so much into her own hands anymore. That would be a start. She'd let the devil out, like Preacher had said. Now leave him out there, she thought. Leave him out there in the dark. He didn't need her help with his work. And she didn't need his help with hers.

She touched her shoulder. With her fingertips, under the collar of her T-shirt, she could feel the lingering bruised and tender indentations Patrick's teeth had left in her skin.

She'd called Patrick and asked him over to her house two nights ago, after her conversation with Preacher about the FBI agent, too wired to sleep after three whiskeys. She'd paced the house for an hour, feeling like she'd burst. She needed a respite, a release from her own head.

Patrick had brought her more pills, though she hadn't asked for them when she'd called him. Stepping through the front door, he'd held out the plastic bag to her as if it were a bouquet of flowers. She'd accepted his gift with an embarrassed grin, whisking it away, swallowing one pill dry as she walked to the bathroom. She knew his bringing these pills to her without her asking for them first constituted a bad sign, and maybe a bad turn in their relationship, but she decided at the time that she'd worry about that later. She had other things on her mind for the immediate future.

In the bathroom, she'd put the pills with the others in an old orange prescription bottle. She took one more with a handful of water. She heard the door open and the bottles clink as Patrick got a beer from her fridge. She hardly drank beer. She realized she kept it in the house for him. She'd looked away from the mirror as she closed the medicine cabinet.

In the locker room, Maureen hung her head. She kneaded her belly with her hands, trying to massage away the billowing disgust in her gut. Trading sex for pills. That wasn't what she was doing, right? Couldn't be. She didn't do that kind of thing. On the other hand, she'd never given him any money for them, and that shit wasn't free. Nothing was free. Nothing. He had never asked for payment. The pills were part of their friends-with-benefits thing, right? They both understood that. Which was why the deal was unspoken. That's what Patrick would say if she asked him. She knew she never would ask. They didn't talk much when they got together.

She'd considered that one day in the future he'd call in a favor from her, take his payment for the pills that way. Whether she'd indulge him would depend on the favor. She'd also considered that he might use the pills against her under the right circumstances, like if he got in trouble with another cop. The wrong cop. She knew firsthand what moral firmaments the bite of handcuffs and a flashlight in the eyes could shake loose in a man. Patrick didn't seem likely to get in trouble with the law, or to rat on a friend; but one never really knew. His drug use was casual, recreational. Actually, Maureen realized, she'd never seen him take anything. She didn't know him that well at all. He was a hell of a cook and a good lay. He liked Harp lager and American Spirit cigarettes.

Sometimes when he stopped over his clothes bore the barest hint of marijuana or another woman. He knew next to nothing about her, but Maureen knew he was smart enough to understand one essential thing. He knew better than to cross her.

She could be that wrong cop if she needed to be.

That night, Patrick hadn't been seated on her couch for five minutes, hadn't been in the house for ten, hadn't drunk a third of his beer before she'd had his pants open, cupping him in one hand and stroking him with the other, him groaning, his teeth digging into her bare shoulder, his pills dissolving into her bloodstream. Calming her ankle. Melting the muscles in her back and her legs. She was already feeling distant, separate, by the time Patrick came in her hands, as if she were watching the two of them from across the room through a veil of gauze.

She'd let him finish his beer as she cleaned her hands in the bathroom before leading him into the bedroom, where, lights out, she let him go down on her.

Her orgasm was slow to arrive, booze and narcotics and exhaustion and noise in her head running interference, making it tough for her to reconnect with her body, but she got there, finally, and when she came the feeling hit her hard and sudden as a car crash, her belly tensing, her fists twisting the sheets. She nearly burst into laughter at the relief, her thighs quivering. It was almost too much. Almost. She pushed his head away, squirming free of his mouth.

Once she'd mostly caught her breath she pulled his face up to hers by his ears. Grabbing his shoulders, her hands traced the muscles of his chest as he climbed on top of her. As her fingertips glided over Patrick's ribs, Maureen thought of the man she had left groaning in the ginger stalks. She wondered which exactly of those precious bones now under her fingers she had she broken in him. Patrick's rib cage expanded and contracted in her hands as he breathed. She thought of that other man's punctured, bubbling, bleeding lung.

Someone nearly killed him, Preacher had said.

She thought of what that man would've done to that little bird of a girl.

Someone nearly killed him.

Good, Maureen thought.

She opened up her legs and lay back, settling her lower back into the crook of Patrick's arm, biting the tip of his tongue as he entered her.

Half-stoned and exhausted, knowing she wouldn't have another orgasm, she relaxed and melted, enjoying his steady rhythm, soothed by the motion inside her. When his breathing quickened again, she gripped the back of his skull, her fingers digging through his hair. She released him when he was done.

She was half-asleep by the time she heard him flush the condom. She was three-quarters asleep when she heard him close the front door behind him. By the time he had unlocked his bike from her fence, she was dead to the world. She slept deeper than she had in weeks, oblivious to the world. She'd woken with a start not long after sunrise, hungover, relieved and terrified at how well she had slept.

In the roll-call room, waiting for her fellow officers, Maureen studied the backs of her hands. Completely clean. Veins, tendons, and wrinkles. No blood under her nails. No cuts, no bruises from the night work she'd done. Her reward for choosing the right weapon. She'd been smart, but she'd been lucky, too. Don't blow this chance to start over, she thought. Don't lose what you came here for. Don't end up shamed like Ruiz, or worse, wash up dead like Quinn. She didn't want to figure in any more stories of how people around her had lost their lives. She had done that already in New York. It was a story she was trying to forget. She drank her cool coffee. Quinn and Ruiz had made their own choices, she reminded herself.

When two male officers came strutting into the room, Maureen saw Ruiz and Quinn. Then she blinked, realizing that was impossible, and saw the men for who they really were. Wilburn and Cordts. Moved to the night shift, she figured, to replace the two lost officers. They nodded at her as they sat a couple of desks away, Cordts touching his knuckle to his hairline as if tipping a cap. Maureen nodded back, raised her hand a few inches off the table in some semblance of a wave. She wondered how much they knew about her. If they remembered talking to her that night at Ms. Mae's.

She took a deep breath, redirected her vision to the front of the room, and tried to settle her nerves. The rest of the night crew shuffled in and filled the desks around her. Patrol officers. Plainclothes officers on the night watch. She recognized their faces, knew most of their last names. Other than Preacher, she hadn't really gotten to know anyone she worked with besides Quinn and Ruiz. She decided one thing she would do with this second chance was change that situation. As the room filled up for roll call, nobody sat with her.

Looking around the room, breathing in the testosterone-heavy smell of freshly showered, freshly shaved men, she realized she needed to be as uninteresting as humanly possible for as long as she could pull that off. She needed to be the most boring cop in New Orleans.

What were the chances of that, really?

Preacher ambled into the briefing room, huffing and puffing as he approached the podium. "Eyes front, chickadees. Put the fucking phones away. I could give a fuck about your fantasy football teams and your dick pics. Listen up."

No matter the outside weather, the roll-call room was always warm and close. Preacher paused and used a bandana to dab at the sweat beading under his eyes. He frowned as he read over the night's paperwork and announcements. The room stayed at a casual attention. No one talked.

"First things first," Preacher said. "The big conundrum on everyone's mind. The city has not gotten back to us on their petition to the DOJ for exceptions to the new detail regulations for New Year's Eve. The state police will be here as usual, but there should be, I say *should* be, OT available for the Quarter, the Marigny, maybe Mid-City, traffic on Poydras and Canal, all the usual spots."

"That's Christmas-shopping credit-card money, Sarge," someone said. "I need to know if it's coming or not."

"I gotta let my wife know if I'll be working, Sarge," another cop said. "It's our year to host the party."

Maureen watched Cordts turn in his chair. "You sure you don't want to work?"

At second glance, Maureen noticed he was kind of cute. He had a mischief in his eyes she liked. She could see it from across the room, like flickering lights.

"We'll get it," Wilburn said, serious and self-important, slapping his partner on the shoulder with the back of his hand. "Nobody important wants it getting out they kept us off the street if someone gets shot on Bourbon. You think Mitch wants that press? Look around this room. It's half-empty. And it's the same story at every district. Forget enough OT to go around, there aren't enough *cops*, no matter how many troopers they send."

"You mean *when* someone gets shot," Cordts said. "This town loves tradition."

"When I know about the OT," Preacher said, "you will know. I'm told the decision is imminent. Off the record, I'm not inclined to dis-agree with young Wilburn's assessment."

"Soon as someone bends over and picks up the tab," someone said.

"Enough," Preacher said. "The day shift's info will be on your laptops when you get your cars. Same as always. And all the cars have working laptops again, as far as I know." He held up his hand. "No promises. But let me know if something goes wrong. I don't think we have any extra, but we can look." He moved some papers around. "All right, I want eyes on that grocery store at Magnolia and Washington. Used to be those dopes wore red. Now it's a different bunch of dopes and they're wearing white. I want to know why that is."

"It's after Labor Day," Cordts said. "Case closed."

Preacher took a long pause. "Two years of college and that's the best you got?" He turned to another officer. "Morello, that's your sector tonight, make some extra passes. Maybe get crazy and get out of the car, get a feel for things, sniff around. Get real crazy and make some notes."

Maureen watched the muscles in Morello's jaw twitch. She suppressed a grin. Morello hated being singled out, which was why Preacher did it. And because everyone in the room knew Morello got out of the car only for meals and, to look at him, to lift weights at the gym.

"The one who's older than the rest," Preacher said. "He's got the white pit bull on a chain. He likes those sleeveless pullovers."

Cordts flipped open his notebook. "The pit bull likes pullovers?"

Wilburn threw Cordts's notebook on the floor. "Would you shut the fuck up?"

"I wanna know who he is, people," Preacher said, "and I'm not talking about his name. I wanna know if that's his white Camaro parked out front every day. That new school a couple blocks back behind the store is up and running now. We got kids coming and going. That part of the neighborhood is on the upswing. Fucking *finally*. I want it to stay that way. I am not giving back one fucking inch of territory. The only colors I want in that neighborhood are the school colors. Believe."

"I hear ya, Sarge," Wilburn said. "But I have a few thoughts."

Preacher's eyebrows hovered high on his forehead. "Proceed, then, Mr. Thoughts."

"The store has started closing at night," Wilburn said. "Eight, nine o'clock. I guess we're not the only ones sick of those assholes." He glanced around the room for affirmation. "That guy with the dog is out there during the day, but it's a different cast of characters at night." He glanced at his partner, Cordts, who intently read a page in his recovered notebook. Wilburn looked back at Preacher, his expression earnest. "And from what we've seen, it's only a couple guys in lawn chairs at night, older guys, not a whole crew with cars and motorcycles and commotion like during the daytime. I can see the day shift getting after this case, but us, I don't know what there is for us to find out. I don't mind the work. It's more of a man-power question. If we know the store is quiet at night, why dedicate resources?"

Preacher leaned forward, squinting at the speaker. He was pretend-ing, Maureen knew, to read Wilburn's name tag. She had no doubt Preacher knew exactly who he was. She saw Morello smile into his hand, happy to see someone else getting a ration of shit.

"Wilburn?" Preacher said. "Is that your name?"

"Yes, sir."

Sir was a good sign, Maureen thought. Wilburn was bright enough to know he'd stepped in it.

"This your first fucking day, son?"

"No, sir. Three years on the job, sir."

"That makes it worse, Wilburn," Preacher said. "Not better." He stepped out from behind the podium, leaned his elbow on it. Maureen felt her stomach drop as Preacher's eyes locked on hers. She was going to get her welcome whether she liked it or not. "Officer Coughlin, you have returned to us from your forty days in the desert. Shalom. You wanna tell us why I want *us* there at *night* when the guy I wanna know about is there during the *day*?"

Wilburn had turned in his seat to look at her, his expression grim. Someone, she realized at that moment, fancied himself an alpha dog among the patrol officers. That spot had been Quinn's. Now it was vacant. Someone, she figured, had to rise and take it. It was the natural order of things. She didn't think Wilburn would make it.

She took a deep breath before she spoke. "Because it's easier to get answers if the guy we're asking about isn't around and watching out for who the neighborhood people are talking to. We roll right up on every-one midday and start making demands, shit gets shut down. Maybe moved to another location, and we're back at zero. Worse, this guy now knows we're asking about him. We want him to be the *last* to know we're looking at him."

Preacher smiled. "A gold star for Officer Coughlin. Wilburn, take notes."

Maureen hated that she'd been forced to play teacher's pet, but directing the question at her, and referring out loud to her absence, was Preacher's way, she knew, of announcing to the squad that he had her back. The attention also meant, she hoped, that Preacher would put her on the store.

"Let's change things up. Morello, you're out of Central City; you're in the Channel tonight, instead. Wilburn and Cordts, you've shown such initiative, y'all take the Washington corridor tonight. My gut tells me the lawn-chair guys are trying to make a statement, trying to reclaim some territory. We may have an opportunity there. They might actually want our help in the neighborhood for a change. Go find out if I'm right."

So much for that, Maureen thought. Getting Washington Avenue meant Wilburn and Cordts got the store. Cordts spoke up. "I noticed those apartments next door, there's 'No Trespassing' signs all over them now. That's new."

Preacher nodded. "If someone is holding a knife to the sweater-vest man's back, I wanna help them sharpen it. Make me proud, gentlemen. On my night shift, we're gonna make real cops outta you yet. ABT. Always. Be. Teaching. That's how I do. Believe." He waited. "Yes?"

"Yes, sir," Wilburn said.

"We believe, sir," said Cordts.

"Halle-fucking-lujah," Preacher said. "In other news, nothing yet on that shooting death from the 2000 block of Second. We're waiting for suspect info from Homicide. I'm thinking someone from the neighborhood, as are you all, but we're waiting for something, anything, more specific."

"Who caught it?" Maureen asked.

"Drayton," Preacher said.

A collective groan went up.

"Enough with that," Preacher said. "Y'all are cops, too. Y'all have people out there you can put the lean on. Here's an idea, do some police work for a change. Who knows what might happen?" He held up a piece of paper. "Maybe something like this, for instance. This here is a memo from Sergeant Hardin of the Eighth District."

Maureen's ears perked up at the mention of Hardin. The Eighth District included the Quarter and the Marigny, where she had been looking for Dice and Madison Leary. Hardin knew they were both part of Atkinson's murder case.

"If you haven't already heard," Preacher said, "someone took a bad beating in the Channel two nights ago."

Maureen's heart sank. This was not what she wanted talked about at roll call.

"Victim is a Caucasian male, mid-twenties," Preacher said. "An unknown person or persons snuck up on him and put down the hurt with a blunt weapon of some sort. Left him lying in the bushes outside a residence with a punctured lung. This was damn close, people, to being a homicide." He shrugged. "But it's not, so it's staying here in the district. Detective Lamb has it.

"The fun part is this. You may also recall we've gotten calls in recent weeks about young women being followed home from bars on Magazine, the Irish Garden, especially. Morello, you caught one of those, I think. We have reason to think this may be our guy. One of the girls said something about a ring. This guy had a heavy college ring on his hand. The young lady who called him in, she had been drinking in the Garden that night. She was arriving home when the beating happened, and it happened in her front yard. Like I said, I think this is our guy, which would make this good news. We'll see if the calls stop coming."

"So that's it, then?" Maureen asked, before she could stop herself. "We're letting Lamb take it from here?"

Preacher was quiet a long time. Maureen worried that she'd said too much.

"If Lamb needs anything from us," Preacher said, "he'll ask, I'm sure. I know he talked to the kid this afternoon. How that conversation went, I don't have details. If you feel really compelled, Coughlin, you can offer your services to Detective Lamb. Can I continue?" He held up the paper again. "Unlike many of you lesser cops, Sergeant Hardin pays attention to shit. This attention-paying compulsion has caused him to notice that this beating, instead of being an isolated incident, fits into an emerging pattern. This is the fifth assault of this kind in the past three weeks."

These assaults we pay attention to, Maureen thought. She crossed her arms and slouched in her chair. We count them. We write memos. God save the young white men.

Preacher ticked off the connections on his fingers. "The victims are male, young, early to mid-twenties, fairly well off, and white. None of them have a record. None of them actually live in the neighborhood where they were assaulted. If you've been by Fat Harry's during an LSU game, you know the type of guy I mean. The five of them are so alike they could be frat brothers."

Maureen folded her arms as she listened. She hadn't realized she'd been so predictable. Just another reason to hang it up, she thought. Patterns got people caught.

"One aberration: last night's beating was the first one of its kind in the Irish Channel. Every victim suffered the same kind of injuries. A pipe, a baton, to the joints or the bones. Whoever's doing it, he wants it to *hurt*. For a long time. I hesitate to use the word *vigilante*, because as far as we can tell none of these guys who got their asses kicked had committed any crimes. But whoever is doing this, he seems to think they had it coming."

"Word gets out there's a pattern," Morello said, "and we're gonna have frat boys all over town wanting police escorts back to their cars."

"That's what neighborhood security is for," Wilburn said. "Let them babysit."

"So robbery is out as a motive?" Maureen asked.

Preacher wagged a finger. "Good question. No, nothing was taken. Which emphasizes to us that the beating was the point. Right now, I'm issuing a be-advised kind of order. If whoever is doing this has started hunting uptown, we need to be on the lookout."

"And girls walking home from the bars at night?" Maureen asked. "We looking out for them, too?"

To Maureen's surprise, Preacher grinned. "Officer Coughlin. We've missed your particular brand of . . . you around here. Not only are we as a police department looking out for those very women"—he tilted his finger back and forth between himself and her—"but *we* are looking out for them, personally, you and me. You're with me tonight on Magazine Street."

A slow clap broke out among the officers.

"You with me so far?" Preacher asked Maureen.

"Yes, sir," Maureen said. "Maybe these beatings, maybe it's something related to those attacks down in the Fifth District, on St. Claude? The Fifth abuts the Eighth. Those were random beatings. Every vic in those cases is a white male."

"Or the kids with the bats on Esplanade," Wilburn said. "The ones robbing the cyclists. Could be something like that."

Preacher shook his head. "The kids with bats only go after bike riders, and the point of those attacks was robbery. And I think we caught those kids. Not that others won't soon pick up the mantle. And the bats." He looked at Maureen. "Anyway, the guys on St. Claude, the three of them live in that neighborhood, and they're middle-aged. They were assaulted by a gang of kids who didn't care if they were seen. Not one of the guys who took these other beatings got the slightest look at who attacked them. They had nothing to offer ID-wise. Nothing. That's impressive work by the assailant. And it points to planning and forethought. To intent. That person doesn't want *anyone* knowing who he is.

"One of the St. Claude guys named a kid from his art class as one of his attackers. Whole different thing. The guy dishing out these other beatings, he's on a mission."

He let his words hang in the air. Maureen thought she heard a hint of respect in Preacher's voice. She was happy to hear the masculine pronouns. "This mission, this crusade, if it has come to the Sixth District, it ends here. *Before* it escalates, 'cause we know that's next. I want no heroes dropping bodies in my district. Not for any reason. Believe."

Maureen looked down into her coffee. Way ahead of you, Preacher, she thought.

13

"I want you to do something for me," Preacher said. "About that store on Washington."

They were parked on a short block of Magazine Street, outside a custom furniture shop, positioned in the middle of a stretch of bars and restaurants that stayed open late. Maureen, in the passenger seat of the parked cruiser, sat looking out the window. Her heel thumped on the floor. She chewed her thumbnail. She turned to Preacher, blinking. "What?"

"You okay?" Preacher asked.

"Yeah, I'm fine. It's tough, you know, sitting here in the car after so much time off. I would've liked the grocery store gig. Talk to people. Move around some."

Preacher said, "That's what I'm asking you about. The grocery store. Believe me, I'm not leaving the whole thing up to Wilburn and Cordts."

He resettled himself in his seat. Being parked for hours at a time wasn't doing him any good, either, Maureen could tell. She knew his back hurt. He glanced at her, then returned to watching the street through the windshield.

"I know you've come back gung-ho," Preacher said. "Which is why I thought you'd be better off easing back into it. That's why you're out here with me, instead of alone in a car of your own."

"I figured it was something like that," Maureen said. "So we're baby-sitting Magazine Street, and you're babysitting me. I get it. Making sure no frat boys get their asses kicked."

Preacher sucked his teeth. "Not that I owe you an explanation for your orders, as your commanding officer and such."

Maureen blew out her breath. She lowered her head in supplication. "I know, I know, I'm being an ungrateful bitch. Again. I'm working on, what's the word for it, *processing*, what happened six weeks ago. It's weird being back, in the car, in the uniform. More so than I thought it would be. Brings a lot of it back. It makes me edgy, the discomfort. Part of me feels like I never left, part of me feels like an impostor. I'm in a hurry to feel normal again, you know?"

"I do, believe me," Preacher said. "I spent a few years, never mind weeks, after the storm trying to feel what you want to feel, but I don't think there's any way to speed up that process. If there is, I never found it."

"It's not just what happened here in New Orleans with Quinn and those guys," Maureen said. She thought of Skinner's admonitions. Who did she trust more than Preacher? "There's things I brought with me here, things from home. From back in New York. This time of year, it makes me kind of squirrelly. Like people here get at the end of August."

Preacher kept looking out the car window, distracted, watching the traffic. Maybe thinking, Maureen wondered, about late August six years ago. He shifted his hips again, trying to relieve the pressure on his low back. Maureen considered the pain pills at home in her medicine cabinet. Wouldn't take but ten minutes, less than that, to pass by her house and get them. One for him, one for her. Did she want him asking, though, where she got them? He wouldn't ask, she realized, he would just know.

"We every one of us got baggage," Preacher said, turning back to her.

"Don't hafta be a cop for that. Three hundred years people have been coming here to be somebody else. It's not new, what you feel."

Maureen was sure he thought she meant she was feeling some boy, maybe some family drama. What would Preacher do, she wondered, if she flat out told him she'd killed people in her past? Imagine saying it, she thought. Imagine spitting out the story like a mouthful of bad milk. She couldn't do it. Not yet, if ever. "You don't want to hear this sentimental shit." She shrugged at him. Smiled. "You're in the car with me, so you get the blowback."

"And that's why *you* are in the car with *me*," Preacher said. "So no one else gets the blowback. I don't know who else could handle you."

Maureen turned in her seat to face him, hands in her lap, her chin raised to him. Work was what they should be talking about. Work. "The store on Washington, you have something you want me to do."

"I want you," Preacher said, "to track down Little E. Tomorrow night, you'll be back in the saddle on your own. Find out what he knows about the guy with the white pit bull. Little E's dealt with you before. He knows you have my trust. He's my best informant. Green as you are, you're the only one on this squad I trust with him. If he's got any info, he will give it to you."

"Gotcha. And thanks for that," Maureen asked. "What do I do for him?"

"Slip him a couple of bucks," Preacher said. "He won't need any more than that. I'll get you back for the money."

"I got it," Maureen said. "No worries. Where's he staying these days?"

"No idea."

"Okay. Where do I find him?"

"Your best bet is gonna be somewhere he's looking for work. Dinnertime, maybe one of the new cafés on Oretha Castle Haley. They don't know him yet. Late night, check the bars. They'll usually let him help clean up at the Fox Den because of his father and the Indian thing. He drinks at Pop's House of Blues, or the Sportsman's Corner. Maybe the

Big Man. Chances are he'll work at one, spend it at another. He moves in a small orbit."

"I got it," Maureen said, grinning.

Preacher frowned at her.

She grinned again. "Indeed."

Preacher stared at her.

"What?" Her throat was dry and tight. Why was he doing this to her? "Why you looking at me like that?" She willed herself to leave her hair alone. She set her hands on her thighs, and immediately started kneading her quads like a cat. Her palms were sweaty. "Big Man. Fox Den. OCH." She gave him a thumbs-up, a gesture she was fairly sure she had never used in her life. "I got it. I'm good."

Preacher continued staring, narrowing his eyes. He was close to breaking her, and Maureen knew that he was aware of it. She didn't even know what it was he wanted her to confess. She broke eye contact with him. Her foot began thumping on the car floor again. She looked at it like it was a sick small animal, like she had no control over it or attachment to it. She felt sorry for it. She thought for a split second about shooting it.

"Out with it, Coughlin," Preacher said. "You mentioned New York. Did you get bad news? Something's got you squirming in your seat like a dirty-diapered toddler. I wanna know what it is. Is it this FBI thing? If you're not ready to be on the job, we need to talk. You have no more room for error out here. None."

She reached for her pack of cigarettes on the dash. She lit up, checked the time on her phone, stalling as she reviewed her options. Where to start?

She could confess that roll call and this night shift now added up to the longest stretch of hours she'd gone without a drink or a pain pill in six weeks. That she could feel the information he'd given her moments ago dissolving in her brain like sugar in hot water. Her head hurt and her mouth was dry and her eyes itched and the chemical void in her bloodstream had her feeling like someone had slipped sandpaper between her skin and her muscles. She hated moving. She couldn't not. Her legs jumped with a twitchy life of their own. Since they'd parked the car, her brain alternated shouting lame excuses to stop by her house with growling bitter admonitions for leaving the pills at home. She had found herself glad and relieved when Preacher's back had started hurting him, and she hated herself for feeling that way.

She licked her lips. What had she been thinking, going cold turkey? Because you didn't need a quit strategy, she thought, if you didn't have a problem. Just one would make it better. Half a one so she wouldn't feel quite this bad.

If she didn't want to talk about what she knew damn well was withdrawal, and she sure as hell didn't, she could bring the conversation back to roll call. She could continue poking around the edges of the investigation into the beatings, trying to see how far along things had gotten and running the risk of exposing herself. Could she find out how much Lamb knew, what theories he had, if any? She wondered again if Preacher suspected her, but she couldn't devise a way to discern that from him without leading him to suspect her, if he didn't already.

He was smarter than she was, and decades more savvy. That she might con or cajole him into revealing his thinking was a ridiculous idea and she knew it. She worried that the real reason they were on the street together was so he could be alone with her, so he could question her without really, officially *questioning* her.

She felt like that loony guy in the Edgar Allan Poe story, the guy with the beating heart hidden under his floor. She remembered the end of the story. The guy was batshit crazy. That was the point and the punch line. He was crazy with rage. With guilt. Too crazy and angry and guilty to shut the fuck up and sit still. Like any other criminal. Was that where she was headed?

"Nothing's up," she said. "I'm fine. I just, I'm anxious, like I was saying before. I feel like a dog that's been cooped up in the house all day, you know, like for weeks." She gestured at the crowded bar a block ahead of them. "I've been in a cage and we drive to the dog park and now you won't let me out of the car. I just, you know me, Preach. I want to be *moving*."

Preacher shook his head. "No. No, you're not the usual you. I've never seen you, never seen anyone crush half a pack of cigarettes like you have in the past two hours. Bored dog, my ass. You smoke like someone who's cuffed up in the interrogation room. Like inside the cigarette is the only place that there's any air."

A neon-green Jeep packed with college kids, the music cranked, caught his attention as it sped past. He watched it continue on in the rearview. Maureen watched his eyes, his hands, his right foot, urging him in her mind to start the car. *Please.*

She dropped her half-finished cigarette out the window. She was that dog again, panting, watching her master stand there ball in hand, waiting, dying for him to throw it.

Instead Preacher said, "How is it you smoke like you do and run like you do? Those things don't go together. You got an extra set of lungs at home in the closet?"

"The nuns in high school used to ask me the same question," Maureen said. "I'm a walking, running contradiction, Preach. It's part of my charm." She lit another cigarette. "I make it happen like I do everything else. Through sheer force of will." She shrugged. "I'm in great shape. I have the resting heart rate of a professional athlete."

"That's the thing," Preacher said. "I know you can run for miles. I saw you cruising around the track in the park. Graceful as a racehorse. But when you stop moving, and I can see you, you don't look healthy. That's my point."

Maureen looked away from him. "What the hell does that mean? That doesn't make any sense."

"It makes me wonder what's driving you. I need to know my officers. I need to know what they carry, and how much it weighs."

She climbed out of the car. "I need to stretch my legs. Boredom, that's what's driving me. And it weighs a fucking ton."

It wasn't untrue; she needed to stretch. Not that she was about to start bending over and doing stretches in the middle of Magazine Street. But she felt better standing than she did sitting.

She walked around to the front of the car, leaned her backside on the hood. The night was cold. The wind picked up. She crossed her arms, rubbed them. She'd left her leather jacket in the car. It would have to stay there. She couldn't even look at Preacher. Not right then. Every now and then someone standing around in front of the bar glanced her way. The wind carried music and voices to her. She jammed her fists into her armpits. She looked down at her boots. The chemical withdrawal was appropriate, she thought. November was now her white-knuckle month.

After her dealings with Sebastian, she'd made it through the New Year before her first meltdown. It caught her by surprise. She thought she was doing great. She hadn't even known what a panic attack was until she'd been having them for two weeks. Once, she had passed out on the staircase in her mother's house, the fall leaving her with a bump the size and color of a plum on her hairline above her right temple.

And days before that accident another attack had left her staggering across busy Amboy Road, fighting to stay conscious and upright, finally crumpling to the sidewalk when she made the other side. A year should feel like a long time, especially because so much had changed. That had been the whole point of everything she had done in the past twelve months.

Yet, right at that moment, standing on a nighttime New Orleans street, a cop leaning against a police car, she could reach back and hear the tires screeching from the cars on Amboy Road that had barely missed her. She could feel the cold concrete of the sidewalk against her cheek as she lay there with her heart fluttering inside her like a dying humming-bird. She almost missed it, the breathless emptiness. The forced surrender of the complete collapse. She thought she might die right there on that

Staten Island sidewalk. She remembered thinking she should feel more afraid of death than she did.

But then her breath had returned and her heartbeat had settled. The bird inside her either died or escaped. Her limbs had gathered underneath her of their own volition and she'd stood, unsteady and wet-eyed like a foal. And something told her she had to get up and get away from the scene of her collapse before the ambulance came. She didn't know what kind of hospital the men in white would take her to should they get their hands on her. She wanted no one strapping her down on the gurney. She'd been captured once in her life. Never again.

Nat Waters, who had been there through the days of the silver-haired man, who in his decades in the NYPD had seen more people short-circuit than he cared to remember, had convinced Maureen to start seeing the shrink early that spring. He was the first one to use the acronym PTSD. The shrink had been the second.

Maureen rubbed her hands over the backs of her arms. PTSD. She'd thought she'd left those letters in the doctor's office. She thought she'd left them, all those names, her *diagnosis*, her *condition*, the reason for her prescriptions, thirteen hundred miles behind her on Staten Island. On the banks of the Arthur Kill where she'd lost her favorite switchblade slicing open one man's throat and stabbing another's leg, where Sebastian's blood had run hot down her arms to her elbows, stinking like copper and steaming off her hands in the cold night air.

This was why, she thought, no one understood her pursuit of Caleb and Solomon Heath, and why she didn't know if she could ever make anyone else understand. Atkinson. Detillier. Even Preacher. She wanted Caleb, she needed him, she *had to have him* because no one else could, no, because no one else *was willing*, to see his future like she could. And she could see his future as clearly as she could see her past. Heath was the larva. He needed to be crushed and smeared before he got too big and too quick to catch.

The trunk of a car. The stink of the Arthur Kill. The roar of the oncoming train.

Maureen had already seen what Caleb Heath would become.

She had already killed him once.

And for the life of her, Maureen couldn't think of a sane way to explain everything she knew to Preacher, or even to Atkinson. Forget Detillier. There was no talking to any of them without sounding like she had Poe's beating heart under her floor. Not without telling them that, on a cold November night very much like this one, she had killed two men with her bare hands. She didn't know how to talk about what she had done. Or how it had made her feel. Not without revealing that deep, deep down inside her, in places where no man's breath or body, where no doctor's probing fingers or questions, where no other human being had ever reached, in the abyss inside her where the darkest things with the sharpest teeth lived and swam and hunted, she missed that killing feeling, the blood running over her hands, through her fingers. The unassailable power of being the one who lived.

Not everyone gets to be the killer. Most don't. Most women who'd been where she had, they became the killed. The dead. The forgotten parts of someone else's story.

Maureen's phone buzzed in her pocket, calling her back to Magazine Street. She checked the screen. The number was private. She answered anyway; she had an idea who it might be. "Coughlin."

"Officer Coughlin, it's Agent Detillier. I thought I'd hear from you tonight. We need an answer from you about meeting with Gage. We want to keep him interested while he's in town."

"I understand," Maureen said.

"I'm sorry," Detillier said. "I have another call coming in. Hang on."

"Sure," Maureen said.

Voices rose outside the Balcony Bar up the street, catching her attention. Two short fat girls in high heels, tight tops, and too-tight skirts had started screaming at each other, thrusting fingers at each other. The front of one girl's top was damp. She'd had a drink thrown in her face. That wet spot was gonna get cold, Maureen thought.

By the door of the bar, Maureen could see the large form of the bouncer rising above the crowd. He had his massive arms folded across his chest, and he was paying close attention to the unfolding conflict. She knew there was another door guy there, too, somewhere in the crowd. A smaller man who checked IDs. Unlike the NOPD, she thought, the bar had enough staff to handle their business. She saw that no boyfriends or wanna-be shining knights had stepped into the conflict. Good news. Alcohol-infused testosterone always made things worse. Always.

Even if the girls came to blows, Maureen would make a move only if a weapon appeared. She'd see it and hear it from the crowd, which would open up like a slow-motion explosion if something got drawn. Unlikely, considering the combatants. Which was fine with her. She really didn't feel like jumping into a drunken catfight. Not the return to action she'd had in mind. In a minute and a half to two minutes, the incident would escalate or defuse.

Maureen turned again, her phone held to her ear, looking at Preacher through the windshield. He was watching the busser at the Rum House across the street sweep under the outside picnic tables. He was picking his nose. What was Detective Atkinson doing right then? Maureen wondered. She thought about the Sixth District task force, the one that specialized in dangerous arrests and warrants. She thought about Homicide, Vice, Special Victims. The fast track to plainclothes work, like Detillier had mentioned, that was what she wanted. Plainclothes, property and persons, they were the way out of uniform and into the bigger and better work. It was never too early to start thinking about the future, now that she was putting past calamities behind her.

"You there?" Detillier asked.

"I'll be happy to talk to him," Maureen said. "Anything it takes to get these guys. Do I need to wear a wire? Because I'm okay with that."

"Won't be necessary," Detillier said. "This isn't an investigation of the man. Think of it as a fact-finding mission, a feeling out, to see if he's worth continuing attention after he settles matters concerning his son. You won't have to wear a wire. You won't have to make an arrest."

"What do you need from me?"

"Give me a time and place where he can meet you," Detillier said. "Someplace you'll be comfortable. Someplace informal."

"You don't want him at HQ? Or maybe at the Sixth District?"

"We don't want the meeting on police property," Detillier said. "He's paranoid. Fearful. We want him to relax if he can. Put him at ease. Again, the meeting should come across like a favor, like the NOPD is reaching out and complying with his wishes, not like an interview or an inquiry. He's coming back to HQ in the morning; we're going to send someone out to him with the details on where to meet you."

Maureen sighed. The fucking feds. They loved to overthink things. Okay, where did she want to do it? Someplace she'd feel more comfortable than Gage would. Someplace that would give her the upper hand. If he was nervous and paranoid, she wanted to use that against him.

"Tell him Li'l Dizzy's," she said, "corner of Esplanade and North Robertson, at one o'clock."

Detillier paused, mulling over her idea. Maureen wasn't entirely surprised. Detillier was local. That meant he'd know Dizzy's.

She waited for his response and watched as a man wrapped one of the yelling girls, the one with the wet top, in a bear hug from behind. He lifted her off the sidewalk and walked her away from the crowd. She *did not* like it, and threw her drink in his face, over her shoulder. The other girl stormed away up Magazine Street, stopping and turning once to point her finger and yell something about "acting the ho."

Maureen, thankful she'd been spared getting involved, closed her eyes and imagined a hot bath. She thought about how a pill and a whiskey would make that bath even better.

"He's not going to like that place," Detillier said.

Exactly, she thought. "Hey, guess what, it's not a freakin' date. I like that place. I feel safe there. And I don't know this guy from Adam. If I get shot at again, I don't wanna be the only gun in the room. That's my offer."

"If we thought your life was in danger," Detillier said, "we wouldn't set it up like this. We wouldn't even ask."

Lies, Maureen thought. She didn't hold it against him. Everyone had to play the part they were given. "My life is always in danger until we chase the Watchmen out of New Orleans." She switched her phone to the other ear. "Listen, Dizzy's is a good place to meet him. Strategic. It's not far from HQ. He won't feel like we're trying to lead him somewhere. Maybe instead he feels special, like we're sharing our turf with him. The café closes at two, so there'll be a natural end to things if I have trouble getting rid of him."

"Fair points," Detillier said after a moment. "Dizzy's it is."

"Thank you," Maureen said. "Any tips?"

"I think you know what you're doing," Detillier said, a laugh in his voice. "Let him talk as much as he wants. Let his thoughts wander. Wait until after he's left to make any notes. I guess the one rule is this, do not let him know the FBI is interested in him. You are a local cop doing a grieving father a favor and that is the extent of it."

"And I'll hear from you when?" Maureen asked.

"I'll be in touch tomorrow," Detillier said. "But if you need to get with me before you hear from me, don't hesitate to call. Thanks for doing this, Maureen."

"You're welcome," Maureen said. "I expect Uncle Sam will pick up the tab for lunch."

"Save your receipt," Detillier said. "I'll see what I can do." He hung up.

Maureen slipped her phone back in her pocket. Behind her, Preacher got out of the cruiser. He came around to the front, handed Maureen her jacket.

"Atkinson?" he asked. "I'm sure someone has told her by now you're back on the job."

"Detillier," Maureen said. "We set up the meeting with Gage. Dizzy's at one."

"Good choice."

Maureen put her jacket on, zipped it. She blew into her hands. The temperature was plummeting, and the night air was turning damp. The moisture in the air blurred the streetlights overhead and the colored lights of the Caribbean restaurant across the street.

"You're doing the right thing," Preacher said. "You have to know there's no traction going right at the Heaths, not unless Caleb himself starts spraying bullets at cop cars on Canal Street. I'm not one to stick up for the FBI, but Detillier is being smart. He's not being lazy."

"Everyone says Solomon's such a stand-up guy," Maureen said. "I think we should give him a chance to prove it. He's got Caleb by the purse strings. I don't care if he's in Dubai, Detroit, or DeRidder. If Caleb's daddy wanted him here, he'd be here." She stabbed her finger into the hood of the car. "Tomorrow. Make everyone's life a lot easier."

"Not happening," Preacher said. Maureen felt him looking hard at the side of her face. "It's not happening. No one is talking to Solomon Heath, not in uniform, especially not even if someone runs into him accidentally jogging through Audubon Park. Were that to threaten to occur"—he made a running figure with his fingers—"that running person would run her skinny little ass right on by. We understand each other?"

Maureen saluted. "Ten-four, Sarge. I hear you. I'm fresh out of the doghouse, I'm not looking to get back in."

Preacher settled his rump against the hood of the car. Maureen felt the cruiser dip under his weight. "Besides, someone in New Orleans is killing the Watchmen, and we can't catch whoever it is. Even if Solomon agrees that his kid is a criminal, he'll never bring him back here while the killer's at large."

He bummed a cigarette from her. "I'm trying to cut back on the cigars. Shit'll kill you." He lit up. "So you haven't heard from Atkinson since you got reinstated?"

"No, I haven't," Maureen said.

"I thought maybe with you getting your badge back, she'd reach out."

"I thought she might call, too. You know, maybe, now that I've been *officially* forgiven. I thought maybe that was what she was waiting for. We haven't talked since I got back to town."

"Aw, give it time," Preacher said. "She's Homicide. They keep their own clock. And it's not like there was a department-wide memo that you're back. Maybe she hasn't heard. Your reinstatement is supposed to be quiet."

"I guess," Maureen said. "I may have blown it with her. I did some things." She found herself getting choked up. Fucking pills. "I don't make it easy."

"Dial it back on the martyrdom," Preacher said. "Your Irish is show-ing. If squeaky clean was the only kind of cop Atkinson had time for, she would've flamed out around here a long time ago. A long, long time ago. She's known, and knows, much worse than you. Believe."

"Anyway," Maureen said, "if I'm talking to her vic's father, I guess she'll come looking for me regardless. She'll want to know what he tells me as much as Detillier does."

"See, there you go," Preacher said. "You two are meant to be together. Like Batman and Robin, the Lone Ranger and Tonto. Fried shrimp and brown gravy."

Maureen lit a cigarette. "So, this meeting I'm having, with the father of a murder victim, on behalf on the FBI. Am I making a mistake?"

"I hope not," Preacher said. "I encouraged you to do it."

"You know what I mean."

"This Sovereign Citizens business," Preacher said, "it's a new thing. I think Detillier meant what he said at PJ's. I think the feds are really behind on this thing. I think they're desperate for information. And I understand his wanting to use you." He paused, grinning. "You figured out the real reason they picked you for the meeting, right?"

"Because I'm being groomed for intelligence work," Maureen said. "The FBI is obviously recruiting me."

"Uh, well, that could be true," Preacher said. "It could be that, sure."

Maureen laughed. "Gotcha. C'mon. We both know Detillier looks at me and he sees a short, skinny *girl*. What he said about my experience dealing with the Watchmen, my connections to the case, about them wanting to help me get even—the entirety of that was bullshit. We both know it. Detillier picked me because Gage will think he can intimidate me. He'll be a lot less cautious with his talk than he would be around a man, or even blond bombshell Detective Sergeant Atkinson, all broad-shouldered six feet of her, and because of that—he'll talk to me. Once he gets over the insult of me being what he gets, he'll run his mouth because he's not afraid of a little girl like me."

Preacher looked at her a long time, like he was seeing her from across the street instead of a couple of feet away.

"What?" Maureen asked. "You're making me nervous."

"This thing happens with your voice sometimes," he said. "Since you came back from the beach. You ever seen a scorpion curl its tail over its back? The poison kind of shining on the stinger? That. You sound like that shine looks."

Maureen looked away. "Whatever. That doesn't make *any* sense."

"Yeah, it does," Preacher said. "You know exactly what I mean."

From inside the car, Maureen could hear the dispatcher raising their car over the radio. Preacher rose off the hood, went to the driver's door. "Like you said, whatever. Let's get back in the car. It's cold out here. Somebody's looking for us, anyway."

Maureen went to her side. She paused after opening the door. "Preach, listen—"

"You make me nervous," Preacher said across the top of the car. He had that faraway look again. The radio kept calling. "I sit next to you, I can hear you ticking. Like a bomb."

"Well, I don't know what you're talking about," Maureen lied. "I don't hear it."

"That right there," Preacher said, "is the problem. I know you don't hear it. *That* is what makes me nervous." He dropped into the driver's seat, reaching for the radio mic.

Maureen climbed into the car, the door creaking as she pulled it closed.

"You got your wish," Preacher said. "We're done sitting here for the night."

"Do tell."

"Anonymous tip. Seems there's a body in Lafayette Cemetery."

"I'd think there'd be plenty of—"

"Don't," Preacher said, slamming the car into drive, hitting the lights and sirens. He was trying not to laugh. "Just fucking don't."

14

Lafayette Cemetery was a box in the middle of the Garden District. Eight-foot-high walls of whitewashed, fern-and-lichen-crusted brick formed the sides of the box, and each wall had a spiked iron gate in its middle that was chained and padlocked at night. With the resident bodies being interred aboveground, the crypts and tombs formed rows of short buildings, their curved concrete and marble roofs peeking over the wall. Maureen had no trouble understanding why New Orleans cemeteries were called "Cities of the Dead." Sections of the cemetery were even named as if they were city neighborhoods, the pathways running through them signed like streets.

She'd been in Lafayette before. She liked it there. She had walked among the tombs on more than one afternoon, nursing a double espresso from the nearby coffee shop. The place was even a popular tourist attraction. But her visits had been during the day, when there were other people, living people, around her. Tonight, she stood with Preacher outside the walls, trying to find a way in. Apparently, there was one dead body inside that didn't belong there.

They had checked each gate, Maureen jumping out of the patrol car at each one to inspect the locks, and the four of them remained secure. However the unaccounted-for dead person had gained entrance, it hadn't been through one of the gates.

"Has anyone called the, uh, custodian," Maureen asked, "or whatever he's called?"

She really wanted to say "cryptkeeper." The guy looked the part. She'd seen him around the neighborhood. A pale, pink-faced older white guy about her height, with long, stringy white hair streaming out from under an endless variety of old mesh-backed baseball caps. He dressed in ratty jeans and stained T-shirts and rode a rickety old bike with a radio and a rusty bell tied to the handlebars. Maureen couldn't think of a job where dress code could be less important.

"That's what I was told," Preacher said. "I guess he's on his way. We have to wait for him to ride over here."

"We couldn't send a car for him?" Maureen asked.

"You're hilarious, Coughlin, you really are. We're a chauffeur service?"

Maureen looked around, hands on her hips. The streets were quiet. She could hear the traffic light change from red to green, one light going out, the other coming on, at the nearby intersection. "Anybody else coming?"

"Beats me," Preacher said. "I bought the call, so maybe it's us until crime scene and the coroner's office gets here. I didn't sense incredible urgency."

"So we went from babysitting live bodies on Magazine Street," Maureen said, "to babysitting a dead one in there."

"It would appear so," Preacher said. "You're wondering now how you could have missed it so much, aren't you?"

Maureen took out her cigarettes, studied the pack, jammed it back in her pocket. She looked at the top of the wall. Wasn't really that high. "Gimme a boost."

"Coughlin."

"C'mon, Sarge. Gimme a boost. I think I hear something inside the cemetery. Voices, I think. We should get in there."

"You think I'm going to fall for that?" Preacher asked. "We wait for the man with the key."

"How'd the dead body get in there?" Maureen asked. "Somebody tossed it over the wall? How'd anyone know about it if the place is locked up tight? Maybe someone is inside." She bounced on her toes. Maureen noticed the security guard in front of Commander's Palace across the street watching them. Here's his excitement for the night, she thought. Mine, too, probably. She made a mental note to make sure she talked to the guard later. He could be the kind of witness who might actually talk to the police. "Who knows how long it'll take anyone to get here? Gimme a boost, help me get over the wall. I can clear the scene at least, make sure it's safe."

"I'm willing to bet," Preacher said, "there is no body. I bet it's a prank, a goof. It happens."

"Better we find out sooner rather than later," Maureen said. "We could save a bunch of people some trouble by checking it out first." She saw Preacher's shoulders droop an inch or two. She knew she had him. And it wasn't her whining that had persuaded him. She knew her logic was sound. "C'mon, let me do a little police work tonight. Please."

Preacher handed over his radio. "I'll get the other from the car."

Maureen secured the radio on her belt, clipped the mic to her shoulder. "Now help me up there."

"Let's go around the Sixth Street side," Preacher said. "The wall is shorter over there."

"You're joking," Maureen said. "You're stalling. The wall is the same all the way around."

"It's not the same," Preacher said. "If you don't know by now that the whole city's crooked, I can't help you."

"Yeah, you can," Maureen said. "Help me climb."

"It's your funeral," Preacher said, chuckling at his own joke. He moved close to the wall. With an elaborate groan, he got down on one knee, leaning one shoulder against the bricks. "Step one is the thigh, step two is the shoulder, after that, reach up and put those young muscles to work."

"Thanks, Preach," Maureen said, and she started her climb.

Standing on one leg, balancing on Preacher's shoulder, the top of the wall was at shoulder height. Grabbing with two hands, sending dust and pebbles tumbling down on Preacher, she pressed her body high enough to swing her hips atop the wall. Surprised, she realized she'd climbed atop a wide marble platform. As she stood, a cold gust of wind knocked her off balance and sent dead leaves twirling over her feet and scratching across the marble's surface.

She steadied herself and looked down at Preacher as he struggled to his feet, dusting her boot print off his shoulder.

"You all right?" she asked. "If I have to get down and help you, it defeats the purpose."

"Don't worry about me," Preacher said. "I'm not the one sneaking into a cemetery in the middle of the night."

"I'm not sneaking," Maureen said, though she did feel like a young girl up to mischief. "I'm doing police work."

"Tell that to the ghosts," Preacher said. "This is one of the most haunted places in the city. In the world, maybe."

"Nice try," Maureen said. "Save it for your tour guide career." She turned in a circle. "I'm on a shelf or something up here. I can see the whole cemetery almost."

She looked over the tops of the vaults and crypts. From her vantage point, the cemetery really did look like a ruined cityscape, maybe an old Greek or Roman village after a century or two of neglect. And okay, she had to admit, the vibe was extra-creepy. Nothing more eerie, she thought, than an empty, silent city. Not that she'd ever tell Preacher how she felt.

"You see our body?" Preacher asked.

Maureen frowned. "I do not."

At second glance, she realized less of the cemetery was visible to her than she'd thought.

Magnolia trees rose in various spots, hiding some of the tombs. Live oaks grew on the sidewalks surrounding the cemetery, and their long, gnarled branches reached over the brick wall, hiding the inside edges and corners of the grounds in shadow. Many of the structures stood close together, creating narrow alleyways, invisible to her from where she stood. The cemetery mirrored the neighborhoods she patrolled, Maureen thought. The closer and longer that she looked at them, the more untended and mysterious, and possibly dangerous, spaces she discovered. She would have to get down from her perch and search the cemetery on foot. The longer she looked at it, the larger the cemetery seemed to grow. Searching the corners and shadows and alleyways alone would take a lot longer than she had anticipated.

"You realize what you're standing on, right?" Preacher said.

"What's that?" The wind was rising again. Maureen thought she heard musical notes. A flute, maybe a toy piano.

"What you're standing on," Preacher said, "is the mausoleum. You know, a big marble-and-concrete filing cabinet, basically, full of two centuries of human remains."

Maureen looked down at her feet, transmitting a silent apology to the spirits of the dead. "I'll let you know when I've found our body."

She walked to the edge of the shelf. She sat, fighting the wind, letting her legs dangle, and then she dropped to the ground.

She landed with a thump. A sleeping stray cat shrieked to panicked life right at her feet, darting into the darkness. Maureen shouted and stumbled backward against the mausoleum. Startled by the noise and the commotion, two more cats shot out of the grass, launching themselves in opposite directions, shadows darting among the crypts. Maureen dropped her flashlight. She had her weapon halfway drawn before she stopped herself.

From the other side of the wall, she could hear Preacher laughing at her. She couldn't be sure, but she thought she might have heard the security guard chuckling as well.

"I'm fine," she shouted. That she'd been so quick to draw embarrassed and frightened her. The panic felt out of character. "God, I hate cats."

She re-secured her weapon and picked up her flashlight, shined it to the left and then to the right down the path of hard dirt and dead grass. Nothing. No body, no ghouls, and thankfully no more stray cats. The surrounding streetlights shed a pale glow on the grounds. At least she wasn't fumbling about in the pitch-dark, she thought. The idea occurred to her, looking around, that this whole scenario could be part of some elaborate welcome-back prank. Please, God, she thought, don't let me shoot one of my coworkers because he jumped out at me wearing a monster mask.

Her radio crackled. Preacher's voice, "This was your idea. Get to work."

She keyed her mic. "We got nothing as to where the body might be?"

"Inside the walls, that's the best we got," Preacher said.

"Fuck me." Should've waited for backup, she thought.

She walked the wide grass path with careful steps, flashlight beam sweeping in front of her from side to side. She was looking for signs of foul play, for signs of a dead body, but it was hard not be distracted by her surroundings. Some of the crypts and tombs were badly neglected, crumbling, ashen, and stained, the angels adorning their peaked rooftops having lost an arm or a wing or a halo, the engraved family names all but worn away by time and weather. Other buildings shone white and new in the beam of her flashlight. Oddly, age had little bearing on condition. On one of the cleanest tombs, the inscription revealed that the most recent inhabitant had been interred more than eighty years ago. Another cold winter gust rushed along the path and Maureen heard the musical notes again. Like someone blowing into the top of an empty bottle.

Maureen caught herself reading the names and the dates and the titles inscribed on the marble slabs on the faces of the crypts. Who had been married, who had been a parent. So many children; New Orleans had proved a hard place for them. Many of them had lived brief lives, only weeks, sometimes only days. Other people had survived into their seventies and eighties, even in the nineteenth century, having lived and died in New Orleans, she thought, before the first of her starving ancestors had ever boarded a ship in an Irish port. She read many Irish names, more than she'd figured she'd see. She both wanted and didn't want to see Coughlin on one of the nameplates. Or Fagan, her mother's maiden name.

At the foot of each nameplate was a small marble shelf, and on some of the shelves passing mourners had placed gifts and offerings for the recent and long-ago departed. Coins. Paper flowers. Tall glass candles. A warped and browned paperback copy of *King Lear.* A filthy white teddy bear tucked into an old urn, Mardi Gras beads placed around his neck, the beads as dull and colorless as the ashen marble tombs. Maureen fought the urge to reach out and touch the bear's little nose, to scratch its frayed ears.

Even those who were interred under simple headstones lay in graves elevated two or three feet above ground. The graves reminded Maureen—and the thought felt disrespectful but she couldn't dismiss it—of flower boxes in a garden. Most of them badly neglected flower boxes, she thought, the headstones cracked and crumbling, trash caught in the high grass that surrounded them. Some of the graves were fenced with wrought iron like the gardens and yards of her neighborhood.

Hanging from a leaning segment of iron fence, Maureen spotted the source of the notes she'd heard in the wind. A set of wind chimes. They were cheap, maybe bought in a card store, or from a stall in the French Market, but they looked new. Whether they'd been placed there as a gift for a lost loved one or as a way to lead her to this particular grave, Maureen had no idea. As she got closer, she started suspecting the latter.

On the other side of the fence, a dark form lay sprawled atop a grave. Maureen keyed her mic. "Any sign of our man with the key?"

"Negative," Preacher said. "You know, I hope dispatch wasn't thinking *we* would call him."

Maureen let that go. Things were certainly getting back to normal. "I may have something here, stand by."

Slowly, she played her flashlight beam along the figure. Cheap blue Keds, bare ankles, cheap jeans, an oversized and misshapen blue-and-white-striped sweater. Not much protection, really, against the cold. The vic was a woman, definitely. There was something familiar to Maureen about the form. Her heart hammered at her sternum. She moved in closer. Blood, a lot of blood, stained the front of the sweater and had run onto the ground, darkening the gravel around the woman's head. Another throat slash. Maureen's stomach turned over. It burned. Oh man, she thought. Oh no.

She shined the light on the victim's face. Stringy brown hair stuck to the pale cheeks, the cracked lips.

"Holy. Shit."

Into the mic she said, "Preach, I've got our body. I think it's Madison Leary."

As if she'd heard Maureen's voice, the woman's eyes shot open. One was green, the other was blue. The woman gasped and gurgled. Blood sprayed into the air. Maureen's hand shook as she held the mic. "It *is* Madison Leary. And she isn't dead. Call a fucking ambulance."

She had nothing to staunch the bleeding. She sprinted for the nearest exit.

15

When Maureen got to the gate, Preacher was already working on prying open the chain and padlock with a tire iron. Over his shoulder, Maureen could see the white-haired man pedaling his way up Washington Avenue. Taking his sweet time with it, too.

Maureen shouted to him, waving her arms. "Would you please hurry the fuck up?"

Swearing, Preacher tossed the tire iron on the sidewalk. He was breathing hard. "Fucking finally. This guy."

Maureen watched as the man eased his bike to a stop at the curb and climbed off. He walked it to a signpost and began the apparently quite complicated process of locking it to the post. Preacher hurried in his direction. "Listen, guy. Just leave it there."

"No way," the man said. "I can't have this bike stolen. The cemetery won't buy me a new one. And my name is Mr. Shivers, not 'guy.'"

Maureen thought she might bite clean through her tongue.

"There's two cops right here," Preacher said. "And there's about to be a bunch more."

"This bike disappears and I'm holding you two responsible."

"We have a woman in here bleeding out in the dirt," Maureen shouted. She shook the gate like it was the door to a cage. "She dies, I'm holding *you* responsible." She could hear the ambulance sirens approaching. "Preach, get me gloves and gauze from the car. There's no time."

"Ten-four," Preacher said, and he headed for the car.

Shivers waddled toward the gate, fumbling with a large ring of keys. "Step back from the gate, please." Maureen took a step back. Shivers adjusted his ball cap. "Farther back, Officer. I can't have you peeking at what key it is."

"Are you kidding me?"

"Coughlin, do it," Preacher shouted.

Maureen backed away from the gate. Shivers unlocked the padlock, pulled the chain through the gate. Then he opened the bolt lock and, very slowly, opened up the cemetery gate. Preacher jogged to her, supplies held out in front of him. Maureen grabbed the latex gloves and gauze packets.

"Down this grass pathway to the left," she said, "almost to the end."

She turned and ran.

Leary had not moved. Her eyes remained open. Maureen pulled on the gloves, knelt beside Leary in the gravel, the stones biting into her knees, examining the wound with her flashlight. Leary had been slashed across the throat, shoulder-to-shoulder, above the collarbone. The wound matched those that Madison Leary had inflicted on her victims.

Maureen set the light down, ripping open gauze packets one after the other. She wiped at the blood around the wound, searching for a place to apply pressure. She didn't know where to begin, everything that carried blood, it seemed, had been opened up by the blade. The cruiser's first aid kit was meant for minor injuries and the small squares of gauze it contained proved useless. In moments, Maureen had succeeded only in smearing the blood along Leary's collarbones and chin, as if she were trying to wipe up a gallon of spilled paint with too small a cloth. Leary's throat now leaked blood in a dying trickle.

That's gravity bringing that blood out, Maureen thought, not a heartbeat.

"C'mon, c'mon, c'mon. Don't you fucking die. Don't die, don't die."

Fuck, should she try CPR? Why do that, she thought, when the blood you pump will only spill out onto the stones? She heard Preacher hustling along the path, his footsteps heavy, his gun belt jangling, calling her name.

"HERE," Maureen shouted. "I'm here," she whispered to Leary. She tossed aside the gore-soaked gauze. She reached for more. "Fuck." None left. She'd used what she had, and it seemed there was more blood on Leary's sweater, on the gravel, on Maureen's hands, than ever. "But I found you. I finally found you."

Never, during any of her searching, had Maureen imagined coming across Leary like this. Wounded. Dying.

The woman's eyes remained open but blank, staring up at the indigo sky. She gave no sign she heard Maureen's words, or was even aware of Maureen at her side. One shallow, rattling breath produced a tiny spray of red mist that settled on the backs of Maureen's hands. The sirens were right outside the cemetery now. EMS would take over soon, thank God, Maureen thought. They'd have better things. Resources. Supplies. They could help. They could—

"Coughlin," Preacher said. "Move away. Slow."

Maureen looked into Leary's eyes. Empty. Dead. The woman was no longer dying; she was dead.

"There's nothing left to do, Maureen," Preacher said. "We have to preserve the scene. Now move away."

She stood. Leary's blood had soaked through the knees of her uniform, and the fabric of Maureen's pant leg stuck to her skin. Her nose was running. Her hands were too bloody to wipe it. She could hear the heavy footsteps of the EMTs as they hustled up the grassy path.

Preacher shone his flashlight at her feet.

"Look at your right foot. There by her hand."

Maureen looked down. Shining in the flashlight beam, inches from Leary's bony fingers, gleaming white against the dark stones of the gravel, lay an ivory-handled straight razor, the blade dark red with blood. Leary's murder weapon of choice. In the Cooley and Gage murders, and possibly others. Dice had described the razor for her. A wanted killer and her murder weapon, Maureen thought, lying at her side. Not hard to figure out what had happened. The questions: Why now? Why here?

"Don't touch it," Preacher said.

Maureen stepped down from the edge of the grave, peeling off her latex gloves. She dropped them on the grave. Numbness spread through her insides. She could feel parts of her break away and dissipate into the night like smoke from a cigarette, like a soul leaving a body. Difference was, unlike the dead woman nearby, Maureen knew her parts would re-form and return to her.

"Leave her there," she said to the EMTs as they arrived, panting. "She's dead. This is a crime scene. Sorry to waste your time."

One of the EMTs stared at her for long moment. "Maybe you should stop by the ambulance before you leave here." He nodded at Preacher. "We'll wait on y'all a little while."

"Don't," Maureen said.

"Thanks," Preacher said. "Give us a minute here."

Maureen walked over to Preacher, standing by the iron fence. He was looking at the wind chimes. "Something to help us find her?" Maureen asked.

"Could be," Preacher said. "Most of the graves in this place have gifts at them, though. And who knows what they mean. Could be for the deceased lying underneath her."

"We should call Atkinson," Maureen said. "She'll want to know about this."

"Indeed," Preacher said. "We will. You okay?"

"Why wouldn't I be?"

"Unless I misrecollect," Preacher said, "this is the first one you've had die on you."

"Nonsense," Maureen said. "I saw Cooley. Shit, I *found* him when he was two weeks gone. I saw Gage the night he was killed."

"They were already dead."

"I saw a friend of mine once," Maureen said. "Well, not a friend, really, a woman I worked with. In a bar. In New York. She'd drowned. I mean, she *was* drowned. Murdered. I identified her body at the morgue."

"I'm sorry to hear that," Preacher said. "I didn't know that." He waited a moment before he continued. "But, again, she was already gone when you saw her. Having them go under your hands, no matter who or what they were, that's a different thing. Believe me."

"She was a killer. Those other bodies I saw here in New Orleans, she's the reason for them. She and that razor she obviously used on herself. On top of someone else's grave. A lunatic. A sick thing is what she was. Afraid to answer for what she'd done."

Preacher said nothing, looking at the ground. He hitched up his gun belt. "Let's have a cigarette, you and me, before we get down to business securing this scene. We've warned off the EMTs. Leary ain't going anywhere."

"You know what somebody called me once?" Maureen said. She felt light-headed. Preacher went in and out of focus. "A little redheaded angel of death. You believe that? Some people. The things they say."

"Let's go to the ambulance," Preacher said.

"I'm fine."

"I know you are," Preacher said. "I believe you. But let's get your hands clean. You've got blood up to your elbows."

16

As crime scene techs got to work on the scene under Preacher's watchful eye, Detective Atkinson and Maureen walked along the main path leading through the heart of the cemetery. Waiting for the detective to speak first, Maureen walked with her hands jammed in the pockets of her leather jacket, which was zipped to her chin. She had her NOPD knit cap pulled low on her head. And she was chilled to the bone. Atkinson walked with her big hands clasped behind her back, no hat, her down coat open. Maureen was embarrassed to be struggling with the weather. Here she was the born-and-bred New Yorker zipped up tight while the native New Orleanian strode along comfortably. Maureen knew, though, it was more than Atkinson's roots that made her the tougher of the two.

They were flanked by the larger, more ornate tombs and crypts as they walked, the stone structures with columns carved in the marble at their corners, with wreaths and Bible verses carved in their walls and with gorgeous white weeping angels draped across their lintels. Everyone inside those temples—and some of the structures bore plaques with more than a dozen names—everyone inside was as dead as any poor slob buried in a potter's field, Maureen thought. As dead as Madison Leary. As dead as Tanya from Staten Island. As dead as Sebastian, who had killed Tanya and dumped her in New York Harbor. She wasn't sure what the display and posturing was for, or supposed to mean. Comfort for the living, she figured, and not the dead. What did the dead care?

Would she and her mother, she wondered, do anything for her father when the declaration came through? And why would they? Here was an instance where the living didn't care, either. His death would be a matter of paperwork. A few clicks on a keyboard. Like getting a driver's license or a new credit card. No real proof the man was dead would exist. No body. No ashes. Certainly no marble temple. Except for me, Maureen thought, there wasn't much extant physical proof he'd been alive, either. Having him declared dead was about the future, anyway, she thought, not the past. And it's about my mother, she thought, not me.

"It's good to see you back in uniform," Atkinson said.

"Not as good as it feels," Maureen replied. "Thanks for saying that. It was a long six weeks. I'm glad to put them behind me."

"So you put the time to good use, then?" Atkinson asked.

Maureen's heart stopped for a moment. There was no way Atkinson could know what she'd been doing at night. No, no way. She chewed the inside of her cheek. *This* is why you don't do shit like that, running around causing trouble and breaking promises, she thought. A guilty conscience gives everything a double meaning. It eats your insides alive.

"If I was having any doubts about where I want to be and what I want to be doing," Maureen said, kicking aside dead magnolia leaves, "I'm cured. The time did that much for me."

"I was pulling for you," Atkinson said. "Still am. Like I said when the shit started going down, you can be an exceptional cop if we can keep you out of jail."

Maureen hung her head and grinned. "Skinner said something similar. I'm looking to steer clear of any more trouble in the department. I'm content with the DC forgetting who I am for a year or so, until I've earned a promotion."

"You know why we haven't spoken before now," Atkinson said.

"No one was supposed to be talking to me," Maureen said. "And you're Homicide, over at HQ. I know Skinner wanted to keep things as much in the district as possible."

"I can't even give the impression," Atkinson said, "that I'm reaching into his shop for my own ends. I can't disrespect him like that."

"I wasn't waiting for it," Maureen said. "For you to swoop in and save me. You, Preacher, anybody. I knew what I had to do. I did it. And here I am. Case closed."

"You've probably heard it already," Atkinson said, "but you haven't heard it from me, and I was there at the river, at the end. And I know my opinion matters to you. Quinn didn't become who he was because you showed up. The rot got inside him years ago. Ruiz, too. Everyone who dealt with Quinn knew what he was, who he was. Some approved, some didn't, some changed their minds about what side they were on after things turned bad for him, but we knew the truth about him. It's not on you. It's not your fault things went so hard for him. And you're not stained with what he did or how he ended up. Not as a cop, and not as a person. Anybody worth *anything* in this department knows that. You should, too."

"You know how it goes," Maureen said. "You can understand things intellectually, but the rest of you can be slow to catch up. It's human nature to look back on bad shit and wonder what you could've done different. I'm getting there. About a lot of things." She unzipped her jacket, reached inside for her cigarettes. She offered one to Atkinson, who accepted. "And maybe guilt-wise I'm not stained with Quinn's bad decisions, but in other ways I am. I'm that girl who that bad thing happened to. That girl cop who was mixed up in that thing with Quinn. I don't want to be that girl that bad thing happened to that one time. I don't want that name."

She paused, weighing what to say next. "I've already been that person. It *sucks*. It's part of the reason I left New York."

"Make a new name for yourself," Atkinson said. "That's your answer."

"You say it like it's easy."

"No, it's not easy," Atkinson said. "And you, you're always in such a hurry. That's what upsets you, that you can't make that new name in a week. I've never met anyone less afraid of hard work and who works with so little patience at the same time."

Patience. Atkinson's favorite word. There was a reason they called her the Spider. She used time as a weapon, wielding silence like a hammer, like no one Maureen had ever seen. Maureen thought of Preacher's comments at the PJ's about going from the shithouse to the penthouse in record time. If there was ever a way to sell her on something, Maureen knew, the promise of a quick trip was it. She remembered that Preacher had said it was Atkinson who'd sent Detillier the FBI agent looking for her. A move that made bringing Maureen back on the job that much more appealing to DC Skinner. Atkinson hadn't saved her, Maureen thought, but she had helped her.

"The FBI guy, Detillier," Maureen said. "He's going to be interested in this. He asked about Leary when I talked to him the other morning. He wanted to meet her."

"You think he knows she's dead yet?"

"I doubt it," Maureen said. "Nobody here knows the FBI cared about her except for me and you and Preacher. He thinks she was the FBI's best bet for information on the Watchmen. So much for that."

Atkinson shook her head. "All those resources and chasing the same homeless schizophrenic we were chasing is the best they can do?"

"That's what I said," Maureen said. "Though to hear Detillier tell it, their resources aren't any more plentiful than ours. I told him he was wasting his time with her. That they should be bearing down on the Heaths."

"Ah. A nonstarter, I'm guessing?"

"What do you think?" Maureen said. "Even Preacher's telling me to drop the subject. Tomorrow afternoon, I'm having that meeting with Leon Gage, the one that Detillier requested. I'm sure I'll be talking to Detillier after that. What do you want me to tell him? How do you want me to handle what happened tonight?"

"Don't worry about me and the FBI," Atkinson said. "I can handle them. If Leary was nothing but a lead on the Watchmen to Detillier, he'll lose interest in her. It's not like she had friends for him to talk to. I'll have the case to myself, which is how I like it."

"The case?"

"Let me ask you," Atkinson said, "what do you think happened here tonight?"

"Suicide, obviously," Maureen said. "She was mentally unstable and off her meds. At least, she was six weeks ago. I can't imagine things had improved for her since then, when she'd been *killing* people. The Watchmen are hunting her. We're hunting her. God only knows what demons she had chasing her all her life. She had no allies, no family, no money. The razor was right there by her hand." She paused. "But somebody called it in. We came to the cemetery because somebody reported a body inside. You think someone else was here while she was still alive?"

Atkinson shrugged. "Maybe, probably. People sneak in here three, four nights a week. Somebody unrelated to the incident could've seen her, thought she was already dead, called it in. That's not what bothers me."

"Why do it up here in the Garden District?" Maureen asked.

Atkinson looked around. "Pretty glorious cemetery. Probably not many paranoid schizophrenics in here."

"Trust me," Maureen said, "there's plenty. They were just rich."

"Fair point," Atkinson said. "But think about this. True, from what we know of her, Leary lived downtown, but the killing she did, at least the ones that we know about, she did uptown. Cooley was killed in Central City. And then Gage was killed, what, a mile and a half from here? So she stole in the Quarter, lived in the Bywater and the Marigny, but she did her murder up here. It's pretty consistent to find her here when you think about it."

"Except for the fact that this time she was her own victim."

Atkinson shook her head. "Nope."

"What is it, then?"

Atkinson raised her hand and touched her cold fingertip to the artery in Maureen's throat. "That right there? With a blade like Leary carried? That's a flick of the wrist. Less effort than it takes to toss a bottle cap across the room. The wound she had? It's vicious. That's a murder wound if I ever saw one."

Maureen touched her throat, put her finger where Atkinson's had been. She could feel her pulse throbbing underneath her skin, still warm where Atkinson had touched it. The detective was right, of course. Seemed obvious now. No matter how much she hated herself, no matter how crazy she was, Leary couldn't cut herself deep and wide like that, couldn't open herself up like that without flinching, without collapsing or dropping the razor.

"So who killed her?"

"That question, Officer Coughlin, is why I get out of bed every afternoon." Atkinson tilted her head back and touched her own jugular. "This. I keep coming back to this. Had to be someone who knew her. Someone who knew how she worked. Someone whose purpose would be served by killing her just this way, the way she killed the others."

"Revenge," Maureen said.

"Who's in town raising hell over his dead son?" Atkinson asked.

Maureen thought again of Dice, of her warnings. She'd have to be careful about what she told Atkinson. But she did have to tell. "Listen, I saw Dice the other night. I was downtown, on Frenchmen, for a show. She appeared out of nowhere, must have followed me to my car."

"I should've heard about this sooner."

"I was suspended," Maureen says. "I wasn't supposed to talk to anyone on the job."

Atkinson frowned at her. "You pick that night to follow the rules."

"Okay, you're right, I could've made it work," Maureen said. "Anyway, I'm telling you now. She told me there were rumors in the streets about someone looking for Leary. Somebody had been working the downtown neighborhoods at night, asking questions about her to the street kids. A man. Dice thought he might be NOPD."

"She give you a description?"

"She hadn't seen the man herself," Maureen said. "She'd just heard that he was looking."

"I thought she was your snitch," Atkinson said. "She didn't bring you anything else?"

"I wouldn't go that far. She's not my snitch."

"What does this person want with Leary?" Atkinson asked.

"Dice didn't say. She didn't know. She just asked me to back off."

Atkinson raised her eyebrows. "Why would she ask you that?"

"You know what I mean," Maureen said, recovering. "She asked me to maybe get this other cop to back off. She seemed concerned for Leary's safety. Like maybe the search was more personal than professional."

Atkinson walked over to a marble bench in front of one of the larger tombs. She sat, leaned her elbows on her knees. That marble has to be ice cold, Maureen thought.

"You think Gage did this?" she asked. "You think he knows Leary killed his son?"

"I'm assuming he knows how his son died," Atkinson said. "What kind of wound he suffered. If she has a history, he might recognize the method. I don't know who she is to him. I don't know what he knows about her, or even about his son."

"Revenge would explain why he's in New Orleans," Maureen said. "Revenge and to shut Leary up if he's involved with the Watchmen himself. He had to figure she'd fall into our hands eventually, by way of a shelter, jail, or the emergency room. There weren't really any other options for her. Asking about the death of his son would be good cover for being in the city." She paused. "But then why tell the cops you're here in the first place if you're in town to commit a murder? Why not do the deed and slip back out of town?"

"Unless he figures there's no way for him to hide being in New

Orleans," Atkinson said. "Like, say for example, he knows the feds are interested in him."

"Fuck me," Maureen said. "Detillier told me the FBI was in the dark on this guy. That's why I'm meeting him tomorrow."

"Detillier told you that?" Atkinson asked. "That they'd never heard of Leon Gage before he came to New Orleans?"

"Not that exactly," Maureen said. "He made it sound like Clayton was the one they were interested in, that Leon had just popped up because of Clayton's death."

Atkinson raised her shoulders, turned up her empty palms. "Making one thing sound like another. Sure sounds like the feds to me."

"That motherfucker."

"Don't feel bad," Atkinson said. "That's how they do. I think sometimes it's unconscious. He might not even know he was playing you." She stood. "And maybe I'm completely wrong about Detillier. Maybe Gage is here for the reasons he gave and didn't think he'd find her and he took advantage of an opportunity. Maybe she set it up, the meeting in the cemetery, like she did the other two killings, maybe *that's* what really brought Gage to New Orleans, and it just went wrong for her."

"You believe all that?" Maureen asked.

"I have to be open to every possibility," Atkinson said.

"But do you believe any of what you said?"

"About as much as I believe Leary's death was a suicide." Atkinson shivered and zippered her coat. Finally, Maureen thought, the cold is getting to her. She's human. Atkinson said, "Can you find that girl again? Dice. I want to talk to her. She's the only person we know in the city who knows a thing about Leary."

"I didn't find her," Maureen said. "She found me."

"I know you've tried to help Dice," Atkinson said. "To build trust, a rapport. That's good police work. If you can produce her, I don't have to send other cops who don't know her like you do looking for her. If you can find her, things'll go easier for her."

"That sounds ominous."

"It is what it is," Atkinson said. "It's not news that the Eighth District and the gutter punks are not real collegial with each other."

"It's not my district. Won't I be stepping on toes?"

"Since when has that stopped you?"

If you only knew, Maureen thought. "I'm trying to stay out of trouble, remember?"

Atkinson said nothing.

"I'll see what I can do," Maureen said. She hadn't been able to find Dice on her own for the past few weeks, and it wasn't like she'd suddenly get good at it.

"Tomorrow," Atkinson said, "y'all will come back and canvass the blocks around the cemetery, right? Should you turn up a witness, if Dice could get us a description of the man asking questions, you see how that could help? Maybe the descriptions will match."

"Detillier can give you a description of Gage," Maureen said, "if that's all you need. Look, Gage is meeting me at L'il Dizzy's at one o'clock. You show up instead of me and arrest him. Easy."

"I don't think Agent Detillier would appreciate that plan."

"Well, fuck him. He put his plan in place before Leary turned up dead."

"Look," Atkinson said, "I don't trust the guy, but that doesn't mean I don't believe in his case. He's chasing guys out to kill cops, out to kill you. You want to get in the way of that?"

"Okay, I'll talk to Gage," Maureen said. "And after, I'll call you, tell you what I've found out about him. I'll let you fight it out with the FBI over him." She looked away from Atkinson, stared back in the direction of where she'd found Leary. That corner of the cemetery glowed now, bright as an operating room. "I'm having lunch tomorrow with the guy who did that."

"You do good police work tomorrow," Atkinson said, "and if he did it, we get him for it. Maybe we get him and a bunch like him before they do worse. There's always worse."

"No pressure," Maureen said. She turned back to Atkinson. "Any advice?"

"Go early," Atkinson said. "Eat before he gets there. He sees you have no appetite you might make him nervous. He shouldn't frighten you, or anger you. None of that. You're not supposed to know anything about him. He's a grieving father from LaPlace and you're a courteous, helpful policewoman."

"So we both show up full of shit and lie to each other. Sounds like a plan."

"Wear your vest," Atkinson said. "And keep one in the chamber."

17

Li'l Dizzy's was a small, busy café in the Tremé, famous for its fried-chicken-anchored lunch buffet. Preacher had turned her on to the place, taking her there a few times during her training days, the café being a central hub of New Orleans's Creole power structure. On any given weekday afternoon, the café buzzed with cops, lawyers, judges, and city politicos on their way to or from the nearby courthouses and police headquarters. A lot of business, city and otherwise, Maureen was sure, got conducted at those lunch tables.

When Gage walked into the restaurant, half an hour late, Maureen knew him right away. Detillier had provided an accurate description. Looking at him, though, trying to get a first read on him as he crossed the room, Maureen realized that despite being told what Gage looked like, she had expected someone much different. She'd expected someone more backwoods, more swamp. She'd expected leathered skin, long hair, and a wild beard. She'd expected camouflage and Confederate flags.

A cliché. Lazy, Officer Coughlin, very lazy. She thought of Atkinson. Stay open to the possibilities.

The man walking toward her was below average height, underfed, cubicle-pale. He kept his thinning brown hair trimmed short, wore a bushy brown mustache. A couple of days' worth of stubble threaded with white whiskers shadowed his cheeks and throat. He wore a yellow shirt under a Carhartt jacket, brown trousers, and a hideous brown-and-gold-striped tie, discount store brown loafers with black socks. His clothes hung on him, Maureen noticed, like they would on a scarecrow. He appeared a man burdened by suffering. If he was faking his grief, she thought, he'd built a hell of a disguise.

"Detective Coughlin?" Gage asked, placing a hand on the back of the chair opposite Maureen, his scratchy voice barely audible above the din of the busy restaurant. He had the bright blue eyes of a different man, a handsome man, Maureen noticed, but not the chin or the cheekbones, and his lips were almost feminine.

Maureen rose, extending her hand across the table. "Officer Coughlin. You can call me Maureen."

Gage hesitated a moment, as if he hadn't shaken a hand in so long he had to remember how. But then he reached for Maureen's hand. He had a solid grip. "Leon Gage. Thanks for meeting me."

The waitress appeared at the table, a slip of a black girl in jeans and a Dizzy's T-shirt, apron tied around her waist, her hair pulled back, nineteen at the most. She'd brought the coffeepot, refilled Maureen's mug without asking. "Something for you?" she asked Gage. Again he looked confused. He looked at Maureen.

"I ate," she said. "But, please, take advantage of the buffet. You'll be glad you did. They'll be putting it up soon."

"No, no, thank you," Gage said. "I ate earlier. A sweet tea, maybe?"

"Maybe or yes?" the waitress asked.

To Maureen's surprise, Gage smiled. He moved one degree closer to handsome when he did so. "Yes, thank you."

Neither spoke until the waitress delivered Gage's tea.

"I take it you know why I'm here," Gage said.

"You have questions," Maureen said, "about the death of your son."

"I do, I do," Gage said. He reached into his bag. He pulled out a digital recorder, set it in the middle of the table.

Maureen eyed the recorder. Gage had turned it on. She covered it with her hand, pushed the device across the table. "We won't be recording this conversation, Mr. Gage. You can put this away."

"Many people would consider your refusal to go on the record as an admission of something to hide," Gage said. "If our roles were reversed, you would use it against me, as cause for suspicion."

"Consider it anything you like," Maureen said. "I'm willing to discuss whatever it is that troubles you about what happened to your son. But we won't be recording anything."

Gage raised his eyebrows. "You've already told me so much. Thank you."

He returned the device to his bag. Maureen wasn't sure he'd turned it off.

"You wouldn't believe what it's like trying to have a simple conversation in this city," Gage continued. "The police, the coroner's office. Or maybe you would. Doing what you do."

He set his elbows on the table, leaned a bit forward. "And I'm not uncomfortable with the word *murder*. Because that's what it was. Murder. I am not a fearful man. Fear is how we lose our truth, by obscuring things from the very beginning of the story. Hiding the truth for the sake of people's *feelings*, or for correctness, or to pass along responsibility for it. My son didn't die. He didn't have a stroke. He didn't drown. He didn't fall down a flight of stairs. He was *killed*. On purpose. As a choice someone made. That difference in wording, that specificity, acknowledges that someone, a free individual, bears responsibility for him being dead." He paused. "I want that acknowledgment made and sustained."

"Consider it so acknowledged," Maureen said, resenting being made to feel like she was on the witness stand. If any one person bore prime responsibility for Clayton Gage's death, she figured, it was Clayton Gage.

He'd made choices of his own. She figured withholding that opinion from his father was best.

"Most people," she said, "don't have your fortitude when it comes to the truth. It'll make this conversation easier if I don't have to hold anything back. And neither should you."

Gage frowned at his tea as if he regretted ordering it. "So you're not a detective, then? You said 'officer' when I sat down. You're not from Homicide?"

"I am not," Maureen said. Why hadn't Detillier told this man, she wondered, that he'd be talking to a patrol officer? For the same reason, she realized, that she'd made him meet her in a restaurant full of black people and Creoles. To knock him off balance. "I am one of the first officers to become involved in your son's case. I was involved from the very beginning."

"So you were with my son when he died," Gage said, using his fingertip to press his glasses against the bridge of his nose. He did that whenever he finished a sentence, Maureen noticed, whether or not the glasses had moved.

"No," Maureen replied. "I was not with him." Time to test Gage's love of the truth. "As far as I know, Clayton was alone when he died." He'd been found lying spread-eagled with his throat cut open like Leary had, Maureen thought. Like her, left in a place where he'd be found not long after he'd died.

"You're the one who found his body, then?" Gage asked.

"I am not," Maureen said. "A college junior named—well, doesn't matter what his name was—found Clayton's body. Outside a bar uptown."

Gage shifted in his chair. He reached into his bag again, tossed a pen on the table. Next came a yellow legal pad. He flipped through several pages of notes written in impossibly tiny, impossibly neat handwriting. "I know about where Clayton was found, how he was found. But maybe I could talk to that boy, then. I'd like to know exactly what he saw. I've been to that bar, but no one there was very helpful. I'll go back."

"Talking to that witness is not going to happen," Maureen said. "No way. And I'd advise you not to return to that bar. Clayton's murder remains an open police investigation. Conducting your own investigation would be considered interference, a criminal act."

"Is that an official warning?" Gage asked. "Are you authorized as a patrol officer to give it?"

"Mr. Gage, I am here to help you," Maureen said, "and as a courtesy to you and your family."

Gage raised his hands, shaking his head, as if only then realizing he'd spoken those last thoughts aloud. "Okay. Of course. Understood. I just, I'm confused." He paused, looked away from her, frowning at a television, not really watching what was on the screen, a rerun of the local news noon broadcast. Maureen watched the images play across his glasses. He said, "So why are you the one I'm talking to? I asked for that detective, Drayton."

Maureen shook her head. "Drayton's no longer on the case. Consider yourself lucky."

"They could've told me that when I called headquarters," Gage said, pen at the ready. "So who has the case now?"

"I don't know," Maureen said, lying, and not sure why she was doing it as she did it. "They don't tell me these things."

"But you knew the other detective had been removed. You knew that."

"Police station gossip," Maureen said.

"But no one gossips about who gets the case?"

Gage took his glasses off, looked at them as if wondering where the moving images had gone. He put them back on. He waved his hand back and forth over the table. "And we're supposed to believe it's not intentional."

"What's that?"

"The lies, the confusion, the manipulation." Gage picked dead skin from his bottom lip, studied it, flicked it off the tip of his thumb. He leaned back in his seat, crossing his arms over his sunken chest. "Did you know that it took the coroner three weeks to find me, to tell me that my son had been murdered?" He pinched his bottom lip. "The little bits, the specks of information we get, so that we think we're getting answers, that we're being paid attention to. They toss us crumbs, like we're birds at the park, and call it a meal. Call it a courtesy."

"I can tell you why it took so long to find you," Maureen said.

"Sometimes I'm shocked they looked for me," Gage said. "I'm surprised Clayton didn't go right to the incinerator like some homeless nobody."

Maureen took a deep breath. She needed to settle him down if she wanted to control the conversation. "I'm sorry it's so frustrating, especially in a time of such grief. Believe me, I empathize. I work in the system. It can be infuriating."

"It's *built* to be infuriating," Gage said, "for anyone who has a thought in his head. That's my point. That's its power. It's the power the tar pits had over the dinosaurs."

"And the rest of us, those of us without thoughts?"

Gage didn't think she was funny. "For the thoughtless, for the passive, it offers enough to pacify. I often wish I was one of them."

"Right," Maureen said. "The crumbs."

She slid her coffee mug aside, folded her hands on the table.

"We couldn't find you, Mr. Gage, because Clayton didn't carry a single valid form of ID. His driver's license wasn't only out of date, it was fake. We had no access to any records of him. We had to use the truck, registered to you, at an address you haven't lived at in years. A house that was condemned and torn down." Maureen paused. "A lot of effort was in fact expended trying to find you. You're a hard man to track down. And that doesn't seem to be accidental. You can't dodge the system and then complain when it doesn't serve you."

Gage looked away, taking a deep breath, using the moment to collect himself. He smoothed his tie with one hand and turned back to Maureen. "When y'all find a car, abandoned, stolen, whatever, and you need to find out about it, what do you use?"

"The license plate," Maureen said, "the registration. If that's no good, like in your son's case, we go to the VIN. We can get a lot from that usually."

"And a gun," Gage said. "You recover a gun used in a crime, or take one off a criminal, you look for the serial number, run it through your computers, see if that gun has a history."

"True. That's why people try so hard to destroy the serial numbers. Destroying that number can hide a lot of bad things."

"When you were born," Gage said, "you got your name, Maureen, which your parents gave you, based on their desires and their histories. Do you know the history of your name?"

"Of the name Maureen? I have no idea. I know my mom wanted me named after her mother, Morrigan, which is the name of some war goddess from Irish mythology. My father thought it was too . . . aggressive. And he worried it was too weird for where we lived. He was a soft, uncreative man. Maureen was a compromise. Another battle my mother lost to my father's charm, to hear her tell it. Or maybe that was Grandma Fagan who said that, the Morrigan of the story." She shrugged. "That's the history as my mother tells it. My father isn't around to argue."

"So, as I said," Gage said, "your name is the product of your parents. Well, the next thing you got when you were born was your Social Security number, which the government gave you. Now why was that?"

Maureen sighed. She had every confidence Leon Gage would answer his own question if she let him. She resisted the urge to check the time on her phone. Why had she agreed to this meeting? This was the guy Detillier had pinned his hopes on? Good luck with that. He carried his share of rage, that was for sure, but she was having a hard time imagining him cutting someone's throat in a cemetery. He seemed like the kind of man who yelled at the television news. Maybe that was why he kept throwing glances at the TV.

"We pay into the system when we start working," Maureen said, "and then we get paid by it when our turn comes. I guess. Sounds pretty simple and fair to me. You give, then you get. I haven't thought about it much."

Gage chuckled. "That's exactly the way they want you. Thoughtless. Oblivious."

"Ah," Maureen said, nodding. "The ominous *they*. I was wondering when *they* would show up." Maybe, somehow, she thought, this conversation would get entertaining.

"You know anyone who goes to work at birth?" Gage asked. He checked his watch, glanced at the television again. His mouth hung open. He appeared to be thinking, calculating what he would say next. He refocused on Maureen. "Why give you a number then? You won't work for at least, what, fifteen years after you're born. Why is that number assigned at birth?"

"Because it's our serial number," Maureen said, shrugging in surrender to Gage's wisdom. "And Social Security is a scam, a veil or distraction to cover up that fact. It's how the government controls us. I have seen the light. I thought you wanted to talk about your son?"

"You're making fun of me," Gage said. "I don't mind. Everyone does. In the beginning. We're conditioned to think a certain way. It's a strange education; I went through it myself. But you wait, you'll find yourself thinking about what I said here today. At night. When you're alone, when you turn on your computer. That's how it starts. The questions make too much sense to ignore."

"Mr. Gage," Maureen said, "do you consider yourself a Sovereign Citizen?" Fuck it, she thought. Why not come right out with it? If he was going to open that door, she figured, she might as well walk through it. She was losing her patience with Gage's condescending tone. If Detillier and Atkinson wanted finesse in the questioning, they could sit with this tedious bastard their damn selves.

Gage gestured for the waitress to refill his iced tea. He waited until she brought back the glass to speak. Maureen noticed he never looked at her once. Never thanked her.

"Do I consider myself a free man?" Gage said. "Do I consider myself a unique legal and spiritual individual, with human rights and freedoms endowed to me by my Creator and enshrined, at one time in history, into man's law by the Founding Fathers? Yes, I do." He fished the lemon from his tea, squeezed every last drop of juice from it. "Do I belong to a specific group whose members answer to that name, or any name? I do not. You can't be the first person I described and also be the second." He leaned forward over the table. "You have to choose."

"Are you familiar with the Watchmen Brigade?" Maureen asked.

"I've heard of them."

"Are you a member?"

"I am a member of the human race," Gage said. "Everything else is subservience."

"Do you believe in their cause?"

Gage grinned. "I get the feeling you and I would define their cause very differently. I believe that patriots exist in this country. That they thrive here. They always have. I believe they do their thankless work in the service of freedom in each of our fifty states. I believe there are many more of them than you know, or care to think about."

He checked his watch, glanced across the room at the television.

"*Freedom*," Maureen said. "You like that word. Your kind always do. Your eyes light up when you say it, like a baby shown a brightly colored ball."

"It's an important word," Gage said. "Everybody loves it. Empires tremble at its sound. It belongs to no one *kind*. It's Joshua's trumpet. Unfortunately, only a few people truly understand what it means."

"I'm gonna guess that you're one of those people," Maureen said.

"The great myth of the past one hundred and fifty years is the end of slavery. The War of Northern Aggression was like every war about the expansion of power by the already powerful. It wasn't about anybody's freedom. It was about the *expansion* of slavery.

"Certainly, our national slavery mutated, like a disease, like a virus, hiding itself in order to survive. Growing, changing, always consuming as monsters do—as the government tossed aside its Stone Age weapons of whips and chains and learned to use its great new modern weapons of debt and taxation. You are a tool, Maureen. A faceless machine with a serial number. You're a car, a computer, a gun with a number used to track your personal history and financial value to the host. You live, you work, you breathe, and you breed to feed the government. You don't buy a house from the men who built it. You buy it from the bank. You don't buy a car from the men who built it. You buy it from the bank. Where do you think the bank's money goes? Up the food chain to the already fat.

"And you, you risk your life every day for this system that devours you, that owns you, that makes you its enforcer. And yet the work you do doesn't earn you a place to live. No, for that you need to embrace forty years of debt to a billion-dollar company so they can buy whatever politicians make sure the system that enslaves you stays in place. You work like a slave, live like a slave, punish the other slaves, and because they let you dress in the blue colors of the American overseer, you call yourself free."

Gage checked his watch again. Maureen wondered why he had even come to this meeting. Why had he arranged it? Clearly he had someplace more important to be, and yet she could see he enjoyed unspooling his lecture. A long time had passed, Maureen figured, since he'd had the chance to lay his sermon on the uninitiated, on someone who hadn't heard every one of his dumb theories a thousand fucking times. She felt immense gratitude for whomever it was waiting on him. She felt sympathy for the poor bartender in whatever backwoods south Louisiana saloon who had to listen to this shit night in and night out.

"I see the spark of truth in you," Gage said, restless in his seat. "Every soul comes to the truth from different directions, like the streams to the sea. There is no one way home. You want to let them lie to you, that's your choice, it's not like you can stop them, but don't lie to yourself. That's the greatest sin. The only prisoner God hates is the one who holds fast to his cell after He has opened the door."

Gage rose from his chair, his face slightly pale. His preaching had taken something out of him. He was so eager to depart that, despite being sick to death of him, Maureen felt compelled to make him stay. To irritate him. He'd leave when she decided he would. She hadn't learned anything useful from him. Not for Detillier or Atkinson. She was determined to pull something worthwhile out of this meeting.

"Do you really want to know what happened to your son?" Maureen asked. "The patriot?" She gestured at his chair, making it clear she wouldn't continue until and unless he sat. Curiosity flickered in his eyes. Gage sat.

"Did you know what your son was doing here in New Orleans?" Maureen asked. "He was running guns for criminals, for gangs that deal in the murder of children and the sale of narcotics, and for organizations classified by federal law enforcement as domestic terrorists. Organizations like the Watchmen that target law enforcement for murder."

Gage leaned over the table. "Slander. Conspiracy." He stabbed the center of the legal pad with his bony finger. "Right here, I want you to put a piece of paper right here that proves those things are true. Something better than the cop-forced confession of a dead black drug dealer."

"Did you know what Clayton was doing," Maureen said, "and if those activities might be what got him killed?"

"A person is what killed him."

"Technically, having his throat opened up with a straight razor," Maureen said, "is what killed your son. I want to know what happened before that. During the days, the weeks before he was killed."

"My son was his own man." Gage's leg bounced like mad under the table.

"Did he come to New Orleans looking for a woman named Madison Leary? Did he come here because she stole from him? Did he come here to kill her?"

Did you?

"My son was a patriot," Gage said. "Which makes him the natural enemy of people like you. That's why you're so eager to believe slanders against him."

"Can you tell me anything useful to catching your son's killer," Maureen asked, "or do you want to talk some more about the Constitution? Do you, Clayton's father, know *anything* about your son's life?"

"Would you believe anything I told you," Gage said, "that didn't conform to the lies you choose to believe?"

"Mr. Gage," Maureen said, "we're trying to figure out if your son's numerous criminal activities, trafficking in illegal weapons chief among them, led to Clayton's tough exit from this mortal world. I vote yes, but we're open to contrary opinions. We stay open to all possibilities. Do you have anything to offer either way? Any specific enemies you can point at? Names, maybe?"

"You do enjoy hearing yourself talk," Gage said.

"Almost as much as you do," Maureen said. "Our interests are aligned, you and the NOPD, as much as that may turn your stomach. We both want to catch the person who killed your son. If you think he had enemies, do tell, I'm all ears."

"I doubt that we have any interests in common," Gage said. "I doubt that very much." He snatched his pen and legal pad off the table, stuffed them into his bag. He rose from his seat. "You know, you're the first cop I talked to who hasn't said 'sorry for your loss' or something like that."

"On the record," Maureen said, rocking back in her chair, "as a representative of the New Orleans Police Department, let me express my condolences. I am sorry for your loss. Off the record, and knowing how you feel about liars, I'll do you the courtesy of the truth. Your son conspired to murder police officers. I am one of those officers. I have bullet holes in my house to prove it. Mr. Gage, the only thing I regret about your son's death is that I didn't get him first."

Gage stared at her. Maureen expected an explosion of rage, it was the response she'd been after, but she could've sworn he stood there fighting back a smile. He said nothing before turning away and striding out the door. Maureen watched him go. Much better self-control then she'd anticipated. So much for provoking him. An amateurish strategy.

When the door closed behind him, she bowed her head, pinching the bridge of her nose. She had certainly fucked that up. She hadn't even raised the subject of Caleb Heath. The name Madison Leary had gone nowhere. Nothing helpful to Atkinson. She'd be going back to everyone empty-handed. She wondered if she could concoct an excuse for another interview. When she thought about it, Gage hadn't gotten anything out of her, either. Why had he even asked to meet her? To recruit her for the cause? A waste of everyone's time.

Maybe she'd ask Detillier for another crack at the man. Maybe when she went looking for witnesses in the Garden District that night she would actually find one. She wanted to go looking for Dice only as a last resort.

The waitress appeared at the table, coffeepot in her hand. Maureen covered her mug. She looked up at the girl. "No thanks. Just the check, please."

The girl pulled a check presenter from her apron and laid it on the table. "I didn't charge you for his sweet tea." She looked at the door. "I didn't like that man."

Maureen opened her purse on her lap, digging for her wallet, her bulletproof vest digging into the small of her back. "Me, either, girlfriend. Me, either."

18

Outside the café, Maureen put a cigarette between her lips and buttoned her coat against the cold afternoon. She lit up and sat at one of the empty outside tables to call Atkinson. The detective's phone went right to voice mail. Maureen couldn't decide what to say, so she left no message. No harm, she figured, in calling Detillier right away. She'd tell him everything Gage had said to her. Maybe that mumbo jumbo the man had spouted would mean something to the FBI. Maybe they'd hear a code in his language, something over her head that the FBI would find useful. Maybe something would surface that helped Atkinson. She wasn't optimistic. She found Detillier's number in her phone, punched it, and put the phone to her ear.

That was when she saw him across Esplanade Avenue, waving at her. His unbuttoned suit jacket and his tie fluttered in the wind. It was awful chilly, she thought, to be out in the street without an overcoat. Detillier stood in the street, on the edge of the traffic, on the balls of his feet, waiting for a chance to cross. The call connected as she watched him, but he made no move to answer. He seemed to be in a big, big hurry. Border-line frantic, she thought, judging by his body language. His head snapped back and forth, back and forth, like a metronome. He was clock-ing more than the traffic. What now?

She stood and looked up and down Esplanade Avenue. Gage was gone. Was that the problem? she wondered. Letting him walk away had been part of the plan. If the plan had changed while she was in the café, no one had thought to tell her. Fucking typical, she thought. Fucking bureau-crats. Detillier's voice mail started speaking to her. She disconnected the call. Detillier had made it to the grassy neutral ground. He waited for an-other break in the traffic. He looked behind him. Went back to watching the street. He was calling her name, like she should rush over there to him.

Maureen's phone buzzed in her hand. Atkinson. Fantastic, Maureen thought. How was that for timing? She answered. "Coughlin."

"Jesus Christ, Maureen," Atkinson said, out of breath. "Oh, thank God. Where are you?"

Maureen's heart had dropped into a hole. "I'm outside Dizzy's, in the Tremé. Right where I told you I'd be. Why do you sound like that? What's happened?"

Detillier was running across the street. He had his gun drawn.

Maureen lowered the phone. She could hear Atkinson ask, no, de-mand that Maureen talk to her. Maureen had never heard her sound anything like this. Shouting, yelling. Panic was something Atkinson didn't do. Hearing it terrified Maureen. A commotion arose inside the café. Maureen turned and looked in the window. Employees and customers alike had gathered, standing under the television. Even the cooks and dishwashers had come out of the kitchen. Maureen couldn't tell exactly what they were watching, but several people had their hands on their heads, or covered their mouths in clear horror. On the screen was an aer-ial shot of somewhere in the city. Sirens in the streets. Lots of sirens. She half-expected to see an overhead shot of her standing on the corner.

She looked up into the sky for the helicopters. Nothing but clouds. Gray and static. And in the distance, she could hear sirens.

Detillier jumped up onto the sidewalk. "Gage! Where is Gage?"

"He left not five minutes ago. He might still be in the neighborhood. I don't know where he parked. I didn't know I was supposed to follow him." She could hear Atkinson calling her name, asking what was happening. "That wasn't the plan. What the fuck is going on? Why is your gun out?"

"Who is that on the phone?"

Maureen felt the air go out of her chest. "It's Detective Atkinson." She felt like a fist was squeezing her heart. A wave of dizziness washed over her, threatened to melt her knees. Like it had a year ago on Amboy Road. She wasn't Atkinson. Panic was something she did often. No. Not now. Not now. "She's calling to see if I'm okay?" Her vision blurred. She could hear the quaver in her voice. "Why is she doing that? Why is she doing that?"

"You can talk to her on the way," Detillier said. He took her by the arm.

Maureen snatched her arm back. The adrenaline surge that came at his touch steadied her, brought her back to earth. "On the way where?"

"We have to move you, we have to do it now."

"What is going on? You said I'd be safe." Maureen looked at her phone. Atkinson had disconnected.

"A bunch of cops have been shot," Detillier said. His eyes moved to the television inside the café. He couldn't help himself.

"A bunch?" Maureen asked, almost laughing at the word. "A bunch?"

"They were ambushed, in different places around the city," Detillier said. "Four of them, so far."

"So far?"

"I'll explain later. We have to get you out of here."

Maureen heard more sirens in the distance now. The screaming seemed to come from every direction. "Are they dead?"

"We have to *go*."

"Are. They. Dead?"

"Maybe," Detillier said, his face dropping. He looked for a moment like he himself might collapse. "Maybe some. I don't know. I don't want to say." He looked over her shoulder. "It's a mess. It's a fucking mess. We can't talk here."

Maureen saw his eyes lock on to something behind her. Whatever he saw rallied his focus. "What kind of car was it the Watchmen used to shoot up your house?"

"A white van," Maureen said. "A commercial van. One with a door on the side that slides open." She turned around and saw what Detillier had spotted. "Just like that one coming up the street. Motherfucker."

A dingy white van idled at a stop sign three blocks back toward Rampart. The afternoon haze threw the shadows of the trees across the windshield. She couldn't see the driver. Maureen ran her tongue over her front teeth. Okay, then. She drew her Glock. She checked the safety. She'd already racked a bullet into the chamber. She spoke to Detillier with her eyes locked on the van. "I didn't see it myself, I was away from the house, but that's what the report said."

The van sat at the sign, a blue-gray plume of exhaust billowing behind it. Traffic had died on Esplanade, the afternoon after-lunch lull setting in. Or was the city on lockdown? Maureen could hear Detillier breathing over her shoulder. Might be an ordinary van, she thought. City was full of them. Every fly-by-night contractor and his brother drove an old, beat-up white van. But the timing, she thought. The timing. The right front headlight was busted. A fender bender? she wondered. Or shot out in the getaway?

"The reports from the shootings," she asked, "they say anything about a van? Any of our guys get any shots off?"

"Not that I heard about," Detillier said. "The shooters walked into restaurants where the officers were eating and opened fire. One guy was killed at the scene, the other pair fled in the panic. That's what we know. This is an ongoing situation. We haven't found anyone yet who saw what they drove."

Maureen swallowed hard. Time to focus. "Okay. We need to get away from the restaurant right now." Or I do, she thought. Since I'm the target. The guys who'd shot up her house, they'd fired hundreds of rounds from some pretty heavy weapons. She had to draw fire away from the café. That was priority one.

"Get everyone inside Dizzy's into the back," she said. "Get them into the kitchen and away from the windows."

The van started rolling again in their direction. She walked quickly toward it, her gun hanging at her side, loose in her hand. She could get to the van before it reached the restaurant. The crepe myrtles on the neutral ground, the parked cars and trees and garbage cans along her side of Esplanade gave her cover. She didn't care if people in the van saw her coming. She *wanted* them to see her coming. She wanted their full attention. She sped up to a trot.

A car came up behind her, the engine revving. She nearly screamed at the sound of it. She drew her weapon. This was no cat in the graveyard. She ducked behind a big plastic trash bin, landing hard on her knees. Stupid, she thought, stupid, stupid fucking girl. She waited for the bullets to fly. She'd have no shot at them. Stupid girl, the van was a decoy and you fell for it. She'd left her back completely exposed, and let herself be drawn out into the open. Two fatal mistakes at the same time. Never let them get behind you, one of the first things Preacher had ever taught her. She could hardly believe there weren't bullets in her back already.

From her knees, her armpits soaked with sweat, looking from behind the trash bin she peeked around the back bumper of a parked VW bug. She watched a noisy old Buick rattle by, an old woman at the wheel barely tall enough to drive. That was her assassin. She emptied her lungs. "Jesus fucking Christ, Maureen. Get a grip."

She wondered what the driver of the van had seen. Did he know where she was? Had he seen where she was hiding? She crept behind the bug, crouched, leaning her hip against its bumper, her gun in front of her in both hands.

The van continued up Esplanade in her direction. Slowly.

Now she could see the dark form of the driver behind the wheel. She couldn't make out his face. Was he wearing a ski mask? Looked like it.

Or was his face darkened in shadow? The windshield was cracked and the driver's-side windows were filthy. She couldn't tell anything for sure. She watched the side door of the van. If that door moved, if it twitched, she would let loose. She wished she'd brought an extra clip. Who knew how many bullets she would need? Where the fuck was Detillier? How long did it take to move a handful of civilians to safety? Why wasn't he backing her up? Had he called for help? Why wasn't he flanking the van? This FBI motherfucker was a *trial*. She raised herself away from the car into a standing crouch.

She sighted the dark shape of the driver over the end of her gun.

That *was* a ski mask he was wearing.

It was, right?

She moved her finger to the trigger. She watched the side door of the van. She pictured the guys crouched behind it, imagined them in camouflage hunting gear, ski masks over their faces, their gleaming weapons at the ready. Like rapists, drooling on themselves, pulling at their big shiny belt buckles. Cowards. Disguised, hiding. They'd start shooting before the door was even all the way open. More rounds per second than she could possibly return. Bullets coming so fast they'd touch off flames where they landed. The gunfire thunder would be deafening, if she lived long enough to hear it. If she wasn't perforated where she stood like a paper target.

Her thighs ached from holding the crouch. Her ankle throbbed. The only good shot she'd have would be the first shot.

So pull it, Maureen, she thought. Pull it and be done with it. Pull the trigger on these motherfuckers. These cop-hating, cop-killing motherfuckers. Fuck being the one to shoot back. Be the one to shoot first. Make sure you're the last one breathing.

She followed the form of the driver with her gun, gritting her teeth, breathing hard through her nose, her palms slick with sweat.

And what if it isn't the Watchmen? she thought. What if you're wrong? What if it's some knucklehead in a dirty old van full of tools? Some poor dope in the wrong place at the wrong time.

She watched that side door. She watched the driver's-side window, waiting for the glass to slide down, for the barrel of a gun to appear over the top of the door.

If that door moves, if that glass moves, I'm shooting.

And what if he's rolling down his window to spit out his gum? Or flick away his cigarette butt? And you blow his head open for him because of it?

Look my way, driver, she thought. Look my way.

"Look at me. Look at me, look at me," she whispered.

Show me who you are, she thought. Because I don't wanna die here but I don't wanna kill an innocent person, either. Because if I kill the wrong person, everything is over. For him and for me. Everything. My career. My life. The great New Orleans experiment. Everything. Shot to hell. I'll die in prison for this mistake, she thought. That's if I don't jump in the Mississippi River first for killing an innocent bystander.

Am I gonna go out like that, she thought, because I let those bully militia limp-dick fucks scare me so badly I ran out into the street shooting at people like a madwoman?

That's what these fuckers want, she told herself. That's their power. This is how terrorists win. With you standing in the street, terrified, a gun in your hand, looking for someone, anyone, to shoot. Doing their killing for them, brainwashed and murderous, no better than a suicide bomber. If you make that fucking awful mistake, she thought, it's them that got you. It'll be them that fucked you, them that killed you and everything you wanted and were and would be.

Don't shoot, she thought. Don't pull that trigger. Stand your ground.

She lowered her gun and walked out into the street.

She heard Detillier calling her name from what seemed a mile away. The van window rolled down, glinting in the sun as it moved. The driver was revealed. He was a smiling guy with a bushy beard in a blue watch cap and a camouflage hunting jacket. No ski mask over his hairy face. He blew Maureen a kiss. She almost shot him for it.

The van picked up speed and headed down Esplanade toward the

I-10. Maureen memorized the plate number. She'd give it to Detillier. He'd call it in. Shooting the guy was one thing. Pulling him over and putting him through the ringer—hell, he'd never realize what a favor she'd done him. She heard Detillier calling her name from closer. He was heading toward her. She figured she should turn and look for him, but she didn't. Each thought she had seemed to take a long time to form and compute, like skywriting.

Maureen felt stunned by the quiet around her, to be standing in it, realizing how convinced she'd been that the air would roar with gunfire. A car, one of those tiny toylike Smart cars, rolled right up to her, the driver leaning on her horn, her phone at her ear. Maureen's reverie broke. She glanced down at her gun, then raised her eyes to meet the driver's. She saw the driver see the gun. The woman shrieked and threw her hands in the air, which Maureen enjoyed. She stood there in the street, staring down the driver until Detillier caught up to her.

He seemed afraid to come any closer and called her name from the sidewalk. Finally, she stepped back to the curb. The Smart car sped away.

"So it wasn't them," Detillier said. He ran his hand over his shining bald head. "Man, we scared the shit out of those people in Dizzy's."

"I don't know who the fuck that was in the van," Maureen said. "I have no idea. Could've been them. Could've been fucking with us. Could've backed down when we spotted them. They don't strike me as the type who get too brave when the prey starts shooting back."

"Speaking of," Detillier said. "You can put that gun away now." He glanced up and down the avenue. "We have to get you off the streets."

Maureen holstered her weapon. "I got the plate for that van."

"Great, great," Detillier said. He remained nervous.

She realized that the van could be making the block, preparing for another pass now that the shooters knew what they were up against. Detillier had started walking away.

"We take my car," he said. "I'll call in the plate from there. We're wasting time standing around here, especially if they've made it to the highway."

"Right. Okay." She pulled her phone from her pocket. She could feel herself returning to earth, could hear the sounds of the neighborhood again. "Okay. Okay." She scrolled through her contacts. She raised her other hand in a "stop" signal. "Before we do anything, I have to make a call. I have to call Preacher."

Detillier stopped walking. He took a couple of steps back to her. "Maureen, Preacher's one of the cops who got shot."

19

"Take me to him," Maureen shouted from the passenger seat of Detillier's sedan. "Take me to him right fucking now."

"I don't know where he is," Detillier said, his eyes fixed on the road as they hurtled up North Rampart Street, dodging traffic, running red lights, speeding away from Dizzy's and the Tremé, headed for the wide boulevard of Canal Street. "He was shot in Mid-City, at a place on Jeff Davis. I don't know what hospital he's going to."

"Get on the radio and find out," Maureen said. "Find out where he is. Find out if he's alive." She pounded her fist on the dash. "Right! Fucking! Now!"

"Let me fucking drive," Detillier shouted back. "There's nothing we can do about Preacher right now."

They caught the green light at the intersection of Rampart and Canal. Detillier muttered under his breath for the foot traffic to keep clear. Maureen braced herself against the dashboard as they sped through the intersection, the sedan bouncing hard over the streetcar tracks, tires screeching as Detillier hung a hard left onto Canal. Maureen saw stars as her shoulder slammed into the door, knocking her head on the window and the breath out of her lungs. They missed crashing into a parked car by half a foot, passing so close that Maureen could see the foam daiquiri cup in the console. She coughed as she fought to regain her breath.

Leaning forward in the driver's seat, Detillier stomped on the gas, swinging around slower traffic where he could, running lights, headed toward the river.

"This is an active-shooter situation," Detillier said. "It's not over."

"I'll find Preacher my fucking self," Maureen said, reaching for the sedan's police radio. Detillier slapped her hand away.

Maureen almost punched him. "What the fuck was that?"

"Are you not listening?" Detillier said. "If not to me then to the radio. We're on the job here, we're in a situation."

Maureen had not been listening to the radio chatter. The fate of Preacher was everything. She couldn't focus on the voices coming over the radio long enough to make sense of the frantic calls and commands rasping out of the speaker. She tried to tune in. SWAT was rolling. The harbor police were involved. Demands for roadblocks at the bridge and on the highway at the parish line, and at the Causeway and the Twin Span. She heard codes and orders that she knew weren't NOPD. Everyone in the area was on deck. Everyone. It made sense to call in other law enforcement, but she couldn't decipher what any of them were doing. She didn't know who was going where. From the sound of things, nobody was really in charge.

Near the foot of Canal, at the big palm-tree-flanked casino, Detillier made a hard right onto the much narrower two-lane Tchoupitoulas Street, bobbing and weaving as fast as he could through the business district toward Uptown. Maureen felt her brain beginning to catch up, to function and put things together in real time. She hadn't asked where

Detillier was taking her. He hadn't said. Now she had an idea, not of the physical destination but of what would be waiting for them when they arrived.

"Where are we going?" she asked. She rubbed her sore shoulder, touched the tender bump rising on her forehead. "We're going after them, aren't we?"

"We are," Detillier said, nodding.

"Where?"

"The Walmart. Pay attention to the radio, get me an update."

"You're shitting me." Maureen gripped the dash again with both hands, her eyes wide because Detillier had them pointed into oncoming traffic. "Whoa, whoa, whoa, the street turns one-way up here, one-way right at us."

Detillier jogged the sedan to the right, shifting off Tchoupitoulas onto Annunciation, sliding back into traffic headed in the right direction. They sped past the World War II museum, ducked under the highway. When they came out the other side of the highway overpass, Maureen could see helicopters in the sky up ahead, none of them over the Walmart.

"Trust me," Detillier said, "They're at the Walmart."

"That is ridiculous," Maureen said, shaking her head. "That's fucking ridiculous."

Detillier turned the car again and again, darting from side street to side street. Maureen clutched at the dashboard and the door handle, trying to prevent getting more damaged than she already had and trying to hatch an idea of how cop killers had ended up at Walmart.

"Preacher was shot in Mid-City," Detillier said. "The other shooting was right around here, on Poydras in the business district."

The overpass that they had just crossed under marked the unofficial border between Uptown and Downtown, Maureen thought. If you wanted to go toward the lake or across the river, or toward Baton Rouge or the southernmost parishes from the business district, you caught the highway here. Several arteries, almost *every* artery, out of town, Maureen realized, linked in this one place. But, she thought, the city streets *underneath* the highway tangled into a spaghetti pile of dead ends, oneways, cobblestone alleys, on-ramps, exit ramps, and construction detours. She knew people born and raised in New Orleans who got turned around enough down there to end up across the river. If you passed straight through and missed the highway, though, Tchoupitoulas shot you out of the spaghetti pile right at Religious Street, which led to the riverside Walmart. She guessed the shooters had panicked and had given up on trying to find the on-ramp that would let them get away.

"They were running for the Ten and got lost, so they went to ground at the most familiar territory they could find. Incredible." She paused, stunned by her own horrifying thoughts. "Holy shit. Well, either they're panicked and stupid and got lost or they're smart and strategizing, and when they were done killing cops they made a planned beeline for the biggest box of guns and hostages they could find."

They raced parallel to the river, the railroad tracks and the shipping wharves hidden behind a high concrete wall. They were back on Tchoupitoulas. Detillier kept making risky passes into the oncoming traffic. Near the river, large trucks made up a fair amount of that traffic. Their bleating steamship horns spiked Maureen's already frantic heart rate. Please don't let us kill someone, she thought. Please don't let us die. I never dreamed I'd want to find a fucking Walmart this bad.

The store materialized ahead of them on their right, the low, boxy building set deep inside its vast, mostly empty parking lot. The lot was massive, Maureen thought. Weird how few cars were there. Whoever had built the place had anticipated a lot of business they weren't getting. No, she thought, it's not the lack of cars that's weird. It's the lack of *police* cars. Of anything with a siren on it.

"Why are we the only ones here?" Maureen asked. She realized she hadn't seen him reach for the radio. If Detillier was so convinced the shooters had fled to the Walmart, why hadn't he called anyone else? FBI? NOPD?

He eased up on the accelerator.

"Why are we slowing down?" Actually, she thought, Detillier hadn't picked up the radio since they'd gotten into the car. He kept claiming not to know anything. Well then, why wasn't he calling someone and asking questions?

"This Walmart does terribly," Detillier said. "It's barely hanging on, and they stopped selling guns after they got looted in the storm." He threw Maureen a nervous glance. "But I'm guessing the people we're after didn't know that. Doesn't mean they're not armed to the teeth already. We should count on it."

"Point made," Maureen said. Her throat was so dry she could barely get the words out.

Detillier pulled the sedan into the very back of the parking lot, and threw the car into park. He stared straight ahead through the dirty windshield at the Walmart a hundred yards ahead.

"We gonna let anyone know where we are?" Maureen asked.

Detillier didn't answer. He watched the Walmart, listening to the radio.

Maureen's eyes dropped to the radio, as if she could read there whatever mysterious signal Detillier was hoping to discern from the chaotic chatter of orders, police codes, and panicked questions filling the car. She ground her teeth. What the fuck were they just sitting there for, doing *nothing*? Her breath got short, tears of rage again welling in her eyes. She palmed tears from her cheeks. She inhaled her snot and swallowed. She took a deep, deep breath, then exhaled long and slow.

She turned to Detillier.

"Can you just call someone? Anyone? There's got to be news about Preacher. I need to know. I can't make anything out of that mess on the radio."

Detillier raised his hand, gesturing, Maureen realized, for her to be quiet.

"And there it is," he said. "That's what I've been waiting for."

"There *what* is? For fuck's sake."

"The response to the first nine-one-one call"—he raised his chin in the direction of the Walmart—"from inside the Walmart. I was right. Those fuckers are in there. Someone fleeing the store called it in." He shifted the car into drive, rolled them toward the store. "Showtime."

20

They cruised slowly across the parking lot, giving the Walmart entrance a wide berth.

Maureen watched as the automatic doors opened and one person then another jogged out of the store, glancing over their shoulders as they ran. She could tell they were scared, but nobody was sprinting. Whatever had frightened them wasn't chasing them, and the danger was away from the front of the store. Maureen knew the Watchmen weren't coming out. Law enforcement would have to go in after them.

"We've got a description coming in over the radio," Detillier said.

Maureen listened as the NOPD dispatcher described the shooters. One male, one female. Possibly a couple. That could matter, be useful, Maureen thought; if they could be separated, maybe they could be used against each other. The dispatcher said the man was white, with a medium to solid build, about six feet, short black hair. The woman was also white, thin, long brown hair, about five-six. The shooters were dressed alike. Camouflage cargo pants, black boots, body armor, fingerless gloves.

An invented, secondhand uniform. This was good, Maureen thought. They'd be easier to distinguish from any remaining customers in the store.

Both were heavily armed, carrying automatic rifles, AK-47s or something similar. It should be anticipated, the dispatcher said, that they carried sidearms as well. And while there had not been visual confirmation on these two shooters, the Mid-City shooter, the one who'd shot Preacher, and who had been killed on-site, had been carrying grenades.

"Jesus fucking Christ," Maureen said. "This is unreal." She looked at Detillier, who watched the front of the store and nodded his head at every detail the dispatcher related. "You ever seen something like this before?"

He went on nodding. "This is how it happened in Vegas. This is how it happened in Memphis. Right down to the fucking Walmart."

"And how did it end those other times?" Maureen asked.

"Ugly," Detillier said. They moved closer to the store as Detillier drove in smaller circles. "These things, with people like this, they can't end any other way. You try to limit the damage."

Maureen pointed a finger at him, sitting up on one knee in the passenger seat. "You know. You know if Preacher's dead or if he's alive and you're not telling me. Why are you not telling me?"

"I wouldn't tell you a thing I'd heard," Detillier said, "even if I had heard something. Because there's better than a fifty-fifty chance that whatever I'd tell you was wrong. Information in these crazy situations is unreliable. Think about that. I need you to focus, Maureen. I need your full attention on the matter at hand. We're walking into an active-shooter situation, a potential hostage situation. You gotta be here now. There's no fucking telling what you're going to be asked to do. You have to be ready for anything."

Detillier parked the car.

He'd put them off to the far right side of the entrance, away from the front doors, the sedan parked at an angle behind a huge black pickup truck they could use for cover. A trio of scraggly parking-lot trees helped to shield them as well. Maureen understood Detillier's strategy. From where he'd positioned them, they couldn't be shot at out the front door. They'd see anyone exiting the store before that person saw them. They'd see anyone who'd slipped out the back of the building and came around the right side of the store. Anyone who slipped out the left side would be more than a hundred yards away from them when they appeared. Detillier had left the Watchmen no direct shots or angles of sneak attack.

"We're not waiting for backup," Maureen said. "Are we?"

"We're not charging in guns blazing, if that's what you mean," Detillier said. "But we do need to gather as much intel as we can. If they've got prisoners in there, we need to know as soon as possible. We need to be able to tell everyone who shows up the lay of the land inside that store. I have gear we'll need in the trunk."

Maureen lit a cigarette. Probably her last one for a while, she figured. No sense in nic-fitting while stalking cop killers in the frozen foods section. Smoke drifted into one half-closed eye as she double-checked her Glock, confirming that first bullet remained chambered. She thought of the places she'd like to send it, like right in between some country motherfucker's eyes. By dressing up and playing soldier, the Watchmen had removed the risk she'd faced outside Dizzy's. She would know, immediately, if the person she aimed at presented a threat. She slipped her weapon back into the holster on her hip. She wouldn't hesitate. Not this time.

They got out of the car. They met at the trunk. Detillier popped it open.

"You're going to have to wear federal colors, I'm afraid. At least they'll protect you from friendly fire once the others arrive."

"I got no problem with that."

Detillier walked away from her, talking into a handheld radio, describing the scene and their plans for the folks on their way. Things were about to get crazy, Maureen thought. In minutes the parking lot would be a forest fire of emergency lights. She took off her leather jacket and tossed it in the backseat. Detillier reached into the trunk, handed Maureen a Kevlar vest. Shaking her head, she tapped her heart. "Already armored."

She grabbed a blue windbreaker that said FBI in big white letters across the back and pulled it on. She tightened her ponytail.

"The female shooter inside," Detillier said, returning to the car and pulling on his own armor and jacket. "That description mean anything to you? Any chance that's your girl, Leary?"

"That's not her in there."

"You sound pretty sure," Detillier said. "Nobody's been able to find her for a month and a half. Could be she found her way back to the Watchmen and that's where she's been hiding."

"We found her last night," Maureen said. "In Lafayette Cemetery with her throat cut open."

"Dead?"

"Indeed," Maureen said. "I was going to tell you after lunch. Other matters took precedence." She could hear the sirens approaching from every direction. The boys were coming, with their big guns and their armor that fit. She'd get cut out of the action. "Let's get going. I feel like I'm standing here waiting for someone else to come and do my job for me. I don't like it."

"If we can do it," Detillier said, "these people are worth taking alive. No matter what they've done. What these guys did today? Trust me, it isn't the endgame; it's the beginning. If we can get from these two what's coming next, we can save lives."

"You don't have to tell me my duty," Maureen said.

"These aren't the two who shot Preacher."

"I'm no vigilante."

"Here's how it's going to go," Detillier said. His radio squawked with multiple voices. He turned down the volume. "You are going to approach from the right side of the entrance so that you don't cross in front of it. When you get there, stay flat against the building. I'm going to loop around to the other side, come at the entrance along the left side of the building. I will clear the entrance. You got that? Me first around that corner. Me. Once I've cleared the entrance, I will signal for you to come in behind me. As we enter, you will cover my back, and I will cover yours. Depending on what we find, or what finds us, we'll use the registers for cover, reconvene, report in, and strategize from there. Got it?"

"I got it," Maureen said.

"See you inside," Detillier said. And for the first time, he smiled at her. He's done this before, Maureen thought as the agent scampered away, and he enjoys it.

Maureen watched as Detillier made his way across the parking lot. He covered the distance in crouching sprints, using cars and trash cans for cover. No sign of life came from the Walmart. No one else came out. She couldn't hear anything happening inside the store, but the approaching sirens grew louder. Two helicopters now hovered low overhead, no doubt relaying the scene back to the approaching forces.

Part of Maureen wanted to wait for backup. That was certainly the safer play. She knew a few people in the Tactical Unit. She'd actually worked with Tactical once, serving a warrant in Central City. They had the armor, the gear, and firepower equal to what the two Watchmen shooters had. They were a paramilitary unit unto themselves. But I'm here now, she thought. And a bigger part of her couldn't wait to get inside the store. She wanted to be the one to make the arrests, and if that didn't happen, to be the one who took down the people who'd killed her fellow officers. There could be hostages. They couldn't be abandoned. She had so much to prove. To the brass, to the other officers in her platoon, to her entire department. To Atkinson. To Preacher.

Detillier had reached the end of his cover. Maureen made her move.

She sprinted across the wide lane in front of the store, jumped up on the sidewalk, and threw herself against the brick façade of the building. She held her gun at port arms.

She watched the glass doors as Detillier ran to take his position on the opposite side of the entrance. In unison, they took slow, careful steps to the end of their respective walls. Detillier made a "stop" sign. Maureen waited. Detillier crouched, then, his gun drawn, staying low, duckwalked toward the doors. They opened when he got close, and he moved into the doorway, making himself small against the wall. Maureen held her breath, waiting for gunshots.

Detillier stayed crouched in the doorway, gun out in front of him, his head turning left then right as he surveyed the inside of the store. He waved for Maureen to follow him. She glanced back at the parking lot as multiple NOPD units rolled in, sirens blaring. A dozen more cops had arrived. And there, on their heels, in their big, boxy truck, was the Tactical Unit. Detillier hissed her name. Maureen took a deep breath and duplicated Detillier's approach. He'd started moving again when she had, and she followed him to the nearest register station. They ducked behind it for cover. She'd been right that the Watchmen had moved to the back of the store. There was no sign of them up front.

Maureen and Detillier sat hip to hip on the tile floor, catching their breath.

"So far so good," Detillier said, his voice low. "They don't want a shoot-out. If they did, they would've been waiting for us right here. Maybe suicide by cop isn't how this ends after all." He looked up at the ceiling. He peeked around the corner of the register station. "Man, this is a big fucking store. It's a lot for two people to cover."

Of course it's big, Maureen thought, it's a fucking Walmart. But she said nothing. She understood Detillier's frustration. The people they hunted could be ten yards away, or they could be a hundred yards away. She certainly understood his urge to act. She more than understood it; she shared it.

As Detillier reported their progress and observations into his radio, Maureen tried to tune him out. Instead, she listened as hard as she could for sounds from the belly of the store. She wanted clues to what might be waiting for them. Unfortunately, she couldn't hear anything but the god-awful piped-in New Country station playing over the speakers. Bon Jovi rejects with banjo thrown in. She was sweating. She wiped her forehead with the backs of her hands. The things you thought about, she mused, when trying not to get shot. What she wanted to hear was voices. When they hadn't been met with gunfire at the door, she'd become more convinced that she and Detillier now faced a hostage situation. She thought she'd hear commands from the shooters, or even weeping and whimpering from the hostages. Nothing came to her, though. Nothing but that terrible fucking music.

"I can't see anything from here," Detillier said. "If we could find the security office, we could use the CCTV cameras to see the whole store."

"They could be anywhere," Maureen said. "They could be gone. They might've escaped."

Back-to-back gunshots roared through the store. Maureen shouted and tried to shrink. Two more shots echoed under the high ceiling in the cavernous space. Detillier had time to mutter "Fuck me" before one more lone shot followed the others. The gunshots had come from the same location, far from where Maureen and Detillier hid. Whoever was shooting wasn't aiming at them. From what Maureen could discern, all the shots had come from the same gun. The source was a single shooter repeating fire, Maureen figured, not an exchange of gunshots. Had Tactical slipped someone inside through a back entrance? Had the shooters been taken out? Maureen doubted it. Detillier was in contact with the world outside; they would've alerted him. That's assuming, Maureen thought, that there's order and strategy to what's happening out front—a big assumption.

As the echoes of the final shot died, Detillier counted down, "Three, two, one."

He didn't have to tell Maureen what to do.

When he hit "one," they scrambled to their feet and ran up the checkout aisle, Maureen hard on Detillier's heels. She could hear him shouting information into his radio as they sprinted through Housewares. She was grateful for Detillier's narration of their location and progress, "Bathroom, Dining Room, Kitchen."

With the shots fired, SWAT, Tactical, and everyone else would come crashing in with guns drawn, and there'd be heavy weaponry involved. The description of the shooters, she recalled, mentioned a man and a woman in matching outfits. A *white* man and a white woman, that was true, and dressed quite differently from how Detillier and she were attired. But considering what had gone down that afternoon, those trigger fingers would be extra-itchy. Maureen didn't even want to think about how far ahead of the brains that commanded them those fingers might run.

Borrowed FBI jacket or not, Maureen thought as she ran, after everything she had survived in her life, she was in no mood to get cut down by friendly fire.

21

Using the direction of the gunshots, Maureen and Detillier tracked the shooters to Sporting Goods, located in the far back corner of the store. Detillier turned down the sound on his radio, in case anyone hiding in the store tracked their approach. They moved through Electronics at a brisk pace, crouched and cautious, guns drawn, held low in two hands in front of them. They breathed hard. They didn't speak. They didn't see any other people.

Maureen, two steps behind Detillier's right shoulder, listened for voices, for sobs, for curses or commands. For any breathing that wasn't her or Detillier. For any movement around or behind them. Every couple of steps she turned and checked their rear. She heard nothing but her own breathing, her own heartbeat, and the piped-in music and a fantasy football report on ESPN playing on a TV in the electronics department behind them.

As they closed in on Sporting Goods, they caught a scent in the air that led them closer to the shooters, the pungent iron-copper smell of spilled blood. Fresh blood. The scent and the quiet told Maureen what they would find. Bodies. She hoped they belonged to the Watchmen.

Detillier gasped and froze as he turned the corner into the fishing aisle. He held his free hand up behind him to stop Maureen from coming closer. He had lowered his gun. It hung loose in his hand by his side. Ignoring his command, Maureen lowered her own weapon and walked up beside him.

She had shrugged off Detillier's "stop" sign on the assumption that its purpose was to protect her from what she'd witness in the fishing aisle. Poor man, she thought. Nice try. Wasn't his fault that he had no idea what she'd already done when it came to death, never mind what she had seen. When she pulled even with him at the end of the aisle, though, she realized Detillier hadn't been trying to protect her delicate feminine sensibilities. His motivation had been more practical. He'd simply not wanted her to step in anything sticky.

The brown-haired woman was seated at an angle, her legs open in a V in front of her. Her arms hung limp at her sides. Her body slouched against a rack of fishing rods, a handful of which had tumbled to the floor around her. A pistol lay on the floor by her right hand. An AK-47 lay across her lap. Except for the guns, she looked to Maureen like any number of drunks she'd seen sleeping one off in a doorway. Well, except for the guns and the fact that the back of the woman's skull was missing. Pieces of it, and a good portion of what her skull had contained, now coated three shelves of heavy test fishing line. Without thinking, Maureen licked her lips. Then she wondered what foul particles she had drawn into her body. She wiped sweat from her forehead with the back of the hand that held her gun. She holstered her weapon. She turned and made eye contact with Detillier. He said nothing, turning away to speak into his radio.

That was when Maureen noticed the man.

He was prone on his belly, a few feet down the aisle beyond the body of the woman.

He wore a yellow "Don't Tread on Me" flag tied around his neck as a cape, like a child playing superhero, over his body armor. A large pool of blood haloed his head. Maureen realized the pool was growing, spreading fast across the dirty tile floor. That told her the man's heart continued beating. Not strong enough to keep him alive much longer. Minutes, Maureen guessed. Moments. His heartbeat was killing him, Maureen thought. Pumping his blood out onto the floor of the Walmart instead of to his body or his brain. She thought maybe she heard a quiet gurgle. She'd heard a similar sound just the night before. She knew what it meant. The man's arms splayed at his sides. There was no weapon anywhere near either of his hands.

She drew her gun anyway, tapped it against her thigh, contemplating.

She glanced over her shoulder at Detillier. She saw that he continued talking into his radio, one hand held up in the air to direct the others to his location. People more important than her were coming to take control of the scene. The thing to do here, she thought, the thing I *should* do, seeing as this guy *is* alive, is tell Detillier, have him call EMS to the fishing department. Today we don't have to wait for the crypt-keeper to come with the keys. Those glass doors slide right open. This guy would give the NOPD and the FBI a living witness to use against the Watchmen. If he could be saved.

Leaning forward, hands on her thighs, Maureen noted that the blood appeared to be leaking from under the man's head or neck. She reached out her foot, with the tip of her boot moved the man's chin a couple of inches. Ah, she thought, there it was. He'd taken a bullet, at least one, right at the base of his throat. I could, she thought, get in there, find and apply pressure to those wounds. She'd tried it for Leary. This guy, though, Maureen thought, he wasn't going to make it, either. She didn't have to be a doctor to see that, with the amount of blood he'd lost. She could see it laid out in front of her on the tile floor.

And, truth be told, she much preferred he died instead of lived.

She sniffed, watched as his feet twitched. His fingertips, too. The last primal circuits in his brain prodding his extremities to do something about the hole in his throat, Maureen figured. Was this guy one of the men who'd shot up her house a month and a half ago? Was he one of the cowards wearing masks and firing automatic weapons from a van in the street who had tried to kill her in her bed? Not enough nerve to get out of the getaway car to finish the job, not having the balls to meet me at my door. I bet that's how you killed those cops today, she thought. A sneak attack. An ambush. Like the fucking coward you are.

Maureen moved closer to the dying man. He didn't seem to be breathing, she thought. She must've imagined that gurgle she heard. Standing over him, she could see one of his eyes. It was blue. It moved.

Surprised, she moved closer to him, not caring that she'd now stepped in the blood. She'd wash it off later. Wouldn't be the first time. Detillier would be pissed, not that there was anything he could do about it. Crime scene integrity and all that.

Maureen squatted beside the man's head, careful not to get down on one knee. Blood on her boots was one thing, no sense staining her pants again. The eye flicked in her direction, seemed to track her as she hovered. She thought of Madison Leary's heterochromic eyes, how they had popped open as if at the sound of her name, and how soon they'd gone motionless and cold after that last flash of awareness, of life.

She thought of the man she'd followed from the Irish Garden, the one she'd left bleeding in the ginger. The one, according to Preacher, she'd nearly killed. She had looked into his eye, too. That eye had been blue like this man's, like one of Leary's had been, but also wild and alive. She had seen everything he was feeling from moment to moment, the agony and the fear broadcast across the surface of that one wild eye. She had seen his life, miserable and terrifying as it was to him at the moment. This dying man's eye was not the same animal. It moved away from her. Came back to her. Moving in tiny increments, it seemed to search the ceiling. A broken thing. What do you see? Maureen wondered. Are there demons coming for you? Do you think you see angels? Or is your dying eye like your feet and your fingers? Unconscious firing of dying nerves. The last of your loose electricity going to waste trying to jump-start your dying brain.

Or maybe, she thought, you know I'm here, and I am all you see. Maybe I am, to you, the devil let out of hell come calling for her due.

"Can you see me?" she teased, whispering. She could hear the smile, the taunt, in her voice, and somewhere deep inside, that smile scared her. She thought of Preacher's talk of the scorpion and rage bloomed inside her. "Do you see me here?" She wiggled her finger at his eye. "Is that why this eye thing is happening?"

She leaned in closer, forearms on her knees. "Can you hear me? Are you hanging on in there, asshole? Good. Don't leave me just yet." She leaned down right above his ear, close enough to whisper. "I'm the one you people wanted the most. Now I'm here to watch you die." She looked at the flag on his back. "Don't tread on me? Fuck you. I'm standing in your blood, you motherfucker, and you are dying at my feet."

Maureen watched his eye, stared right into it, as the last of the life remaining in him departed. She saw it go. Nothing on or in him moved. He was as dead as the woman who'd shot him. She stood. She waited for the sensations that had come when Leary had died, the parts of her breaking free and fading. She felt none of that this time. She missed Preacher.

"Coughlin!"

Her shouted name hit Maureen like a slap in the face. She turned. Detillier. Damn. Forgot about him.

"What are you doing?" Detillier asked.

"I, uh, I thought he might not be dead, so I checked." She looked down at the corpse, then back at the FBI agent. "But he is. I can say for sure he's deceased."

"Now you're the medical examiner?" Detillier asked. "Step away, please."

He was disturbed, Maureen could tell, by finding her looming like a reaper over the dead man's body. How long had he been standing there, she wondered. What had he heard her say?

"Just, geez," Detillier said, "you're standing in the blood. C'mon, we need to be professional here."

"All right, all right." Maureen backed away from the body, gave the dead woman as much distance as she could as she headed over to Detillier at the end of the aisle. She left bloody boot prints on the floor.

"The woman," Detillier said. "Do you recognize her?"

"Should I?" Maureen took another look, as a courtesy to Detillier, but she knew it wasn't anyone she had known. "Because I don't."

"She look like someone you've heard discussed? Maybe by Quinn or Ruiz?"

"Nope."

"What about him? You got a good-enough look."

"I don't recognize him," she said.

"You see anything useful on him," Detillier asked, "during your closer inspection?"

"I saw that he's got a big fucking bullet hole in the base of his throat. Gotta be where she shot him. I think he was on his knees, waiting for it. I wonder if he was begging her to do it, or begging her not to do it. We'll see when they turn him over if he had the guts to open up his armor to her." She shook her head. "Leave it to the man to lose his nerve when it counts. Anyways, she put a couple of rounds into the shelves behind him. Those were the first shots we heard, her trying to get him. The single shot that came last, that was her finishing the job. Suicide pact is my guess."

"Makes sense," Detillier said. "For some reason, these types never want to stick around for the glorious revolution. Less work to be a martyr, I guess. They never live long enough for me to ask them."

"Revolution," Maureen said, shaking her head. "Martyrdom. Is it really that deep, or are they just bananas? Seriously, if these two hadn't found the Sovereign Citizens and the Watchmen, wouldn't someone else be cleaning up the same mess in a trailer park somewhere over meth or dog fights?"

Detillier shrugged. "Anything's possible."

"You've seen this before?" Maureen asked.

"I have," Detillier said. "And I get the feeling I'll see it again."

"Well, whatever happens next," Maureen said, "it won't involve these two."

22

With the bad guys dead, Maureen didn't have anything to do.

She hung around the fishing aisle, thinking someone might want to
ask her questions about what had happened there, but nobody did. Everyone who came through went right to Detillier. As the crowd grew, she
grew more and more eager to leave. She wanted to lose the FBI jacket
and get out of her heavy vest. She wanted to go home, be alone, and have
a drink and a long shower. For right now, she'd be happy to get outside
and breathe cooler, less blood-laden air. Outside she could find someone to ask about Preacher's condition. Christ, she had a shift that night,
which was hard to even think about.

Who would do roll call?

Sporting Goods swarmed now with NOPD detectives and FBI agents,
large, anxious men arguing in hushed tones over who was in charge of
what. The FBI was labeling the afternoon's shootings acts of domestic
terror, which came under their jurisdiction. As far as Maureen could tell,
the NOPD didn't give a shit about terminology and jurisdiction. They

wanted an all-out manhunt. They wanted blood. However much of it pooled on the floor of the fishing aisle, that blood wasn't blood they had spilled. It wasn't enough. That blood didn't count. Maureen understood. She watched as a calm and determined Agent Detillier struggled to explain to whoever from the NOPD would listen to him, which appeared to be nobody, that the investigation was paramount now, that the three known shooters from that afternoon were dead.

At the moment, Detillier insisted, there was no one to hunt.

Maureen wasn't so sure that was true. Somebody, she thought, scratch that, *everybody* should be looking for Leon Gage. Detillier had to be thinking the same thing.

She suspected, though, that he feared the raw wrath and bloodlust of a gut-shot NOPD. Anyone connected to these attacks who the city cops got their hands on tonight wouldn't live to see the morning. Any information a prisoner gave up before dying would be beaten out of him, and that information would be useless as a prosecution tool. As badly as she wanted Leon Gage caught or even dead, she understood Detillier's strategy. He needed Gage, needed the information in his head.

As the voices of the men surrounding her got more heated, Maureen decided that hanging around corpses and angry men did her no good. From a distance, she made eye contact with Detillier and pointed toward the front of the store. He nodded and put a finger to his lips. She got the message. Talk to no one. She decided she might heed his wishes. She might not. Someone had to find Leon Gage. She'd blown the hunt for Madison Leary. She wouldn't make that mistake again. Detillier made a hand signal at his ear that meant he'd call her later, like someone would make to a friend across a crowded barroom. The gesture seemed so absurd, Maureen had to fight back laughter.

On her way out of the Walmart, she passed through the grocery section and grabbed a cold bottle of water. She'd pounded half of it down by the time she got outside.

23

Maureen felt as if she'd escaped from a maze as she stood outside the front door, people in uniform hustling past her. She ran her fingers along her scalp, enjoying the cold air, wondering how she'd get a ride to Dizzy's to pick up her car.

As she peeled off her FBI jacket, a familiar voice called her name.

She turned to see a smiling man, large and muscular, approaching out of the swirling crowd of law enforcement filling the parking lot. Dressed in full paramilitary gear, with his wraparound shades, flattop haircut, and an automatic rifle strapped across his chest, he looked like a soldier dipped in blue ink. Maureen recognized him right away. Sansone. One of the muscle-bound boys from the Tactical Unit.

"Why am I not surprised," he said, "to see you in the middle of this mess, Cogs?"

"What can I say? You guys were too slow. The pros had to step up." She took off her shirt, and unstrapped her vest and pulled it off, dropping it to the ground behind her with a grunt. She put the jacket back on. She rolled her shoulders. In her thin sweaty T-shirt, she shivered in the cold. "Much better."

"I heard you were rolling with the feds on this. Badass."

"That's an exaggeration," Maureen said. "One fed. Guy named Detillier. He's working the Watchmen case, the guys who shot up my house. I was with him when this shit went down. It was Detillier who knew they'd be here at the Walmart. We were halfway here before the first nine-one-one call came in from the store." She patted her pockets. "Tell me you have a cigarette."

"For you," Sansone said, "of course." He produced a pack of cigarettes and a Zippo. He lit hers, then lit one for himself. "Tell me you got 'em. *Please* tell me it was you and not that fed."

"I hate to disappoint you," Maureen said, "but they offed themselves before we got to them."

"Fucking *cowards*," Sansone said, stomping on the pavement. "I hate that shit. *Hate* it. So much for my hard-on." He growled. "But I'll get it back tonight. We'll be out busting many heads tonight. I'll be sporting a fucking table leg. I'll be staggering."

Maureen took a long pull of her cigarette. "What've you heard about Preacher?"

Sansone shrugged, looking away from her, exhaling a long plume of smoke. "He was alive when he went in the ambo. Conscious, too. Talking, of course, because he's fucking Preacher."

Her relief was so overpowering she lost her balance. She found a concrete planter by the door, sat on the edge. "You were there? You saw him?"

Sansone shook his head. "Fuck, no. This is my day off. This parking lot is the first place that I've been. I'm just now catching up myself. I missed *everything*."

"And?"

"Straight into surgery is what I heard. He got that far."

"Nothing since?" Maureen asked.

"It hasn't been that long," Sansone said. "Not much more than an hour since the first calls came in to nine-one-one."

"Holy shit. An hour? I feel like I've been running for days. This is fucking insane." She crushed out her cigarette in the dirt of the planter. She was absolutely fiending for a drink. Preacher hadn't been the only officer shot. Waiting to hear it wouldn't make the news any better. "What about the others? What's the word?"

"Bad, bad, bad." Sansone nodded at the Walmart. "Those two dead pieces of shit in there walked into the Reginelli's on Poydras and opened up. Pulled AKs out from under long coats, like in a fucking movie. Mays and Harrigan from the First were in there on lunch, splitting a pizza, sitting right by the door. They never had a chance. Not a chance. Died with their weapons in their holsters." Sansone coughed into his hand, covering the cracking in his voice. "Harrigan's old lady had a kid like six months ago. Fucking family man. Mays wasn't even thirty yet. This is a fucking nightmare."

Maureen looked away from him. She focused her gaze on a leafless, half-dead tree on the edge of the parking lot. She let her tears run. "What happened with Preacher? Can you tell me?"

Sansone looked over his shoulder. "Landry, you know him, the fat kid from the day shift? His girlfriend is an EMT. She was there." He sniffed. "According to what Landry's girl heard, Preacher was in Neyow, in Mid-City, eating lunch with some guy named Bridges, a lieutenant from the Fifth District. It's a regular thing they do, I guess. Every Tuesday.

"The shooting, it was like with Harrigan and Mays. Guy walked in quick, drew down with an automatic rifle. Went right for the cops and started shooting, not giving a fuck, not about civilians, nothing. People screaming, diving out of the way. Busser caught a round in the hip. I think a patron caught some shrapnel. Preacher had his weapon with him. He was sitting in the back of the dining room facing the door, saw the man walk in. Dropped him. Killed the *fuck* out of him. Emptied the fucking clip from his seat is what I heard. Took a couple of rounds before it was over. Bridges had his back to the door, took a bullet in the back, another in the shoulder. I think the lieutenant caught the worst of it. It was bad. Way bad. He's hanging in, though, the word going around. But who the fuck knows, you know?"

"I heard the shooter had grenades strapped to his chest," Maureen said. "Is that true?"

"I heard that, too," Sansone said. "After what these two here did, I'm thinking Preacher saved a lot of lives. I bet you that fuck was gonna blow the whole place, pull the pin and go out in a blaze of glory, that kind of shit."

"Mays and Harrigan," Maureen said. She bummed a second cigarette. "They were working, they were in uniform, right?"

"They were. Why?"

"Preacher was supposed to be running the night shift in the Sixth tonight," Maureen said. "And the lieutenant, was he on duty?"

"I don't know."

"I bet not," Maureen said. "How did these guys know Preacher's a cop? If they were randomly driving around Mid-City looking for cops to kill, didn't they see a unit in their travels? They didn't see anyone else in uniform? Instead they go after two guys in civilian clothes?"

"Preacher's being a cop," Sansone said, "means he's been making enemies in this city for thirty years. Lots of people know him, know his face. You know him: if he's in the room, everybody knows it. He's done some things, did some things back in the day, I mean, he's Preacher, but you know how it is." He frowned at the sky, trying, Maureen could tell, to fit the pieces together. "But personal shit would've been just people going after him. What happened today is plain crazy. Nobody does shit like this, not the Mob, not the gangs. Blowing away cops two at a time? Four in one day? Honest guys, every one of them. Nobody was mixed up in *any* shit."

"Detillier's been telling me about these guys," Maureen said. "The shooters. They're a new breed, part of a bigger movement, a national thing. They've gone after cops before, been doing it for years, across the country. Ambush. Suicide-mission sneak attacks on random cops. Or they set traps, create emergencies, and pick off law enforcement as they respond."

"What the fuck for?"

"Protest," Maureen said. "Revolution. Martyrdom. You know, because their noble deaths will inspire their brothers-in-arms to put down the remote and pick up their guns. To fight the New World Order or whatever."

"You are fucking kidding me," Sansone said. "This shit is national?"

Maureen nodded. "It is. All it takes is a Google search to find out about it."

"Then why am I only hearing this from you now in a Walmart parking lot after four cops get shot? What the fuck?"

Maureen shrugged. "Detillier said the FBI is running behind on the matter. But they're catching up. That's why he was talking to me."

"Wow," Sansone said. "Just, fucking *wow*."

He stood, his hand over his mouth, for several long moments. He set his hands on his hips, blew out his breath, crossed his arms over his chest, his shock morphing into rage. Maureen realized she'd made it that much harder for Detillier to keep the department calm after these shootings. She'd informed soldier boy number one here that the NOPD was now under siege. That they were at war. He'd tell his friends. He'd tell a lot of people.

"What happened to Harrigan and Mays fits the profile," Maureen said. "But Preacher, they hunted him."

"They targeted you, too," Sansone said. "Weeks ago."

"That they did."

She'd sat at a table with Leon Gage, she thought. Had a conversation with him. She'd been a sitting duck. She hated to admit it, but he probably could've killed her pretty easily. So why hadn't he? Was killing her dirty work left to the guys in that van? Had the white van really come to kill her? Where was it now? Outside her house? In the confusion, Detillier had never called in the plate number. Someone needed to find Leon Gage and ask him these questions. And do it in a way and in an environment more conducive to answers than lectures.

"Jesus, Coughlin," Sansone said, "what the fuck did you do to these guys?"

Madison Leary had killed two of their foot soldiers, Maureen thought. But me, I did something worse. I drove their financier out of the country, the source of the cash they used to buy their weapons, the source of their stash houses and hideouts in New Orleans. I cost them Caleb Heath. And he wasn't coming back, Maureen realized, while she and Preacher remained a threat. "I canceled their meal ticket," she said. "And they took offense."

Sansone's radio squawked and he turned his head to listen.

Maureen looked back into the Walmart for Detillier but couldn't see him. In Sporting Goods, giving directions, she figured. And he'd probably be a while; he had enough of a mess to clean up.

"We're standing down," Sansone said. "Headed back to the district."

"To do what?"

"Man, I don't know. Whatever's next on the to-do list, I guess. This is gonna be bigger than us, Cogs. The Staties will come in. The FBI is already on it. I'm here to take orders. I'm sure there's some weed dealer who missed his court date who needs his door kicked in. You?"

"I'm working tonight," Maureen said.

"Hey, listen," Sansone said. "A bunch of us, we're gonna grab something to eat before we go back to the Sixth. You wanna come with?"

Maureen thought about it. She wanted to go, but she wouldn't. She was afraid. The others had been on the force so much longer than she had. She was afraid they'd start telling back-in-the-day, remember-when stories about the two officers who'd been killed, or about Preacher's lieutenant friend who'd been shot in the back, people the other officers knew but who were strangers to Maureen. Or worse, they'd tell stories about Preacher. Eulogizing him. Memorializing him. Already talking about him as if he were dead while he lay opened up on the operating table. She couldn't deal with any of it.

"I gotta take a pass," Maureen said. "My car is in the Tremé. I gotta go pick it up, then somehow get my shit together for work tonight. It's not like they can give us the night off for bereavement or whatever."

"Well, stay frosty, Cogs. You're a true soldier." He raised his sunglasses up onto his head, squinted into the distance. "Where are your people again? Jersey, right?"

"New York," Maureen said. "Staten Island."

Sansone pointed toward the wall of law-enforcement vehicles forming a perimeter around the Walmart parking lot. Along the outside of that perimeter, the TV news crews had gathered, the vans side by side, their satellite dishes pointed at the sky. Maureen could see the reporters lined up, standing with their backs to her as they talked into the cameras.

"If this isn't a national story yet," Sansone said, "it will be any minute. You should call your people and let them know you're okay. I mean, who fucking knows what those media people are saying."

Maureen checked her phone. She'd gotten no calls, which was a good sign. Her mother and Waters hadn't heard the news of the shootings yet. "I'll do that. When I get a minute, I'll send a text."

Sansone shook his head. "No, no, no. Not a text. Let them hear your voice. You like acting like you're a lone ranger, but you're not. Show respect for your people."

"Okay, okay," Maureen said. "I'll call."

"Ten-four." Sansone moved to turn away, then came back to her, standing closer than he had before. "Whatever it is that happened at the river, whatever went on before that with Quinn and Ruiz, consider that over and done with. Maybe it gets revisited down the road, maybe it doesn't. That depends on you, mostly. But right now we're under the gun, and you're one of us. We gotta stick together. You need something, you call, you reach out. Ya hear?"

He waited for an answer.

"I hear you," Maureen said.

"And whoever else there is to get, we'll get 'em. Only a matter of time." He grinned and pounded his armored chest with his gloved fist. "Believe."

Maureen felt tears rising to her eyes again. They ran down her cheeks when she tried to blink them away. She knew who else there was to get. She knew at whose doorstep the blood trail ended. Forget the goddamn weed dealers, Solomon Heath's door needed kicking in. She wanted to pin the man down, hold a broken bottle to his throat while he called his sons in Dubai. She wanted to, but she wouldn't. Not then. Not yet. She returned Sansone's grin and nodded at him. "Right," she said. "We'll get 'em. Believe."

But she was lying. She didn't believe.

She watched Sansone as he marched away from her to join the rest of his crew before they went out to eat together, which they would do before they spent the night working together. Maureen knew she'd have to dart out of roll call in a hurry if she was going to get on the streets alone tonight. And she needed to do that. Work alone. She didn't need anyone asking her questions about where she was going and what she was doing.

Carrying her vest and wearing the FBI windbreaker, she walked to Detillier's car. She left his jacket in the backseat and put her leather jacket back on. She turned and looked back at the scene. She shouldn't leave. Eventually, somebody would want to talk to her about what had happened inside the Walmart, and outside Li'l Dizzy's. Then again, Detillier had been there for everything. He was the one everyone wanted to talk to, and he could tell the story as well as she could. She realized they hadn't discussed her conversation with Leon Gage. Perhaps that had been what the "call me" gesture had been about.

Maureen couldn't think of anything from that conversation that would've tipped her off to what was happening across the city while she sat with Leon. She couldn't think of anything that might tell her what would happen next, either. He'd babbled at her, killing time while his people killed cops. Overall, she felt pretty fucking useless. Detillier would want to talk about Leon Gage. And he'd want to talk about Madison Leary. A call to Atkinson, Maureen thought, was probably a good idea.

She pulled out her phone and walked off to the side of the parking lot, away from the reporters. But before she spoke with Atkinson, she had another call to make. She found the number and waited for an answer, the phone to her ear.

"Maureen," Amber said, "what's the matter?"

"Ma, every time I call," Maureen said, "that's how you answer."

There was silence, which was Amber's way of either refusing to argue or starting an argument, Maureen was never sure. But the silence was a good thing. If Amber were aware of what had happened in New Orleans, she'd be hysterical, not pouting.

"Last time I called and you answered like that," Maureen said, "I had good news."

"And that was two days ago," Amber said. "What are the odds you've got more good news already?"

This time Maureen was quiet. Her mother had a point. She didn't have good news, unless she counted the fact that she wasn't one of the cops who'd been shot, which was kind of a big deal.

"Am I right or am I right?" Amber asked.

"Some stuff went down at work today, Ma," Maureen said.

"Stuff? What do you mean by 'stuff'?" Already Maureen could hear panic creeping into her mother's voice. "Do I need to turn on the TV? Is the city flooding again? I thought hurricane season was over. Let me find Nat and tell him to turn on the TV."

"Before you do that," Maureen said, "listen to me. No, we're not flooding."

She decided she'd tell the truth, up to a point, and tell it fast. She felt immense relief that her mother had Nat there with her, in her life. That fact would help her be more honest. "It's bad news. It is. Four cops were shot here today. They were ambushed in restaurants. Two of them were killed, two of them were badly hurt."

"Oh my God. Oh my God. Where are you? Where are you calling me from? Are you okay?"

"I'm fine," Maureen said, though she wasn't and she knew her mother could hear it. "I'm calling from a parking lot. I wasn't shot. I wasn't hurt. I'm fine."

She could hear her mother yelling for Nat. For once, Maureen didn't want to talk to him; she wanted to talk to her mother. She wanted her mother's attention. But she felt her throat closing, acid rising from her belly to the back of her throat. She had to get the story out, had to finish telling it quick, before she lost control of herself. Hysterics on her part would only make her mother more upset, and she wasn't sure how many of her fellow officers could see her. The conversation couldn't last. Only one key piece remained to tell. She choked out the words.

"Mom, Preacher got shot. He got shot. He could die. They shot Preacher."

With that, the levee broke.

Dizzy, weeping, her nose running, exhausted beyond reason, Maureen eased down onto her knees as best she could before she collapsed. Everything that had held her upright since she'd spotted Detillier outside of Dizzy's crumbled underneath her. She could barely hold the phone to her ear. She could hear Nat's confused questions in the background. She could hear her mother's voice. "Oh, my baby. Oh my God."

On her knees in the Walmart parking lot, Maureen wept, her mother's voice in her ear, the sobs coming hard like kicks to the stomach.

24

Shortly after nine that night, Maureen stood outside the front gate of a two-story apartment building on Coliseum Street, across from Lafayette Cemetery.

Before lighting the cigarette between her lips, she offered the flame to the tall woman standing next to her. The woman, named Beatrice, was thin as a cocktail straw, her mahogany bob streaked with gray. She leaned down to the glow in Maureen's cupped hands. Her long wool coat reached the tops of her tennis shoes. She wore heavy makeup, and her waxy lipstick left a crimson ring on the filter of her long white cigarette. She had wine on her breath.

She exhaled to the sky, asking Maureen, "Will it be much longer?"

"The detective is on her way," Maureen said. "It's been a long day."

"Of course, of course," Beatrice replied, looking away, resting her elbow in her palm as she held her cigarette close to her face. "I only meant, if there's a better time . . ."

That afternoon Beatrice had called the Sixth District wanting to talk about something she'd seen the night before, something possibly related, she thought, to the murder in the cemetery. Her message had been lost in the chaos following the shootings, and had only been passed along to Maureen a couple of hours into her patrol shift. Beatrice, returning home after walking her dog, had been quite surprised to find Maureen waiting for her at the gate more than four hours after her original call. Maureen had conducted a brief preliminary interview, deciding the woman could have something useful to offer, and had called Atkinson to let her know they'd found a witness. They'd been waiting nearly half an hour.

Beatrice turned and looked up at her dog, a serene white shepherd mix watching from the metal staircase that led to the second-story. "A few more minutes, dear." She looked at Maureen. "He always gets a treat after a walk. He'll sit there and wait all night for it."

"I know the feeling," Maureen said. A white sedan turned the corner and headed their way down the potholed center of Coliseum Street. "Here she comes now."

Atkinson parked close to them and climbed out of the car. She wore faded black cords that flared over her cowboy boots. Her broad shoulders stretched the limits of her bright red down jacket. Her huge hands were bare despite the cold. She carried her radio in her left hand and extended the other to Beatrice as she got closer. She offered Maureen a curt nod. "Officer."

"Detective Sergeant," Maureen said.

Atkinson shook with Beatrice. "I'm Detective Sergeant Christine Atkinson, Homicide."

Beatrice released Atkinson's hand. She glanced at Maureen then dropped her gaze. "Someone did die. There was talk in the neighborhood, I was hoping it was wrong."

"She was alive when we found her," Atkinson said. "Unfortunately, she'd lost so much blood from the murder wound, she died before we could get sufficient help. Really, though, the wound was so catastrophic, a terrible gash to the throat, I don't know if there was any saving her no matter when she was found."

Beatrice, who had turned pea-soup green, dropped her cigarette and grabbed the fence, steadying herself. Atkinson, thankfully, stopped talking. The dog trotted down the stairs and barked once at Atkinson. Then he wagged his tail while growling at her, as if simultaneously scolding, forgiving, and warning Atkinson for making his owner feel bad. Atkinson looked at Beatrice, trying and failing to raise a fake smile. "He's a wonderful animal."

She's so much better with the dead, Maureen thought, than she is with the living. It's the one hole in her game.

"The reason we found the victim when we did," Atkinson said, "is because someone called the nonemergency number to report a dead person in the cemetery. Was that you?"

"No," Beatrice said. "I didn't call anyone until this afternoon."

"Can you tell me," Atkinson asked, "what you saw that caused you to call us today?"

"I have a studio downtown," Beatrice said. "I'm a painter. I work odd hours, sometimes until dawn. I always take Cosmo out for a walk when I get home. Usually, he's been alone a long time by then, and it helps me unwind. I like the Garden District best late at night. It's rather mysterious and beautiful, especially when there's a good heavy fog coming in off the river."

"So you were coming out of the gate here," Atkinson said, "when you saw? What?"

"As I told Officer Coughlin," Beatrice said, "I was coming through my gate with Cosmo, around midnight, and I saw two people hopping the wall there by the entrance, climbing into the cemetery."

"Two people?" Atkinson asked.

Beatrice turned, gesturing toward the cemetery gates. "I saw two people go over the wall. Maybe others went before them and they were the last two, but I saw two."

"Why didn't you call anyone last night?" Atkinson asked. "Neighborhood security? The police?"

Beatrice shook her head. "I didn't think anything of it. I see people, kids mostly, sometimes tourists, climb over the wall constantly. It's so short there." She shrugged. "For mischief, to smoke some pot. For sex. For the creepy thrill of it. The tour guides are always going on about vampires in this neighborhood. There's hardly trouble from it, not even vandalism, really. The neighbors know it happens. Nothing bad has ever come of it that I'd heard of. Until last night."

"And these two people," Atkinson asked. "What did they look like?"

"One was a woman. Thin, long hair. Baggy clothes but definitely a woman. She climbed over second. Her friend stood atop the wall and helped her over. A boy, it looked like, if I had to guess. A young man, maybe. I couldn't see his face. He was short, slender, wearing a long coat with the collar turned up. He seemed to have short hair."

"Would you know the male," Atkinson asked, "if you saw him again?"

"That might be difficult," Beatrice said. "I didn't see his face, the woman's, either." She slid another cigarette from her pack. Cosmo let loose a short howl. "I swear he knows these mean we're staying outside."

Maureen offered her lighter again and Beatrice lit up. She said, "Do you think the boy was the one who killed her?"

"That's where we'll start things," Atkinson said. "Did you hear voices? Did either of them seem frightened or angry? Like maybe they didn't want to go over the wall."

"They didn't speak that I could hear," Beatrice said. "Although, once they were over the wall, the woman started singing."

"Definitely a woman?" Atkinson asked.

"Absolutely," Beatrice said, nodding, proud of her certainty. "More than anything, that voice told me one of them was female. I was walking away with Cosmo by then, and I don't remember the song, none of the words or anything. But I stopped to listen, just for a few seconds." She pressed one hand to her heart, her eyes getting wet. "He cut her throat? Excuse me." She coughed into her fist. "The woman had the most extraordinary voice. Mesmerizing. It's such a shame. Such a terrible shame. Horrible."

"It is," Maureen said.

"Do you think you'll catch the man who killed her?"

"I like our chances," Atkinson said. "Thank you for calling us. You've been very helpful."

Beatrice seemed startled the interview was over. Maureen could tell her mind was lingering on the singing she'd heard coming over the cemetery walls. "All right, then. I'm sorry I couldn't give you more. Officer Coughlin has my information if you need to speak with me again. I keep my phone off when I'm at the studio—I can't be disturbed while I'm working—but, as I said, I keep odd hours, so call anytime."

Atkinson handed Beatrice a business card. "Same goes for you. You remember anything else, if you see that man again, please call me. Day or night."

"Of course," Beatrice said. She pulled open her gate. "Well then, good night, ladies. Good luck."

"Thank you," Atkinson said. She waved at the dog. "Good night, Cosmo." He growled at her before trotting up the stairs to wait for his owner at their apartment door, his tail wagging.

"Oh, Beatrice," Maureen called, "I forgot one thing. Please tell the detective about the object."

"The object?" Atkinson asked. "That sounds ominous."

"I'm so sorry, of course," Beatrice said. "Before she climbed the wall, the woman passed something up to the boy, for him to hold so she could climb. I saw him bend down and take it from her."

"Any thoughts on what it was?" Atkinson asked.

"I couldn't really see it," Beatrice said, "but there was this musical tinkling. I swear it sounded like wind chimes. I didn't think anything of it at the time. People often leave gifts for the dead in there. Helps with the guilt of going on living, I suppose."

25

Three hours later, Maureen sat in her patrol car, chain-smoking.

She was parked under a big magnolia tree and between two streetlights, having positioned the car in a convenient pool of shadow. Her
location, unknown to her fellow cops, put her not far from Audubon
Park and not anywhere near where she was supposed to be at that hour.
In addition to the cruiser's engine, Maureen had turned off the lights
and the radio. She needed to concentrate. An hour ago, word had gone
out that Preacher had survived his surgery. He had been moved into re-
covery. He certainly wasn't well, but he wasn't dying. Wasn't close to it.
Earlier reports, Maureen had learned, had exaggerated the direness of
his condition. With the news about Preacher, the emotional scaffolding
inside her had collapsed, leaving her physically wobbly and mentally
zombified.

To resharpen her focus, she'd rolled down the car window, inviting
in the damp nighttime chill. She turned her face to the wet cold, breathing it deep into her lungs. Between drags on her cigarette she blew into

hcr cupped hands. Running the engine so she could use the heater tempted her, but the steady warmth would put her right to sleep. She needed to be cold. Also, she needed to remain inconspicuous. Better if no one saw her sitting there. She wasn't on a street, or in a neighborhood, that the common street cop often visited, not without an invitation.

This particular short, narrow, smoothly paved dead-end street existed to access the two enormous homes on it. Homes that faced the park. One of them, the brick behemoth in Maureen's rearview, belonged to a retired federal prosecutor. The other home, the one she watched, was the regal antebellum mansion belonging to Solomon Heath.

The house was dark, and had been since Maureen had arrived. If Heath was home, he either slept or was sequestered deep inside the house. A lone gas lamp burned beside the back door, the reflected flame igniting glowing crystals in the door's cut-glass window. That was the same door Solomon had made Maureen use the night she'd met him, when she'd worked a security detail at this very house. That was the night he'd bribed her, or had tried to, depending on how she interpreted things. She'd done nothing for the man, but she'd kept his money.

Recalling that security cameras watched every inch of the Heath property, she had parked the cruiser beyond their range. She'd found a spot to be invisible, as she had in the Irish Garden. What she had to decide was what to do next. She wasn't tucked in a barroom booth, a big sweatshirt hiding her appearance. She was in a police cruiser tonight, in uniform.

Maureen settled deeper into her seat, her arm hanging out the window. She fixed her gaze on the gas lamp's dancing flame.

She didn't know what she had expected to discover sitting outside Solomon's house. Even if the lights were on, what did she hope to see? She felt he needed watching, so she watched. Her thought process hadn't advanced much beyond that basic instinct. Did she think he'd have a late-night visitor arriving at the back door? Or did she think she'd be able to accost *him* as he came creeping home in the wee hours from nefarious doings about town, maybe with a young girl or young boy on his arm? She had tailed him on and off for a month and had found no indication of such behavior. If only he would make it that easy, she thought. If only he were that sloppy. That ordinary. But you didn't get to where he was, and remain where he had managed to stay, by being sloppy. He wasn't the kind of man to commit common sins.

After weeks of watching his house, of following him to work, she had witnessed no wrongdoing of any kind. She had gained no leverage against him, had none to provide to Atkinson or Detillier. She could sit outside his house a hundred nights in a row and Solomon would give her nothing. Anything useful she got from him, she was going to have to take.

26

Before ending up outside Solomon's house, Maureen had visited the construction sites of the new jail and then the new hospital. She'd even smoked a couple of cigarettes parked by the demolition site of the Iberville projects. She stared down security guards who stared right back at her, hoping she'd move along so they could go back to sleep or smoke another joint.

As she moved from site to site, she had started wondering—as she stared at the deep holes and the rising structures, at the boards and the bricks and the girders, at the silent enormous machines that tore down and built up, at the placards on the fences with the Heath Design and Construction logo alongside their licenses and permits and their long list of worksite rules—about who was *really* in charge of the world she lived and worked in. Her house had been shot up, she realized, only days after she'd taken money from Solomon that he'd intended as a bribe, only for her to work against him in the end. Who had really given that first order to kill her weeks ago? Had it come from Caleb? That was hard to imagine. He was a spoiled punk. He had provided the Watchmen her street address, but he hadn't picked up a gun against her.

A group like the Watchmen—angry, violent people who fancied themselves *revolutionaries* in their grandest, suicidal fantasies—wouldn't look to a weak man like Caleb as a leader. He was the rich kid they let hang around the clubhouse because he had money to buy guns, because he knew people who had information and influence. They didn't embrace him; they tolerated him. They would follow someone else.

Solomon wouldn't lead the Watchmen directly, wouldn't dirty his own hands with their particular brand of USA crazy. Were he involved with them, Maureen thought, whether for his son's sake or for other reasons, he'd exert his authority through a proxy.

Maureen figured Leon Gage, despite his middle-school math teacher looks, was that leader Solomon used. He had the air of the pulpit about him. She could see him raging at a crowd, those blue eyes blazing. She knew she had no evidence connecting Solomon to the doings and dealings of the Watchmen, no proof that Leon took his orders from Solomon.

Light from inside the house suddenly filled the back door's window and spilled onto the slate steps. Floodlights illuminated the yard and the back door opened. Solomon stepped out of the house. Maureen could see his breath as he pulled the door closed behind him.

He wore, as he always did, khakis and brown loafers. Against the cold he wore a thick down vest over a red flannel shirt. He had a wool snap-brim cap pulled low on his head and wore leather gloves. He carried something in his left hand. Maureen sat up straight for a better look. A thermos. He clutched it to his chest like a football as he walked in her direction.

Maureen zipped up her leather jacket, pulled on her knit cap, and got out of the car. Fuck it, she thought. She unbuckled her weapon. For weeks, you've been hoping to stumble into exactly this moment. And now there's no one else around, no joggers in the park, no construction workers at the worksite. And no Preacher to rein her in and scold her.

Maureen decided as she stepped into the street that Solomon had ordered the hit on Preacher. She had seen Solomon recognize him in the park. And he had revived the kill order on her; she was sure of that, too.

With Caleb safely sequestered in the UAE and the NOPD working overtime to erase Quinn's dirty history and look the other way at the circumstances surrounding his death, Maureen decided Solomon had convinced Leon Gage that now was the time for starting his war against the NOPD, using Gage to get rid of the cops that threatened his son. Gage was a leader to his men, but he was a weapon for Solomon—as Quinn had been, one of his countless tools.

Maureen figured that Leon, who was mourning a son who had crossed over much more than an ocean, hadn't needed much prodding.

She closed the cruiser door, keeping her eyes on Heath, who had stopped his approach when Maureen left the car.

She realized as she straightened her gun belt on her hips that her return to work, to the NOPD's good graces—hell, there was no reason he couldn't know about her work with the FBI—had spurred Solomon into action. Being a cop again made her a threat again. He'd waited to see if she'd quit the department and leave New Orleans like Ruiz had done. Instead, she had rubbed her continuing presence in his face. So Solomon had acted and had done so in the way that men like him preferred, through others, by putting those others' baser instincts and desires to work for him. Leon Gage fancied himself a man with a cause and an army. Solomon Heath gave him an enemy. A target. Then he sat back safe and distant in his big house and watched the bodies drop.

But she must have done something right, Maureen thought, because here he finally was. The man himself, the man that neither the NOPD nor the FBI would touch, had come to face her in the street. He was twenty yards away. Closer to her now than he'd gotten with his golf club.

Those other two cops, Maureen decided, the ones who had died, Mays and Harrigan, they'd been collateral damage, camouflage and distraction for the Watchmen's real intentions as they came after her and Preacher. In fact, she was pretty sure that Leon Gage had been setting her up for the kill that afternoon. She should have opened fire on that passing van. It had to be the van. Should've lit those fuckers up. Gage couldn't take the shot at her himself, because if he did he couldn't be sure he'd walk out of the café. Not in a place as popular with city law enforcement as L'il Dizzy's. Maureen wouldn't be the only one in there with a gun, which wasn't something that Gage would know, but Heath would.

Heath gave the orders and Gage had escape plans, Maureen thought, because the so-called leaders never did the dirty work themselves. Gage, like Solomon, passed off the risk and the bloodshed to underlings. The ones who made the speeches never did the dying. Bin Laden didn't pilot one of the planes. The guy who held the press conference wasn't the one who climbed aboard the bus wearing the suicide vest, or the one who drove the car up to the embassy entrance. That job always went to the poor schmuck who the fake patriots and false prophets had convinced that dying in a bomb blast or a hail of bullets was the only thing worth living for. Only their death could make their lives worth anything in this world and the next. Solomon Heath and Leon Gage were those salesmen. In that way they were alike.

She'd picked Dizzy's to irritate Gage, and in defiance of Detillier's protestations, Maureen thought, and had quite likely saved her own life in the process. Had Solomon come outside to finish the job by himself, she wondered. Had she become worth that much to him? It had been a long time, she figured, since Solomon had done his own dirty work. Here she was, though, standing in the street as living proof that if you wanted something done right . . .

She watched as Solomon tucked the thermos under his left arm, jamming that hand into the pocket of his vest. He raised his other hand in a salute, telling her with the gesture that he'd come no farther without her permission. Maureen raised her hand and waved him closer. His leather soles scratched on the asphalt as he walked toward her.

Maureen knew that for Solomon, killing her and Preacher was the only way to make New Orleans safe for Caleb's return. Once she and Preacher were dead, with Quinn dead and a discredited Ruiz fled to another state, there'd be no one left to link Caleb to the Watchmen and the New Orleans drug gangs they worked with to hide and move their guns for their war. She was sure by now that he knew Madison Leary, the one other threat to his son, was dead.

Solomon smiled at Maureen as he got closer, walking with both hands buried deep in his vest pockets. Here was a man, Maureen thought, who had never in his life thought twice about approaching a police officer with his hands in his pockets. And despite everything she thought she knew about him, she'd let him come this far without protest. Were he a twenty-year-old black man, she thought, she'd have asked to see his hands before he crossed the street. And this was a man she knew wanted her dead.

"Am I in danger?" Heath asked.

"Excuse me?"

"I asked, am I in danger?" He continued smiling. He had perfect teeth.

"And why would you think that?" Maureen said.

After a chuckle, Heath said, "Because there is a police officer parked outside my house in the middle of the night."

"And that means danger to you," Maureen said, "the presence of the police."

"Has there been a threat against me?" Heath asked. "You're out here to protect me from something. I was wondering what that is."

"If you're worried for your safety," Maureen said, "why leave the house?"

Heath nodded. "I'm under surveillance?"

"Not as far as I know. But the bosses don't tell me everything. I'm just a foot soldier."

Heath looked over his shoulder. "We can have this conversation in a much warmer place, Officer. You're welcome to come inside."

"I'm fine right here," Maureen said. "Thank you."

"I saw the events of the day," Heath said. "The whole city has by now, and the whole country, I'm sure. If not the world. Horrific beyond words. I don't know what kind of statement those animals thought they were making. My heart goes out to you and your fellow officers. I understand that you and Sergeant Boyd are especially close?"

"He was my training officer," Maureen said. "It's probably unprofessional to admit it, but I take what happened to him very, very personally. Above and beyond even the murder of the other cops."

"Odd that a man out of uniform was targeted," Heath said, lowering his eyes, "when the other officers were in uniform and seemingly picked at random."

"I wasn't aware," Maureen said, "that information had been made public."

"You and I both know," Heath said, raising his eyes to hers, "that I'm not stuck relying on WDSU for my information."

"Is there anything you know, then," Maureen said, "that maybe we don't?"

He held out the thermos to her. "I brought this for you. For your vigil. It's coffee. *Good* coffee." He smiled. "It has a bit of the Irish in it. I hear you have a taste for that."

"Thank you, I'm fine."

"You mind if I do?" Heath asked.

"Be my guest," Maureen said.

Heath set the thermos on the hood of the cruiser. He unscrewed the plastic cap. Maureen watched as he poured the coffee, steam rising into the cold night air like a genie from a lantern. He raised the cup to his lips, blew on it, eyebrows high on his forehead. Maureen sighed as the earthy roasted aroma of the coffee filled the air around her, the sharp wood-smoke tang of the whiskey dancing like heat lightning through the cloud of coffee. Her mouth watered.

Am I really this easy? she wondered.

Now that she was here, and had figured things out, what was stopping her, she wondered, from throwing Heath down in the street and arresting him? Or from beating him senseless like she had those other dangerous men. She had the ASP in her pocket. She unzipped her jacket and reached into that pocket. Nothing was stopping her, that was what. Specifically, the nothing she had to offer as evidence of his involvement in any conspiracy to kill cops, or of any wrongdoing whatsoever. She'd be the one in cuffs, not Solomon. Tonight she wasn't an anonymous assailant.

Instead of the ASP, she produced her pack of cigarettes from her jacket pocket.

If she got in trouble again, there'd be no cover-up this time, no mercy, no deals. She'd be lucky to make it to prison and not end up in the river. She lit up.

The other option, she thought, was killing him. They weren't far from the river. They were out of range of his cameras. Most likely.

"Would you mind?" Heath asked.

Maureen held out the pack to him. "Wouldn't have figured you for a cigarette smoker."

Because of course you can do that, she thought. No problem. You can kill one of the five richest men in Louisiana, the mayor's buddy, dump the body in the Mississippi, and walk away from it. She had killed before, but that was in a fight for her life. Sebastian's flunky, who'd put her in the trunk of a car. And then Sebastian himself had his hands on her, was trying to murder her. Only one of them could live through those moments. Plain and simple like nothing she'd ever been through before or since. Now she was mixed up in something much more complicated. Everything about her life now was much more complicated.

Heath slid a cigarette from the box by pinching the filter. "It's been a while. I do prefer cigars, but unless we're going inside." He shrugged. He put the cigarette in his lips and lowered the tip to the flame of Maureen's lighter.

But was this situation truly so different, Maureen wondered, from what had happened on Staten Island with Frank Sebastian?

This man Heath, who is standing right here smoking one of your American Spirits, wants you dead. He's different from Sebastian how? He deserves due process because he had other people pulling the trigger? Can you afford to wait that long? she wondered. Look at what he's done already.

There's one key thing to remember, though, she told herself. This idea that Solomon is the source, this theory that he's using the Watchmen to kill you and Preacher to protect his son, viable as it sounds to you—right now, you're the *only one* who has this idea. And you have no proof that it's true and no one, with Preacher in the hospital, who you can take it to without ending up in that new jail or that river. Who would believe it?

Heath slurped his Irish coffee. "It does cool off quick out here."

Gage had you one-on-one in L'il Dizzy's, Maureen thought, and you walked away. You spent weeks alone and unprotected and no one came for you. From the outside, how does all that look? Suspicious as hell, Maureen thought. Maybe it was Coughlin, people might wonder, who told Gage and the Watchmen where to find Preacher.

Get a grip, Maureen, she told herself. You're losing it. Stop thinking that way. Think like a cop, not like, not like . . . whatever else you've been thinking like.

Heath gestured at the thermos. "You're sure?"

"I'm on duty," Maureen said.

Killing Solomon Heath, she thought, wasn't whipping some frat boy's ass in the bushes to teach him a lesson. Killing a scion of the city, committing vigilante *murder*, she thought, even to save herself and avenge her fellow cops, doesn't catch the other bad guys. It's not self-defense because he came at you with Irish coffee and charm. Vengeance is not in the job description. And it's a hell of a long way farther back from secret blood justice than it is from cracking somebody's ribs in the dark. That's supposing there is a way back. You've had a hard-enough time, she thought, finding your way back from the bank of the Arthur Kill.

"Who's going to know you took a little nip besides you and me?" Heath asked.

Killing Solomon Heath solves nothing, she thought. Maybe it brings Caleb home, but who wants or needs him by then anyway, with the big fish gutted and grilled?

"And after a day like today," Heath said, "who would begrudge you? This is New Orleans, after all."

Taking out Solomon Heath does send a message to the Watchmen, Maureen thought. It shows how far the cops go to protect their own. She watched as Heath produced a second plastic cup from his vest pocket and set it on the hood of her cruiser. He unscrewed the thermos and poured. No. No, killing him wouldn't send the right message, she thought, the coffee-whiskey aroma blooming into the air again.

Killing Solomon, she thought, shows how far one crazy cop would go to get her own sick version of revenge. Shit, she'd told the FBI she had it in for him. Killing him wouldn't do the most important thing she needed to accomplish, which was put an end to the Watchmen and their war against the NOPD.

There had to be a way, a legit or at least passably legal way, to tie Solomon Heath to the Citizens and the Watchmen. To pull his whole house down on top of him.

She thought of Preacher and of his constant reminders of their true mission, of their real job. Catching bad guys.

She reached out and took the plastic cup from Heath, blew on its contents as he had.

Maureen got the feeling that once she and Preacher had been eliminated, Leon Gage wouldn't last much longer. Their surviving the day probably kept him alive that night. Actually, he was a goner either way.

Maybe he wouldn't even survive the night. She wondered who Solomon had in the wings sharpening their claws against Gage. Solomon would find a way to turn Gage's people against him and hang on to their loyalty for himself. Of course, the wet work would fall to others, someone weaker, ambitious, deluded. Someone broke. Heath wasn't any better than the drug dealers outside the Washington Avenue grocery who Preacher had talked about at roll call last night. Killing. Conniving.

"You asked me about information," Heath finally said. "If I had any."

"I did."

"Napoleon Gage. He is the man you should be looking for."

Maureen laughed to herself. She wondered if Solomon would offer her the job of killing Gage. The pay would be good. Better than good. Was that why he'd gone after Preacher? To make her that much more willing to kill Gage? He'd get her or she'd get him. Either way, Solomon came out the winner. It made sense.

She wondered if Solomon had an envelope full of money in the pocket of his khakis, and if he would offer it to her right then and there. Like a bounty. She wondered if she would take it. "We had that idea. Where to find him would be much more useful information."

"What do you know about the man?" Solomon asked.

"Enough."

"You really think so?" Heath said. "You don't know enough to find him tonight, do you?"

"If not tonight, tomorrow," Maureen said. "But we'll get him. What I wonder about is what he's going to tell us when we do."

Heath shrugged. "I'd imagine the man has left town. Wouldn't you? I would imagine that right now y'all have impressive resources at your disposal."

"You and I both know," Maureen said, "that you have a deeper well to draw from than we do." She set the empty plastic cup on the car. She wasn't feeling it yet, but the coffee had more than *a little* of the Irish in it.

"I'm not sure," Heath said, "that I'm the kind of man you think I am."

I know exactly the kind of man you are, Maureen thought. And there's one very important thing about me that you don't know. That nobody in New Orleans knows. The last one like you I met? The only things that remained of him were a black shoe and bloody, greasy gravy smeared like wet paint across the front of a speeding train.

Don't tread on me, indeed.

"I know what kind of man you are," she said. "And I know what kind of man your son is, too."

"My son," Solomon said, "is certainly not what you think he is, or what you have told people he is. He had nothing to do with what happened today. He's had nothing to do with anything that's happened to you. Those Watchmen people would kill him, too, if they could. I sent my son where he would be safe. There's nothing more to it than that." He set his empty coffee cup on the car, poured a refill.

"I'm out here talking to you because I want the same thing you do, Officer Coughlin. To see the Watchmen undone, before any more blood is shed. And there will be more. We're on the same side, you and I. We always have been. I know Quinn tried convincing you of that."

What struck Maureen, listening to him, was that Solomon believed everything he said to her. She knew firsthand that no limits existed to the fictions people could convince themselves were truth. A good detective, Maureen thought, considers every angle, every possibility, no matter how improbable. What if Solomon Heath was nothing more than a father trying to protect his son? What if he wasn't, she thought, for the sake of argument, a criminal mastermind? If she didn't allow for that possibility, she thought, she could waste a lot of time and energy, neither of which she had to spare, going after the wrong man. What if there wasn't any evidence linking him to the Watchmen because he wasn't connected to them?

"I brought Caleb into the family business, gave him properties to run. I gave him the River Garden development. I gave him Harmony Oaks. To teach him responsibility, how to be answerable and accountable to other people. To at least give him something to do besides running around the swamp with those crazy people."

"Is this the part of the story," Maureen said, "where you tell me he was never the same after his mother left New Orleans. Or was it Katrina? Was it the storm's fault? Poor lost lamb, Caleb. Please."

"You don't think I warned Caleb away from those people?" Heath asked. "You don't think I warned him of the consequences?"

"Posh digs in Dubai," Maureen said. "Some consequences. He can't do anything without you. Without your blessing or your money. You've rebuilt half the city. You build shit across the world. And you couldn't get your son to find different friends? Ones who don't want to be terrorists? You didn't give a shit what your son did, until today. And even now I'm not so sure."

"What makes you think you know anything about me and my family?" Solomon asked. "Because you stood outside a garden party looking in through the fence for a night? Because crooked, disturbed cops you knew nothing about told you stories?" Heath folded his arms, staring her down. "And you did everything, I'm sure, that your parents told you to do."

Maureen laughed. "I smoked cigarettes and raided the liquor cabinet. I didn't arm cop killers."

Heath stared at her, solemn and angry.

She'd seen that look in a parent's eye before, in dealings she'd had with parents worth a lot less money and with a lot less power than Heath. Parents who listened to the detective say right to their faces, "We have witnesses, we have the gun," and who shook their heads and said, "Not my son." Maybe certain things really were universal. What wasn't universal, Maureen thought, was access to plane tickets to Dubai.

"I've known this Napoleon Gage almost half my life," Heath said, "though he used to go by a different name. In the eighties, he led a congregation of sorts. I gave them, gave *him*, money. Large amounts of money. Several of us did. Here in New Orleans. In Baton Rouge. He had pull in the lower parishes. He was good at getting people to vote, and vote a certain way. Local elections, state elections. He had a good racket going. He could play the game."

"In a way that made you and your friends the big winners, I'm guessing," Maureen said. "What happened? He finally caught on?"

"He expanded," Heath said. "He came to New Orleans. And when I saw him up close, I realized that *he* wasn't playing games."

"He got tired of being the good soldier," Maureen said, "and wanted an empire of his own, like you."

"You've seen those people in the Quarter," Heath said, "with the big white crosses, the banners with the flames, screaming about hell and the devil and damnation. It was like that, the crew he led, but worse. Much, much worse. They wore fatigues. They marched through the streets of the Quarter, chanting. I went to see him once on a Fat Tuesday, in Jackson Square. It's a big day for those types, too. You'll see. The rage that came from him, that he inspired. The vitriol. The hate. I'd never seen anything like it. Haven't since."

He paused, shaking his head at the recollection. "I cut him off after that. Turned my back on him. I got the others I'd persuaded to finance him before to cut him off as well. His resources dried up. I heard there was infighting in his ranks."

"You undermined him."

"He had to go. It was clear. People like him never get *less* angry. Letting it out only lets it grow."

"I'd imagine he didn't take to that," Maureen said. "To you shunning him."

And I can see, she thought, what he wanted with your son. Knowing Caleb's money came from Solomon, Gage built his movement, his army with Heath money all over again. Until it cost him his own son. The sins of the father weigh heavy, indeed.

"I admit I felt a twinge of admiration," Heath said. "All the time I thought I was using him, he was using me right back." He finished his cold coffee. "And I admit that after I stopped the money I was afraid of him and his thugs. I spent a good six months looking over my shoulder.

Then there was a terrible fire, a lesbian bar on the edge of the Quarter. Multiple deaths. He was never connected to it, but he disappeared from New Orleans before the ashes went cold.

"I'm telling you these things," Heath said, "because you need to believe that Leon Gage is the real thing. The worst kind of true believer. He's a dangerous man, and completely capable of the atrocities that happened today. And I have no loyalty to him, no reason to protect him."

"It works out real well for you," Maureen said, "if we believe that someone else is the real threat here. The radical, the fringe player, the lone wolf. You'd love for us to believe there's only one rat in the kitchen. That there's not a big, teeming nest just out of sight."

"You're so terribly new to all of this," Heath said. "This place, its history. Our history. You're in so far over your head you don't even know you're drowning. Wake up. Why do you think Detillier picked you as the canary in the coal mine? Because you have no idea who Leon Gage really is. You couldn't have a conversation with him if you did. You couldn't stomach it. And because he'd never talk to a cop who might remember who he was."

Maureen handed Heath back the plastic cup. She couldn't look at him. She had to get away from him. Talking to him was worse than talking to Gage, because what Heath said made sense to her. "Thanks for the coffee."

"Do yourself a favor," Heath said, taking the cup from her. "Ask your FBI friend about a man named Leo Freeman and an abortion clinic in Baker, Florida, what happened there in 1993. Ask about the dead doctor. Ask him about the girls' shelter in Crestview, about the fire there in 1995. The eight bodies pulled from the ruins."

He offered her the thermos. "Take the rest, bring the thermos back another time. You need all the help you can get."

"That's okay," Maureen said, and she climbed into the cruiser. "I have what I need."

Before dawn, she decided, she would find proof of who both Solomon Heath and Napoleon Gage really were, one way or another.

She started the car and turned on the headlights. She pulled into Solomon Heath's driveway, the headlights shining into the first-floor windows. Then she backed out of the driveway, easing the car alongside Solomon. "Good night for now, Mr. Heath. I have things to do tonight. But you'll see me again. Believe that."

27

Maureen parked the patrol car at the back of Touro Infirmary, by the loading docks and service entrances, away from the cops and the press crowding the front of the hospital.

As she got out of the car, two security guards came to meet her. Without a word, they escorted her into the bowels of the hospital. Maureen knew they were being overly careful and she let them. She didn't expect to get shot at tonight. The Watchmen had slunk back into their hiding places, she figured, as is typical of bullies, because they were cowards at their core. Now we know about them. Now we're on the lookout. Not just me—every one of us cops, Maureen thought, is living under a death threat. And every one of us knows it. Who she'd been avoiding by sneaking around the back was not the Watchmen, but other cops. She didn't want to talk to them. Maybe later she would, maybe in the morning, but not right then. Every ounce of energy she had left, physical and emotional, was devoted to getting to Preacher's hospital room.

Once inside the hospital, Maureen's uniform let her move freely.

She realized as she waited alone for the elevator that no one she had passed as she moved through the building, not doctors, not nurses, not orderlies, not patients, would so much as look at her. Everyone lowered their eyes. Did they know who she was? Maureen wondered. The story of her house getting shot up was in the news again because of the day's events. Did the people she walked past know that she had been the Watchmen's first target? That the NOPD had failed to stop them from striking again?

We'd had warning, Maureen thought, and we did nothing. The morning her house was shot up, Skinner had come to the house to speak with her and to survey the damage. To make promises, to her and to the cameras, like a good politician. And maybe he would've done more. But then Quinn had gone in the river with a prisoner and neither of them had come out alive, and the department turned its focus to squashing the scandal that had threatened to emerge around Ruiz and Quinn and the Heaths. The feds had only taken an active role in the case several weeks after the incident. Maybe they'd been watching all along, but so what if they had? What mattered was they hadn't done anything to help until it was too late.

We devoted our energies to covering our asses, Maureen thought, instead of defending ourselves. We played politics. As Preacher would say, we let them get behind us. Even me, she thought. I was too busy running drunk through the downtown streets at night, chasing impossible revenge against a man I've already killed, to do the work that would have protected Mays and Bridges and Harrigan and Preacher. The suspension wasn't my choice, Maureen thought. But the choices I made about how to handle it, giving in to the selfishness and rage and self-pity, that was all me.

The elevator arrived. Maureen let the doors open and close without getting on.

She hadn't put Preacher in this hospital; she knew that. Her ego wasn't quite that outsized. But could she have kept him out of it? Could she have found Madison Leary before she ended up dead? Lost to herself and no use to anyone else. Maureen grinned at her warped reflection in the silver elevator doors. I find her, Maureen thought, I keep her alive, and maybe Atkinson learns something. Maybe she shakes loose from Leary's tangled brain some iota of information about the Watchmen that stops today from happening. She shouldn't have been drinking while she was out, Maureen thought. She shouldn't have been distracted by the men, like the one from d.b.a. or even the one from the Irish Garden. She should have stayed focused. She could have worked a lot smarter.

Shit, everything she had ever done since she was about twelve she could've done smarter one way or another. Just ask her mother about that.

And now, tonight, she *should* be out for revenge. She *should* be on the warpath, along with every other cop in the city. But she felt none of that. She didn't feel dangerous and frightening. Not like she had when she'd stalked the streets with her ASP. Right then, she felt so exhausted with anger, confusion, and grief that she feared she might fall over. She had no idea what to do. She couldn't even see the rest of her shift past this visit with Preacher. She felt like the doctors here might not let her out of the hospital, and she wasn't sure she'd fight them on it.

Under the harsh, mundane fluorescents of the hospital hallways, waiting for the elevator to return, the theories of vengeance and conspiracy she'd spun in the isolation of her patrol car's front seat became fantastical. Half-mad and paranoid. Was it so impossible, so outlandish that Solomon Heath was a rich white man with a black sheep son he couldn't control? Was she becoming as delusional, Maureen worried, and not for the first time that night, as the woman who'd died in the fishing goods aisle of a half-empty Walmart? Was that the way she was headed? Living in fear. Driven by rage. Seeing webs of conspiracies and armies of enemies wherever she went. In the end, putting a bullet in her brain for the sake of a false flag. Or maybe dragging a razor across her throat to silence the voices.

The elevator door opened. She stepped aside to let an orderly pushing a woozy young girl in a wheelchair pass, pale and bald from chemo.

What she felt was fucking helpless. And she *hated* it.

How're we going to protect anyone, she thought, from anything if we can't protect ourselves? How are we going to get these guys? She stepped into the elevator this time, just before the doors closed.

She rubbed her eyes, thinking of those long frazzled moments on Esplanade, the driver of the van in her gun sights. How long before one of us pulls the trigger on the wrong white van, on the wrong guy in a pair of camouflage cargo pants? Under this kind of pressure, she knew it was only a matter of time before someone who shared her uniform made a tragic mistake, either by pulling the trigger at the wrong time or by not pulling it at the right time. And wouldn't that prove Leon Gage's point? Wouldn't that play right into his hands?

But who could blame us for having itchy trigger fingers? Maureen thought.

These guys wear grenades. They've got bigger, better guns than we do, and they buy them in suburban convention centers, Maureen thought. They're not afraid to die in the act of killing us. If I wanted this, if I wanted a gig in counterterrorism, she thought, I would've become a Marine instead of a cop. At least then I'd have the necessary combat training. And better guns.

This situation with the Watchmen *cannot* be allowed to continue, she thought. Somebody has to step up. Even if by some miracle no one else got shot over the next few days or weeks, the psychology of the threat was too corrosive. She'd heard the chatter. Starting tomorrow, solo patrols were over. The change would cut deep into the number of cars the department had on the street. This with football season in full swing and the holidays coming on hard.

She checked her phone. Nothing from Detillier. No word from him all night. She'd called him twice. Both times her call went straight to voice mail. The longer she went without hearing from him, the more strongly she suspected that he was in trouble. He had fucked up by sending her to meet Gage, she figured, and by missing entirely the multiple-shooter operation, the terrorist attack, that had been executed right under his nose.

Well, fuck the FBI, then. Fuck the feds. She didn't need them. She hadn't been around for Katrina, but waiting for the agents of the federal government to come riding to the city's rescue was not a favorite New Orleans pastime. She'd learned that much already.

The elevator doors opened onto Preacher's floor. She felt a familiar sting at the back of her eyes. Maureen was tempted to let the doors close and take her back down the way she'd come. She'd have to go farther back than the ground floor of the hospital, she realized, to start this day over.

28

Outside Preacher's hospital room, Officer Morello, the night's guard, slept, arms crossed, chin on his chest, in a plastic chair far too small for him, an empty Popeyes box under his chair. Maureen could smell the heavy, buttery odor of the fried chicken fat and the greasy carcass of bones, even stronger than the medicinal antiseptic odor of the hallway. She was almost disgusted. Who could leave that trash sitting there like that? In a hospital, no less. Morello defined lazy, took it to new heights. Or was it lows?

Then she realized that if the smell reached Preacher, he wouldn't complain. Popeyes would be a finer bouquet to him than any bunch of flowers.

Frayed and exhausted, listening with envy to Morello's deep rhythmic breathing, Maureen stood for several long minutes in the corridor outside Preacher's room, letting the wall hold her up. Nurses in scrubs hustled by, their heads down, their white sneakers squeaking on the tile. Somebody groaned in her sleep down the hall.

Maureen positioned herself at an angle to the door, in a spot where she could see Preacher, but she figured he couldn't see her.

To her surprise, Preacher was awake.

His eyes were half-closed. His head was turned to one side, resting deep in the pillow. He had a slight smile on his face, as if he were fighting sleep while listening to someone tell a good story. Maureen could hear the murmur of the other person's voice, but couldn't see him or make out any of his words. Though Preacher was about as pale as buttermilk, he looked better than she had anticipated. In fact, her relief at the sight of him was so great she wanted to melt down the wall and puddle on the floor.

All night when she thought about Preacher her imagination had painted him, Maureen realized, maybe because of the manner in which he was shot, as a battlefield casualty. She'd anticipated a bloody mass of bandages and wires and tubes. She'd expected machine noise worthy of an assembly line keeping him alive. Looking at him lying there, Maureen saw tubes and wires and monitors, bags of liquid suspended over his bed, but right in front of her eyes Preacher's body performed its essential functions on his own power source, not relying on one plugged into the wall.

She should've known. There couldn't be many people in New Orleans harder to kill, Maureen thought, than Preacher Boyd.

So now what?

Preacher being conscious was a stroke of luck, actually. Seeing him alive and breathing with her own eyes had been the point of her visit. She hadn't planned on being able to talk to him, though she wanted to. She needed to know more about what had happened at the restaurant if she was going to do anything about it. After tonight, she wouldn't have the freedom to move, the liberty to investigate the day's events that she had now. She had wasted hours obsessing over Solomon Heath. Was there another connection out there to the Watchmen, other than Leary, other than Heath, that she had missed?

She heard murmurs again in the hospital room. Someone was

definitely in there with Preacher, talking to him. She studied him, a sheet-covered mound in his bed, framed in the doorway. Maybe she shouldn't talk to him quite yet. He needed rest, she figured, more than he needed anything else. She should leave him alone and work the streets like a law-enforcement professional. Like Preacher had trained her.

"You gonna stand out there the *entire* shift feeling sorry for yourself?" Preacher called from his bed. "Or you gonna come in here and offer your condolences?"

Maureen peeled herself off the wall and walked into the room, her hands clasped in front of her belt buckle, shamed like a child called in to see the principal. She said, "Condolences are for the survivors of the dead."

"And there will be plenty of those to go around," Preacher said.

Maureen stopped short, not because of his words, but because of Preacher's company.

In an armchair pulled alongside the bed sat a hefty man in loose jeans and a dirty gray Saints T-shirt. The man reminded Maureen of hired muscle, of a security guard or a bouncer, maybe a gangland legbreaker, gone to seed. He had dark chocolate skin, a large round and bald head, and an expansive, expressive face with wide brown eyes. He was about Preacher's age. He needed a shave. His stubble had a dusting of gray at the jawline. He nodded to Maureen and said nothing.

At the edge of the bed, he and Preacher held hands.

"I thought you couldn't see me," Maureen said to Preacher. "I'm sorry to intrude." She broke into a smile. "Man, I was expecting so much worse. The stories going around. You wouldn't believe."

"I couldn't see you," Preacher said. "But I sure could smell you. How many cigarettes you smoke tonight anyway?"

On cue, Maureen coughed. "All of them."

Preacher turned his head to the man beside him. Their hands stayed clasped. "Officer Coughlin, this is Doctor Anthony Green." He turned back to Maureen. "My partner."

Maureen almost said *In what?* but she caught herself. "Well, shit."

Preacher grinned. "You had no idea? Coughlin, I must say I'm surprised. And here I was admiring your discretion."

"I have no gaydar," Maureen said, shaking her head. "None." She shrugged. "Even after all those years in the bars in New York. It's kind of embarrassing. It's a blind spot."

Anthony patted the back of Preacher's hand, careful of the IV, a smile curling his lips. "This is the one in such a hurry to be a detective? The talented one? Your last great trainee."

Maureen nodded, hands on her hips. "I can see the attraction." She walked over to him, her hand extended. "Nice to meet you, Doctor. You work here at Touro?"

Anthony gripped Maureen's hand, rising slightly from his seat. He shook his head at her question. "I'm an orthodontist. I have a practice in the Gentilly, near where we live." He raised his eyebrows. Tears welled in his eyes. "What happened to this one today. Years, decades with hardly a scratch. Then this."

Preacher reached out, wincing from the effort, touching the back of his hand to Anthony's face. He lowered his arm, settled his hand on his chest, tossing a quick, commiserating glance to Maureen before exhaling to release the pain of moving. "I was the lucky one today. Fucking bad fucking day. Goddamn."

"Fifteen years," Anthony said. "For fifteen years I've been making fun of him because every time we go out to eat, this one has to sit with his back to the wall, somewhere he can see the door. You're not Wild Bill Hickok, I said. This isn't Tombstone. Then today happens."

"So this means I don't have to hear that anymore, right?" Preacher said.

Anthony shook his head.

Maureen raised her hands. "What did happen, Preach?"

Preacher raised three fingers. "I took three, believe it or not. One in the left side, one in the left hip, one in the right thigh. The two on the left, they were through and through. Graze wounds, really. Caught mostly body fat and took some of it with them. The one in the thigh, that was a bit more complicated. That one they had to go in and get. I got it around here somewhere." He pushed himself up against the pillows stacked behind him. The pain took his breath away and he gasped. Sweat speckled his forehead. "Maybe another time."

"Yeah, absolutely," Maureen said. Anthony was squeezing the armrests on his chair. Maureen sensed his patience with her visit was waning. "Preach, relax," she said. "I'll take your word for it."

Preacher glanced at Anthony, then looked at Maureen. She could tell he felt Anthony's impatience. And that he wanted to tell the story. That he had been waiting for another cop to walk in at the right time. He'd been waiting, she thought, for me.

Preacher licked his lips. "Guy walks into the joint calm as you please. Solo. Long coat like a gunslinger. I think about it that way now, I didn't then. Nobody did. Nobody was thinking gun. Why would they? Because he has a long coat? It's wintertime, practically. And all the shit that's gone on in this country and we still don't think about it. But something about him tripped the wire, eventually, you know, if not at first? He caught my eye. He had that hinky vibe. Not that I had much time to analyze; he came right for us, and the place ain't that big."

"Like he knew you were there," Maureen said. "Knew who you were."

"Yeah," Preacher said. "Yeah. The way he crossed the room, the look on his face, he wasn't choosing from a random array of targets, he was searching for someone specific. At first I figured he was meeting people, and that's who he was looking for. But then he locked on target when he saw me."

Anthony wiped his hand down his face. "You're making me ill."

"Then he made a move," Preacher said. "I could see it—the first, like, microgestures, something in the shoulders or his hips or something— and I knew shooter's stance was his next position. My brain added it up, the little things wrong about him. I hesitated for what felt like half a second. Less. Wesley had his back to the whole thing. I saw him see something in my face. He had a forkful of pork chop hanging there halfway to his mouth the whole time, white bean gravy dripping onto the tabletop. I couldn't decide what to do: if I should say something, or try and push Wesley aside."

He paused, catching his breath. Anthony set himself to rise from his chair, changed his mind and stayed seated. Preacher said, "That's what cost us, in the end. I was too slow. My brain had it put together, but this fat, old cigar-smoking body . . . In that half moment, the shooter got his gun up and let loose."

"Preacher, please," Anthony said.

"Wesley caught the first couple of rounds in the back," Preacher said. "I think he saved my life taking those. I would've taken those bullets in the guts. He definitely bought me time to return fire. I got my gun up and squeezed. It was so fucking fast. One moment this mope was walking in, the next my whole lower half is on fire, I got three holes in me, I'm on my back, blood is on the walls, plates are breaking, people are scream- ing. I only knew the shooter was dead 'cause he had stopped shooting."

Pausing for breath, he looked at Anthony, as if checking to see if his partner could stand the rest of the story. Preacher turned back to Mau- reen. He seemed to sink even deeper into his pillows, a wounded bear settling into the snow. "I was never more scared in my life than when it was over, when I was lying there bleeding. I thought, what if there's another one, what if he's not alone? I thought I was dead, thought I was dying, I thought I was dreaming, I thought I was having a heart attack. Fuck." He was out of breath.

Anthony held up his hand. "I think maybe this visit has gone on long enough. Thanks be to God, y'all will have plenty of time to talk about this, but, Preacher, you've been shot. Three times. You need to rest."

"I'm good," Preacher said.

"Maureen . . . Officer," Anthony said, "we're glad you stopped by. We are. I know he was worried about you. And I'm glad to meet you."

"I wish it was under better circumstances."

"I'm right here, Anthony," Preacher said. "Don't talk about me like I'm not."

Maureen pressed her lips together, suppressing her laughter. Heinous as the situation was, she could hardly believe that hours after she was frantic with grief and worry that he was dead, she was standing there watching Preacher have a spat with his dentist boyfriend. Fucking New Orleans.

"Maureen will come back before her shift tomorrow night," Anthony said.

"She has to go out there again *tonight*," Preacher said. "These people came after her first. I *told* you about that. They're out there."

"Anthony's right," Maureen said. "And the Watchmen tipped their hand. They're gonna go to ground now, these fucks. I'm safer tonight than I've been in weeks."

"Because terrorists always do the logical thing," Preacher said.

"Because they're cowards," Maureen said. "And cowards run when you chase them. They scatter when they lose the advantage. All fucking bullies are the same."

"Okay, okay," Preacher said. "One more thing. There's something I need to tell you tonight, Coughlin. Something you could tell Detillier about."

She decided not to tell Preacher about Detillier's disappearance. Why give him any more to worry about? And if Preacher gave her good-enough cause, she'd go looking for him one more time. "Whatcha got?"

"I'm going for a soda," Anthony said, clearly flustered. He got up, the chair squeaking loudly on the floor, and walked toward the door. "Make it quick, you two."

"It's out of love," Preacher said. "He's been waiting to meet you. He has. It's the circumstances, like you said. He doesn't even drink soda."

"I think he's doing great," Maureen said. "If it were me, I'd be spitting nails and out for blood."

"You mean you're not?" Preacher said. "How are you holding up, by the way? You look terrible. Like, I hope I don't look as bad as you."

"He's gonna be pissed if I'm here when he gets back," Maureen said. "What was it you wanted to tell me?"

"Always the artful dodger," Preacher said. "When we were talking to Detillier, he wanted Madison Leary because she connects to the

Watchmen, right? She was the only lead we had left. Quinn, Ruiz, Bobby Scales, Caleb Heath, the other loose ends are tied off."

"She's not talking to anyone," Maureen said. "Ever. You know my feelings on this. We should be squeezing Solomon Heath. Now. We'll never have more leverage than we do tonight."

"Fuck him," Preacher said. He raised an admonishing finger. "In fact, you make sure you stay away from him. You have impulse-control problems. Besides that, I have a better idea. An easier target. One less likely to get you in trouble if things go . . . sideways."

"I'm all ears."

"Who connected Caleb Heath and the Watchmen to Bobby Scales?" Preacher asked.

"Quinn. We've gone over this a hundred times." This was old news. How much blood had Preacher lost? Maureen wondered.

"But it *wasn't* Quinn," Preacher said. "There was a middleman. Remember?"

Maureen got it. Fucking A. "Shadow. Quinn and Ruiz had Shadow on a string. He was the matchmaker, the one who connected Heath and the Watchmen with Scales. And that motherfucker is out there on the streets." She sat in the chair, inched it closer to Preacher's bedside. "That's a great idea in theory. Shadow is definitely a forgotten link to the Watchmen, but, man, that cat is harder to find than Leary."

"That's where you're wrong," Preacher said. "This shit with the white Camaro, around that grocery store, I'll bet anything it's drawn him out of whatever hole he's been hiding in since Quinn put Bobby Scales in the Mississippi. A shift in power, a change in ownership of the territory in front of that store? I *promise* you Shadow is hovering on the edges of that shit. It's what he does. The problem has never been seeing him. It's getting anything to stick to him. He just glides over the surface of things. It's why he's called Shadow."

"Little E might know something," Maureen said. "You think he's the way to go?"

"No doubt. He's dug into the neighborhood like a tick. That's why I wanted you looking for him over at the grocery store before this other shit went down."

"What if he doesn't know," Maureen asked, "or he won't say?"

"Coughlin, I'm in a hospital bed," Preacher said. "For the forseeable future. I gotta do your job for you from here?"

"I don't want to fuck this up is what I'm saying. I wanna move as fast as possible and make sure I get results."

"Cops are dead over this," Preacher said. "Today isn't the end of it. They'll come after us again, and Shadow connects to the men who did it. You said it yourself: there will never be a time when you have more authority, and more freedom to use it to get the answers you need, than you do right now, tonight. Use it, Coughlin. Tell the rest of the squad. Hit the neighborhood like a fucking hurricane. Answers, Officer. By any means necessary. Believe."

Maureen rose from the chair, stepped to the bed. She reached out, set her hand on Preacher's. She figured she had until morning before the powers-that-be got their shit together. She had a lot to do before then. Miles to go before she slept. "I'm going to take care of this, Preach. I promise." She walked to the door.

Before crossing the threshold, she stopped, turned back to him. "The other two cops, that was opportunity. But you. They came after you because of me. Your connection to me got you shot."

Preacher blinked at her, waiting a long time to speak. "So."

"Well, I just want to—"

"You apologize to me," Preacher said, coughing, wincing at the pain. "And I will get out of this bed. So help me God, I will put you over my knee."

Maureen sputtered. "I mean, I—"

"You're right," Preacher said. "I was targeted because I'm close to you. So what? What if instead of hunting me they hit the streets today gunning for someone else? That's better? It'd be better, you'd *feel* better, if instead of coming after an old warhorse savvy enough to see them coming, they went after two more young'uns with pretty wives and little kids? They don't come for me, and maybe we have four dead cops today instead of two. Think about that."

Maureen put her hands on her hips, hung her head. She blew out her breath.

"I love ya, Coughlin. I do. But you gotta quit thinking you're at the center of everything. This city was fucked up when you got here. It'll be fucked up when we're dead and buried. You're just another marcher in the fucking parade. The sooner you learn that, the happier you'll be. Welcome to the party."

29

Shortly before three a.m. Maureen rolled up on Little E in a dark and quiet section of Central City. Madison Leary had been hard to find. Finding Shadow would be a challenge. Little E was not tough to track. His accessibility was part of what made him a good snitch.

E sat on the wide, dirty concrete steps of an abandoned house, next door to the Big Man Lounge, a can of beer between his feet. Maureen pulled up slowly, roof lights off, bouncing the creaking patrol car over the curb, halfway onto the cracked-up sidewalk.

On the steps of the house, three other men sat with Little E. Each of them was positioned on a different step. Each of them nursed the amber glow of a cigarette, or maybe a roach. They sat with their thin shoulders hunched deep into their old second- and thirdhand coats. None of them had so much as flinched at the arrival of an NOPD cruiser. They knew that had Maureen been looking to make trouble for them, she would have arrived with much more bluster.

She got out of the car, zipping up her black leather NOPD jacket. An old soul tune played in the bar, floating out into the street. She closed the car door, dug her knit watch cap from her jacket pocket, and pulled it snug on her head. She blew into her fist as she stepped up onto the sidewalk. She had gloves in her pocket but was saving them for later. Behind her, she heard the rattle of a metal gate. She turned to see the bar owner, his brown face a scowl in the shadows, locking up the Big Man. The music cut off mid-song. The neon beer signs and colored lights in the small windows went dark. The men watched her from the steps. She studied their emotionless faces, hoping to recognize someone in addition to Little E. She didn't like that E wasn't alone.

On the one hand, because he had company, Little E could be less likely to talk to her. He couldn't have the whole neighborhood knowing he was an NOPD snitch. He at least couldn't let it be this obvious. And if he did talk, an outcome to which Maureen was especially committed, his cover would be blown as soon as Shadow got picked up. At worst his life would be in danger, at best E might be useless to her and Preacher as a snitch anymore. The trick to negotiating the situation, she realized, would be what she and any other cops did with Shadow. They didn't want to arrest him, not tonight. Not if it could be avoided. She could let that be known, make it part of Little E's message. Tonight they wanted information. That might be enough to save Little E from too harsh a retribution. Maybe.

"Mr. Etienne," Maureen called. "Come down from the steps and see me, please."

E glanced at his compatriots, who looked away from him. They gazed past Maureen, their faces blank, and over the neighborhood, demonstrably ignoring not only E but her as well. No matter what happened in front of them, Maureen realized, they would see and hear nothing. Tonight, she realized the men were letting her know, lots of things otherwise forbidden would get a pass.

Abandoned to his fate, E leaned forward, groaning, to grab his beer.

He stood, unsteady, and came carefully down the marble steps, one hand at the small of his back, as if Maureen's visit had interrupted a long night of heavy lifting.

"Fellas," Maureen called out, "why don't y'all head back inside the bar? It's cold out here, anyways."

"They closed," Etienne said, sniffling. "That's why we out here in the first place."

"They can take a walk," Maureen said to him, her voice calm and low, "or I can call another unit and you and me can take a ride together to lockup." She paused. Let the message sink in. It was smarter, she thought, better neighborhood politics, to let E negotiate the next moves with his friends than for her to push them around. She lit a cigarette. Patience, Maureen thought, that's what Preacher would counsel. "I hate to break up a party, but we're in a bad mood tonight."

"Mos def," Little E said, turning. "I got you. Fellas, I'll catch up with y'all around the way." He gestured at Maureen with his beer can. "I got some parole thing I gotta clear up. Ain't no thing. Just be a minute. Nothing to worry about."

No way they believe that story, Maureen thought. Nobody, especially not a beat cop, comes around following up on "parole things" at three in the morning. But the men got the message they needed. They stood, picked up their beers, and sauntered down the steps. One of them muttered an "all right" as they walked away into the darkness, shaking the cold out of their backs and shoulders.

She noticed Little E eyeing her cigarette. She gave him one from her pack, lit it for him.

"OC, I been hearing *things*," Little E said, animated now. "Crazy shit." He leaned in close, as if there were anyone else on the block to overhear them. He stank. "I heard the Klan got Preacher. That true? No way that's true, right?" He swallowed hard. His emotion, his concern, it wasn't an act, Maureen thought. Etienne was upset. Not because cops who were strangers to him got killed, she knew, but because Preacher, who had done Little E an untold number of small favors, had been shot.

"First off," Maureen said, "Preacher is alive. And he's going to make it. I saw him not too long ago tonight."

Etienne smiled and clapped his gloved hands. He pumped his fist. "Yes, indeed. Ol' Preach. He a tough motherfucker." He tapped his fist over his heart. "You tell him, you tell him Little E got prayers up for him."

"I will," Maureen said. "He'll be glad to hear it."

"So it *was* the Klan then?" Little E said. "I heard they was back around. Hard times. Hard times."

"Not the Klan," Maureen said. "Something like it, but different. Something new. They're antigovernment, anti-police. They call themselves the Watchmen Brigade."

Etienne was skeptical. He shrugged. "Nigger-hating country white boys with guns. Am I right? Maybe they don't call theyselves *Klan*, but they *ain't* nothin' *new*. Believe that."

"The two cops that were killed, they were white," Maureen said.

Etienne shrugged again. "I'm just glad it weren't niggers that shot them cops. Not that I'm glad they got shot. I don't like nobody getting shot down like that." He paused. "Even y'all. It's bad all around."

"The Watchmen Brigade," Maureen said. "What do you know about them?"

"They *sound* like people I would hear about?"

"They've been doing business in the city since the summer. Especially in this neighborhood. Buying guns, selling guns. Throwing lots of cash around, talking about a war. A revolution."

Little E nodded. "Now that you mention it that way. They the ones doing business with Bobby Scales, hiding their guns at his place." He pointed to the NOPD emblem on her jacket. "I thought y'all put a stop to that business when Bobby went in the river with that cop."

When Bobby went in the river, Maureen thought. Pretty diplomatic of you, Mr. Etienne. She wondered how much he had learned from Preacher. "So you knew Bobby Scales, knew his business?"

E slugged his beer. "I knew *of* him. I kept my distance from his business, believe that." He looked away, down at the street. "You see where it got him."

Maureen recalled the times she'd observed Preacher working an informant, smooth and rhythmic in the way he talked, his questions and tone guiding the snitch this way then that way, massaging, like a man gently polishing clear a smudged marble surface. She thought of watching Atkinson hammer a suspect in the box, direct and relentless as a pile driver. This was a time for Preacher's way. The information you wanted, she'd learned from him, you had to circle it, come at it from the side, indirect. If you led the person right toward the prized information, the one important answer, they'd anticipate what you wanted, they could see the next question coming, and the question after that, and they'd start planning their answers, lining up their lies. You'd never get a clear picture through the smudges.

"Preacher and me," Maureen said. "We were working on something before he got shot. He said you could help with it. He told me you *specifically*. He'd be here himself, you know, if today hadn't happened. I'm here with you because he needs your help."

"Makes me sad," Little E said, "what happened to him. Preacher's a good man. We've had our things, you know, our differences, like friends do, but he done right by me most of the time. By a lot of people in this neighborhood. A lot of fellas in this neighborhood making ends instead of doing time because Preacher a real-world person. He know when someone need a break. Always." Etienne dragged his wrist under his runny nose. "Fuck. I was eight years old, selling peanuts up Napoleon Avenue on the parade route first time I met Preacher. He used to come in the Fox, drink a beer with my old man on Super Sundays."

Maureen smiled. "Selling peanuts? Exactly how'd you 'meet' Preacher?"

"Yeah, well, you know." He couldn't stop his grin. "Pick up a lost wallet or two. Lot of people drop their wallet while they chasing beads. It happens. You work Mardi Gras, you'll see."

"I bet I will."

"But I don't know *nobody*," Etienne said. "I don't know *nothin'* about nobody out killing cops."

Maureen waved the idea away. "It's not that. I know that if you knew something that would put me on the Watchmen, you would've told me by now. You wouldn't waste my time with memory lane. Not with Preacher nursing bullet wounds. I want to know about the grocery, the one on Washington and Magnolia."

Etienne's eyes darted sideways for an instant. Bingo. She had him.

"It a grocery. Chips, cold drinks, nothin' special."

"I'm not looking to go shopping," Maureen said. "The white Camaro. The dude with the white pit bull and the sweaters. What's the story?"

"You the police," Etienne said. "You tell me."

"Couple weeks ago, the boys out front were in red. Nowadays, they're different boys and they're wearing white. I wanna know why."

"You asking about shit that's over my head. I don't run with fellas like that. Red or white."

"I'm not asking for the whole operation," Maureen said. "Tell me what you're hearing, what's floating around in the air. Rumors. Talk."

Little E let out a long sigh. Maureen lit two cigarettes, gave him one. He said, "The dude with the dog, Big Mike, I don't know him. Them boys with him make like they a Josephine Street crew, and maybe Big Mike is, I don't go around asking, and maybe some of them J-Street boys is over there with him now, but word is them boys hanging around wearing white is *really* downtown muscle. The reds, they was two uptown neighborhood crews really, and they started beefing with each other, like internally. Right about that time the Iberville started getting torn down, which eliminated prime Fourth Ward territory."

"So Big Mike," Maureen said, "he's making a move on this neighborhood by bringing in those Fourth Ward boys, using them for muscle in exchange for kicking something back to them."

Etienne shrugged. "Their spots in the Iberville are torn up now. Their neighborhood is gone. Ain't there no more. Nobody living there, and the new place is going to look like that Harmony place across from the grocery, nice and shit. Prob'ly put a school there, too. Times are chang-ing, I guess."

"So how did news of two uptown crews beefing get down to the Iberville?"

"You got me," Etienne said. "Small city, you know. Everybody in the same business, basically. Word travels."

Maureen moved half a step closer to Etienne. "No. No. There's more to it than that. It's a big leap, a big power move, bringing people from way down the Iberville up to Central City. Especially for someone like Big Mike, who's not real known as far as I can tell, certainly not outside this neighborhood."

"I mean, I don't know," Etienne said. "I've never been *in* the game. I use every now and then, I ain't gonna lie, but I ain't like *in* it, ya know?"

"And yet you do seem to know quite a bit," Maureen said.

E stepped away from her. He straightened his coat. "No offense, but shouldn't you be after those boys that shot y'all's own? You know how we do. You don't like Big Mike, give it six months, someone else be out in front of that store with a different car and a different dog and everyone be wearing, I don't fucking know, whatever the fuck, purple or some shit."

"Back to Big Mike," Maureen said. "Here's what I'm thinking. There's one key thing that he would need to exploit a crisis like a gang beef with new muscle from outside the neighborhood. He'd need a broker, a go-between."

"I have no idea what you're talking about," Etienne said. "I'm not smart enough to follow you. I'm just a convict. And I'm getting cold."

"An inside man," Maureen said. "A matchmaker would make a move like Big Mike's so much easier. An inside man would get himself paid and protected greasing the wheels for a man like Big Mike, a big mover like him."

Little E raised his beer can to his mouth, but he'd drunk it dry. He studied the empty can, tossed it in the gutter, jammed his hands in his coat pockets. "If you say so, Officer. You're the one trained in this shit."

Maureen closed the distance between them again, steeling herself against his stench. "I want you to stand there and tell me you haven't seen Shadow hanging around these past couple of weeks. Everything that's gone on, you haven't been hearing his name?"

"Shadow?"

"Yeah, Shadow. I'm stuttering? This alliance with the Iberville guys, you think that doesn't have Shadow written all over it?"

Etienne's mouth hung open as he thought of what to say.

"Don't you fucking lie to me," Maureen said. She touched the leather over her ribs. The ASP rested in an inside pocket. She'd carried it with her everywhere she'd gone tonight. She didn't want to use it on Little E. He was small and scared, cold and weak. Not the kind of person she carried it for. But that didn't mean she wouldn't use it if he left her no choice. "Don't you lie to me, E. Not now, not tonight."

"I heard things," Etienne said. "I heard this was Shadow's big move. Y'all saw to that, you gave him the opportunity. Getting rid of Scales like y'all did opened up the game for Big Mike."

"One goes down," Maureen said, "and another steps up."

"Only, you know Shadow," Etienne said. "He never the man on the throne. He the man behind the man, that's how he do. Someone else always get to take the fall."

"Not this time," Maureen said. "This time it's him I want."

"Get in line," Little E said. He stamped his feet against the cold. His discomfort was making him brave. "Nobody know where Shadow stay. You think you're the first cop to ask me that? Damn, OC."

Maureen reached into her jacket pockets. She pulled out her leather gloves. E's eyes got wide. She'd been standing there with her hands turning blue to preserve that effect. She slid one hand into a black glove then the other. "I'm not the first cop to ask that, but, and this I promise you, I am the most persuasive. I'm the one asking tonight." She flexed her fingers in her gloves. The leather creaked. "Where is he?"

"Whoa, whoa, Officer." Etienne went to step back, his hands in the air. "Preacher wouldn't do me like this."

"Preacher ain't here," Maureen said, moving in closer. "He's laid up in a hospital bed, and Shadow knows the guys behind it." She reached out, put her hand on E's shoulder. Her touch was light. "Where is he?"

"I don't know that," Etienne said. "I don't. There's no way I would know that. Shadow is a player. I'm a piss stain. You know that. C'mon, now. You scaring me."

"How many fucking times you gonna make me ask you the same fucking question?"

She twisted the shoulder of Etienne's coat in her fist. A thought occurred to her. Solomon Heath wasn't the only one who could've given Preacher away.

She said, "Preacher took three bullets. Preacher was having lunch in street clothes. How did the Watchmen know who he was unless someone told them? You ask me, that rat was Shadow. He knows who Preacher is, what he looks like. He knew the Watchmen before Scales did. It connects."

"If you say so. I got no love for Shadow. Fuck him. It ain't about that. I plain don't know where he is."

What if I beat the daylights out of him, Maureen thought, and he doesn't know shit? She released his shoulder. Then he's useless to me. Tonight and every other night going forward. And it's not impossible someone finds out how he got torn up, she thought, especially if he ends up in the emergency room like the last guy she'd tuned up with the ASP. This encounter's not anonymous like the Marigny and the Irish Channel, she thought; there are witnesses this time. Three guys saw her pull up and ask for Little E. Three guys heard her chase them away so she could be alone with E. Tonight, she was out in full uniform. She wasn't skulking around town in a hoodie. She wasn't sneaking up on anyone. She zipped up her jacket. Besides, odds were Little E *didn't* know where Shadow stayed. But he would know someone who did. That was a fact.

Maybe there'd be two, three degrees of separation, but E would have a connection he could tap for information. He'd been around the neighborhood too long, had absorbed too much. He might not even know he had it. But she'd *inspire* him to find that connection. She would simply stop asking, stop giving him chances to deny her and treat him as if he'd already agreed to help.

"Come with me to the car," she said.

Little E grumbled but he followed. At the front of the car, she said, "Wait here."

Maureen opened the passenger door of the cruiser, grabbed a plastic shopping bag off the seat.

In the bag was a prepaid cell phone she'd bought for cash at an all-night convenience store on Broad Street. The transaction would be on the security video, but she'd done what she could to obscure the item she was purchasing. She tore open the hard plastic packaging and made sure the phone was activated. She took out her own smartphone, found the number for the Big Man Lounge, and programmed it into the prepaid. Then she handed that phone to Little E. He stared at it like Maureen had handed him a live hand grenade with no pin.

"I'm a snitch," he said. "This is starting to feel like some kind of mission."

"Here's what's gonna happen," Maureen said. "You're gonna go around the way and catch up to your boys, and the four of you are gonna make like messenger pigeons and get word out to Shadow that the NOPD wants to speak with him. You put it out there, no arrest, no jail. We want to talk only. Tonight only. When the meeting's over, he walks away. It's a chance for him to score some points with us. Points he *will* need to cash in one day."

She jerked her thumb over her shoulder. "You're going to call me at the Big Man on that phone I gave you. The number's in the phone. Sun's up in about three hours. My shift is over in four. That's the duration of this offer. We don't see Shadow tonight, we're tearing the neighborhood down. SWAT, Tactical, the state police, the FBI, everybody's coming. Because when I go back to the district to file my report, I'm putting Shadow and the Watchmen together, I'm telling everyone that you told me Shadow was laid up in Central City and we're coming looking—for him and for you.

"We're hitting Big Mike and his crew first. And I'm gonna make sure Mike knows you had a chance to stop the storm from happening and didn't get it done. And Shadow won't be helping anyone else up onto the throne because there won't be a throne. There won't be a kingdom. I'm coming through and burning *everything* down. You think the Iberville got torn down? You ain't seen nothing."

"I, uh, no disrespect," Little E said, "but the Big Man closed."

"Let me worry about that," Maureen said. "You get word to Shadow. You call me when he's on his way to the Big Man."

Etienne looked at the phone in his hand and Maureen knew his thinking. He could get five, maybe even ten dollars for that phone, a burner with all its time on it, within five blocks in any direction of where they stood. He could toss it down the nearest storm drain and tell Maureen someone had taken it off him. He knew enough that even if the 82nd Airborne came through the neighborhood the next day, their interest in him wouldn't last. He was too small-time. For the game. For the law. His smallness was what allowed him to survive, and E knew it.

"I want you to think about something," Maureen said. "I want you to think about the times, the many, many times, that Preacher did right by you. The times he caught you fucking up and let it slide. You think about the jail you didn't do because of Preacher. You don't like me, you don't want to do nothing for me, that's fine. But I'm here representing him, and I'm calling in his favors."

Little E stared hard at the street, his chin on his chest. Maureen had no idea if she'd reached him. She'd threatened him, reasoned with him, appealed to his better nature. She didn't know what else she could do, other than let him loose. The clock was ticking and she'd emptied her bag of tricks.

"Hit it," she said. "And let me hear from you soon."

An idea struck her as Little E walked away, something to add emphasis to her request and some urgency to Shadow's response. She called Little E back to her. Shadow had become involved with the Watchmen because Ruiz and Quinn had something on him, something they used against him. What it was, Maureen had never learned, but Shadow didn't know that. E looked at her expectantly.

"You tell Shadow that I've been talking to Ruiz. Tell him it's been passed on to me."

"That's it?"

"Make sure you tell him that," Maureen said. "He'll know what you mean. Trust me."

E walked away from her, murmuring to himself.

30

After E turned the corner in search of his friends, Maureen walked over to the Big Man.

She rapped on the gate over the front door with her flashlight. She leaned in close to the door, listening for sounds from the inside. She heard faint jukebox music. No doubt the bar's owner was there, trying to relax while he cleaned and counted, swept and mopped and sorted. Maybe sipping the night's first cold beer, smoking the first unhurried cigarette. She knew the drill, she'd done it herself countless times, which meant she hated bothering the man. But times were different now, and there was shit she needed to get done.

She rapped on the gate again, adding, "NOPD. Open up."

She glanced overhead. She saw that a security camera peered down at the entrance. The owner could double-check that it really was police at his front door. After she'd had a chance to talk with the man, she'd have to convince him to turn off that camera, and any other cameras in his place, for as long as she needed. She banged again with the flashlight, harder this time. The music went off inside the bar. Don't do that, she thought. Don't pretend you're not in there. Don't make this harder than it has to be.

The door opened a few inches. "I didn't call. There's nothing going on in here."

"It's not about that," Maureen said.

"I don't know nothin' about them boys on the steps," he said. "Every now and again, they drink in here. Neighborhood fellas, they're never any trouble for me. If they're trouble for anyone else I don't know nothin' about that."

"This doesn't involve them," Maureen said. "Not directly."

"It's been a long night, Officer," the man said. "I won't get out of here for at least another hour as it is."

"That's actually a good thing," Maureen said.

The man frowned at her.

"I'm Officer Maureen Coughlin. And you are?"

"Gus LaValle."

"Mr. LaValle, the NOPD needs a favor from you."

LaValle looked down at the floor. "I know y'all have had a bad day. I don't know what I can do."

"We're pursuing leads about the shootings today," Maureen said. "And we have to act quickly. We need your place for a meeting, tonight. Sometime between now and dawn."

LaValle chuckled. He opened the door wider, propped one arm up on the frame. He kept the gate between him and the outside world locked. "You want me to do the police a favor? In this neighborhood? What do you think that does to my business? I feel bad about them young officers getting killed, and them other two getting shot up. But not everyone around here feels like I do, you know what I'm saying? And I gotta live here, do business here. It was out-of-town crazies that shot at y'all. White boys. It wasn't nobody from this neighborhood."

Maureen felt rage squeezing her throat closed. She fought to keep her head clear. She kept thinking about the fear in Preacher's voice as he told his story. She imagined the wails of the wives of the two young officers who'd been killed. Patience, she told herself. Diplomacy. Don't start with threats. They don't leave much wiggle room. Get results right now, she thought, opening and closing her gloved fists. She couldn't go back to Preacher's bedside having blown up everything with her temper. He'd forgive her, maybe, but she'd never forgive herself. This night was her chance to make things right. To prove herself. To prove she wouldn't always be the Sixth District problem child.

"There's things going on," she said, "ties to this neighborhood that would surprise you. You work with me, nobody gets hurt. Nobody even gets arrested. I'm explaining the reality of things to you. Right now, I'm the one running things. I'm the only one who knows what's going on. In a matter of hours, that is going to change. Everyone on the NOPD will know what I know. The FBI will know what I know. I'm going to have to tell them that I came to you for help, on the day four officers got shot, and that you turned me away."

She rested her hand on the metal gate. "You have to live with your neighbors, that's true. And, believe me, I know how many of them are, especially about cops. But you have to live with us, too. We're part of the neighborhood. Forever. Longer than Bobby Scales. Longer than Big Mike. And longer than whoever comes after him. We're not going away. And we never, ever, *ever* forget."

LaValle's face had hardened. "What exactly are you saying, Officer?"

"I'm saying you can deal with me tonight," Maureen said, "when I can control what happens. Or the circus comes to town tomorrow, and there's not a damn thing I can do about it. You, either." She paused. "All I need from you is a table and chairs inside and a little bit of time and patience." She flashed a smile. "Maybe a drink or two." She raised her eyes to the camera. "And for you to turn off the recorders when I ask you."

LaValle stared at her for a long time through the metal bars of his security gate.

"You can stay in the office," Maureen said. "You won't even know we're here."

She heard LaValle suck his teeth. Then she heard the brass bolt slide home as he unlocked the gate.

31

Once she was locked inside the Big Man Lounge, Maureen was stuck doing the one thing she hated the most: waiting. She flipped a chair and sat at a table where she inspected her gun. She eyed the whiskey bottles across the room behind the bar. She put her gun back in her holster, sitting and waiting, tracing her fingers over the scratches in the tabletop. Names. Curse words.

LaValle was locked in his office, doing his numbers for the night. He'd taken three cold bottles of Budweiser back there with him. She'd halfheartedly tried to get him to leave her the key and go home. She realized right away she'd have an easier time getting answers out of Shadow than she'd have getting LaValle to turn his bar over to the cops.

When she got tired of sitting, she got up from the table, put a dollar in the jukebox, played Otis Redding and Dr. John and Muddy Waters. Otis sat on the dock of the bay. Dr. John walked on gilded splinters.

Everything, everything, everything gonna be all right this morning, Muddy sang.

I fucking hope you're right, she thought, pacing the smooth, cigarette-burned wood floor as the music played.

When the music ended, she sat on a barstool, swiveling her seat, drumming her fingers on the bar, chain-smoking, staring at the phone behind the bar, listening to the New Orleans night's activities on her police radio. Please keep this a quiet night, she thought. She prayed nothing happened that the other cops on patrol couldn't handle. No all-calls tonight. Please. For one night let the neighborhood knuckleheads be reasonably well behaved. Let our bad reputation work in our favor for tonight, she thought.

Maureen worried as she sat there that she'd misjudged Shadow's involvement with the Watchmen. What if he was *more* hooked into them than she was guessing? Their connection was live if she was right about Shadow being the one who gave the description of Preacher. But wasn't that what she was sitting there hoping for? That Shadow was in deep with the Watchmen. What if he led the Watchmen and their white van right to her? What if he walked in willing to do the job himself? Wasn't likely Little E was going to pat him down first. She'd set herself up but good for another attempted assassination, she thought, for another shoot-out.

Alone in this bar, she was cornered. Cases of bottled beer blocked the back door; she had checked, and it was padlocked anyway.

She had backup in the neighborhood, but who knew if they'd respond fast enough.

Not long after Little E had left, Maureen had reached out to Wilburn and Cordts. They stopped by the bar and she filled them in on her plan. It wasn't very complicated. Get Shadow to the Big Man. Make him talk about the Watchmen. By any means necessary. Wilburn and Cordts agreed to hang around the neighborhood and stick close to the bar as much as they could without completely neglecting their patrol assignment. That way, if something unexpected happened with Shadow, they'd only be blocks away. But that also meant, Maureen thought, if something unexpected happened, they'd be blocks away.

Whether the meeting with Shadow went poorly or well, she'd be alone with him for most of it. Not that she was afraid of being alone in a room with Shadow. He'd taken her out once before, had surprised her from behind a blind corner during a foot chase in the Quarter and punched her right in the throat. None of that tonight, she thought. She was tougher now. Meaner. And she hoped she was smarter.

When word came from Little E that Shadow was on his way, she'd call Wilburn and Cordts. She'd ask them to meet him outside the bar, make sure he was alone, and pat him down. She hadn't decided whether she wanted Wilburn and Cordts inside the Big Man for her conversation with Shadow. She might not want witnesses to what she did. They couldn't talk about what they hadn't seen. She wanted to offer them that protection. If they needed it. She hoped things with Shadow didn't go that route; she wasn't looking to hurt him, simply reserving the right to do what was necessary.

Maureen got up from the bar, walked around behind it. Whether or not she had booze on her breath wouldn't be a deal breaker. Wasn't like anything that happened in that bar would be spoken of again. Wasn't going to be any paperwork. She searched the bottles. No Jameson. Disappointed but not discouraged, Maureen poured herself a double Jack Daniel's in a plastic cup. She checked the wells. LaValle had burned his ice. So much the better, she thought. Not exactly the setting for kicking back with a cocktail. She downed the double shot. She felt the heat rise into her sinuses, felt the scorch in her throat, the match strike in her belly, felt the sparks drip lower. Grease for the machine. Her mouth filled with saliva, and she spat in the sink. She tossed the plastic cup in the trash, rolled her head on her shoulders. She laid a ten on the bar for the drink, tucked under her full ashtray. She lit a cigarette, pulled the smoke deep inside her.

The phone behind the bar rang. Maureen answered. "Speak."

"That nigger Shadow coming to you," Little E said. "That's what I was told."

"Well done," Maureen said. She hadn't fully believed until that moment that she wouldn't see the sunrise with nothing happening. She reached for the bottle of Jack, poured a single. Well, she thought, an Irish cop's idea of a single. "I'm gonna tell Preacher you came through for him. Count on it."

"So we straight, then?" Little E said. "You and me, we done?"

"For tonight," Maureen said.

"What you want me to do with this phone?"

"Whatever the fuck you want," Maureen said. "I was you, I'd toss it, and I'd stay far away from the Big Man tonight."

"You don't gotta tell me twice. I'm out. Peace, OC." Little E was gone.

Maureen downed her shot. She checked her gun. She thought of going back to LaValle's office, telling him if he needed a piss after those three beers that now was the time. She thought she'd tell him that Shadow was on his way. LaValle was a grown man, she thought. He had a phone in his office. He knew what it meant when it rang. And his bladder wasn't her worry.

She reached into her pocket and took out her cell phone.

The right thing to do, the professional thing to do, was to call Detillier and tell him about Shadow. He was more qualified to do the questioning, especially in a huge case like this. The reason she'd been paired with Detillier in the first place was so the FBI could put her connections to the Watchmen to use, to better use than she and the NOPD could. And if Detillier was in the doghouse, she thought, giving him a fresh lead might be the thing to get him out of trouble. And if that were the case, wouldn't he owe her a huge favor? How was that for turning the tables? She had no loyalty to Shadow. Sure, she'd promised through Little E that he would walk away free from the meeting with her. But, in the end, fuck Shadow. Too bad for him if the FBI needed him. Keeping promises to career criminals wasn't a top priority for her.

She scrolled through her contacts, found Detillier's number. She hesitated.

And what if he shows up with a dozen other guys and whisks Shadow away in a van? What if it would be hours, or days, before the feds got anything out of Shadow? What if lawyers got involved? That happens and here we are again, Maureen thought, waiting for, counting on the feds to come through and pluck us off the rooftop. No thanks. And really, what leverage did the FBI have? Shadow presented the same problem as Solomon Heath did. Unless he was suddenly inspired to incriminate himself, nobody had any proof that Shadow was *guilty* of anything.

And what if another attack happened while the feds were dicking around with Shadow? Maureen thought. More shootings? A bomb, even? Who knew what else the Watchmen had up their sleeves. The FBI couldn't, they wouldn't, go after Shadow like she could. She had a freedom, at least that night in that bar, the FBI didn't have.

On the other hand, she thought, with Madison Leary dead, Shadow was the one lead, the *only* extant lead into the Watchmen that anybody, feds or local, had right now. She was done, *done* in the NOPD if she blew that lead. What if another attack happened *then*? How would she live with herself? She'd already maybe failed, despite what Preacher had said in the hospital, to stop the first attack by failing to find Madison Leary. What if she failed again?

She took a deep breath. Okay, then. Me first, then him. We can both have him, she thought. I can make this work. She called Detillier. When he answered, she could tell he'd been asleep. I hope I never learn that, she thought, to sleep on a night like tonight, when there's so much work to be done.

"I might have something for you on the Watchmen," Maureen said.

"Might? Where are you?"

"I'm working. Get up, make some coffee. And be ready to move. I'm gonna call you back in thirty minutes."

"Excuse me?" Detillier said. "You know who you're talking to?"

Maureen disconnected, slipped her phone back into her pocket.

She went back to her table. She righted another chair, set it across the table from where she'd sat before. She put an empty ashtray on the table. She lit the mason-jar candle. Then she sat and waited again. This time the waiting was easier. This time she knew the wait would be short. She unzipped her leather jacket, making the ASP easier to reach.

32

Twenty minutes later, she heard someone bang three times on the metal gate. Either Wilburn or Cordts. The three bangs was their signal that Shadow had arrived and everything was copacetic. She got up from the table, found LaValle's office in the back. She rapped a knuckle on the door. "They're here," she said. "Do not come out of this office for any reason until I come back and give you the all clear. For safety's sake. Your safety. Am I understood?"

LaValle hollered back that she was.

Maureen walked to the front door and opened it.

Shadow stood on the other side of the iron gate, a bored look on his face, his hands loose at his sides, his eyes so red Maureen thought he might have burst a few blood vessels. The weed stink off him made her own eyes water. He was slender with a small potbelly, and looking at him face-to-face Maureen realized he was not much taller than she was. She remembered him as a bigger man, taller and more rangy. Then again, she'd only gotten one good look at him, and that was from across the street before she knew who she was looking at. Back then, months ago, she'd had no reason to pay close attention; he was an older boy yelling at a younger boy she was talking to at a crime scene.

After that he was the guy who ambushed her with a throat punch. She hadn't seen him that day, not coming at her, not running away.

He'd shorn his braids since she'd seen him on the streets, keeping it close now, and he had a long, wispy goatee hanging from his chin like Spanish moss. His puffy down vest was open, and against his chest, over his thermal tie-dyed shirt, lay his telltale cowrie-shell necklace.

Behind Shadow stood Wilburn and Cordts, each gripping one of Shadow's upper arms in one hand. The officers were stone-faced. They hated what she asked of them, Maureen thought, which was bodyguarding her while she questioned a known fugitive and possible conspirator in cop killings, and did so off the record. Too bad, she thought, if they hated her. Or maybe, she thought, they just hated the pungent dogshit odor of the high-grade marijuana. Shadow sighed.

"He's unarmed," Wilburn said.

"Only love," Shadow said, raising his chin, eyelids heavy and low. "Only love."

This guy, Maureen thought, was gonna be her big breakthrough? If there were ever a time and occasion, she thought, that required Preacher's touch . . . but tonight, there was no Preacher. There was only her and what she'd learned from him in too short a time together.

Maureen searched Shadow's face for any indication he recognized her. She found nothing. She wasn't sure he knew where he was or what was happening. She was surprised at his condition. There might be more than THC in his system, she thought. Out of character for someone with a reputation as a consummate operator. Then again, in her short time on the force, Maureen had found the common criminal element pretty disappointing. With very few exceptions, nobody lived up to the rep that preceded him on the streets. Not the criminals, not the cops. Maureen was determined to be one of the exceptions.

"Bring him in," she said, opening the gate. "You guys, too."

Wilburn and Cordts traded glances, then marched Shadow into the bar. They wouldn't question her in front of a criminal. Wouldn't leave her alone with him, either. She was counting on these things. *Stick with me, guys*, she thought.

"Shadow," Maureen said, "follow me to the table over there." To the other cops she said, "Can you guys wait at the bar?"

Wilburn rolled his shoulders. He spoke in a low voice as they watched Shadow stroll over to the cocktail table. "That's three of us, Coughlin, off the streets when we should be out there. If we get a call, we have to roll. I'm not gonna broadcast anything, but I'm not gonna lie about where I am. You do what you gotta do, we'll cover for you as best we can, but . . ." His voice trailing off, he completed his sentence with a shrug.

"That's plenty," Maureen said. "This shouldn't take long. I appreciate your help."

"If you can get a coherent sentence out of that guy," Cordts said, "about anything, you deserve that detective shield, like, tomorrow."

Maureen left them at the bar and crossed the barroom to sit with Shadow. He slouched deep in his chair. She said, "You've been told what this is about?"

Shadow slid a cigarette from the pack Maureen had tossed on the table. He lit it using the candle. "Some kind of parlay." He coughed one time, sharp, like a bark. "I do for you or the wrath of God burns down the neighborhood." He waved a dismissive hand. "Some shit like that."

"Yeah, some shit like that," Maureen said. "You heard what happened today."

Shadow nodded slowly. "White boys killing cops. In a big way. Crazy, for sure. But not nothing that had to do with Shadow."

"But you're here."

"Not for you," Shadow said. "For I."

"You remember a guy named Cooley, another guy named Gage? Clayton Gage?"

"The things I do," Shadow said, "I meet a lot of people. Shadow diversified, you could say."

"Well, I believe you met them during one of your diversification efforts," Maureen said. "White boys from outside the city. They call themselves Sovereign Citizens. They were raising a militia called the Watchmen Brigade. They wanted to move guns, lots of guns, into and around New Orleans."

"Sounds to Shadow like they got that shit done."

"Because you helped them," Maureen said.

Shadow held out his hands. "See these hands? These hands never so much as picked up a gun." He pressed his palms together. "That's not Shadow's way."

"You connected Cooley and Gage to Bobby Scales. You set them up in New Orleans."

"*You* set them up in New Orleans," Shadow said. "Your people. It was a cop that made Shadow make that connect. What happened today? What goes around, comes around, feel me? Y'all did this to y'all selves. Karma. Payback a bitch."

He eased deeper into his chair, grinning, confident in his wisdom.

Maureen flipped the table, cigarettes, ashtray, and burning candle flying.

She kicked Shadow in the chest, boot heel hard to the sternum, toppling him and his chair backward onto the floor. His cigarette flew through the air. Wilburn and Cordts were halfway to her before she stopped them with a raised hand. She knew they were rushing in not to defend Shadow, not to restrain her, but to assist in the beating they saw coming. All day, every cop in New Orleans had been waiting to kick someone's ass. Anyone. But they stopped at her wordless order. They stood frozen, panting like dogs waiting to be let off the leash.

Shadow was slow to recover. He managed to slide out of the chair and roll over onto his back. Maureen circled him. She crushed out his lost cigarette under her boot.

"Fucking mother*fucking* pigs," he spat, his stoner cool evaporated by fear and rage. A surprising amount of rage, Maureen thought, for someone so stoned. "That's it, huh? Shadow going in the river, too. Fuck y'all. I hope them white boys kill all y'all."

Maureen strode toward Shadow, him crab walking on his back to get away from her, coughing, fighting for breath. She'd struck him a good one, knocked the wind right out of him. His eyes were tearing. Even if he could get to his feet, he had nowhere to run. Maureen knew it. Shadow knew it. She could see the knowledge, the fear, electrifying his eyes. She wanted to see just how much electricity she could generate.

She reached into her leather jacket, pulled out the ASP. She flicked her wrist and the weapon extended with a metallic snap, the end quivering with the weight of the leaded end. She put her foot on Shadow's chest, pushed him flat on his back on the floor. He was transfixed by the vibrating tip of the ASP, drool running onto his bottom lip.

Maureen looked at Wilburn and Cordts. "Y'all do not have to be here for this. I got it from here."

"If he's got something to say," Cordts said, "I wanna be here to listen."

Maureen narrowed her eyes, trying to read the other cops. Cordts was both eager for and frightened by what might happen next, like a kid at the top of that first roller-coaster peak. Wilburn was clouded and distant. And hostile. What he wanted, and feared, was harder to read.

She thought of the strange men she had taken down in the dark. She had to admit it. This might be better. She didn't have to hide behind a hood. She tightened her grip on the ASP. She could feel Shadow breathing hard under her boot. His red eyes stayed wild with terror. Maureen realized she was sweating like crazy, beads of it trickling into her eyes. When had the bar gotten so warm? The ASP became as heavy as a sledgehammer in her hand.

Looking down at Shadow shaking under her boot, Maureen tried conjuring the fresh memory of Preacher in his hospital bed, tried to hear the fear in his voice as he told the story of being shot. She tried to imagine the cries of the widows when the most horrible news of their lives came to their doorsteps. She tried to think of these things, and she failed.

Instead Maureen could only feel her heart beating so hard it made her body shake. She could smell the black mud of the Mississippi. She saw again how Officer Quinn had put Bobby Scales's head under his boot, pressing his face into the mud at the riverside to suffocate him. She breathed in the brackish waters of the Arthur Kill and recalled how a year ago she had scrambled and crawled through the muck and the cattails of the dark shoreline to get away from Sebastian as he marched toward her, fists clenched, destruction on his mind.

Both men were to her in those moments nothing but monsters.

Is a monster, Maureen wondered, what she came to this city to be?

She lifted her boot. She collapsed the ASP, tucked it back into her jacket. "I told E to tell you that you would walk away from this meeting. That is how this will go."

Shadow raised up on his elbows. Maureen righted his chair, pointed to it. Never taking his eyes off her, Shadow climbed into the chair.

"The Watchmen," Maureen said. "Talk."

Like a pendulum, Shadow's red eyes moved from the hidden ASP to Maureen's face and back again. He straightened his vest. "What? Yeah, I made introductions. It wasn't my idea. Ruiz and Quinn, they wanted Shadow doing it. Either that or they tell Big Mike I'm gonna hit him with the double cross when he makes his big move. Big Mike hear that kind of talk and he's gonna hit Shadow with two in the chest, feel me? So I make the connect for the cops. What the fuck Shadow care what white boys do? They wanna play soldier, get y'all's attention for once, that works for me."

"So you meet Edgar Cooley," Maureen said. "At the daiquiri place."

"Right, right."

"But then there's a second meeting," Maureen said. "After Cooley left the picture, you met with Clayton Gage."

"If you say so," Shadow said. "Fuck if I remember they names."

"I do say so. This second meeting, this was back at the daiquiri shop again?"

Shadow shook his head. "This Gage didn't want to do nothin' out in the street. I got the feeling things didn't work out so well for the first guy, know what I mean? Gage was more careful. Cooley and the other one who came around, the money man." Shadow hung his head, snapping his fingers as his brain tried to resurrect the name.

Maureen could see that, in spite of his circumstances, Shadow was starting to enjoy himself, almost even forgetting he was talking to a cop. She realized that his role in solving the puzzle fed his ego. She could see what drove him on the streets. Knowing things, moving the pieces around. Systems, relationships, conspiracy. Moving parts. He didn't want to drive the race car; he wanted to build it and watch it run in circles around the track. And he wanted to be able to walk away when the car hit the wall and burst into flames, driver be damned. A man who could build a good race car could always find another driver. She'd have learned none of these things, she realized, if she'd left him picking his teeth off the bar-room floor.

"Heath," Maureen said. "Caleb Heath is the name you're looking for."

"Yeah, that's it. Cooley and Heath, they was into it"—he switched into his version of a white man's voice—"being down, being gangsta, whatever the fuck. But Gage, he was business, and he was cautious."

For all the good it did him, Maureen thought. "So this second meeting, where was it?"

"At Gage's apartment," Shadow said.

"Clayton Gage had an apartment in the city?" she said.

Holy shit, she thought. She was getting it done. Shadow was giving them one fucking lead after another. Wilburn and Cordts had caught her excitement. They rose from their barstools again. Cordts tapped his wrist. She had their attention, but she was running out of time.

"I was there," Shadow said. "It was nice. New. New paint. New shit.

We had to go there late at night, when shit in the 'hood was quiet. Not the kind of place you can be bringing guns in and out of. Which was pretty much the point of me being there. Finding other places to stash the guns." Shadow straightened up in his chair. He put his hand on his chest. "I gotta say, Officer. You scared me some there."

"The apartment," Maureen said. "Where is it?"

"Around the way," Shadow said. "In them new places. The Harmony Oaks. In a building where no one was renting yet."

"The houses that Solomon Heath built," Maureen said. "Gage worked out of an apartment he rented from Caleb Heath."

"If you say so," Shadow said. "You got another cigarette?"

"They're around here somewhere," Maureen said, her mind spinning. "I guess I should put the table back."

She righted the table, set the ashtray back on it. The mason jar holding the candle had smashed on the floor, spilling wax onto the wood. She walked to the bar and laid another five over the ten she had tucked under the ashtray. She hoped LaValle hadn't heard too much of the commotion. Shadow brought his chair back to the table and sat. Maureen tossed him the pack of cigarettes and her lighter. Shadow lit up, set the pack and the lighter back on the table.

He said, "So what now?"

"Any chance you remember an apartment number?" Maureen asked.

"It was months ago, and I didn't go but that one time." He sat up straighter. "But it's easy to find. First floor, in one of the brick buildings right off Louisiana, one of the old ones they saved from the projects." He laughed. "They got like a *pool* and shit there now. In the old *Magnolia*. Looks nice. I only seen it through the fence."

Maureen adjusted her ponytail. It was helpful information, sure, about the apartment, but her earlier excitement was waning. Clayton Gage had been dead six weeks. The apartment had probably been cleaned out and rented by now. But Caleb Heath had bolted after Gage was killed. Maybe he hadn't had time to clean up. He didn't seem the type to do much of that to begin with. And Maureen doubted Caleb had told Solomon what he was doing with the apartments he was supposed to be supervising on his father's behalf. It was worth a look. They might get lucky.

Shadow stood up. "If there's nothin' else you need from me."

"I think that'll do," Maureen said. She tapped her own chest. "Sorry about that. Bruise'll heal in a couple of days."

"Ain't no thing. Shadow's had worse. Believe that."

He straightened his down vest. Stretching his neck, he touched his cowrie-shell necklace with his fingertips. He seemed to be lingering, Maureen thought, in order to savor the fact that the cops were letting him go. "I have to admit, Shadow thought for a hot minute he wouldn't walk out of here."

"Thanks for your help," Maureen said. "I'm sure you've got business to attend to."

"Shadow always has the business to do." He turned, sauntered to the door. He tipped an imaginary cap to Wilburn and Cordts. "Irie, gentlemen."

Wilburn stared him down, but Cordts was smirking. "We'll see you soon, Shadow. Real soon. We'll tell Big Mike you stopped by."

That last crack almost broke Shadow's cool. Almost. He threw a glance over his shoulder as he slipped out the door.

"Big Mike'll fucking kill him," Maureen said, "if he hears Shadow talked to us. About anything."

"Fuck that mope," Wilburn said. "We'll be better off, and it'll be an easy solve for Homicide. Everybody wins."

"Just giving him something to think about," Cordts said.

"You're the one about kicked his heart out his back," Wilburn said, stepping forward. "Now he's your pal."

"I was working him," Maureen said. "Aggressively, but it was work. These are extreme circumstances. He's not my pal."

Wilburn stormed outside, slamming the door behind him. Maureen could hear him shouting curses then calling for his partner.

"I take it we're done here, too?" Cordts said.

"I gotta make a call," Maureen said, "start moving on Shadow's information. And I'll let LaValle know he can finally go home. But, yeah, we're done. Thank you, the both of you, for having my back. And for showing some flex."

"Watching you work," Cordts said, "was interesting. Keep us posted on how it goes from here." He tilted his head at the door. "Don't worry about Wilburn. He could give a fuck how you treated Shadow. I think he's just pissed you let the mope walk. Long day today, for all of us."

"I'm gonna make sure someone pays for it," Maureen said.

"In case you hadn't noticed," Cordts said, "we're all chasing that same result. Including the two guys who helped you conduct your secret interview with a wanted man." He duplicated Shadow's hat-tipping gesture and walked out the door.

Maureen took several deep breaths before calling Detillier. She poured another shot but didn't drink it. Detillier was fully awake when he answered this time.

"I have new information on Clayton Gage," Maureen said. "The location of an apartment he used in the city until his death."

"Should I ask where you got this information?"

"Through a CI of Preacher's," Maureen said. "It's reliable. It makes sense. It's an apartment that Caleb Heath provided the Watchmen through his father's stock of properties. That it's connected to Heath makes me think it's legit. He also puts Caleb Heath in that apartment with the Watchmen. He gives us back what we lost with Quinn and Scales and Leary."

"Where's the apartment?" Detillier asked. "You have an address?"

"Not an exact one," Maureen said. "It's in Harmony Oaks, the CI said, in one of the two brick buildings. One of them is part of the rec center, so there's only one building it can be."

"There are some logistics I have to work out," Detillier said, "but I bet we can get in the apartment by morning."

"By morning? How can you wait that long?"

"Listen to me, Maureen, very carefully," Detillier said. "The Sovereign Citizens and people like them, they booby-trap their homes before they go out on their missions. I've seen it several times before. We have no idea what could be waiting for us there. Please trust me on this. Don't go looking around there yourself."

"I believe you," Maureen said. "It's just, it's our best lead."

"It is," Detillier said. "And I'm taking it very seriously. I'm on it. I'll roust a couple agents out of bed and send them to sit on the building overnight."

"I can do that for you," Maureen said.

"Y'all are shorthanded enough as it is," Detillier said. "Believe me, I have the manpower I need after today."

"Don't cut me out of this," Maureen said. "This is my lead. I tracked this down. I want to be there and see what comes of my hard work."

"I wouldn't dream of freezing you out," Detillier said. "But I'll take it from here. Keep your phone close. Trust me."

Maureen laughed out loud. "And what do I do until I hear from you?"

"You keep doing your job," Detillier said. "And you wait." He hung up.

Maureen slipped her phone into her pocket. She picked up her plastic cup of whiskey, looked down into her drink. She raised it halfway to her mouth and stopped. It came to her what the look on Wilburn's face had meant, the tough-to-read frown he'd worn as she'd roughed up Shadow. She knew that look. What Wilburn saw when he looked at her was what she had seen when she'd looked at Quinn, when she'd seen him for what he really was.

She knew it wouldn't make a real difference to anyone, but she poured the shot of Jack down the sink anyway.

33

Maureen waited outside the Big Man for LaValle to lock up, then walked him to his car. He said nothing to her when she thanked him for his patience. When she offered him a business card, he wouldn't take it from her. She stood a few long moments in the street after he'd driven away. One of his taillights was out. She'd stop by the bar one night and let him know. Before he got pulled over and ticketed.

On her way back to the car, she pulled out her phone and called Atkinson.

"Very strange," Atkinson said. "I was about to call you."

"Where are you?"

"In the East," Atkinson said. "A domestic double. Father and son, it looks like. Just when you think you've seen it all." Maureen heard the *snick* of her lighter as she lit a smoke. "We pulled a second print off the handle of Madison Leary's razor."

"Any idea who?"

"An idea, yes," Atkinson said, "but we haven't heard back on it yet.

I may have to hit up Detillier for help, those FBI resources. Anyway, what's on your mind?"

"I may have something for you on the Watchmen murders."

"Do tell."

"Me and the others have been working CIs in the neighborhood," Maureen said. "We've uncovered an apartment that Clayton Gage used in the weeks before he was killed. We know he did Watchmen business there. And we know Caleb Heath was there, too."

"An apartment where?"

"Right here in Central City," Maureen said. "In the Harmony Oaks development."

"Wow. Okay. That makes sense. You found Cooley's body right across that empty lot from there. And it explains what Gage was doing uptown when he was killed. Could be where he was headed with Madison the night you pulled them over."

"I was thinking the same things," Maureen said. She leaned against the hood of the cruiser.

"So you're there now?" Atkinson asked. "At the apartment?"

"No," Maureen said. "I'm on the street. I'm going back on patrol. I told Detillier about it."

"Does he think Leon Gage is in there?" Atkinson asked. "There's a weird logic to it. A hide-in-plain-sight thing."

"I didn't get that impression," Maureen said. "Though Detillier told me he was dispatching agents to watch the building. We don't know exactly which apartment it is, but we know which building. He's getting a warrant and a team to search the place in the morning. And of course, they'll pick him up if he tries to get there, or if he's in there and tries to leave."

"Did you tell Detillier about Caleb Heath being at the apartment?"

"I did not."

"Keep it that way," Atkinson said. "As an extra precaution. I'm sure you asked him to let you in on the raid?"

"I did. He said he'd keep me in the loop."

"Listen, I may need a favor from you," Atkinson said. "As a professional courtesy, early tomorrow morning, Detillier *should* let me know that he's found this apartment, since I have a murder victim with a history there. He should invite me over for a look around. If he doesn't do that, I'm going to need you to let me know what's happening so I can be there. I want a look at that apartment whether the FBI has their manners or not."

"You got it," Maureen said. "I'll keep you posted on everything."

"I have to ask," Atkinson said. "How did you make this happen?"

Maureen tried to suppress the pride she knew would flood her voice. "We got to Shadow."

"Really?" Atkinson said, astonished. "You have Shadow? You flipped Shadow?"

"I *had* Shadow," Maureen said. "I had to do some dealing to get the information. So he's back on the streets. But he walked away thinking that I now have whatever Quinn and Ruiz had over him, so I don't know if he's flipped, but he might be useful to us in the future. At least until he finds out I'm full of shit."

Atkinson said nothing for so long that Maureen started getting nervous. Then the detective said, "That is good goddamn police work, Maureen. Well done. This is how good cops make a name for themselves, this right here is exactly it. Hell of a job, Officer. Preacher's going to be real proud." She paused. "I know I am."

"Thank you," Maureen said. She had decided only a year ago to be a cop, but Atkinson's praise sounded like words she'd been waiting her whole life to hear. She didn't know whether to jump up and down or burst into tears. "That means a lot. I'm just happy to help, on a day like today, especially."

"You're welcome," Atkinson said. "Have you seen Preacher? I heard he came through surgery okay, that he's doing pretty good."

"He is," Maureen said. "He's in pain, and he's rattled, but who wouldn't be? I'll probably stop by one more time before I head home, whenever that is. I'll tell him you asked after him."

"Anthony's with him, I take it?"

Maureen stammered. Atkinson chuckled. "C'mon, Maureen. I thought you wanted to be a detective?"

"Some day," Maureen said. "In the way, way distant future, apparently."

"All right, I gotta go," Atkinson said. "The music never stops. Don't forget to keep me updated on the apartment. Keep up the good work."

"Will do," Maureen said. She ended the call.

She eased off the hood of the cruiser, her whole body humming with what Atkinson had said to her. She felt high. She knew that when she got back to work, when the car started rolling and the radio chatter started, the spell would be broken. She wasn't ready to give it up just yet.

Instead of getting into the car, Maureen walked over to the abandoned house where she'd found Little E. She sat on the concrete steps. She tilted her head back and howled at the stars. A yard dog in the neighborhood answered. She rubbed her palms on her thighs, looked at her hands. What inside her, she wondered, had stayed her hand in the bar? She didn't really care about Shadow's welfare. She hadn't cared about Bobby Scales's at the river. That wasn't why she'd tried to save him from Quinn. Complete exhaustion had done her in, then? Maybe. The fact that other cops were watching her? Could be. But they didn't care about Shadow, either. They knew the stakes. They'd done things like she was doing. There was more to it than that.

She'd done a lot of damage over the past six weeks, she realized, to others, to herself, and the result of her efforts had been only the desire and the opportunity to do more and greater harm. She'd been here before, she realized, snared in this ugly cycle of using pain to justify pain. Like an alcoholic. Like a junkie. The snake eating its tail. In New York, she'd done it with married men and cocaine. Now, in New Orleans, it was pills and violence. Eventually, she knew, sometimes it took weeks, sometimes it took months, but eventually she came back to wielding her weapons at the same old target. Herself. She broke her own heart. She bloodied her own nose. Sabotaged herself. Over and over again. Too many ways. Too many times.

She thought, of all things, of what Solomon Heath had said about Leon Gage. *People like that never get less angry.*

What had Nat Waters said to her on the day they'd met? *You have to protect yourself, Maureen,* he'd said. *Nobody else can do it for you.*

She rested her elbows on her knees, folded her hands in front of her. She closed her eyes. There wasn't a sound on the street. She took a deep breath and held it, listening for the grinding gears of the machine in her belly. She couldn't hear it.

She released the breath, pulled in another. She heard the rattle in her chest, the one she got late at night from too many cigarettes. Nothing after that. A cat screamed in the distance. But nothing happened inside her. When had that quiet started? When she saw Preacher? When she'd seen the look in Wilburn's eyes? All bad things must end, she thought. She had to stop killing herself sometime. Now seemed as good a time as any. She had already started being a better cop. Atkinson's words were proof of that. She took one more deep breath, made the sign of the cross, and came down the steps. Back to work. She couldn't live on magic spells.

She lit a cigarette and climbed into the cruiser, started the engine. She felt good, very good, but that didn't mean she didn't need coffee, and need it bad. She thought of Solomon Heath and his thermos. She had an idea. She'd promised him she'd be back. She hadn't necessarily meant that night, but, she thought, she had given Little E and Shadow the chance to do the right thing, and they had, in their way, come through. She wanted to give Solomon Heath the same choice, the same chance.

He'd told her unbidden that the Harmony Oaks apartment complex was under Caleb's supervision. It *was* possible that Solomon didn't know about the apartment the Watchmen had used. Would she tell him what Shadow had said about Caleb? What he did when he heard the news that the NOPD had a living witness connecting his son to the Watch-men, a witness who had spilled in front of not one but three cops, would tell her an awful lot. Solomon's next decisions after that would tell her everything she needed to know about him.

She was on a roll, doing the job Preacher had told her to do. There was only one thing to do, Atkinson had said so herself. *Keep up the good work.*

She put the car into drive and pulled away from the curb.

34

When Maureen returned to Solomon Heath's house, she found the back door ajar. She couldn't think of anything more unlike him than that. She walked up the steps and glanced at the security camera above the door. Looked like it was working. A break-in? If so, she wondered, where was the alarm? Where was the security company that should be responding to it? She backed down the steps and swept the yard, the butterfly box, and the shrubs with her flashlight. Nothing. Not even footprints in the grass. She reached for the radio mic clipped to her shoulder, changed her mind. For the second time that night she was in the one place both Preacher and the FBI had warned her not to be. No sense flushing her career down the toilet because Solomon Heath had a senior moment and left his back door unlocked.

Maureen stood on the path leading to the door, chewing the inside of her cheek. What she should do, she thought, was go get that coffee. A big one. She wouldn't be going home after her shift. She would be there when Detillier searched that apartment in a few hours. Depending on what they found, it might be another twelve, eighteen hours before she slept again. So. Coffee. A lot of it. But instead of moving for the car, she stood there on the path, staring at the golden vertical line between the open door and the doorframe. But, damn, she thought, Solomon Heath didn't seem the kind of man prone to senior moments. What if something had happened as he returned to the house? What if he'd fallen? Had a stroke or some kind of emergency. Just to be sure, she thought, for safety's sake, I'll take a look. She returned up the path.

She knocked on the door before reaching for the knob. "Mr. Heath?" She waited. She settled her other hand on her gun. Nothing from inside the house. "Mr. Heath? It's Officer Coughlin. Everything okay?" She waited. No answer. She bumped the door with her shoulder. It opened into a small, second kitchen. She saw no sign of Heath, or of anyone else inside. The thermos they had shared sat on an island in the middle of the room. She entered the house, easing the door closed behind her.

There, behind the door, the golf club he'd held in the park stood propped against the wall. She checked the keypad on the wall above the golf club. The alarm had been deactivated. With the club in its place and the alarm off, Maureen figured nothing bad had happened at the back door. She looked around the kitchen. A familiar scent tickled her nose. Bourbon.

She stepped deeper into the kitchen. She considered calling out to Heath again, hesitated. Broken glass crunched under her boot. Fragments, she saw, of what was likely a highball glass, lying in a pool of spilled bourbon. She backed up. That, she didn't like. Why would Heath drop a drink and leave it there without cleaning it up? Because, she thought, something much more urgent had commanded his attention. She checked the kitchen tile for footprints, saw a couple of dirty work-boot prints that were probably not Heath's. All right, she thought, someone else is in the house. The story so far: After she leaves, Heath comes in the back door, turns off the alarm, sets the thermos down on the island, makes himself a drink. Everything is cool.

Then, later, something brings a sleepless Heath to the back door—a

knock, maybe a voice. He opens the door, fresh drink in hand, and whoever is there backs him up into the kitchen, then does something scary
enough to make Heath drop his drink. Which hadn't happened that
long ago, she thought. The ice cubes had hardly melted. A gun? Heath
drops the drink and puts his hands up? He tries to set the drink on the
island and misses because something else, like a man with a gun, has
his strict attention. She had a good idea who that man with a gun might
be. It was then Maureen heard voices coming from deeper inside the
huge house.

She turned the volume down on her radio. Maureen was very glad
she had not made more noise coming through the back door. Two men,
arguing. One declaring, the other persuading. Her best guess: Gage
delivering a lecture, Heath pleading not to die at the end of it. She could
tell they were moving through the house. Away from her. She glanced
at the back door. Solomon, you arrogant idiot, she thought. You let him
in thinking he'd come to you, his old benefactor, for help one more
time. That you'd keep him here for us, or maybe that you'd finish him
yourself somehow. That he'd never come to hurt you, that no one would
ever come to hurt you, in your big, safe house.

Maureen unsnapped her holster. She figured she didn't have long to
find them. Gage loved a good lecture, loved to hear himself talk, but
he had to know his time was running out.

She pulled her gun, held it low by her hip, and considered her options. Gage surrendering, she figured, was not one of them. She knew
from the Walmart sporting-goods section that the Watchmen were not
the surrendering type. Gage, if he couldn't kill her and escape, would
want his blaze of glory for the effort. And he'd want to take her and
Heath with him when he went. For all Maureen knew, his pockets
bulged with grenades. He couldn't know she was there.

She could call for backup, wait for others to help her search the
house. That was the sensible course of action. But the radio would make
noise. She was in a quiet house. If the men inside hadn't been arguing,
they might've heard her calling out or stepping on the broken glass.

Maureen glanced again at the ice on the floor. Waiting for backup would cost her a fair amount of time. Heath's house opened onto Audubon Park. Gage could easily disappear into the park with his hostage. He could have a getaway car on Magazine Street, on St. Charles, on any number of side streets that ended at the park. They could vanish in any direction. That was most likely the plan. They were not far from the river, not far from where Quinn had disappeared under its currents. The river road, dark and winding, would lead Gage right out of town whether he was taking a hostage with him or leaving another corpse in his wake. She reached into her pocket and pulled out her phone. Atkinson: she worked all night like Maureen. Straining to follow the path of the conversation through the dark rooms of the mansion, her gun in one hand, Maureen thumbed a silent message to Atkinson. Her location, the men in the house with her. She sent the text and slipped the phone back into her pocket. Help would come, then, Maureen thought, she just didn't know how long it would take to get there.

The voices in the dark grew heated. Someone struck a blow. The other man hit the hardwood floor. In stages, it sounded like. Knees then hands. Gage urged Heath to get on his feet. Maureen heard doors thrown open. A cold wind blew through the house. They were headed for the porch, Maureen thought, and for the park. She couldn't let them get away, couldn't let them disappear. As quietly as she could, she moved from the lighted kitchen into the deep, dark belly of the big house, moving forward into the cold November wind.

35

It is too damn dark in here, Maureen thought. Gage must have made Heath turn off the outside security lights, leaving virtually no ambient light in the house.

The men had stopped talking, and she was losing her sense of how far away they were. She did not want to bump into them. She did not want to get too close. Her biggest advantage was Gage not knowing she was there. She moved slowly through what she thought was a small study into a wide living room. She held her gun in front of her in both hands, pointed at the floor. One set of French doors leading onto the wraparound front porch stood wide open. A trap? Had Gage heard her in the kitchen, and decided to lead her outside? To what advantage? They'd gone outside through the middle of three sets of French doors. There really wasn't any place for Gage to hide and ambush her. He couldn't know she was tracking him.

On the porch in front of her, Maureen could see the motionless silhouettes of Heath's rocking chairs. She listened for footfalls. Nothing. She moved into the doorway, crouched behind one of the rocking chairs. It wasn't much cover, but the darkness that Gage wanted for himself could help her, too.

She scanned the front yard. Nothing in the yard but the black shape of the barbecue. She looked beyond the grill, peering into the darkness under the huge live oaks that bordered the park. The branches grew so large and hung so low to the ground that ten men could hide under them. She strained to see a different shade of darkness, a lighter or darker shadow. She considered retreating into the house. If Gage and Heath had gone deep into the park, there was no way Maureen could track them by herself. She'd be letting them get away. How would she ever explain herself? How would she live with herself if she let Gage get away to kill again?

She rose to her feet, started backing into the living room. Out of the corner of her eye, she saw two figures emerge from the blackness of the trees. Gage held a gun to the back of Heath's head. They walked slowly toward the path that ringed the lagoon. There was no time to call anyone now, Maureen thought. Everything was on her.

She strode forward, gun out in front of her, the same way she'd marched on the white van on Esplanade Avenue. She jumped down off the porch, landed as lightly as she could, never taking her eyes from the two men. She kept walking forward, chin up, shoulders back. She kept her gun trained on Leon Gage. Too tough a shot from as far away as she was, especially in the dark. Gage had his arm out, digging his gun, Maureen guessed, into the back of Heath's head. She didn't want an accidental, panicked trigger pull taking out his hostage. She'd seen enough splattered brains for one day. She fought the urge to call out to Gage. She needed control of the situation. She'd have one try at it. The longer she waited, the better.

She was closer now. The men were stepping out from under the trees, their skin turning silver under the lamps lining the jogging path.

Gage was running his mouth again, an angry snarl, at the back of Heath's head. Heath held his hands in the air. Even from yards away, Maureen could see him shaking.

Off to the right of the two men, Maureen could see the bench where she'd talked to Preacher about the FBI only days ago. Where he'd warned her to stay away from Solomon Heath. Extenuating circumstances, Preach, she thought. She was sure he'd understand. Ducks slept under the bench, their heads tucked under their wings. Maureen passed through the darkness and came out into the lamplight. Gage forced Heath to his knees, lowered the gun to the back of his head, still talking, talking, talking. He was talking about his dead son. If he'd shut up for even a beat, Maureen thought, he'd surely have heard her approaching.

"Do not fucking move," she shouted. "Gun down, hands in the air."

Gage turned to face her. The gun he held to the back of Heath's head did not move. "Why are you here?" he asked Maureen. "This is business between men. Old, old business."

"I'm making it my business," Maureen said. "Back away from Mr. Heath and set that gun in the grass." She took two steps closer. She had a good shot if she wanted it. Gage wore his Carhartt jacket. There was no telling what he had in his pockets. She thought about grenades. "I want both your hands where I can see them, Gage. Now. Right now."

"I raised an army for him," Gage said, "and he left me in the wilderness. He destroyed my only son. He *owes* me."

"I don't care," Maureen said. "Put down the gun and get on your knees with your hands behind your head. Nobody wants to hear you talk."

If there was anyone she'd get a medal for gunning down, Maureen thought, here he was. But was that the kind of hero she wanted to be? Because, she thought, here also was the head of the Watchmen, wanted by the FBI, by the NOPD. He knew the Watchmen's plans. Shit, he *made* their plans. He knew what they had planned next. Taking him alive would save lives. Many lives. And she had him caught. He had nowhere to go. She'd held her fire earlier that day. She could do it again. Then his gun hand whipped right at her.

Maureen squeezed off two rounds, and blew Leon Gage off his feet.

Heath ran screaming into the water.

Bird Island erupted into a deafening, squawking riot. Shrieks and beating wings filled the night sky. Maureen marched toward Gage, who rolled around in the grass, moaning in pain. He rose to one knee, drooping, fighting for breath. He still held his gun.

Maureen knew she'd hit him, put two rounds right in his ribs. She raised her weapon, sighted his chest. Center mass this time. He needed convincing, this one. She was right on top of him now. "Gage, drop that fucking gun."

His elbow bent, his gun hand moved again. But Gage wasn't raising the weapon at her this time, Maureen realized. He was going for his own head. Oh, *fuck* no.

She jumped forward and stomped on his arm at the elbow, knocking Gage onto his back, the joint breaking under her boot. His gun tumbled from his hand and into the lagoon. Maureen held her balance as Gage squirmed in rage and pain under her foot. She tested his ribs with her other foot. He wore body armor, which was why her first two shots hadn't killed him. Which was exactly what she'd hoped for when she'd shot him in the chest and not the head. She moved her right foot from his elbow to his throat, applying pressure until he quit moving. He grabbed at her ankle, but he had no strength left in him.

"You know what I decided?" Maureen asked him. "No one else dies today."

In his flailing, Gage had lost his glasses. His blue eyes blazed up at Maureen, enraged. She saw in them all that fierce, undying hate that Heath had talked about. She never wanted her eyes to look like that.

Hey, she thought, speaking of Heath . . .

Maureen looked across the lagoon and saw Solomon Heath sitting on a big gray rock on the banks of Bird Island, his right shoulder and hair covered in streaks of white egret shit.

"You can come back now, Mr. Heath. I've got things under control." Smiling, she looked down at Gage. She lowered her gun so it pointed at the spot right between those fierce blue eyes.

"Don't I, Mr. Gage?"

36

At nine the next night, standing outside the late Clayton Gage's Harmony Oaks apartment, Maureen watched as the door opened and Atkinson walked out, ducking her tall frame under the yellow crime-scene tape guarding the doorway.

"Anything? Maureen asked.

Atkinson locked the door behind her. She shoved her hands deep in her coat pockets, and shrugged. "Nope. Not that I expected there to be."

They walked away from the brick building, heading for Maureen's police cruiser, parked on Louisiana Avenue. While Atkinson searched the apartment, Maureen had made a coffee run. Two large, hot dark roasts awaited them in the cruiser. On the passenger seat sat three Hubig's pies that she'd have to smuggle to Preacher around Anthony's vigilant watch.

Atkinson looked over her shoulder. "Couldn't let it go without checking it out one more time. Thought maybe, with no one else around, I might see things differently. Changing the way you look at things, and

I don't mean that in some deep philosophical way, I mean stand on a chair and look around, change the light, can make a bigger difference than you'd think. You never know. Having the place to myself didn't make a difference this time, but now I can forget about that apartment as part of the case."

"Detillier and his guys took everything, huh?" Maureen said. She tucked loose strands of hair up under her NOPD knit cap.

"He let me in with his team this afternoon," Atkinson said, "once the bomb squad gave us the all clear. He let me get a good look around. He did right by me."

"He gonna let you have a run at Gage?" Maureen asked.

"Oh, I doubt that," Atkinson said. "That's all right."

"Seriously?"

They'd reached the car. Maureen opened the door, leaned into the front seat for the coffees. She handed one to Atkinson, who winced and spat as soon as she sipped.

"Too hot?" Maureen asked.

"I think I got yours," Atkinson said. They switched cups. "Damn, Maureen, that is *a lot* of sugar."

"Enough to stand up the spoon."

Atkinson raised her coffee cup for a toast. "Here's to that."

"Why don't you want to question Gage about Madison Leary's murder?" Maureen asked. "He was in town for revenge, no doubt about that. Attacking the cops, trying to murder Heath, and those blueprints for Heath's projects that Detillier found in the apartment? And bomb-making instructions on top of that?"

Atkinson chuckled. "I'm with Detillier on that. No way Gage doesn't blow himself to bits building a bomb. I'm glad we got him before he took out half of Harmony Oaks with him."

She leaned on the cruiser, looked back at the development, picturing, Maureen could tell, the smoking carnage they'd prevented. Atkinson was good at that, Maureen had noticed, imagining horrible things. She'd put in decades on the New Orleans streets, coming up through the ranks, the model of what Maureen wanted to do. Atkinson hadn't left the city in the days and weeks after Katrina, her own Mid-City house rotting under six feet of water while she slept in the backseat of her unmarked car. Maureen wondered how much of what Atkinson saw was imagination, and how much of it was memory. Was that the price of admission to get where Atkinson was, Maureen wondered, a head full of horrible things? What did it really take to be able to do what the detective could do?

Atkinson turned to Maureen, faking a grin. "I wonder if Solomon's attitude toward his beloved son will change much when he finds out it was Caleb who got those plans for Gage."

"It won't," Maureen said. "Not in any way that we'll see. He'll deny Caleb had anything to do with it. It's one more reason to leave him overseas. That's a family that closes ranks against all others. Believe that." She bumped her shoulder against Atkinson. "You're really not going to question Gage?"

"Do you believe," Atkinson said, "that it was Gage going over that graveyard wall with Leary? Carrying wind chimes?"

"He matches the description we got from the witness," Maureen said. "He's the right height, the right build. He's even got the right haircut."

"In that hat," Atkinson said, "from far enough away, so do you."

"That fingerprint you found on the razor," Maureen said. "I'm guessing it wasn't his."

"It was not," Atkinson said. She set her coffee cup on the trunk of the car and reached into her jacket. "But I found out who it does belong to."

"That was quick," Maureen said.

"I told you Detillier did right by me," Atkinson said. She pulled a folded piece of paper from inside her coat and handed it to Maureen. "He helped with tracking the print. Said it was a Watchmen thing. Which it is, technically."

Maureen opened the page. It was a copy of a photo. A mug shot of a young woman. Hardly more than a girl. Her bony shoulders were bare. She had a Mohawk haircut. Two red streaks adorned her right cheek. Not blood or bruises, but stage makeup. She'd also painted a red band over her eyes like a bandit's mask, or like war paint, Maureen thought. Under the face paint bloomed a freshly inflicted black eye. The girl's bloody top lip curled in a swollen sneer. Maureen wondered if the arresting officers had knocked the girl around. She looked the type who'd resist, not just arrest, but *everything*.

The girl in the picture looks very familiar, Maureen thought, around the eyes and nose, especially, but she couldn't place her. Like an actor in a movie, she thought, and you can't remember where else you've seen her before, but that face, you know you know it.

The initials scrawled across the bottom of the photo read "LAPD." That didn't help. "California?"

"The photo is a couple of years old," Atkinson said, nodding, "so you have to use your imagination."

Maureen looked again. At second glance, the name that went with the face arrived. It clicked. Of course she knew that face. Her mouth fell open and she turned to Atkinson. "Is that who I think it is?"

"Officer Coughlin, meet Natalie Sparrow. You know her as Dice."

"Wow," Maureen said, handing Atkinson the paper. "Damn. Her fashion sense has improved somewhat. I wonder if I looked so *furious* at that age." She noticed Atkinson was not amused. Something in the air around them had changed, darkened. "Oh, you don't think . . ." Maureen grabbed the paper, checked the back for additional information. She looked at Atkinson. "This photo, what was the charge?"

"Multiple." Atkinson fought back her grin. She restrained all of it except for a tiny twitch at the corner of her mouth. "Homicide. Three counts. She crushed three guys against a bus with a stolen car."

"Allegedly," Maureen said.

Atkinson laughed. "What? Young Sparrow doesn't look like that kind of girl to you?"

"We're all that kind of girl," Maureen said, "when we have to be." She blew out a long sigh. "She and Leary were friends. She admitted that to me. It's why I started working with her in first place. It's not so outrageous her prints were on the razor."

"What if Madison Leary never killed anyone?" Atkinson said. "What if someone else killed Leon Gage's son, Clayton, and the Watchmen body we found before him, Edgar Cooley? Just consider the possibility Leary didn't commit those two murders." She paused. "It's fucking genius, if you think about it. The best lies are wrapped around a grain of truth. What if everything Dice told us about Madison Leary was *her* life story, pieces of it, at least."

Maureen did think about it. She thought about how Dice was the only person who seemed to know anything about Madison Leary, about her mind and her history. She thought of Dice sneaking up on her on Frenchmen Street. Had she been hiding that razor then, in a pocket of her long coat? "You think Dice, this Natalie Sparrow, killed Leary?"

"I think Sparrow killed Cooley, Gage, *and* Leary. I think she was Leary's avenging angel when the Watchmen came to town looking for her."

"Hell of an angel," Maureen said, "who cuts the throat of the woman she's protecting."

"Leary must've weakened," Atkinson said. "She might've become a threat, maybe started talking of getting help. Sparrow might've tired of watching her suffer. One thing for sure, she didn't like doing this one. That's why she left the razor behind this time."

"There's still a ton of evidence that points right at Leary being the Watchmen killer," Maureen said, but her mind had turned, she'd felt it, from disbelieving Atkinson to simply playing devil's advocate. "We have everything that Dice said about her, for example."

"Exactly," Atkinson said. "We have *only* the stuff Dice told us. Did anyone talk to Leary about any of it?"

"Talk to Leary?" Maureen said. "How exactly were we going to talk to her? She was a paranoid schizophrenic living on the streets and off her meds."

"You're making my point," Atkinson said. "Think of the condition Leary was in. She ate three meals a week. She weighed maybe a hundred pounds when she died. Maybe. She lived on cheap street drugs and air and whatever electric crazy ran through her brain. And we believe she stalked these backwoods militia guys through the streets of New Orleans, picking them off one at a time with a razor blade? Because some homeless punk rock girl told us so?"

She held up the picture. "A punk rock girl with one terrifying fucking history. Her first contact with the police was in New Mexico, where we *think* she was born. There are a lot of gaps in her history. She was twelve. She and a boy, one with a rep at school as a bully, were 'playing' on the roof of an abandoned warehouse. The boy fell through a hole in the roof. He died."

"Accidents happen," Maureen said. "Sounds more like bad parenting to me."

"I read the report," Atkinson said. "Lots of kids played on that roof. None of them remembered that hole being there before that kid fell through it. Two weeks later, Sparrow disappeared from her foster home. She doesn't pop up anywhere until that day in California."

"Leary knew the Watchmen," Maureen said. "She was with them in LaPlace for we don't know how long. And maybe these Watchmen assholes aren't half the badasses they think they are. Maybe that's why they shoot when no one else is looking. They're fucking cowards."

"You put it like that," Atkinson said, "and it sounds like you're rooting for Sparrow."

"I was," Maureen said. "Until five minutes ago." God, why did she feel so *sad*? Like someone she knew had died. "Anyway, it doesn't matter. We can't fucking find her. Six weeks we looked for them both. Though I'm guessing we weren't looking real hard."

"We are now," Atkinson said. "Believe that."

Maureen reached into her pocket, pulled out her phone. She should've saved those messages, the voice mails she'd gotten from Leary, well, no, from Sparrow where she sang Maureen those creepy songs. "You know, I thought, maybe for a little while, I could sleep through the night. Walk the streets without looking over my shoulder. Be a regular cop."

"Oh, I don't know," Atkinson said. "She seems to have a type, for killing, I mean, and you're not it. In fact, she seems to like you."

"I know. That's what I'm afraid of," Maureen said.

"When you saw her," Atkinson said, "what did she say to you? Anything useful? Think about it again. Look at her differently now."

"Oh, Lord," Maureen said. "She told me she couldn't wait for Mardi Gras. That she was super excited to experience her first one."

"So you think she's planning on staying here?" Atkinson asked. "Or maybe she was bullshitting you, blowing smoke. And that was before she killed Leary. That murder may have changed her plans. She may already be long gone. She does know how to disappear."

Maureen opened the photo again, studying the warrior-painted face, the wild ink-black eyes that stared back at her, into her, across the years. "I think she's in New Orleans to stay. I think she's home."

That makes two of us, Maureen thought. It's you and me, Sparrow.

She folded the photo, tucked it into her leather jacket.

May the best woman win.

ACKNOWLEDGMENTS

Thanks first and foremost to the McDonald, Murphy, Lambeth, and Loehfelm clans for their unwavering support of every kind.

Thanks to Jarrett, Kelcy, and the rest of the Executive Tuesday Krewe, past and present. Real recognize real. And thanks to the owners and staff of Joey K's for putting up with us.

There's one name on the cover but it takes a big team to make a book. I'm lucky enough to be part of a great one:

Tremendous gratitude to my amazing agent, Barney Karpfinger, and to Cathy and Marc at the Karpfinger Agency. No way this operation stays afloat without them.

Huge thanks also to Sarah Crichton, editor and publisher extraordinaire, for her thoughtfulness, thoroughness, and enthusiasm, and to John, Abby, Marsha, Lottchen, Rachel, Spenser, Elizabeth, and the whole amazing team at FSG and Picador. Special tip of the cap to Alex Merto for conjuring another mind-bending cover. And to Jill and Ian for keeping me pointed in the right direction on tour. I know I forgot some people, just because I always do. Forgive me. Y'all are the best. Thanks for giving me a happy writing home.

Each writing project has an extensive playlist. As you might expect, the New Orleans books (and their author) rely heavily on New Orleans music. That music includes but is not limited to: Dr. John, Anders Osborne, Kelcy Mae, Juvenile, the Revivalists, the Soul Rebels Brass Band, the Hot 8 Brass Band, Luke Winslow King, Trombone Shorty and Orleans Avenue, Galactic, the Rebirth Brass Band. Inspiration also from the Dead Weather, Band of Skulls, Juliana Hatfield, Metric, Matt Mays, Black Rebel Motorcycle Club, the Tragically Hip, Jason Isbell, Gillian Welch.

As often happens, I took some liberties with time and place in New Orleans for storytelling purposes. I beg my fellow New Orleanians' indulgence and forgiveness.

Though Marques Greer gets a break in this book, AC and I remain supportive of the Roots of Music and their musical and educational efforts: www.therootsofmusic.org.

We also support the work of Steve Gleason, Team Gleason, and their ongoing efforts on behalf of people living with ALS. Find out more at www.teamgleason.org. No White Flags.

And finally, as always, all my love to my amazing wife, AC Lambeth, my best friend, favorite person, and the wellspring of any and all good work I do.

A NOTE ABOUT THE AUTHOR

Bill Loehfelm is the author of *Doing the Devil's Work, The Devil in Her Way, The Devil She Knows, Bloodroot,* and *Fresh Kills.* He lives in New Orleans with his wife, the writer AC Lambeth, and plays drums in a rock-'n'-roll band.